SUDDEN IMPACT

AirQuest Adventures

Sudden Impact

Jerry B. Jenkins

ZONDERKIDZ

This title is also available as a Zondervan ebook.
Visit www.zondervan.com/ebooks

Requests for information should be addressed to:

Zonderkidz, 5300 *Patterson Ave., S.E., Grand Rapids, Michigan* 49530

978-0-310-73311-9

Art direction: Laura Maitner-Mason and Julie Chen
Illustrations: Dan Brown
Cover design: Cindy Davis
Interior design: Ruth Bandstra
Interior composition: Greg Johnson/Textbook Perfect

Printed in the United States of America

13 14 15 16 17 /DCI/ 20 19 18 17 16 15 14 13 12 11 10 9 8 7 6 5 4 3 2 1

Contents

Author's Note

I had as much fun writing this trilogy of books as any other kids' books I have written. Want to know why?

Besides using two of my kids' names (Chad and Michael), the story allowed me to imagine being in a family that has gone through a huge personal loss, but which also gets to be involved in all kinds of adventures.

My own father was a police officer, which was cool enough. But wouldn't it be something to have a dad who flies planes all over the world?

I hope you enjoy reading these books as much as I enjoyed writing them. And if you do, I'd love to hear from you.

Jerry B. Jenkins
Box 88288
Colorado Springs, CO
www.jerryjenkins.com

CRASH
at Cannibal Valley

To Dallas, Chad, and Michael.

May you remain ever young at heart.

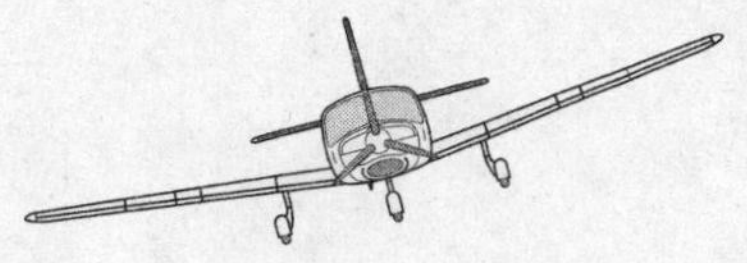

Contents

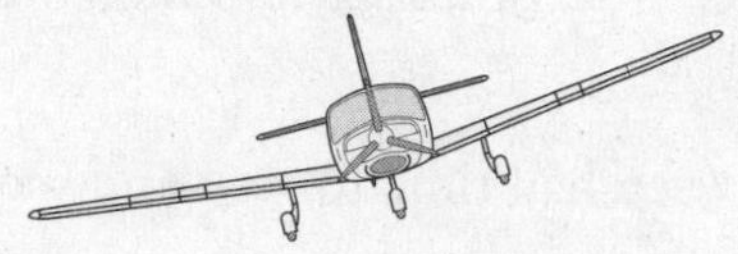

Misery in Mukluk

Chad Michaels bounded out of Mukluk Middle School in northern Alaska. He ran as fast as he could despite his huge boots, down-filled snow pants, mittens, and hooded parka.

At noon, he and the other sixth-grade guys usually engaged in daily snowball fights against the seventh graders. Chad hated these fights; he would have skipped them if it weren't for the name-calling he'd have to endure. Today's snowball fight couldn't ruin his day though. He had two special things to look forward to that afternoon, and that's what he thought about as he ran out into the snow.

The winter sun set early in Mukluk, so the whole school was let out for recess before lunch every day. That meant there were just too many kids to watch at once, and the boys could get away with breaking the no-snowball rule. Besides, these guys had been snowball fighting for so long, they knew where to play without getting caught. Chad glanced over his shoulder. The other sixth graders were right behind him.

Chad hadn't even had time to stop and scoop up a ball of his own when he saw Rusty Testor, his least favorite seventh grader, standing a few feet away, a huge snowball in his palm. The icy wind stung Chad's exposed cheeks as he sprinted for all he was worth, but the bigger, older Testor had the angle on him and was closing fast.

Rusty had a gap-toothed, freckle-faced grin that gave Chad nightmares. *I'd love to pop him, just once*, Chad thought. He imagined himself rushing Testor, driving his head into the bigger boy's stomach, and knocking the wind right out of him. That's what his friends would do.

But not me, Chad thought as he ran. *Rusty's right. I'm a wimp.*

Chad headed for the highest, deepest drift he could find, planning to hurtle over it and fight back from the other side. But from the corner of his eye he saw Testor draw back his throwing arm. Chad mistimed his leap over the snowdrift and left the ground too early. He spread his arms and legs, but instead of flying over the top to safety, he flopped face-first into the side of the drift.

As he called to his friends for help, Rusty's snowball smacked his cheekbone and drove ice and water into his ear and eye. It burned, and he wanted to cry, but he would never do that. It was bad enough he was a klutz; he wasn't going to be a baby too. At least he wouldn't show it if he was.

Chad turned and saw Rusty scooping more ammo from about ten feet away. Several other seventh graders joined in, grinning just like Rusty. Chad squatted, covering his face with his arms and drawing up his knees to protect himself as the fusillade pummeled him.

Here was the perfect opportunity for his friends to charge the seventh graders from the rear, while they were all occupied with him. But where were they? Was he sacrificing himself for no purpose? He peeked through his hands in disbelief. They just stood outside the circle of older kids, looking at him in disgust.

"You're too easy," Rusty said. "Go hide somewhere."

Chad wanted to charge him, to throw ice balls at him, but not if his so-called friends wouldn't help. He was tired of being a sitting duck. He stood, shoulders sagging, hands at his sides, as the seventh graders turned their attention to the other sixth graders. They would put up a better fight, which was more fun for the seventh graders than terrorizing Chad.

When they trudged back into school for lunch, one of Chad's friends caught up with him. "What's the deal, Michaels? Every day it's the same thing! You're big enough, you're strong enough, you're fast enough. You're as good at basketball as anybody in the class. But outside you're like a pansy."

Chad just shook his head as he peeled off his snow gear. Maybe he was a wimp, but he wouldn't let anything ruin this special day, even if he wasn't the rugged outdoorsman that most of the boys at Mukluk Middle School seemed to be. They fished and hunted, camped and hiked. He had nothing against that, and his father had taught him a lot about the outdoors. Thc truth was, he just wasn't good at all that stuff.

Chad would rather sit at his computer, surfing the Internet or maintaining his files on his favorite pro and college sports teams in the lower forty-eight states. He loved downloading scores and statistics in the morning before school; because of the time difference, all the results from the night before were already listed on the news and wire services. No one in the school knew as much as he did about sports.

After lunch Chad's teacher, Mrs. Wright, called the class to attention. "For the third straight time, I'm happy to announce that Chad Michaels is our student of the month." She added, "Congratulations, Chad," as most of the boys shook their heads and grimaced, while several of the girls turned and smiled at him. Chad's dad said the guys were just jealous, but there were days when he wished he were an average student. He didn't need something else to be ridiculed about.

"And," Mrs. Wright said, "Chad has two things to share with the class, don't you, Chad?"

Chad felt the heat creeping up his neck. "Uh, no, not really."

"Oh, come on," Mrs. Wright said. "Come on up here and tell us what will be happening this afternoon."

Chad shot her a pleading glance, but he could see it would do no good. He shuffled to the front and turned, feeling as if he were facing a firing squad.

One boy groaned. "Is this where we get to hear about his dad the hero again? Does he still call you Spitfire, Michaels?"

Mrs. Wright shushed them. Chad stared at the floor. "Well, first, my sister, Kate, is speaking to our class in about half an hour."

"A fifth grader?" someone said, snorting.

"Kate will tell us when she comes in," Mrs. Wright said. "But what else—"

"Radios, of course," one of the girls said. "She knows everything there is to know about radios."

Chad nodded. "She knows even more'n my dad about radios."

"I knew he would come up," a boy said.

"Now that's enough," Mrs. Wright said. "Chad, tell us what's so special about today. "

They don't care! But there was no getting out of this. "Well, uh, Kate and I will leave school early today to go with Mom to the airport. The peacekeeping mission is over in the Middle East, and my dad landed near Washington, D.C., several hours ago. He should be in Anchorage soon, and then he'll fly here."

"Did he kill anybody over there?" someone shouted.

"I don't know," Chad said. "He could have. He flies— "

"Fighter planes; yeah, we know."

Face burning, Chad sat back down, more sure than ever that the other kids were jealous. None of their fathers did anything as exciting as his dad did. Even when he wasn't being called into duty by the Air Force, he flew charter flights all over Alaska, Canada, the northeastern United States, and even the Pacific. Dad owned his own company—he called it Yukon Do It—which included ten planes and employed several pilots.

The other kids could mutter all they wanted and make fun of him, but Chad knew they wished their dads were as daring as his. The school assemblies that Bruce Michaels spoke at each year were always the most popular and talked about. And when Chad's class took a field trip to his dad's hangar, and the kids got to take rides in one of the small charter planes, Chad lived for days on the attention. For a while, some of the kids even called Chad Spitfire like his dad did. Mr. Michaels had told him a Spitfire was a World War II plane that could be quick and deadly. "And that's you," his dad often said. Chad secretly liked it when his dad called him Spitfire, but he asked his dad not to do that in front of his friends anymore.

An hour later, Chad was again amazed at what his sister could do. She didn't even seem nervous when she arrived with her radios and oscillators and gave her little demonstration. A bit shorter and thinner than Chad, she had his blond hair and green eyes, and it wasn't unusual for people to ask if they were twins.

After a few interruptions from the class clowns, Kate quickly won them over with her knowledge of the history of the discovery of radio waves, and her explanation of how quickly the technology had grown, even in just the last five years. "You know," she said, "that television signals are really just high-frequency radio waves. Some day we'll be wearing TV phones on our wrists and looking at each other while we talk."

She also told about her recent trip with her father to an Asian radio-manufacturing plant, and all she had seen and done there. When she finished she received loud applause and cheering. “I have to get going now,” she said, smiling, “because in about half an hour, my mom—”

“We know, we know!” some boys hollered. “We’ve heard all about it!”

Kate blushed as she packed up her things.

Chad and Kate squabbled as much as any other brother and sister, but now he sat beaming. He was proud of her, and while he might not admit that to her, it felt good. He was glad she was his sister.

Chad found it hard to concentrate on anything during the next half hour. He had his stuff arranged and was ready to go. His dad had been gone six weeks now. It had been longer the time before, and he had shot down an enemy plane that time.

Chad’s mother was good about not showing her worry. They prayed for Dad every night, of course, but she didn’t cry or talk about the danger all the time. She said there was just as much danger when he flew his charter flights, and they weren’t going to waste their lives away worrying about things that may never happen.

Chad stared at his watch, trying to make the time go faster. The seconds seemed to tick like minutes. At two o’clock he was to go by Kate’s classroom and walk with her to the office where his mother would meet them, sign them out, and then they’d head for the airstrip, forty-five minutes away.

Finally his watch showed two o'clock sharp. With a nod from Mrs. Wright, Chad quietly left the room. "Say 'hi' to your dad for us," someone whispered. He nodded. He could even put up with Rusty Testor on a day like this.

"So, how'd I do, Chad?" Kate said as they made their way to the office.

"It was all right," Chad said.

"Just all right?" she said. "Really? Just all right?"

"You were great, of course," Chad said. Why couldn't he ever tell her how he really felt? What would be wrong with that?

"You sound like you'd be happier if I'd made a fool of myself," she said.

"Nah," he said. "You did good."

"*Well*, you mean."

"Yeah, you did well."

Chad was surprised his mother was not already at the office. He and Kate peeked outside at the parking lot to watch for her while the receptionist took a call. "Kids," she said then, "your mother's been delayed. It'll be a little while."

Chad squinted and said, "Was that her on the phone?"

"Um, no. But they told me she's been detained."

"Detained?" Kate said. "Who told you that?"

The receptionist looked nervous. "I didn't catch his name."

"Listen," Chad said, "my dad will touch down in an hour, and we're supposed to be there waiting for him. He'll worry if we're not—"

"It won't be long," the receptionist said, "before we'll know something definite."

"About what?" Chad frowned. Why wouldn't the receptionist look him in the eye? "Who was on the phone?"

"I just take the messages, kids. I don't explain them. Your mother has been delayed, so you might just as well take a seat."

"For how long?" Kate said.

"I honestly don't know, honey," she said, turning back to her work. "You know as much as I do."

Chad and Kate looked at each other, and Chad shrugged. He guessed there was nothing to worry about, like Mom always said. But it would have been easier not to worry if it were his mother on the phone. She would have asked to speak to him.

Chad and Kate sat fidgeting while they watched for their mother out the window. Eventually, a police car stopped at the entrance, and the uniformed cop glanced at them as he hurried in. What was going on? He bent to whisper to the receptionist, who immediately went and knocked on the principal's office door. She and the officer went in then and shut the door.

A minute later the principal and the receptionist came out. The receptionist went back to her desk without looking at the kids. The principal, a grandmotherly woman with white hair, came and bent before Chad and Kate. "Would you join Officer Flanagan and me in my office, please?"

Chad wanted to ask what it was all about, but deep in his stomach he was afraid he knew. After he and Kate entered the principal's office, the principal shut the door. Officer Flanagan sat at a small table and pointed to two chairs. The kids sat.

The officer was not smiling. "Chad and Kate, is it?" he said.

They nodded.

"Chad, I need to get some information from you. What time is your father expected?"

"In an hour. Why?"

"And you and your sister and your mom were going to meet him?"

"What happened to him?" Chad said.

"I'm afraid I have some bad news for you," Officer Flanagan said. "But it's not about your father."

Dad's Announcement

"I wish there was another way to tell you," Officer Flanagan told Chad and Kate, "and I wish I could wait until your dad was here with you. But there would be no keeping it from you. Your mother was in an accident on the way here. It wasn't her fault. The other driver ran a red light and hit her car broadside."

Chad noticed Kate trying to speak, but it seemed she couldn't make a sound. So Chad spoke for both of them. "How bad was she hurt?"

"I'm sorry, kids," Officer Flanagan said. "Your mother was killed."

Kate's eyes grew wide, and she began to shake and then cry. Chad wished he could cry. He wanted to reach over and hold Kate, but he couldn't move. This had to be a bad dream. He would wake up soon and start the day over.

The principal put her arms around Kate, and Officer Flanagan kept an eye on Chad. Chad didn't know what the officer expected him to do, but there was no need to worry. Chad felt himself growing cold. He couldn't even seem to move his eyes. He stared at the officer's face, but everything else seemed to turn dark.

His mind whirred. What would happen next? How would they tell Dad? What would they do without Mom? A happy day that couldn't even be ruined by a seventh-grade bully had suddenly become the worst day of Chad's whole life. The policeman asked Chad if there was a relative or a family friend he would like to have with them.

"No," Chad managed. "Our closest relatives are a couple of hours away, and I want to see my dad as soon as he gets off the plane."

"I can understand that. Anyone you'd like to have ride along with us? Your pastor? A teacher? A neighbor?"

Chad shook his head. He could probably think of someone if he tried. But he just wanted to get to his dad as soon as possible. "Are you going to take us?" Chad said. "Because we'd better get going."

All the way to the airport, Chad and Kate huddled together in the backseat. Kate cried and cried, but different emotions welled up in Chad. He was angry. How could this have happened? Who ran a red light and killed his mom?

He had worried about his dad getting back. Nothing had better happen to him! He was all they had left.

Usually when Chad was in trouble or bad things happened, he prayed. Now he couldn't pray. What would he say? "Take my mom to heaven"? He knew that was already answered. "Send her back"? That wasn't going to happen. "Where were you when this happened?" That sounded disrespectful, but it was what he was thinking.

How could God have let this happen? Chad knew that being a Christian didn't mean your life was perfect, but how did this fit in with the faith of their family? They had prayed for each other, that God would "bless Mom and Dad and Kate and Chad," for as long as he could remember. Didn't "bless" include "protect"?

He didn't feel like much of a Christian right now, but it didn't seem like his fault. How was he supposed to feel? He was scared and he was mad. Worst of all, he knew this ugly news would stay with him forever. All he wanted now was to see his dad.

When they arrived at the small airport, about thirty miles north of Mukluk, Officer Flanagan took the kids into the waiting area. "Your dad's gonna see me and size this up pretty quick," he said. "I need you to give me a minute with him, okay? I need to make sure he hears it right, then you can have him all to yourselves."

As Chad and Kate sat in the molded plastic chairs, scanning the sky for their father's small plane, Chad felt a tightness in his chest that made him want to shout. He wanted to break something, to throw something, to hit someone. But who would he hit? This sure wasn't Officer Flanagan's fault. Or Kate's. Or his dad's. He hated this feeling. The news was so terrible he didn't want to think about it, but he wondered if he would ever be able to think about anything else.

His dad would look for their welcoming smiles, but there would be none. If anything was worse than hearing that your mom was dead, it was thinking about how your dad would feel when he found out.

Kate was the first to spot the black speck in the cloudy sky. The day was already growing dark, though it was only mid-afternoon. They stood and watched as the small plane touched down and then taxied back to let off its only passenger. Bruce Michaels appeared on the steps of the small craft, stretching and running a hand through his sandy brown hair. He was stocky and muscular, and Chad noticed he had already changed out of his uniform into khaki pants and leather jacket.

Dad peered toward the little terminal, then helped the pilot unload his bags from the underbelly of the plane. As they carried the stuff in, Bruce Michaels was clearly looking for three familiar faces. Chad and Kate hung back as Officer Flanagan stood by the door.

Dad's expectant smile faded as he saw the policeman. And when Officer Flanagan quickly told him what had happened, Dad staggered and had to sit down. He looked for the kids, and they ran to him. Dad wept openly, and Kate sobbed again. Chad wanted to cry more than ever, but that anger, that heaviness inside him, wouldn't allow it. He buried his head in his dad's chest and held on as if he would never let go.

During the next several days, relatives and friends and people from the church filled the Michaels' house, and some stayed with Chad and Kate as Dad made the funeral arrangements.

It was nice to hear all the wonderful comments about his mother at the funeral, but Chad couldn't help wondering, *If she was so great, why didn't God leave her here?* It didn't help when he learned that the other driver in the accident had been drunk. And unhurt.

Many people said they had never seen a church come together so quickly over a tragedy. Kathryn Michaels had been a Sunday school teacher, and several kids said they had received Christ in her classes. One girl said she had been putting off her decision, but now realized that you never knew how much time you had to come to Christ.

"Maybe that one girl was the reason for what happened," Dad said.

Chad wondered why God couldn't have reached her without letting his mother die.

Over the next couple of weeks, Dad and the other adults did a lot of praying. Chad couldn't even pray silently by himself. He didn't understand what had happened, and he didn't like the explanations the grown-ups kept giving him.

He didn't want to burden his father with his troubling thoughts, so every time Dad said, "How ya doin', Spitfire?" Chad just nodded. Kids at school didn't know what to say, so they mostly said nothing. Nobody bugged Chad about dropping out of the daily snowball fight.

Kate started clinging to their dad as if she never wanted him out of her sight again. They worked on radios together and talked a lot.

The last thing Chad wanted to do was talk. He kept to himself and his computer. When his dad passed and laid a hand on Chad's shoulder, he shook it off.

"I'm worried about you," his dad said one night at supper. "You need to talk instead of closing up."

"Talk? Why? Will that bring Mom back?"

"Chad!" his sister said, tears welling.

"Sorry," Chad muttered.

"Chad," his dad said. "Anger is natural, but we all have to get past it."

Chad shrugged. He didn't want to talk about it.

As the school year wound down, Chad's grades dropped, even though he still did better than lots of the other kids.

"Brain drain?" his friend Erik said.

"Shut up," Chad said.

Frequently, Chad found his dad on the phone talking business. Something was up, because whenever he came into the room, Dad changed the subject or quit talking.

Finally, one night about a month before the end of the school year, Dad called a family meeting. It was the first time they'd had one without Mom. Chad and Kate sat in front of the fireplace.

"You kids know I'm a plain guy," Dad began, stoking the fire.

"A plane guy or a plain guy?" Kate interrupted, giggling.

Dad smiled. "Plain, as in ordinary."

"I wouldn't call being a fighter pilot ordinary," Chad said.

"That's history, Spitfire," Bruce Michaels said. "Now I'm just a businessman with ten small planes, a crew of pilots, and too much work to do. At least I was."

"I wish I had a nickname," Kate interrupted.

"I could call you Sparky," Dad said. "That's what they call the radio techies in the military. But Kate is already a nickname. You were named after your mom, but a nickname never seemed to fit her. I always called her Kathryn."

The three of them sat in silence for a moment, the only sound the crackling of the fire. It was hard to think about Mom.

Finally, "What do you mean, 'At least I was'?" Chad said. "You're not still Mr. Yukon Do It Man?"

Dad shook his head. "You know I quit flying so I could be here before and after school. But still I have all the other pilots and flights to worry about."

"I know," Kate said. "Seems like you're always busy."

"Well, that's changed now." He went on to explain that he had sold his business, planes, cargo, routes, and even the contracts with his pilots.

Chad had never thought of his dad as anything but a pilot. "You're not going to fly anymore?" he said.

"I'll always fly," Dad said. "Don't worry about that. But I had to get in a position where I don't have to be away. This sale gives me that freedom."

"So, are we rich now?" Chad blurted.

"There you go, Spitfire," Dad said. "Jumping the gun as usual. The truth is, we've never been poor. You know there's never anything you really want or need that we can't afford."

"Then why do we have to chip in on everything?" Kate said. "You always make us pay half out of our allowance if it's anything big or special."

"True," Dad said. "Because that's how life is. Anything worth having, like all your electronics stuff, is worth working for. Nobody will ever just give you things. You'll be glad we raised you that way. Growing up, my family never seemed to have enough. We had to work for everything."

Chad was still reeling from the news, but he didn't know how to say it. "So are we rich now or not?"

"Let me put it this way," Dad said. "I was taught that if you work hard, treat people right, and, as the Bible says, 'do everything heartily as unto the Lord,' you'll be all right."

Chad couldn't sit still. He moved closer to the fire and watched the light from the flames shining on his dad's cheek. "Yeah, you do all that stuff and then your wife gets killed. You call that being all right?"

"Chad!" Kate said.

"It's okay, Kate," Dad said. "I've had my questions about all this too. I don't understand why your mom had to die either. I've had some long nights over this. But God is good. He's in control. Who knows? If that one girl became a Christian because of it, you know your mom would have—"

"I know," Chad said quickly. "I don't need to hear that again, okay? Are you going to tell us whether we're rich now, or not?"

Chad was surprised his dad didn't simply send him to his room for talking like that. Dad hesitated. "Yes, we are," he said finally. "I want to tell you both this because it's important. It's an answer to prayer, but it comes with tremendous responsibility. I'd been praying about changing my life so that by the end of the school year I could spend more time at home. I didn't know it would mean selling my business, but that's what it came to."

"But you love your business!" Kate said.

"I love flying, and I'll still do that. It won't be hard to give up the rest of it. But this is the important part. I sold the business for much more than I ever dreamed I would."

"How much?" Chad said.

"I'm not going to tell you, Spitfire," Dad said, "because you wouldn't understand it much more than I do. Let's just say it's almost a hundred times more than I ever expected to see in my life."

"Wow," Kate said. Chad whistled.

"Of course there are huge taxes, but I wouldn't be able to spend the rest in two lifetimes. I'd never have to work again if I didn't want to. But that's not how I was made. I feel a tremendous responsibility to use this money the way God would want us to. So we're going to give half of it to God's work."

Chad rolled his eyes at the "tremendous responsibility" bit. Chad wished *he* had that kind of responsibility!

"I want you two to pray about forming a new company that would be made up of just the three of us. I want to use my flying skills and this extra money to help with the work of God around the world. Would you do that?"

Kate was excited, but Chad shrugged. He didn't want to hurt his dad, but he wondered why he would want to give so much to God—money and time and everything—when God had let his wife die.

Over the next few weeks, Kate and Dad talked about the new company every chance they got. They dreamed of flying all over the globe as a family, helping missionaries wherever they could.

Chad just listened and tried not to be sarcastic. When Dad wasn't around, Kate tried to find out why Chad wasn't excited. "Think of what we can do and where we can go!" she said.

"I don't want to go anywhere," he said. "Who wants to go halfway around the world? Who knows what kind of food they would have or whether they even have running water?"

But finally it became official. The little family of Chad, Kate, and Bruce Michaels would become AirQuest Adventures. Dad would let missionary groups know that he was available for anything they needed.

He could build planes, fix planes, fly planes, fill in for someone who was home on furlough, whatever they needed. He could even repair radios, with Kate's help. He would go only when Chad and Kate could join him, because he never wanted to be separated from the family again. Most of their missions would be over the summer, but if Dad were needed somewhere else during the school year, he would even take the kids out of school and either hire a tutor or teach them himself.

Then one day Dad announced that immediately after school was out for the summer, the family would leave for Indonesia. Inter-Indonesian Mission had asked Dad to evaluate their small fleet of single- and twin-engine planes and recommend whether they needed new ones. He would also fill in as a pilot as needed.

Chad would rather have done anything but go to Indonesia.

The Trip

One evening, about a week before the family was to leave for Indonesia, Dad knocked at Chad's bedroom door.

"I'm online," Chad said as his dad quietly entered.

"I'll wait," Dad said.

"I'm just writing to Uncle Bill in Portland."

"About?"

"You know."

"Chad, I don't want you to stay with Uncle Bill after all. You're going with Kate and me."

"*What?*" Chad quickly saved his work, exited the system, and shut down his computer. "Why?"

"Because the whole point of our new company is being together. I know you miss your mom. So does Kate and so do I. That's why I want us together. You kids are growing up fast. I want as much time with you as I can get."

Chad didn't know how to answer that. He knew he hadn't been acting like anyone his dad would want to spend more time with. "Dad, you know I'm not into all that outdoor rough stuff. Indonesia, especially where we're going, is full of jungles. And I'll bet they're not even on the Internet."

"Well, maybe you can help get them up to speed."

"Dad, I don't know why I have to go."

"I don't want to have to make you go, Chad. But neither Kate nor I would want to go without you."

"Kate wouldn't care."

"If you believe that, you don't really know Kate. She loves you. And you love her too, even if you've gotten out of the habit of telling her."

Chad stared at the dark computer screen. Of course he loved Kate, but not enough to want to go to Indonesia with her. "So you're making me go."

"Like I said, I don't want to have to do that."

"But I don't have any choice?"

"When you put it that way, no."

Chad shook his head.

"And I'd like you to have a good attitude about it."

"To fake it, you mean?"

"I want you to not make the trip miserable for your sister and me with your negative attitude. You don't have to like it, but we don't want to hear about it all the time, okay?"

Chad sensed his father's anger.

"Okay?" his dad pressed.

"I'll try," he said.

"I also want you to be fair and open-minded. You might like this new experience. It's an unusual opportunity that few kids your age ever have. You'll learn a lot, and you might just become more of the outdoorsman you want to be."

"Who says I want to be that?"

"You complain about it all the time."

"That doesn't mean I want to be a nature-loving guy."

"Yes, it does," Dad said.

Chad hated when his dad was right.

They flew from the airstrip north of Mukluk to Anchorage in Dad's own plane, then to Los Angeles by jet. From there they flew to a series of South Pacific Islands, through Sydney, Australia, and on to Jakarta, capital of the huge island of Indonesia.

After a few days of getting used to the sticky heat and the new time zone, they flew more than two thousand miles to Sentani, near the Irian Jaya–Papua New Guinea border. They stayed at the Inter-Indonesian Mission compound near Sentani. And until they headed back to Alaska, all their flights would be on tiny single- and twin-engine planes.

Chad hated every minute of it. The heat, the humidity, the bugs, the inconvenience—everything made him wish he was home, or at least with his uncle Bill in Oregon. As exhausting and strange as the trip had been, Kate seemed to love getting to know the missionaries and their families. She got to learn about radios she had never seen before. Chad kept his distance, but he had to admit that he enjoyed seeing his dad happy again.

Dad spent the first ten days mostly in the Inter-Indonesian Mission hangar at the Sentani airstrip. Kate flew several test flights with him, and Chad watched him get greasy from head to toe, tearing engines apart and putting them back together again. Dad recommended to IIM that they upgrade the technology on several of their planes, and when they balked at the cost, he insisted on ordering the parts and paying for them himself.

Chad kept begging his way out of the flights into the jungle. If he couldn't handle snowballs, how would he do with boa constrictors and poisonous insects? He wouldn't admit he was a little jealous when Kate came back with stories about the tribespeople of that area and their strange clothes and food and huts. They had a long flight planned in a few days, but Chad wanted no part of the jungle. This time, though, his dad put his foot down.

"You're going with Kate and me tomorrow when we take Dr. Howlett to Yawsikor. "

Visions of snakes and scorpions filled Chad's mind. "Who's Dr. Howlett?"

"You met him. Dr. George Howlett is the Inter-Indonesian Mission president. He's making a delivery to missionaries working with a tribal group in the jungle near Bime (Bee-may). Then we take him on to Yawsikor on the other side of the island, about 250 miles from here. He's going to a missions conference there, and then he'll be flown on to Jakarta for a flight to the United States."

"Can I go with him?" Chad said.

"Not on your life. Now get some sleep. We leave before dawn."

"Before dawn!"

"Of course. The flight curfews are late morning here because of the winds. We have to fly to Bime, then to Yawsikor, and all the way back here, all in the morning."

"Oh, brother."

"And I don't want any attitude, you hear?"

Chad pursed his lips and nodded.

At five-thirty the next morning, Dr. Howlett loaded his luggage onto the twin-engine plane, carefully weighing it first. "I've got lots of goodies for the kids in Bime and Yawsikor," he said. "They always expect it. And see this cooler? You could drop this from the plane and it wouldn't break open. I'm taking some food from a Chinese restaurant in Jayapura for the missionaries."

Chad secretly liked Dr. Howlett, because he didn't seem like a typical executive. He dressed like a normal person with a light pullover shirt and shorts, and usually tennis shoes, though today he wore tall hiking boots. He was a robust man who had himself flown these rugged jungle areas for years.

When they boarded the tiny twin-engine four-seater, Dr. Howlett helped the kids into the rear seats, Chad behind his dad and Kate next to Chad. Then Dr. Howlett climbed in next to Mr. Michaels to help with the preflight checklist. Dad stretched the microphone cord back so Kate could lean forward and reach it. As they taxied onto the runway, she spoke, "Kilo double Hotel forty-forty-eight to tower."

"Tower, go ahead."

"Preflight finished, ready for takeoff to Bime, continuing to Yawsikor."

"You're clear, forty-forty-eight. Blue skies. Bime and Yawsikor wind curfews are nine-thirty this morning. Ours is ten-thirty, so hurry back."

"Roger, tower."

And they were off.

Dr. Howlett turned, straining against his seat belt to talk with Chad and Kate. He had to shout over the engine noise: "Our first stop is right in the middle of a 1976 earthquake area," he said. "I remember flying over it a few years after the earthquake, and seeing where the vegetation had been stripped from the sides of the mountains, and rivers had been dammed up. To look at it today, you'd never know there had been one of the biggest earthquakes ever in this region."

Dr. Howlett peeked at Bruce Michaels' flight map. "We won't be able to stay long at Bime, but the next leg of the flight will take us over the mountains. You'll be able to see Mt. Juliana, which is about fifteen thousand feet high. Just over the other side you'll see an area we call Cannibal Valley. The small Braza tribe there is cannibalistic, and we have been unable to get to them since the earthquake."

Kate leaned forward, straining to hear. "I thought you said that earthquake was more than thirty years ago!" she shouted.

"It was, but it closed off the way to them by river. It actually caused the Braza River to change course, and now there's no way to get to the Brazas unless they would allow us to land a helicopter there. And they won't."

"And they eat people?" Chad said.

Dr. Howlett nodded. "They used to. There have been no reports of cannibalism in these jungles for many years, but without any recent contact with the Brazas, we just don't know."

"Don't they need water?" Chad's dad said.

"The change of the river's course produced a sort of freshwater lake for them, but they're pretty much limited to a small area now. They would have to walk a long way to put a craft on the river and travel anywhere. We think it has kept them from warring with other tribes, but it has also kept them from hearing the gospel."

During the flight to Bime, Chad's dad explained how he always kept an emergency landing spot in sight between airstrips.

"They are just openings. You'd never choose to put down there, but if you have to, you have to. I find a spot and keep my eye on it until I can't see it anymore. I figure if I can see it, I can reach it if we have engine failure. Back home there are all kinds of places to land in an emergency, but here, where there are no roads and very few landing strips, you have to keep track of your spots."

Chad leaned close to the window and stared at nothing but treetops. Engine failure? Emergency landings?

"All our pilots do this," Dr. Howlett said. "They spend almost their entire time looking for the next clearing."

The flight was smooth, and the landing on the tiny airstrip at Bime was bumpy but exciting. Bruce Michaels landed the twin-engine plane uphill, and parked at the high end of the runway, not far from one of the mission houses. Dr. Howlett explained it was necessary to land uphill. "That slows the plane and allows you a shorter runway. When we take off again, we'll start downhill to get up enough speed to get airborne."

"But there's a mountain at the end of the runway going that way," Chad said.

"So there is!" Dr. Howlett said, smiling. "And it rises to fifteen thousand feet, so when we take off again, your dad will have to fly in circles until he's high enough to get over it."

The planc was quickly surrounded by missionary families and tribal people. Chad felt as if he and Kate were in a movie. He had seen pictures of people like this, but he had never expected to see them close-up.

They were barefoot, wore hardly any clothes, and some wore bones through their noses. Dr. Howlett explained that they lived nearby in a village of thatched-roof huts, and the missionaries were learning their language and telling them about Christ. "That's what I did with the Brazas, more than twenty-five years ago."

"You worked with the *cannibals*?" Chad said.

"I wasn't the only one," Dr. Howlett said. "Mr. Coleman, who runs this mission station right here, and I went the long way around and arrived by canoe. We made contact with just a few of them. After several secret visits they warned us we were in danger from some of their violent tribespeople, and so were they, if they saw us again. We had learned just enough of their language to present a simple gospel. One man they called Jonga tried to say my name. He called me George-George and Mr. Coleman Man-Man."

Dr. Howlett and AirQuest Adventures were on the ground in Bime for less than half an hour. Kate looked over the little ground radio setup and made a quick friend of one of the missionary children. Dad helped Dr. Howlett unload two boxes of supplies, then went looking for Kate and her new friend. Chad explored the mission house.

The elderly couple who lived there, the Colemans, had served in Bime now for more than forty years. Mrs. Coleman told Chad that their own children had grown up there and were now involved in their own ministries. "You'll have to run along now," she said, "because we have an important meeting with Dr. Howlett. When we're finished, you'll be on your way."

As Chad left, Dr. Howlett entered the mission house with a grim-faced young man about twenty years old. Chad tiptoed onto the makeshift porch of the stilted frame home and sat under the screenless window, listening. It might not be any of his business, but he hadn't asked to land in this wild country either.

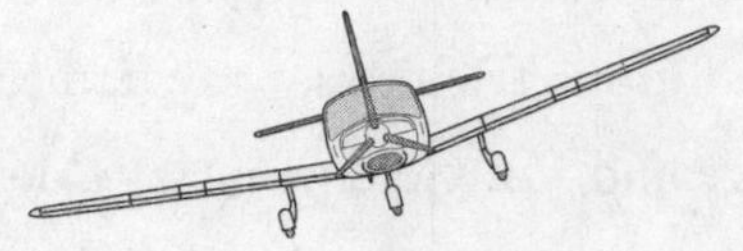

Cannibal Valley

From what Chad could make out, the Colemans suspected the young man, Waman, of teaching children from his village that the Christians were liars, and that the superstitious beliefs of the tribe made up the only true religion.

Mrs. Coleman had confronted Waman and he had denied it, but she had heard from others she trusted in the nearby village that much in Waman's life was not as it appeared when he showed up at the weekly church service. "What breaks my heart," she said, "is that we love him. We led him to the Lord. We know he understands the truth."

Dr. Howlett sounded grave as he spoke to Waman. "We want to understand what is confusing you because your actions and your words do not seem consistent. If you choose your own religion over the truth of the Bible, that is your choice. But to pretend to be a believer and then to work against the church, that is deceitful." His voice dropped so that Chad could barely make out his words. "The Colemans love you, but they don't feel they can trust you. Since you couldn't come to an agreement, they have asked me to become involved."

He paused, and Chad could not hear the young man's response.

"Waman," Dr. Howlett said, "I must tell you my decision. You will not be allowed to work for the Colemans as long as you are working against the gospel. You must stay in your own village and not come to the mission compound. If you wish to confess, however, the Colemans will forgive you and welcome you back."

Chad turned and peeked through the window. The Colemans were crying and nodding. But Waman looked angry. He began to shout in his own dialect, and Chad couldn't understand him.

"Yes," Mr. Coleman responded in pidgin, "there is a young woman from your village who works here and who is not yet a believer. But she doesn't claim to be one and then live another way. You once claimed to be a Christian."

Waman stood and argued again. It sounded to Chad as if he was saying that he rejected the accusations as well as Dr. Howlett's authority. He no longer wanted to work for people who would think such things of him. Chad had to wonder, what if Dr. Howlett was wrong?

Dr. Howlett spoke softly to the Colemans. "I must ask you once again, are you certain that you are right to suspect him?"

They both nodded sadly.

"Then your offer of forgiveness stands and you must regretfully accept his decision."

With that, Waman ran from the house, yelling. Chad was startled when Waman flew past him. Waman's look of pure hatred chilled Chad to the bone. He wanted to follow the young man, but he was afraid the Colemans and Dr. Howlett might see him and know he had been listening.

"He curses us," the woman said. "It's so sad. We have always loved him, and we thought he understood the gospel."

"We'll pray God speaks to his conscience and that he returns," Dr. Howlett said.

Chad sneaked behind the house and went to find his dad and Kate, who was saying good-bye to her new friend.

They headed back around to the other side of the mission house and boarded the little plane for the next leg of the flight. Dr. Howlett appeared and talked about the compassion of the Colemans.

"That's why we're here," he said. "When I see how devoted these missionaries are to getting the good news to these tribes, I want to do anything I can for them. I miss being on the front lines myself."

While the little plane struggled to gain altitude, Kate was obviously working hard to hear, but the big man couldn't turn any farther in his seat.

"How about I trade places with you, Chad?" Dr. Howlett said. "I want to tell you more about when I worked with the Brazas years ago."

Chad had wanted to sit next to his dad anyway, so he quickly agreed. While Dr. Howlett carefully climbed into the back, Chad clambered over him to the front, next to his dad, and strapped himself in. It was easier for him to turn and listen, and now both he and Kate could hear Dr. Howlett. The older man then told them how he had learned to greet Jonga and a few other Brazas and to tell them he had come in peace.

"We used the wordless book, a book with a green cover and four inside pages, all blank and in four colors—black, red, white, and gold. With the black page I tried to show them that, like all of us, their hearts were dark with sin. The red page showed that God's son, Jesus, shed his blood and died for them, paying the penalty for their sin. That brought them to the white page, which showed that their hearts could be as white as snow. The gold page represented heaven. I walked them through those pages several times. I even left a few copies of the wordless book."

"What is the green cover for?" Kate said.

Dr. Howlett got a faraway look in his eyes. "Green signifies growth, the way Christians are supposed to grow in Christ. I simply wasn't there long enough to know whether they understood and became believers, let alone whether they grew at all. The last time we tried to land a helicopter there, the Brazas shook their fists and waved weapons at us."

"What did their language sound like?" Kate said.

"*Treetzee* is a Braza word that means warm, sunshine, peace, friendly—all those things at once."

"It sounds like an ice-cream cone," Kate said, and they all laughed.

"*Shaka* means hello. And the word *benboon* means gift or present."

Kate began saying, "Shaka, treetzee, benboon," over and over to Chad, to her dad, and even to Dr. Howlett, who repeated the same back to her. "Do you have a benboon for me?" she said, laughing. "Those cannibals wouldn't have any idea what I was saying, besides benboon, would they?"

Dr. Howlett smiled at Chad and Kate as they made up other words and pretended to converse in Braza dialect. Then he grew quiet, yawned, and stretched his legs into the tiny opening between Chad's and his dad's front seats. "Hey, you kids can start looking for Cannibal Valley pretty soon," he said. "Let me know if you see any of the nationals—people who are native inhabitants of this country—or any smoke from cooking fires down there."

He folded his arms then, lay his head to one side, and soon fell asleep.

Dad turned a crank under the instrument panel several times.

"What're you doing?" Chad said.

"Letting out the radio antenna wire."

"What's that?"

"Fifty feet of wire that extends out the back of the plane."

"What's it for?" Chad said.

"Tell him, Kate."

"The radio antenna wire makes the plane a bigger target for radio signals," she said, "especially when you're flying in the mountains. You reel it out when you're up and reel it back in before you land."

As Dad set their course for Yawsikor, Chad grew tired of looking for Cannibal Valley. It all looked the same to him. There was a valley all right, as far as the eye could see. The entire side of the mountain range was overgrown, and he saw nothing of anyone or anything else. He tried to see where the river had changed course, but he had no idea what that would look like, so he didn't know what to look for.

In fact, there were no clearings anywhere. What would they use in case of an emergency? Chad wondered if his dad had his eye on any spots. He glanced over, but his dad was no longer scanning the horizon. He seemed more concerned with the instrument panel, especially the fuel gauge. He tapped it, then rapped hard on it. Chad leaned over to take a peek.

"Does that say what I think it says?"

"It has to be a gauge problem," Dad said. "I fueled this plane myself."

"Shouldn't you be looking for clearings?" Chad said. "Like before?"

Dad ignored him, so Chad searched for clearings himself. Still, he saw nothing but trees and jungle. Except for a few muddy rivers, nothing lay below them but green, green, and more green. Even the mountainsides of the Great Dividing Range were covered with foliage.

Despite all the flights he'd been on with his dad, Chad had never before been on a plane that was in trouble. He stole a glance at Kate in the seat behind him. Had she noticed that Dad had changed his routine, that he was tapping hard on the fuel gauge? But Kate was idly drinking from a bottle of distilled water and looking out the window.

Up to this point, Chad had almost been glad he had come on this flight. But now something was definitely wrong. He didn't want to worry Kate, and Dr. Howlett was still asleep.

"Dad," Chad said, "is there anything I can do?"

"I don't know yet. I just hope this is an instrument problem."

Dad, studying the horizon again, got on the radio. "Bime radio, come in, please. Kilo double Hotel forty-forty-eight to Bime radio."

Dad repeated his call several times. Chad knew that the radio at small stations was usually on only a few hours a day, but surely someone monitored it for a little while after a takeoff.

Dad tried his transmission again, and Mrs. Coleman came on.

"This is Bime radio, go ahead."

"Roger, Bime. We just took off from there, and I've got a low fuel reading."

"Did you fuel at Sentani?" she said.

"Roger."

"Then you should be good to Yawsikor. You think it's an instrument problem?"

"Hoping."

"Roger. You want to be safe and set back down here?"

"Negative, but I don't see any clearings here either. We're across the divide, pointed at Yawsikor. Is there any place on this side where I could put down if I had to?"

"Roger, you should see some clearings in about fifteen minutes."

"Roger."

"We'll be praying for you."

"Thanks!" Dad replaced the mike.

"She doesn't sound very concerned," Chad said.

"I'm sure this is everyday stuff for them," Dad said.

"I just hope you're right about the gauge," Chad said. "It says we have no fuel left, let alone fifteen minutes' worth. We couldn't even get back to Bime if we ran out now, could we?"

"Well, no," his dad admitted, "but that won't happen. There's a small reserve fuel tank. I just have to switch over to it."

"Good!"

"Maybe not so good. The first tank shouldn't even be close to empty, and both tanks feed the engine from the same line. If the problem is in the line, we may have plenty of fuel and no way to get it to the engines."

Chad bit his lower lip so hard he tasted blood.

His dad reached under the instrument panel. "The reserve-tank switch handle is right under here. Ah ..." He smiled at Chad. "It's only a loose wire running from the fuel gauge. I was worried for nothing, as usual."

Chad breathed a heavy sigh of relief. "Hope I didn't do that," he said.

"It was probably our passenger," his dad answered. "When you two switched places, he must have caught it with his foot. I might even have done it when I was letting out the antenna wire."

Chad nodded and began looking for clearings again, just in case.

"I see a valley, but I don't see any cannibals," Kate grumbled behind him.

And then the engines began to cough and sputter. Within seconds both engines had died, and Chad's dad was maneuvering the controls as if playing a huge musical instrument. Chad watched as Dad quickly switched to the reserve fuel tank and frantically tried to restart the engine. Loose wire or not, faulty gauge or not, enough fuel or not, the plane had no power. They were going down!

"Dad!" Chad shouted.

"Quiet!" his dad said, and quiet it was. The racket of the noisy engines had stopped, and now Chad heard only the dead stillness of gliding at high altitude. His heart slammed in his chest.

"Why did you turn it off, Dad?" Kate said, leaning forward.

No one answered.

"Should we wake up Dr. Howlett?" Chad said.

Dad shook his head. "Nothing he can do," he said. "And we won't glide long. I'll use the flaps to level us. I just don't want to hit nose-first."

"Can't you restart it?"

"I'm trying!"

He manipulated the controls, but Chad could feel the momentum change from forward to downward. Kate began to cry, and Chad wanted to.

"What can we do?" Chad said.

"Pray!"

"I already am!"

"Me too!" Kate said.

The nose of the plane turned down even more, and Chad felt the pressure build in his ears as they descended. He knew his dad was doing everything he could to keep the plane level, but what good would that do if they had nowhere to land? And if those fuel tanks were full, the plane would explode the second they hit!

"If the engines don't restart," Dad said, "the best I can do is skim the trees and hope for a clearing. If we're shut off when we hit, we're going straight down."

"Will that kill us?" Kate said.

"I hope not," Dad said.

"Will we wake up in heaven with Mom?"

"I believe it!"

"So do I," Chad said, "but I'm scared."

"So am I," Dad answered. "Is there any room in the back? We need as much weight back there as possible!"

Chad looked back to where Dr. Howlett had stored his cargo. They had unloaded only a couple of boxes at Bime. "Kate and I might be able to fit back there. You want us to try?"

"You'd better. Now hurry!"

"Will that save us?" Kate said.

"I don't know," Dad said. "But we have to try!"

Chad and Kate jarred Dr. Howlett awake when they scrambled past and climbed in among the cargo. Chad felt his stomach rise as the plane shuddered and shook against the wind resistance. The cargo suddenly shifted forward and pushed at the restraints. Chad and Kate held on to keep from tumbling to the front of the plane. Dr. Howlett seemed suspended forward, held by only his seat belt.

He clutched the back of Dad's seat. "What's happening?" he said. "Throttle up!"

"No power!" Dad said. "We lost our fuel somehow!"

Dad adjusted the flaps to fight the wind. The plane went from a steep dive to another long glide, which made Chad feel better for only an instant. They were still about to crash, that was certain. He only hoped that somehow they could survive.

But Dr. Howlett grabbed his Bible from his briefcase on the floor and held it tight to his chest. "Lord," he said, "spare us with a miracle or take us all at once. Don't leave one of us alone in a place like this!"

The Crash

“One more sweep away from the mountain and we’re going down!” Dad shouted. “Hang on!”

Chad had never been so scared as they plunged toward the earth faster than any roller coaster he had ever ridden.

Dr. Howlett reached back with his long right arm and pressed his hand against one of his cargo boxes, just under where Chad and Kate lay. “You kids get as far back in the plane as you can!” he shouted.

The plane was vertical now, nose almost straight down. Every time Chad’s dad adjusted the flaps, the cargo slid away from the tail a foot or so, and Chad and Kate hooked their toes on the edges and pushed hard with their hands to keep from dropping to the front of the plane. Chad could see Dr. Howlett straining to keep the cargo from crushing him, one hand jammed against it and the other clutching the back of Dad’s seat. His face was red and covered with sweat, as if he knew he would be sandwiched between the ground and the cargo if they hit.

Chad caught sight of the flaps on the tiny wings struggling to level the plane one more time. Metal and plastic squeaked and groaned as the free-falling craft picked up speed. When the blue outside turned to green, Chad waited for certain death. He and Kate embraced each other, and they heard Dad yell, "I love you kids!"

Chad turned to look at Kate. Her face was a mask of terror. It appeared she wanted to say something, but no words came. They hung on to each other, and as the plane made its last desperate swoop from vertical to almost horizontal, Chad felt the pressure on his body give way. There was now a foot and a half or so of space between the cargo and the tiny rear of the plane.

He pulled with his toes and yanked Kate with him. As he heard first leaves and then branches batter the bottom of the plane, they tumbled into the crevice in the back. Huddled there, their bodies and heads jammed together as if they were one person with eight limbs, Chad heard Kate moan as the plane blasted into the tops of trees.

For the briefest instant, in spite of the noise, it seemed as if the treetops had violently slowed the plane and that it was level. But then they were spinning. From the racket and the direction of the lurch, Chad knew a wing had caught a branch or the trunk of a tree. They were whirled in a circle so fast that Chad almost lost consciousness.

Something ripped a hole in the tail of the plane, and Chad glimpsed the wing that had just been sheered off teetering in a treetop and then cartwheeling to the ground. Kate seemed unconscious already, and Chad wished he was. He didn't want to feel whatever it was that might finally knock him out.

Leaves and branches and vines banged the hurtling plane and made a deafening roar. Chad shut his eyes tight as the plane spun and bounced end over end. The remaining wing bashed into something and the plane seemed to stop dead in the trees, all the weight shifting forward. If they hit the ground, Chad's dad and Dr. Howlett would surely be crushed by the heavy, shifting cargo.

With Kate limp by his side, Chad watched the cargo break through the restraints and smash into the two back seats, ripping them from their bolts in the floor and slamming them into the backs of the front seats. A great groan came from Dr. Howlett.

Chad and Kate slid over the top of the seats and hurtled toward their father, who was trying to protect his head and face with his forearms as the side of the mountain and the jungle floor rushed to fill the windshield.

There seemed to be no space between the cargo and the cockpit now, and no sign of Dr. Howlett. But just before the plane crashed to the ground, it was jerked in yet another direction and bounced crazily on its side.

Barely conscious and hanging on for dear life, Chad could see out the front where the glass had blown out. The plane was hanging from some fibrous, viny tree only a few feet off the ground.

For an instant there was complete silence. Chad was aware of the heat, the humidity, the lack of any wind or even the slightest breeze to move the leaves, some sticking crazily through the holes ripped in the side of the plane. He heard liquid splashing. That had to be fuel, but from where? Would they now explode and burn?

With a squeal and a squeak, what was left of the plane dropped onto its right side, pulling free from the foliage and landing on what felt like solid rock. They'd hit the side of the mountain two hundred feet from the valley floor, and now they began to slide.

For a few seconds, nothing blocked their path. Chad's body was pasted against the side of the plane scraping down the mountain, and he fought to move away from the quickly heating metal.

"Kate?" he called out, as the sliding mass of twisted steel picked up speed again. No answer. And he couldn't see her.

"Dad?"

Nothing.

He didn't call out to Dr. Howlett. His body had to have been crushed between the cargo and Dad's seat from the first great weight shift.

When would this end? The plane kept skidding, sliding through the underbrush, scraping the side of the mountain. It hit something and spun, then dropped another twenty feet or so, blowing open another hole and dumping out cargo — and Dr. Howlett.

Where was Kate? Had she already been thrown clear? And Dad! What would he find if he survived this last plunge? When would it stop?

The next several seconds seemed like minutes on a crazy carnival ride. Something made the careening carcass of what used to be the twin-engine plane spin halfway around again. Now they were dropping backward, tail first, down a ravine. By the time the wreckage finally came to a stop at the bottom of the mountainside, all that was left inside the mangled fuselage were Chad's father, the two front seats, the instrument panel, and Chad, gripping mightily a dangling nylon strap that had once corralled the cargo.

Stunned, Chad heard nothing but the ringing in his ears from the racket of brushing treetops, banging, crashing, hanging, sliding, bumping, sliding cargo, and finally slamming to a stop. Chad let out a huge breath and realized he had been holding it in since the last time he had called out for his dad. His stomach and chest heaved with the effort of catching his breath, and he felt the sobs well within him.

Had anyone else survived? Had God left Chad alone in this horrible place?

"Dad?" he called weakly.

Chad suddenly realized that if he'd stayed in his original seat, he'd have been crushed like Dr. Howlett. Where was Dr. Howlett anyway? Where was Kate? "Dad?" he called again.

Everything in him screamed to move forward, to pick past the debris to his dad. What would he find?

Move! Move! Chad kept telling himself. But his fingers seemed paralyzed, forced into a fist around the nylon strap. He was crouched, almost as if he had surfed down that mountainside. He tried to straighten up, but his knees were swollen and sore and there wasn't room to stand inside the fuselage.

Chad reached with his free hand and pried his fingers from the strap. He tried to move again and his legs gave way. He slumped and sat, his back against the crumpled side of the plane.

Was this some kind of crazy nightmare? Would he wake up, and where? Home in Mukluk?

Or had he and his dad and sister really flown halfway around the world to Indonesia? Would he awaken in the mission home in Jakarta? Or at the compound near Sentani?

Though his mind was reeling, down deep Chad knew the truth. This was no dream. Sweat poured from him, and he felt a chill in spite of the overwhelming heat and humidity. Painfully he straightened his legs and noticed he'd lost both his shoes. As he stared at his puffy ankles, he moved his toes in circles and clenched and unclenched his fists.

Finally, the numbness left, but he almost wished it hadn't. He didn't think he had any broken bones, but he was suddenly sore all over. "Dad!" he called. He knew he had to crawl through the wreckage, but he was terrified of what he'd find.

Without warning, a great fatigue washed over Chad. His mind was foggy. Something made him want to sleep, to roll onto his side, curl up, and close his eyes.

He could not. He *would* not. *Maybe I'm in shock.* He didn't know. As he fought the urge to drift from consciousness, his hands began to shake. Soon his legs quivered too. Then his whole body convulsed into shudders he couldn't control.

This uncontrollable shivering terrified him. Did he really want to sleep? Did he want to die right then and there? If he lived, where would he go for help? Dr. Howlett had said this mountain was 15,000 feet high. How long would it take him to climb through the underbrush all the way up and then all the way down again to the mission station at Bime? Could he evade the Brazas? More important, could he stand or walk at all?

From where he sat, Chad could see the top of his dad's head. He was afraid to see more than that. Between the bowed front seats were the radio headphones, seemingly the only undamaged things in the plane.

Chad fought to stop shaking, then rolled to his side and drew his knees to his chest. Overcome by hopelessness, he tucked his chin to his knees and the sobs came. Chad heard himself wailing in the otherwise eerie silence of the jungle wilderness, and he realized he had not cried since before his mother died.

Kate was gone. Dr. Howlett was gone. Dad wasn't making a sound. The plane was a wreck. And Chad hardly recognized his own body.

Almost without thinking, Chad called out, "God, help me." He didn't expect things to suddenly return to what they were just minutes before. He knew he wouldn't be given some kind of superpower. He wasn't even hoping for that. All he wanted was help. And there was no one anywhere to give it to him. Except God.

Moments later, Chad stopped crying. He still shook, but

he somehow knew that even though he couldn't do much, he might be the only one left who could do anything.

He sat up and clenched his fists painfully. *No more crying*, he told himself. No more sleeping or wishing he'd died. He wanted to do what his dad would do, what his mom would be proud of, what his sister needed.

Chad struggled to all fours, his knees tender as he crawled out of the wreckage. Then, as he tried to drop a couple of feet to the ground, he caught his shirt on a metal shard that hung him up for an instant before tearing loose. He fell hard on his hands and knees. Anger swelled in him. He could hardly walk, hardly move, and he couldn't even jump two feet.

Chad looked up the mountainside at the swath cut by the hurtling plane. He hoped the damage would be visible from the air, in case Bime or Yawsikor sent out a search party. Somewhere up there were Dr. Howlett and Kate, but first he had to think of Dad. He didn't know whether his dad was dead or alive, but he knew one thing for sure.

He couldn't leave his own father in a sweltering box of steel in the middle of nowhere.

Getting to Work

Above all else, even more than the intense feelings of fear and grief, Chad felt alone. He had no idea where—or if—he'd find Kate or Dr. Howlett. But his first task was to somehow get Dad out of the wreckage.

Chad stumbled to the front of the plane and peered in the broken window. His dad was twisted in the seat, his head sagging sideways. Except for a gash in his cheek that had bled all over his neck and shirt, his face was mostly scratched and scraped. His legs were pinned in the cockpit at an odd angle. "Dad, can you hear me?" Chad said.

Dad was obviously unconscious, but was he breathing? Chad fought tears as he leaned in and pressed his head against his father's chest. There it was! A faint heartbeat! Chad jerked back and banged his head on the edge of the window opening, but he barely felt it.

He leaned in again and took Dad's face in both hands, turning it gently toward him and looking for other signs of life. He used his fingers to open one eye, but clearly Dad was not conscious, not seeing anything.

Chad put his ear to his dad's nose, but he heard nothing. What was it they did on TV? Didn't they put a mirror under the nose to see if any vapor formed? Chad wondered if a piece of shattered window glass would work just as well. He leaned in over his dad and grabbed a piece from between the seats. He held it under Dad's nose and waited. Sure enough, Dad was breathing. It was very slow and seemed weak, just like the heartbeat, but his dad, at least for the moment, was alive.

"Dad!" Chad cried. "I need your help!" He wanted to slap his dad's cheek and get him to wake up, but he had to be careful; he didn't want to make any injuries worse. "I have to know where you're hurt!" Dad did not move.

Chad hurried to the other side of what was left of the plane and searched for anything he could use to wake his dad. Had all their distilled water bottles been thrown from the plane? He finally found one under the other front seat. It had been punctured and was nearly empty, but a few inches of lukewarm water remained at the bottom. Chad splashed it in Dad's face, but nothing happened.

He had feared his dad was dead, and now it looked like he was going to die if Chad didn't do something! He crouched on the seat next to his dad, staring at this man who looked so broken. His head hung motionless, now dripping water. With a sudden inspiration, Chad leaned close and blew in his dad's face. As hot and muggy as it was in the jungle, air on water would have to create a change of temperature on the face.

His dad stirred.

"Dad, wake up!"

Dad's eyes slowly opened, and he winced. He tried to speak, but he could form no words.

"Dad! It's Chad! We crashed!"

Dad struggled to bring his hands to his face, but only his left arm was working. He wiped his mouth and turned to stare at Chad.

"Dad! Can you hear me? Where are you hurt?"

"K-K-Kate?" Dad managed in a whisper.

"She was thrown from the plane. Dr. Howlett too. Tell me—"

"Kate," he rasped. "Find Kate!"

"I will. Tell me where you're hurt, and let's get you out of here first. Then I'll look for them."

Dad nodded and took several seconds to form his words. "I'm okay. Are you hurt?"

"I feel awful, but nothing's broken," Chad said. "Where do you hurt?"

Dad sighed and his shoulder slumped again. It was as if talking at all was too much for him. Chad called out to try to keep him conscious. His dad reached across his body with his good hand and pulled Chad close.

"Chad," he said slowly, then took a breath, "I'm hurt bad all over. I think both my legs are broken. You may not be able to get me out of here, but you've got to find Kate. *Now.* If she survived, you have to let her know where we are and help her."

"But you can't stay here like this."

"Just put something behind my back so I can sit up straighter and breathe."

"Like what?"

"Anything."

"Everything was thrown from the plane. There's nothing soft. How about these earphones?"

Dad moved his eyes; Chad guessed he was unable to turn his head. "Did you have a water bottle?"

"Part of one."

"Try that."

Chad helped his dad sit forward so the bottle could slide down behind him. Dad's scream as he moved was the most painful thing Chad had ever heard. He knew now what it meant to wish someone else's pain was your own. Dad had always been the strong one. When he was hurt, he never showed it. He had nearly cut off a finger on a table saw once, but he had actually smiled on the way to the emergency room.

"Dad, will you be okay for a few minutes?"

"There'll be plenty of time for me," Dad said. "But listen, Spitfire. If anything happens to me—"

"Don't say that. You're not going to die."

"I'll try not to, buddy, but we can't play games anymore. If anything happens to me, you and Kate and Dr. Howlett need to try to get the radio rigged up and get a message out."

"I don't even know where the radio is!"

"It's right here."

"But it can't be working."

"I'll check it. You go look for them."

"Dad, you—"

"Go!"

It was so painful to watch Dad try to talk that Chad was almost glad to get away from him for a while. On the other hand, he was scared that without him there for encouragement, Dad might give up.

As Chad headed up the path the plane had taken, he felt as if every bone in his body had been crushed. He was stiff and sore, and he limped on both feet. He felt pain in his feet, his ankles, his knees, his hips, his back, his neck, his arms, and his head. *What else is there?* he wondered.

Chad climbed about a hundred feet, pulling himself

along slowly and painfully by grabbing foliage. He didn't know what kinds of creatures to expect in this jungle. He just knew he didn't want to step on anything that would bite. Until he found something to wear on his feet, he would move very slowly.

Chad was tempted to call for Kate and Dr. Howlett, or to call down to Dad to make sure he was all right. But he didn't want anyone else to hear. Who knew how close a Braza village full of cannibals might be?

Chad stopped every so often to listen, but for what he didn't know. A cry from Kate? A shout from Dr. Howlett? Once when he stopped, he heard something. Did these cannibals, the Brazas, have poison-dart guns? Spears? Knives? Did they set traps? Or would they just surround him or run him over in a pack?

What was that? Footsteps? The wind? The jungle was so moist and hot that Chad welcomed even the slightest breeze. And then he saw it. About twenty feet up the path, in an area that had been cleared by the plunging plane, a wisp of a breeze was gently flapping what appeared to be pages.

Chad quickened his pace. This must be something from the plane. He couldn't imagine anyone ever having been in this part of the jungle before. The clearing was just a ten-foot shelf, a leveling in the mountainside. It was where the plane must have hit that last time, throwing out Dr. Howlett.

Chad reached the source of the faint noise and picked up Dr. Howlett's well-worn Bible. The years he'd spent in this climate had dried the cover and made it crumble. The book's spine was broken, maybe by use or maybe due to the plunge from the plane.

Chad needed to continue his search for Kate and Dr. Howlett, so he closed the book and set it down. The slight breeze made him shiver. He felt an urgency to hurry, but he was in so much pain he found it difficult to move.

Where were they, and what position was the plane in when Dr. Howlett was thrown clear? Chad guessed that Dr. Howlett had fallen through the opening on the left side of the plane. He looked in that direction and saw one of Dr. Howlett's hiking boots, the sock still inside. Crazily, the boot was upright. Chad walked farther and saw another boot sticking out of some brush, only this one was pointed toe upward, as if worn by someone lying on his back. Which Dr. Howlett was.

Chad had seen only two dead bodies before. One was at the funeral of a classmate who had drowned. The other was his mother's, also at her funeral. He mustered his courage and checked for a pulse on the man's wrist and at the pressure point in his neck. He bent low to listen for breathing too. Nothing.

Dr. Howlett, Chad knew, was probably crushed by

the shifting cargo the first time the plane stopped. Chad promised himself he'd come back and bury the man later. It would be the only right thing to do. But for now, he took a deep breath and unlaced the man's remaining boot and carried it over to the other one. He sat awkwardly and put them both on. They were several sizes too big, but he could move much better now. He hoped he would find his own hiking boots somewhere up the path; more than that he hoped he would find Kate—alive.

He figured Kate might have been thrown from the plane at least another hundred feet up the side of the mountain. He hadn't actually seen her fall, but he recalled that she was missing before Dr. Howlett was thrown. Chad started the difficult, slippery trek up, painfully raising his legs high on each step so the long soles of Dr. Howlett's boots would not drag on the mountainside.

Five minutes later, about forty feet off the path down a tricky ravine, Chad spotted two cargo boxes still intact, plus the cooler Dr. Howlett had bragged about. He'd been right. After dropping from the plane, it hadn't even broken open. Chad only wished he and his family and Dr. Howlett had been as fortunate.

About twenty-five feet farther up the mountain were two more huge crates, but these had split open and cargo was strewn about. One left a trail of things for several yards. Chad didn't bother to see what it all was. If by some miracle Kate had survived, he wanted to get to her as soon as possible.

Chad felt his heart racing and his lungs heaving, and he stopped to rest. He was dizzy and exhausted; the climb in his condition took more from him than he realized. He couldn't get the images of his dad and Dr. Howlett out of his mind. It had been only minutes since the crash, and he had seen more horror and tragedy than ever before in his life. It was too much to take in, too much to think about.

Chad wanted to call out for Kate. Who knew how far from the path she might have been flung? In the silence he heard only his own breathing. He became frantic to get back to his dad. He waited for his breath to return and his pulse to slow, then he set his sights toward the gouge in the trees where the plane had first come down. Kate had been in the plane for several hundred feet past that. Unless she had been thrown so far that he couldn't see her, she would probably be on one side or the other from that point downward.

Chad bent at the waist and set his shoulders forward, grabbing leaves and branches as he trudged up the mountain. It wasn't long before his breathing became labored again and his throat grew dry, but he didn't want to stop. He wanted to find Kate so at least he could tell Dad something.

It would be bad enough to return with the report of Dr. Howlett's death. He hoped against hope that he could tell Dad he'd found his sister—alive.

Suddenly, Chad stopped dead in his tracks. Something caught his ear again. In the stillness he heard movement in the underbrush. This was no rattling paper, no breeze in a clearing. Something was moving, something bigger than a small animal.

God, Chad prayed silently, *please don't let that be a cannibal. Not now!*

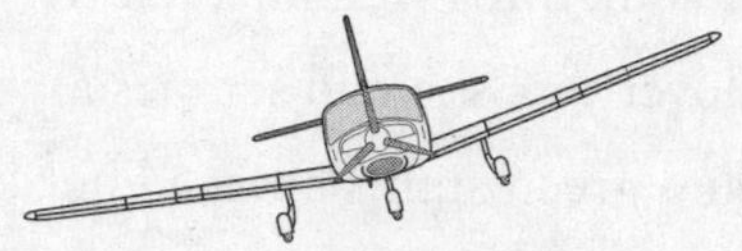

First Things First

Chad carried nothing with which he could defend himself. Maybe he should have picked through that strewn cargo. Had this animal, or Braza, or whatever it was, seen him? Fortunately, there were plenty of places to hide. The movement came from his right, so he stepped quietly to the left, away from the narrow clearing cut by the crashing plane.

Chad crouched in the underbrush, panting, but trying to keep quiet. Was it a war party? He didn't even know if the Brazas had such a thing. But what would he do if they surrounded him? He was no match for a seventh grader with a snowball, let alone a cannibal in the jungle! Now he saw movement in the leaves across the way. He prayed that whoever it was did not have friends to sneak up from behind, or drop from the trees, or jump from the grass.

He held his breath as the form emerged into the path. Kate! She stopped and turned one way and then the other, as if looking for something or someone. In tennis shoes, shorts, and pullover top, she had scrapes all over her body. Pieces of bark and green stains covered her legs and arms and face.

Chad hurried to her. "Kate?" he whispered. He wanted to hug her, but he was afraid he might make any injuries worse.

"Oh, hi, Chad," she said, as if she had just run into him at school. "Do you know where Mom is? I can't find my parka anywhere."

"Your parka!" Chad almost shouted. "Kate, it's a hundred degrees out here!"

"Mom doesn't want me out without my parka and my gloves." She looked down and stamped her foot. "And these aren't my boots! Where are my boots? Are those my boots you're wearing?"

"These are Dr. Howlett's," Chad spoke more softly. "Kate, you're hurt. You'd better sit down."

"I'm not hurt," she whined, eyes darting. "I'm just cold, and Mom's gonna be mad at me."

"Come with me," Chad said. "We'll find your coat."

He took her hand, and they carefully made their way back down the mountain.

"This isn't our yard, is it?" she said.

"No, it's not," Chad said. "Do you know where we are, Katie?"

She shook her head. "Nope."

Chad knew she couldn't deal with it right then. After a bit, they stopped to rest and Chad took a closer look at her. She must have been thrown right into a tree, face-first, and slid to the ground. Tiny branches and twigs and bark had scraped her face and arms raw. And who knew what internal injuries she might have? She had probably been unconscious until just before he found her. Chad couldn't believe she had been thrown from a plane and was now walking. He wondered how long that would last.

When they reached where Chad had found Dr. Howlett's body, he distracted her. "Oh, look, Kate! Somebody's Bible, right here in the path."

"Probably Mom's," she said. "Where is Mom?"

Chad slipped and let go of Kate to keep from pulling her down. He grabbed the Bible and struggled to his feet as she stared at him.

"What happened to you?" she said. "You've got bruises all over."

"We were in a plane crash, Kate," Chad said. "Do you remember?"

"No, we weren't! Dad's in the war in the desert. Mom's going to pick us up from school, and we're going to go get him at the airport."

Chad put his hand gently on her shoulder. "Kate. Listen to me. Do you know where we are?"

"No."

"Mom's in heaven, remember?"

Kate squinted, appearing to try to make sense of it all. "Mom was in an accident," she said finally.

"Yes," Chad said. "Now you remember."

"The drunk guy didn't stop at the red light. He killed Mom before she even picked us up from school!"

"That's right. Dad got to the airport, and we were there without Mom, remember?"

She nodded and began to cry. "The policeman told him. It was supposed to be a big, happy time, but he was crying. Chad?"

"What, Katie?"

"I think I'm hurt."

"We're all hurt, Kate. Dad's hurt too. We're going to go see him right now, okay?"

She took Chad's hand again and stumbled down the slippery, grassy, rocky pathway. Dad still sat in the plane, rigid with the empty water bottle behind him. He gave a weak wave with his good hand.

"Dad!" Kate reached in and grabbed his good hand.

Chad noticed that the shoe on her right foot looked tighter, as if her foot was swelling. "Let's get that shoe off," he said, and she finally let him sit her down. Her foot was so swollen that the laces were hard to untie. He struggled to slip the shoe off, then peeled off the sock.

Oh, man! What am I supposed to do about this?

The toes on her right foot were swollen, and he figured they must be broken. He didn't want to be there when she began to feel that pain. "You stay right here, you hear?" he said.

Chad limped to his father. "We've got to get you out of there," he said.

Dad winced as he tilted his head to get a look at Kate. "She looks awful," he said in that gravelly voice. Chad told him it looked as if she had slammed into a tree. "Probably right," Dad said. "I'm so sorry, Chad."

"You're sorry? This wasn't your fault."

"I know. I'm sorry about all you're having to do by yourself."

"I don't have any choice. I'm the only one who can move much."

"Did you find Dr. Howlett?"

"He's dead, Dad."

"Oh, no. How will we ever tell his wife? They've been married more than forty years."

"When will we ever tell his wife, Dad? We're not getting out of here."

Dad turned slowly to look directly at Chad. Every word was a chore. "Come here and listen to me," he said. "We're not going to give up ever, are we?"

Chad looked away.

"Are we?" Dad repeated.

"No, sir."

"Say it like you mean it. Nothing less than our best will get us out of here."

"It's impossible!"

"Nothing is impossible. You know that. God spared us for a reason. I can't believe he would let us survive that crash, only to die a few days later."

"I can't believe that either, but I can't do this! You know I'm no outdoorsman! We're—"

"Chad, what have I taught you all your life?"

"I know."

"Tell me!"

"To be a can-do person, not a can't-do person. But this—"

"I know this is the biggest test anyone could ever face, Spitfire. But either we're going to make it because we're determined to do everything God gives us the strength to do, or we're going to be quitters. Chad, I can't move. All I can do is help you decide what to do. But I promise I'll do my part if you'll do yours. I promise I won't give in or give up. We all need each other. Let's beat this. What do you say?"

"I'll try, but what can I do?"

"First, check your own damage. Start with anything life-threatening. Do you have any injuries that might kill you?"

"I don't think so."

"Any broken bones?"

"Maybe, but they all seem like sprains."

"Sounds like you just got knocked around pretty good. You'll be sore a long time, but I'm guessing you're not critically injured."

"It won't be long before Kate won't be able to walk."

"Then deal with her next."

"Dad, I don't even know where to start."

"Now you're talking."

"I am?"

"Yes, that's what I want to hear. When we start wondering where to start, that's when we start prioritizing. You remember what that means?"

Chad nodded. "Deciding what to do first."

"Right. Now, what time is it?"

"My watch is gone," Chad said. "What does yours say?"

Dad slowly brought his left arm up in front of his eyes. "Unless this has stopped, it's almost eight-thirty in the morning."

"Seems like we've been here all day," Chad said. "It's hot already."

"It'll get hotter, believe me, especially here. I already feel dehydrated. The first thing you have to do is get me out of this little seat."

"I'll really try, but how?"

"Well, ignore my screams, for one thing. The way it hurt when you put that bottle behind me is nothing compared to what I'll feel when you drag me across the other seat and onto the ground. I'll try to help you with my left hand, but it's going to take some leverage and some pulling. You'll have to do it, no matter what I say or do. Then, once you get me set up under some kind of shade out of the sun, I can tell you what to do next."

"What should I do about Dr. Howlett?"

"Bury him before the sun gets too high. We don't want animals getting to him."

"Or cannibals."

"I wouldn't worry about them just now."

"Why not? They can't be far away."

"I don't think they'd come to investigate a racket like we made, do you? It should scare them more than make them curious."

Chad sure hoped his dad was right. "How can I bury a big man like that?"

"Spitfire, you'll do it, with God's help, because you're the only one who can. You're going to round up all the cargo you can find, and set us up a little stash of supplies. And somewhere, somehow, you're going to find or make the tools you need to do what you've got to do. One thing I'm sure of: You'll sleep well tonight."

Kate limped over to them.

"Kate!" Chad scolded. "I told you to stay put!"

"But I'm hurt! What happened?" Suddenly she sounded like herself.

"It's all right, Chad," Dad said. "Katie, listen. Chad's gonna pull me out of here, and you'll hear me scream. Just cover your ears. I promise I'll feel better when it's over, all right?" She nodded. "And you're going to be brave for me, okay?" She nodded again, but Chad didn't think she thought things were okay any more than he did.

In the past half hour, Chad had been through more than anyone, let alone a kid, should have to go through in a lifetime. But Dad was right. There was more work to do. He had to do the toughest stuff first, and he had to do it soon.

Getting Dad out of the plane was even harder than he'd expected. The plan was to pull him out on the right, so Dad leaned over on the front passenger seat. "My right arm is obviously broken, so be careful of that. My legs may be broken too, but I can't feel them. I don't know how we can avoid hurting my hip. I'll try pushing and pulling with my left arm, and I want you to drag me by my belt until you can get a grip on one of my legs."

It seemed to take forever, and as Dad had predicted, he screamed with every move. But every time Chad hesitated or let up, Dad yelled, "Keep going! Keep going!"

Dad had begun by leaning over and pushing himself away from the left side with his good arm. Then, once he was on his back on the right seat, Chad put his hand under his father's good shoulder and grabbed his belt. He jerked and yanked until Dad's torso was almost out one side of the plane and his mangled legs were in the pilot seat. With a surge of energy, they worked together until Dad flopped out onto the ground, his legs still up in the doorway.

"Dad, I'm killing you!" Chad said.

"Leaving me in there would kill me," Dad said, the pain clear on his face. He used his good hand to try to hold his hip in place as Chad took his feet and pivoted his body free of the plane. "Now, if you can just get me over by that tree, I can stretch out."

It took Chad several minutes to drag his father, holding him under his arms, across the ground. Finally, Chad situated him with his back against a tree about fifty feet from the wreckage.

"Get Kate near me. Then you've got to start carting the cargo down here. Anything you can salvage, we'll probably need. If you find any pieces of the fuselage up there that you can handle, they might make a good lean-to."

By the time Chad left his dad and sister to head up the mountainside again, Kate lay whimpering in obvious pain.

Chad turned his eyes away when he came to where Dr. Howlett's body lay. He had no idea how he would bury him. How would he ever get that large man down the mountain?

For now, all he had to worry about was finding the cargo. He decided to start at the highest point where he'd seen anything and keep pushing stuff down before him as he went. Just getting up and down the mountain was a chore. He wondered many times whether he could do this.

At the point closest to where the plane first hit the trees, Chad spotted the radio antenna wire draped high in some branches. He couldn't reach the low end of it, and jumping or climbing a tree was the last thing he wanted to think about it. Maybe he could get to it later if he needed it.

The next thing he found was the top of one of Dr. Howlett's trunks. It was a three-foot by four-foot lid that had broken off its hinges, and it would make a perfect sled. He turned it over and loaded it with as many useful items as he could find. He included vines and twigs to use for setting and wrapping sprains or broken bones.

In a duffel bag hanging from a low branch, Chad found some of Dr. Howlett's personal belongings, including a leather belt and a long, heavy, sharp machete. That huge knife might come in handy. He first used it to poke a hole in the trunk lid, then he threaded the belt through the hole and fastened it. That would keep the trunk from sliding off the path, or all the way down the mountain. Once he got the lid loaded, he used the weight of the sled to help him walk upright, and then he followed it down by hanging on to the belt.

Two other trunks still had side handles attached, so after checking on Dad and Kate, he struggled back up after them. He heaved and pushed them to the path, and then let them slide down the same way. After an hour, Chad made a large pile near Dad. It was everything he could find that had bounced out of the plane.

Among the pile he found his own socks and boots; he had expected to wear them after a soccer game at Yawsikor. They would make it much easier to climb and walk. He also found an extra shirt for both himself and Dad. Dr. Howlett's personal suitcase held lots of clothes and toiletries that would be useful. Kate could wrap herself in some of his clothes to keep warm that night. Chad also found a copy of the wordless book Dr. Howlett had told them about.

He opened the last trunk to find a treasure of snacks and treats! Dr. Howlett had packed a couple dozen boxes of fruit punch, the kind with straws attached. He also found a dozen bottles of distilled water, six candy bars, and an entire box of individually wrapped packages of crackers and cookies. Chad and Dad figured they could live for days on that alone. But in addition, Dr. Howlett's indestructible cooler contained a Chinese dinner feast that would feed six or eight adults. Everything had spilled and run together, but if they could keep it from spoiling, the three of them could make it last for days — if they had to.

"Chad, did you find my backpack?" Dad said, looking around.

"Yeah, over there. I found all three of them."

"Great! Mine has a first-aid kit in the bottom. There should be some gauze and bandages and even some antiseptic."

Chad found the kit and helped Dad clean and dress the cuts on his face and his side. The smell of blood mixed with his dad's sweat made Chad queasy, but he kept at his work. Then he bandaged Kate's many scrapes and cuts. He spent several minutes pulling huge splinters from her face and arms and trying to clean her up as well as he could. Then he sprayed antiseptic on her forehead and made her shriek.

"Now, Kate," Dad said, "you may not want to watch while Chad and I try to set my broken arm."

Chad felt dizzy when he saw the bone sticking through the skin. Dad coached him on how to pull his right forearm from the wrist and elbow until the protruding bone clicked back into place.

"I can't do that, Dad!"

"You have to, Spitfire. It'll be okay." Dad put a roll of gauze in his mouth to bite on. Tears poured down Dad's cheeks as Chad worked. At one point Dad reached over with his good hand and helped pull on the arm himself. Then Chad bound the forearm crudely with sticks and a vine.

"Is he gonna do that to my toes too?" Kate said.

"No," Dad said, hissing in pain. "We're not sure they're broken. It's almost impossible to set toes anyway."

Kate lay back in the shade, whimpering. Her foot looked horrible, even more swollen. Chad's heart sank. It was clear that he was the only one left who could walk.

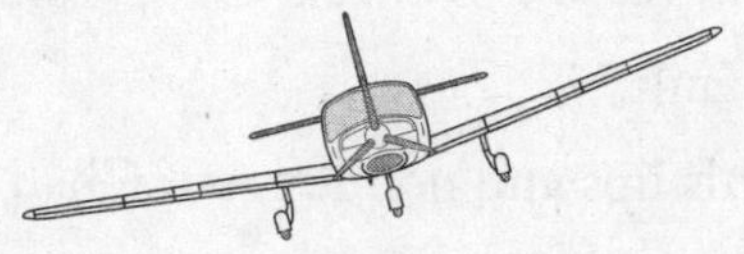

Progress

Chad's dad called him close. "It's driving me crazy trying to figure out what went wrong," he said. His throat was still weak and talking sounded painful. "Did you hear that splashing sound before we started to slide?"

Chad nodded.

"That had to be the reserve fuel tank. That means there was a problem in the line. It was either blocked or had a leak. More likely, it was a leak. If there was a block, we never would have gotten out of Bime. There had to be a hole in the line that emptied the first fuel tank, and then when I switched over to the reserve tank, there was already air in the line."

"How could that have happened?"

"I don't know. We were good coming out of Sentani. The landing at Bime was a little rough, and we may have kicked up a stone. I should have checked."

"There was no reason to check, Dad," Kate said weakly. "It wasn't your fault."

Dad pursed his lips and nodded, but Chad knew he blamed himself. To change the subject, Chad told Dad that he had a plan to pull Dr. Howlett's body down the mountain on the trunk lid, the same way he had moved a lot of the loose cargo.

"Chad," Dad said slowly, "you may find this hard to understand right now when so many other things seem so important. But I think Dr. Howlett's family will really appreciate your efforts."

"Why?"

"Well, they will know, just as we know, that he is gone. His body is just a shell he used when he was here. But they love him, and will be relieved to know you did your best. You understand?"

"I think so."

"Just be careful."

With Dad's advice in mind, Chad made the difficult trip back up the mountain, pulling the trunk lid behind him. How could he do this? How could he touch a dead body, let alone wrestle it onto this homemade sled? Would he even fit? He hoped Dr. Howlett would not be much heavier than the loads he had followed down already.

Chad was weak and tired and wanted to collapse, but he knew how important it was to see that Dr. Howlett was properly buried.

Chad closed his eyes and tried to avoid looking at the man's cut, bruised face. Finally he took off his own shirt, wrapped it around Dr. Howlett's face, and strained to roll the big man onto the trunk lid. Slowly, step-by-step, Chad held tight to the belt he had fastened to the trunk lid and followed the load down the mountain.

"Bring me Dr. Howlett's Bible," Dad said. "We'll have a little ceremony, then you need to bury him. Not too deep, but enough to protect the body from the elements until we're rescued."

"If we're rescued," Chad said.

"*When* we're rescued," Dad corrected.

Chad retrieved the Bible and Dad leafed through it, looking for something to say. "Oh, kids," he said, his voice thick with emotion, "look at this."

He showed them the inscription in the front of the book: "To my beloved on our wedding day." It was signed by Dr. Howlett's wife.

"And look," Dad said, "you can't turn to a page anywhere in this Bible without seeing some underlining or a note. We'll have to keep this safe so we can give it to his wife."

Chad told Dad about finding the wordless book. "She's probably got a whole bunch of those," Chad said. "But she might want the one he had in his suitcase when he died."

"She just might," Dad agreed. "Now, before you bury him, let me just say that this was a man who really loved the Lord and loved his Word. I don't know what else we can say about him. I didn't know him well, but I know he was a good husband and father, a missionary statesman, and someone who cared about winning people to Christ. Let's pray.

"Lord, thank you for the privilege of knowing Dr. Howlett. We know he is with you right now, because that is what your Word promises. Comfort his family when they hear of this. And help us, Lord."

Dad suggested that the grave should be on the other side of the plane, opposite their little camp. "That way, if the wreckage is spotted from the air, they'll see that you dug a hole and covered it over, and they'll know there were survivors."

"They'll know at least one person died too," Chad said.

"They won't be surprised," Dad said.

Chad developed blisters on his palms while digging the shallow grave with Dr. Howlett's machete and his bare hands. He knelt and covered the body with a mound of dirt. The whole time he prayed that this nightmare would soon be over.

He made his way back to where Dad and Kate were half-dozing in the heat. "I have to rest, Dad," he said. He flopped to the ground in a dirty, broken heap.

"I know," Dad said, "but first let Kate give you her ideas about the radio."

"The radio isn't working," Chad said. "It doesn't even switch on."

Kate roused. "The battery cables probably came loose in the crash. If the battery wasn't smashed, it should still work."

"But how do you know it isn't ruined?"

"We won't know until we can get some juice to it," she said.

"Anyway," Chad said, "we're almost three miles down in a valley. The antenna wire is stuck up in the trees."

"Really?" Kate said. "You saw it?"

He nodded.

Kate looked at Dad. "You didn't reel it in before we went down?"

"I was hardly thinking about that."

"I couldn't reach the wire, though, Kate," Chad said. "I'd have to climb a tree to get to it."

"Leave it where it is," she said. "First see if the battery and the radio both work. Then get them out of the plane and take them up the mountain to where you can hook the antenna wire to the radio. Having the wire strung out through the trees is probably the best."

"The best for what?"

"For search parties."

"They're not gonna see a little wire in the trees."

"No, but they'll be sending and listening for radio signals. We want our radio to be where they can hear it or reach it."

"Do I have to stay up there by the radio?"

"Not for long," Dad said. "Assuming it even works, we're already past the wind curfews. No one will be flying into or out of Bime until tomorrow morning. We'll be missed at Yawsikor soon, and they'll communicate with Sentani and Bime. It won't be long before Mrs. Coleman lets them know when she heard from us last. She'll tell them we were complaining of fuel gauge problems, so they'll likely start the search just over the divide from Bime."

"Should we have a fire going or spread something out in the trees that they might see from the air?" Chad said. "We're pretty deep in the bush here."

"You can try putting something up there that they could see, but we'll have to be careful of fires and smoke if we don't want nationals in this area to know we're here."

Chad's heart skipped a beat. "The cannibals, you mean?"

"Dr. Howlett himself said there have been no reports of cannibalism for years," Dad said. "But this is the Brazas' area. I can't imagine they even know we're here, but there's no sense frightening them and making it obvious either."

"But doesn't it get cold here at night? If we can't have a fire, how will we keep warm?"

"The tribal people smear their bodies with pig fat. Short of that, we may have to make some sort of a stove that hides the light of the fire and sends smoke up only after dark."

Chad knew that being seen from the air or heard over the radio were their best and probably only chances of being rescued. Tired and sore as he was, he trudged to the plane and began pulling sheets of metal from its crumpled sides. He bent them back and forth until they snapped. When he had a half dozen pieces of from a foot square to about three feet square, he knew he had enough. He would place them along the path the plane had sheared into the mountainside. Hopefully the sun would hit them and reflect their light to search planes. The search party might see the sheared-off wing in the trees too, but Chad would place these so it was obvious they weren't just the result of the crash. He would shape them in a circle or a cross so the searchers would know there were survivors.

Kate explained how to remove the radio from the control panel in the cockpit, and Dad said Chad should find the battery in the nose cone of the plane. "The nose never hit the ground, so the battery may still be in one piece. We can hope."

As Chad climbed into the tiny cockpit, made even smaller by the crash, he hurt to think about Dad and Kate. Dad had confided to him, when Kate couldn't hear, that any one of the three of them might have serious internal injuries. They might be bleeding inside. What that meant to Chad was that time was everything. Who knew how long they could survive, especially unprotected from the elements?

Chad was amazed, as always, at what Kate knew about radios. She was right. He needed no tools to get the radio out of the control panel. There were only a couple of wing nuts to loosen, and one had snapped off anyway. "They make these easy to get out," Kate had said, "because they're easier to work on in the hangar than in the plane."

It was more difficult to get into the nose cone, but when he did, Chad discovered that Dad was right too. All the shaking and rattling from the crash and slide had jarred the battery loose from the wiring. It was not connected to the radio or anything else on the control panel, and it was far from the long-dead engines.

The battery was heavy, and Chad could hardly budge it. A short, plastic lifting belt was built into it, but even with both hands he couldn't lift it the necessary two feet to get it out of the nose cone. He noticed then that part of the metal nose was on hinges, and it appeared that a huge crease along the other side could possibly be bent again and again until the cone was split in two.

One piece could probably be molded into a perfect small furnace. The other might be straightened and be the beginning of that lean-to his father had suggested. These thoughts were encouraging, but even so Chad was overcome by fatigue. His head ached and his joints seemed to cry out. He slumped to the ground, his back against the plane. How could he go on like this? He wanted to trust God, and he wanted to believe it was possible to survive. But he could do only so much. He knew Dad and Kate would help if they could, but their survival and rescue depended on him.

He looked forward to showing Dad the pieces of the nose cone, as soon as he could muster the strength to tear them apart. And even though that would make the battery easier to get to and drag out, how would he ever lug both the battery and the radio all the way up the mountain and attach the radio to the antenna wire? He would have to use Dr. Howlett's belt again, but would it damage the battery to drag it? He'd have to use the trunk lid again as a sled. There seemed to be solutions for everything, but that didn't make his job any easier.

As he sat thinking, he felt his body wanting to shut down. If only he could take a nap. Didn't he have until early the next morning to rig up the radio anyway? Maybe if he could make the furnace, shape the lean-to, and make sure the battery worked, then he could take a break. But could he last till then?

Suddenly he spotted a long, narrow plume of smoke rising on the horizon maybe two or three miles away. This was his worst nightmare. That had to be a cooking fire, and it could only be coming from the Braza settlement.

Did those cannibals know his family was here? Had they seen the crash? In that instant Chad realized time was one luxury he could not afford. There was a lot of work to do, and it had to be done now. He made it his goal to create an invisible source of heat, make a shelter from the wind, give some of the snacks and food to Dad and Kate, get the radio functioning, and get it up the mountain to the antenna wire, all before dark.

Come dawn and the early morning flights out of Sentani and Bime, he wanted to be on the radio and visible from the sky. He also knew they had to avoid being visible to the Brazas on the ground. Was that even possible? No matter how overwhelmed and exhausted he felt, he had to try.

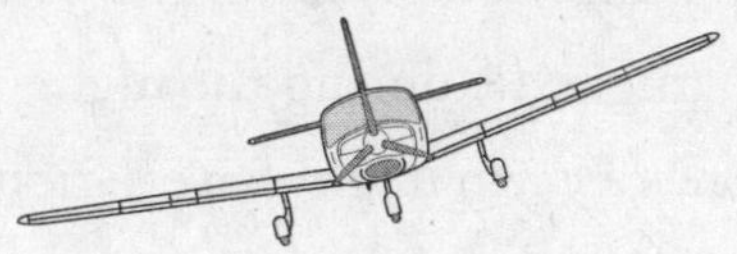

News

Chad started building their shelter with the cargo he found. After several trips back and forth to the plane, he finished the job by reshaping one half of the nose cone and building a little furnace out of the other half.

Dad was impressed and said so, but Chad was uneasy. He had made the difficult decision not to tell Dad or Kate about the smoke he had seen on the horizon. And the jerry-rigged lean-to, made from airplane skin, nose cone, and a variety of trunks, backpacks, duffel bags, and junk, blocked their view of the smoke.

Dad looked worse with each passing hour. He barely moved, and a sheen of perspiration covered his face. Kate, pale and weak, breathed heavily. That, Chad knew, was not a good sign. Maybe she had injured a lung, or maybe there was other damage. He couldn't know. And he didn't know how to help her anyway.

Chad tried to push from his mind the possibility that one or both of them might die during the night. Dad was right, of course, any one of them might have serious internal injuries. If they weren't hurt so badly, and if one of them could help Chad, maybe they could hold out for a few days. But not this way. Neither Dad nor Kate was likely to improve enough to walk in the next few days. Whatever Chad had to do to get them out of there, he had to do as soon as possible.

Chad pulled the belt out of the trunk-lid sled that had served him so well and took it back to the plane. He threaded it under the plastic carrier on the battery, then fastened the buckle and slipped the other end of the loop over his right shoulder.

The battery was so heavy it made the belt dig deeply into his shoulder. He lowered it to the ground and decided to make sure the battery still worked before he lugged it all over the place. He sat straddling the box and studying it. Just like a car battery, it had negative and positive poles, one black and one red.

How do you know when a battery is still good? he wondered. He pressed his left index finger on the negative pole and felt a tingly sensation. Then he reached for the positive pole with his right hand.

The next thing Chad knew, he was on his back. He had completed the circuit, and the charge had driven his elbows back so fast that his upper body followed and slammed the back of his head on the ground. *I'm stupid!* He should have known better than to do that from elementary school science. He certainly didn't need more injuries. He was already sore enough.

So the battery's fine. Now, if the radio was okay, the battery should make it come to life. He would need Kate's advice in hooking it up, however. He looped the belt over his shoulder again, carried the much lighter radio and headphones in his left hand, arm extended to provide some balance, and hauled the battery back to their campsite. By now Dad had maneuvered into a prone position on his back and was sleeping. Chad didn't know if that was good or not, but he certainly didn't want to wake him.

He sat by Kate. "Maybe you should get some sleep too," he said.

"I will," she said. "But let's see if that radio works first."

Chad dragged the stuff over by her. Any time she moved, even to reach and point at something, she winced.

"Just tell me," Chad said. "I can do it."

She patiently walked him through the process for attaching the wires.

"Be careful not to get a shock," she said.

He almost laughed. He wasn't about to admit his stupidity. How strange it was to smile—even briefly—in the middle of all this horror.

Two connections were to be made in an area so small that Chad had to rummage through Dr. Howlett's toiletries to find a pair of tweezers and make the attachments. Once everything was connected, Kate said, "Just flip that switch. If the red light comes on, you've got power."

He did and it did. "Yes!" they said in unison.

"Now," she said, "play with that tuning button. You won't hear anything except maybe some static until you're hooked up to the antenna wire, but that green light will tell you if you've locked onto any strong frequency."

Chad turned the dial until the green light burned faintly. He played it back and forth until the light was solid and bright. "Good news, right?" he said.

"Best I've had all day. Now click on the microphone like you're going to transmit. If it makes the green light go out, it's probably working too."

Chad held down the switch on the mike. The green light still shone.

"Not so good," Kate said. "Check the connection and move it around a little. Keep the switch on."

When Chad pushed the connector in and out or twisted it a little, the green light wavered. "Good?" he said.

She shook her head. "If it goes completely out, you can be heard. If it just gets faint, you'll sound crackly and faint too. If it goes on and off, they'll catch only a little of what you say. You'll just have to try it. If they can hear you, you'll know. With the headphones on, you'll know right away whether you can hear them. Once you get it hooked to the antenna wire, keep it set at the strongest frequency and try calling Bime."

"In the morning, you mean."

"I guess. If there's no one flying until then, there won't be much radio traffic now."

"I'll find out," Chad said. "First, I'm going to get something for us to eat and drink. Think we should wake up Dad?"

"He looks like he's really resting," she said. "Maybe I'll wake him up in an hour or so. It sure is hot."

"Sure is," Chad said.

It felt like over a hundred degrees and as humid as jungles can get. Their clothes were soaked through.

"Aren't you hurt?" Kate said. "I feel so bad that you have to do all the work."

"Yeah, I hurt, but mostly I'm tired. I've already worked harder in just this one day than in my entire life."

"That wouldn't be hard," Kate said, smiling weakly.

"Hey," he said. "Be nice or I'll leave you here."

It felt so good to actually be teasing again.

"I sure don't want to go up that mountain again," Chad said as he dug through the foodstuffs and found some cookies and water. "This won't be very cold. Later, maybe I'll try cooking some of that rice from the cooler."

"You'd better eat, Chad."

He nodded and stuffed some cookies into his mouth. Then he took a quick drink. The water was warm, but quenched his thirst. He felt an almost immediate surge of energy from the cookies. He stood and stretched his sore muscles and joints.

"Better get going before I can't move at all," he said. "I'll leave this stuff close enough for Dad to reach."

Chad was tempted to tell Kate what to do if she needed him while he was gone. He knew he could hear her from a couple of hundred feet up the mountainside if she called out or screamed. But he didn't want to give her any ideas. If she called out or screamed at all, the noise would surely bring the Brazas right to the camp. He would just pray they didn't come this way before he got back. Of course, he didn't want them to ever come around, but at least if he was in the camp, he would have the machete. That was something he couldn't carry up the mountain this trip.

Chad believed this would be his last climb of the day, but he had no idea how difficult it would be. The battery pulling at the belt over his shoulder was heavy and painful and awkward enough, but trying to carry the radio, headphones, and microphone was nearly impossible. He was left with no free hand to help him climb.

He wrapped the microphone cord and the earphones around the radio, worrying he might be damaging them. He tucked the whole mess under his free arm, but he couldn't get any leverage. When he tried to reach with his arm that carried the battery, the belt slipped and the battery swung and bumped him, knocking him off balance.

Chad felt like giving up, and he slumped in the path. He stole a glance at the horizon. Now two columns of smoke billowed from a mile or two away. He must think of something. He finally decided to suspend the belt over the top of his head and let the battery hang down his back. It was the way he had seen the nationals carry loads. And it was better than making two trips almost straight uphill, more than two hundred feet.

He set the battery down and sat in front of it. Then he reached back and slipped the belt to the top of his head. He pulled his feet up under him and rose slowly, feeling the weight begin to press into his head. Finally upright, he felt the battery swing into his back. It felt lighter, balanced in the middle of his body. But he wasn't sure how long he could endure the pressure on his head. He had to hold his neck straight and stiff.

Then Chad squatted again to pick up the radio. He quickly straightened with the radio in one hand. Now he had one hand free to grab at rocks and branches as he climbed. Every few feet he stopped to adjust the belt. By the time he reached the tree where the low end of the antenna cable dangled, he had stopped several times just to catch his breath.

"Lord," he prayed silently, "I can't do this by myself."

The ground by the tree trunk lay at a steep angle, and he had to push the battery into the soft underbrush to keep it from tumbling back down the mountain. He lodged the radio and all the cords on the upside of the tree, then sat to gather his strength before climbing. He had never felt more hot, more sweaty, more exhausted. He remembered the sheer terror of the plunge down the mountain in the plane, but now he felt another deep fear. Could the Brazas be watching without his even knowing?

Chad scoped out the tree from where he sat and spotted a fork in the trunk where he could set both battery and radio, if he could get them up there. The antenna wire hung close enough for him to reach if he stretched. He would have to carry the battery atop his head again, so he'd have both hands free for climbing. He decided to climb the tree empty-handed first, and pull the wire into position. The climb was easier than he expected, but the wire was surprisingly tight. He was careful not to pull so hard that the whole thing gave way, and he was finally able to pull the end down to where he could sit and work with it in the fork of the tree.

Chad held his breath then and heaved himself and the battery up into the tree, all in one move. He couldn't wait to get the belt off his head, and he nearly dropped it while slipping his head out of the loop. The battery lodged neatly in the fork with a little room left for the radio, if Chad straddled the larger branch.

One more trip down and up the tree with the radio and attachments, and everything was in place. Kate had shown him where to insert the antenna wire to the radio, but he hadn't expected it to be loose. He didn't have a tool to crimp the wire and make it stay, so he grabbed some leaves and stuffed them into the connector. He didn't want to have to wiggle the antenna wire—something he knew he would have to do with the microphone cord. If this whole contraption worked, it would be a miracle.

Chad rigged up the battery to the radio, the way Kate had shown him. When he flipped the switch he got static. He plugged in the headphones and put them on, then played with the tuner until the light shone bright green. He didn't even plug in the mike, because he didn't expect anyone to be transmitting or receiving at that time of day. No planes had been in the air since ten-thirty that morning. He wanted to get his little radio shack set up and tuned in. Then he could turn it off for the night to save the battery and come back at the crack of dawn.

In the middle of the static, however, when the green light was clearest, he heard a voice and nearly fell out of the tree. He pressed the headphones closer to his ears as he teetered on the branch and tried to stay upright by pressing his sore thighs tight against the limb. He couldn't let go of the phones.

"Can you give us an update, Langda, over?"

"What was the latest you heard, Koropun?"

"Only that they should have landed Yawsikor early morning. Left Bime in plenty of time. Last contact was with Bime shortly after takeoff. They could be in this area."

Chad reached for the microphone and nearly bumped the radio out of the tree. He jammed the cord into the unit and pushed the button, shouting, "We're down in the mountains, just the other side of Bime in line with Yawsikor!"

But the green light had never gone off. He knew no one could hear him. He mashed the button again, but he couldn't remember the name of either base. "Hello? Hello? Is anyone there? Mayday! Mayday! Crash site to Bime!"

He jiggled the connection, and even though he heard the static, apparently no one else on the air did. He listened some more.

"Mrs. Howlett will be flown into Bime at daybreak, over."

"Roger, we heard that. Several planes from the different agencies will help out. Only a float plane is available from Yawsikor. They will set a course directly toward Bime and fly as low as possible."

"What do you make of no radio contact, over?"

"Not good. There's supposed to be another briefing broadcast at eighteen hundred hours, over."

"Roger and thanks, over and out."

Chad had no idea what time it was now, but he knew eighteen hundred hours was six o'clock at night. He also knew the sun went down fast in the tropic zone and it would be getting dark by six. He couldn't wait to tell Dad and Kate. He wanted to try to make his microphone work again, but with both stations off-line, they wouldn't hear him anyway. He wondered what a briefing broadcast was. Would all the stations be on? He didn't think Yawsikor could pick up stations on the other side of the divide, but maybe they relayed messages. Where were the two stations he had just heard? They had to be on this side of the divide in order to hear each other and for him to hear them. And they had to be fairly close to Bime if they thought the plane could be near them.

Chad made sure everything was hooked up and in place.

Then he shut it all off and scampered down the mountain, slipping and sliding, grabbing and falling, but not feeling the pain as he had before. He knew he would feel it later when he slept—if he slept—and for sure he would feel it in the morning. But for now, he just wanted to get down and tell Dad and Kate the good news.

He would round up shiny stuff to stick on the trail, and no matter what, he would be back to the radio before six o'clock. Even if he couldn't make them hear him, he was sure that planes looking for them between Bime and Yawsikor would spot something.

Finally, he thought. *We're getting somewhere.*

The Attack

Though they weren't in any condition to jump around, Kate and Dad were as excited about the radio transmission as Chad had been. His news was balanced, however, by their news.

"We can't think of any way to start a fire," Dad said. "We have no matches, no flint, nothing."

"How about rubbing two sticks together like the Indians used to do?" Chad suggested.

"Have you ever tried that?" Dad said. "You have to have patience and perfect conditions. Maybe we could use the sun, magnified through Dr. Howlett's reading glasses. We could point it at a cotton ball soaked with alcohol, but then a fire might make it obvious to everyone where we are. We know no search planes will be out till tomorrow morning, so the only people we would be signaling might see us as enemies."

"There is a way to start a fire after dark," Kate said, "but I don't think you want to hear it."

"What?"

"You take about an eight- or ten-inch piece of the antenna wire and connect the two poles of the battery. It'll shoot out sparks that would ignite dry leaves or paper."

"But how am I supposed to get the fire back down here?"

"You'd have to bring the battery down here to do it," Dad said.

Chad shook his head. There was no way he could unhook that battery after the six o'clock transmission, bring it down in the dark, and then get it back up there in time to listen for search planes in the morning.

"Isn't there any other way to keep warm tonight?" he said.

"We can bundle up with the extra clothes from Dr. Howlett's suitcase."

"Will that work?"

"It'll have to."

"I won't be able to cook you any of that Chinese dinner."

"We're not hungry."

They didn't look hungry. Actually, both Kate and Dad looked awful. Their eyes looked heavy, and they hardly moved. Dad said he was getting some feeling back in his legs, but he still had to use his good arm to move them.

Dad's abdomen appeared swollen, but Chad didn't mention it. There was nothing he could do anyway, and surely Dad had to have noticed it himself.

Kate's toes were discolored, and Dad mentioned that there might be a blood-circulation problem. "What does that mean?" she said. "I could lose my toes?"

"No, sweetheart," Dad said, "it would take a long time for any real damage to set in. We'll be out of here long before that. Meanwhile, try wiggling your toes as much as you can to keep the blood flowing."

"Dad," Kate said, "my toes won't even budge." She grimaced as she tried to wiggle them.

"You might have to move them with your hand, Kate," he said.

She tried, but the pain brought on fresh tears.

"It's important," Dad said. "Want Chad to do it for you?"

"No! I'll do it myself." She forced herself to pull her toes back and push them forward. She cried out, which made Chad instinctively scan the horizon. He quickly caught himself and tried to appear casual, as if not looking for anything special.

But then, to his horror, he noticed a cooking fire that was only half as far away as the ones he'd seen earlier. Either a settlement of Brazas was closer than he thought, or a group was moving toward the crash sight. Could it be a war party?

Chad tried to sound relaxed. "What time is it, Dad?"

"Almost five-thirty. You'd better take my watch. You've got to get stuff up in the trees before dark and be by the radio at six."

It was still hot and humid as Chad rustled through the cargo and found lots of Dr. Howlett's clothes. Many of them were dress clothes, including white shirts and even two suits. It seemed strange to be piling them next to Kate and Dad with the sun still so warm. But Chad knew when the sun went down in the mountains, the temperature would drop quickly.

"Better take something warm with you too," Dad said.

Chad chose a light-colored denim vest with lots of pockets. It hung almost to Chad's knees. He loaded himself up with the sheets of metal from the plane and started, this time for sure, his last trek up the mountain for the day.

After all he'd been through, Chad was amazed he could keep going. He knew, as his mother used to say, that he was "running on nervous energy." Would he just collapse and sleep when he ran out of gas? Maybe, but there was too much to do first.

Chad climbed the familiar trail and higher where the plane had plowed through. He carefully arranged the sheets of metal in the form of a cross. No one in the air could mistake that for crash debris. It would be obvious someone had put them there on purpose. If searchers saw them, it wouldn't be long before they spotted the plane wreckage with the fresh grave off to one side and the little encampment fifty feet to the other side.

It was getting dark as Chad carefully made his way back to the radio. Sharp pain shot through his muscles, and dull pain seemed to have settled into every joint. His head throbbed, and he was hungry again. At the base of the tree he sat to rest and thrust his hands into the deep pockets of Dr. Howlett's vest. He felt something small and hard at the bottom of one pocket. A cigarette lighter! Dr. Howlett was not a smoker, but he probably knew that a lighter was handy in the bush.

Chad's fingers quivered as he tried it. It produced a flame on the second spin! He almost cried out in joy. He could surprise Dad and his sister and start a fire.

But now, as the sun slipped away and a full moon began to rise, Chad slowly climbed into position. He checked Dad's watch. In about five minutes the radio briefing would begin. What would be better than getting someone to hear him? They would be turning on their sets about now, he decided, and so he did the same.

Chad put on his earphones and heard only a faint hiss. He carefully held the end of the microphone cord straight and steady and pushed it into position. When he clicked the thumb switch on the mouthpiece, the green light went out. He blinked, wondering if he was seeing things. He clicked it again and again until finally the light went out.

If that meant he could be heard, Chad didn't want to wait. He wanted to be on the air when everyone else switched on for the briefing. He watched the green light carefully every time he clicked the button. When it went out completely, he spoke quickly.

"This is the crash site calling. Mayday. Mayday. Crash site, does anyone read me? We're on the other side of the divide from Bime and crashed in the valley on course to Yawsikor. Does anyone read? Come in, please!"

Chad waited a minute, listening, then tried again. He looked at his watch. It was a few seconds before six. Soon other stations came on in rapid succession, and Chad realized there was some sort of a relay system. The only voices he could hear clearly were from the two stations he had heard earlier, Koropun and Langda. They seemed to be getting messages relayed from all kinds of places. He heard station names like Sentani, Mulia, Bokandini, Nalca, Eipomek, Bime, and Okbap.

Chad decided not to interrupt while each station was identifying itself. If his transmission really did work, he didn't want it to get lost in the traffic. Once everyone was on, the operator at Langda begin relaying the messages from Bime, pausing between each sentence:

"Here's the latest at eighteen hundred hours. This is coming directly from Dave Coleman at Bime. Three planes and a search party will arrive Bime as close to oh-five-thirty hours as possible. Mrs. Howlett will be in that party, but will remain at Bime during the search, which will begin at oh-six-thirty hours.

"So far there has been no word of sighting from Yawsikor. No radio contact. As you all know, last radio contact with Pilot Michaels came at about oh-seven-thirty hours with a report of fuel or fuel gauge problem. He was on course to Yawsikor, but no word on where or when they might have gone down."

There was a pause and Chad quickly clicked on. The green light went faint, but he plunged ahead anyway. "Crash site is on the air!" he shouted. "Mayday! Mayday! Does anyone read me?"

"This is Koropun. We temporarily lost you there, Langda. Repeat after no word when or where they might have gone down, over."

"Nothing further on that, Koropun. I lost Bime there for a second too. Stand by. Here's more from Bime. Coleman says they have had a development. A houseboy disciplined by Howlett and the Colemans heard of the loss of contact with the plane and has confessed to hurling a shovel at the plane while it sat empty on the runway at Bime. This would have been minutes before takeoff. Houseboy is regretful and wants to be involved in search effort. Coleman hasn't decided whether that would be a good idea."

"What damage could have been done, over?"

"Bime, this is Langda. Koropun is asking what damage the shovel might have done, over."

Chad tried cutting in again. "Crash site to Langda or Koropun! Come in, please! Mayday! We lost fuel from the main tank and couldn't get reserve fuel to the engines! Does anyone read?"

"Langda to Koropun, stand by; we're hearing from Bime, but with interference."

"Breaker! Breaker, Langda, this is Koropun. Did you hear—?"

"Stand by, Koropun! Losing Bime."

"Breaker, Langda! Emergency breaker! This is Koropun, and we're hearing from crash site!"

"Koropun repeat, over!"

"Stand by Langda and all stations. Crash site, this is Koropun. Repeat please."

Chad mashed the button and shouted into the microphone. "Mayday! This is crash site!"

"Back off from the mouthpiece a bit there, son. What's your location and situation?"

Chad was so excited he was shaking and couldn't slow his words. "We're in the valley on the other side of Bime!"

"Check your connection, crash site. Repeat, please."

Chad tried again, keeping an eye on the green light. It went off completely only for a second.

"All we got was 'valley,' crash site. Survivors?"

"Other side of Bime!" Chad tried again. "Three survivors."

"I didn't get any of that," the voice at Koropun said. "Langda?"

"This is Langda. He said three something. Stand by, all stations. Koropun is getting something from the crash site, but it's breaking up. It's a young boy on the radio, and we've got valley for a location and possibly three survivors. Stand by."

Chad kept trying, but the mike connection was bad and getting worse.

"Koropun to crash site, stand by. If you can read us, listen. Your transmission is bad. Hold for a moment."

"This is Langda. Bime says the boy would be the pilot's son. Any word on Dr. Howlett, the daughter, or the pilot?"

Chad tried to break in. "Three survivors!"

But no one could hear anything now. He wrenched the

connection around and around, but all he heard was static when he tried to transmit.

After the word spread throughout the stations that radio contact had been received from the crash site, the operator at Langda tried to summarize. "We've lost the transmission, but we and Koropun will stay on for another hour just in case. We each read a little from the boy, so the site has to be on this side of the divide. Let's assume the best, that Michaels got to the clearings about fifteen minutes past the bottom of the valley and was able to get down somehow. They can't fly out of there, and they can't climb out either, so we'll need to locate them and get a chopper in there. Stand by. Go ahead, Bime."

There was a pause as Langda listened to Bime. "Dave Coleman reminds us that they could be in Braza territory. Crash site, if you can hear us, we have no relationship with that tribal group. They might be unfriendly and violent. Avoid contact, if possible."

Chad tried answering, but the green light stayed on.

"We'll take from those clicks and that static that you can hear us and that you acknowledged that."

Chad clicked several times again.

"We're reading that, crash site. Give me a double click if you read."

Chad double-clicked.

"Roger! Work on that radio! We'll stay on the air all night and will monitor this frequency. You'll make it a lot easier on us if you can help us locate you in advance. Give me a double click if you reached clearings and were able to put down safely."

Chad waited.

"Give me a double click if the plane is damaged."

Chad clicked twice.

"Any casualties? Any dead, I mean?"

Chad clicked again.

"Injured?"

He clicked again.

"Son, I'm going to walk you through a series of questions, and by your response you can give us a lot of information. Let's determine who's alive and how serious the injuries are. There's a mission hospital at Angaruk. Then we'll try to pinpoint where you are. Do you read?"

Chad clicked again, but before he heard another word footsteps sounded in the tall grass beneath him. He froze in fear and switched off the radio. But he was too late. Two strong hands grabbed his dangling ankle and jerked him from his perch.

Chad landed hard on his side and felt the air rush from his lungs. The headphones were slipping from his ears, the cord pulling the radio from the tree. He gasped, and in the moonlight between the branches, the fierce face of a young tribesman stared down at him. As the warrior reached for his spear, Chad grabbed the earphone cord and pulled with all his might. The radio slipped from the fork in the tree, then hung suspended as it tightened its connection with the battery. Chad tugged again, and the radio pulled free of the antenna wire and dislodged the battery. Radio, microphone, and battery tumbled out of the tree, and the battery smacked the tribesman in the shoulder. He screamed and raised the huge spear high over his head with both hands.

Chad didn't even have time to pray as the heavy spear rushed down at him.

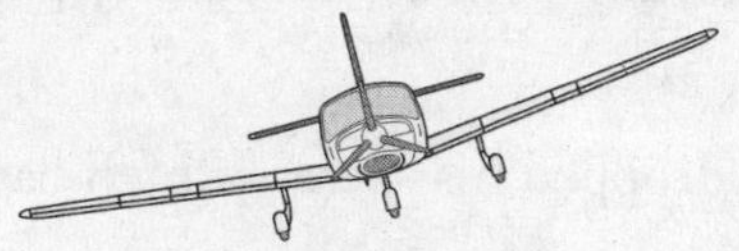

The Standoff

Chad covered his head with his arms and rolled quickly to his stomach, but he was not the target of the tribesman's spear. The spear drove into the radio and smashed it to pieces. His attacker felt the battery with the toes of one foot, then tried to push it out of the way.

Chad knew he could lie there and be killed and maybe even eaten, just as he had taken the snowball attack from the seventh graders, or he could fight for his life, and the lives of his dad and sister. If he hadn't suffered through so much already, he might have remained paralyzed with fright, but now he had nothing more to lose.

He leaped to his feet and faced the tribesman, who now pointed his spear at Chad. He then hefted up the heavy battery and held it in front of him, poles facing the warrior. When he saw the man coil, as if ready to thrust the spear,

Chad rushed him and pressed the battery poles against his bare stomach.

The warrior dropped his spear and fell back, screaming. He spoke quickly in words that made no sense to Chad, then seemed to call out to someone. Chad's heart sank as he heard more footsteps in the dark jungle.

The man bent to retrieve his spear, but Chad thrust the battery toward him again. The warrior backed off a step, so Chad dropped the battery and grabbed the spear. But rather than holding it on his opponent, Chad threw it down the mountain as far as he could. The warrior looked terrified.

Chad picked up the battery again and forced the man to back out into the path created by the crashing plane. Three other tribesmen, also armed with spears, appeared from the other side of the path. Chad's attacker spoke to them quickly, pointing at the battery, and to Chad's amazement, they all threw their spears over his head and down the mountain.

Chad wasn't sure how long he could stand there holding the battery, but as long as they were scared, he was in control. When he finally set it down and straightened up, he sensed the tribesmen, who he was sure were Brazas, tense again as if ready to either attack or run away. Chad pulled the lighter from his pocket and produced a tiny flame.

The Brazas stumbled back and stood staring at the lighter and then into Chad's face. Now what should he do? They were big, muscular men, barefoot, with huge, wide feet. They wore something at their groins that he could not see clearly, and their stomachs were bound with twine or vines, wide belts so tight that they changed the men's shapes. Blocks of wood stuck out of two of the men's earlobes, and the other two had bones or sticks through their noses. Chad didn't know what cannibals were supposed to look like, but these four sure seemed to qualify.

It felt so strange to have the advantage, at least for now. Chad's first instinct was to scream out for Dad or his sister, but they could do nothing, and he didn't know how many more Brazas were in the area. He knew something they didn't know: If they merely rushed him, they could overpower him easily. Then how long would it be before they discovered Dad and Kate?

They were afraid of the battery, for good reason, and of the flame, because it seemed to appear out of nowhere. Chad knew he had to conserve the tiny supply of butane in the lighter, so he let go and the flame died. But each time the Brazas moved again, he flicked it back on. They were at his mercy. At least for now.

If he charged them and scared them and made them run off, could he and his family hide from the rest of the Brazas until the search planes flew over in the morning? He didn't think he could even stay awake that long. There was no way he would try to fight these people.

The longer they all stood there, and the more he thought about it, the more Chad realized that he was the outsider. He was the threat. This area was their home. How would he react if he saw an alien in a tree in his backyard, talking to and listening to a squawky box?

He still feared these dangerous warriors and maybe even cannibals, but he couldn't blame them for attacking or being scared of contraptions they had never seen before. If only he could remember those words Dr. Howlett had taught him and Kate! Nothing came to mind. He remembered that the words were strange and different and that one of them had sounded to Kate like an ice-cream cone.

"Tastee Freeze," he said.

The Brazas flinched, wide-eyed, and looked first at him and then at each other. One of them tried to repeat the word, but in his guttural dialect, it was impossible to understand.

Chad knew Tastee Freeze must not mean anything in their language. What were those words? And would they have the same meaning twenty-five years after Dr. Howlett and Dave Coleman had met this tribe? If only Chad could remember the greeting, the word for gift, and the word for friendliness. He didn't want to be an enemy of these people. He just wanted to stay alive long enough to be rescued.

What was it Dr. Howlett said the Brazas had called him and Dave Coleman? Yes! George-George and Man-Man!

"George-George," he said.

Again, one of them echoed him, but there was no sign that they had any idea what Chad was saying.

"Man-Man," he said, and this time they didn't even try to repeat it.

"George-George?" he said again, this time as a question. "Man-Man?"

Nothing. Of course, these tribesmen were children or maybe not even born when Dr. Howlett and Mr. Coleman had made contact with that small party years before. They were probably the age now that Jonga was then, the one Dr. Howlett said had taught him and Mr. Coleman a little of their dialect. Could Jonga still be alive? Would any of these men know him?

"Jonga?" Chad tried, and all four men recoiled at once, startling Chad and almost falling over each other. They stared at him in shock. Now he was on to something.

"Jonga!" he said with confidence.

"Jonga!" the four said together. They looked at the one who had attacked Chad. He spoke quickly, obviously running together several Braza phrases and sentences, but

Chad understood nothing except for the one name he heard twice. Jonga.

Chad repeated it in as friendly a tone as he could. Now the warrior spoke even more quickly and was harder to understand. But he appeared to want to communicate with Chad. His tone was softer and more insistent. Chad held both hands out, the lighter still in one, just in case. He said the name as a question, hoping they would understand that he was asking where the man was.

"Jonga?"

The warrior was excited and moved closer to Chad as he spoke. He pointed to the west. Was it possible Jonga was nearby? Or were they just saying anything they could think of in hopes it would allow them to escape? He didn't want to hold them. But when the warrior stepped still closer, Chad lit the lighter one more time. He couldn't take any chances.

The man stepped back, still afraid of the flame. Chad let it die, and gesturing toward the west, said kindly, "Jonga. Jonga." He nodded and pointed as if urging the men to go get Jonga. Would they bring him back, or would they return with an entire war party?

The four began to move back and step away, keeping their eyes on Chad as if to make sure it was all right that they retreat. He tried to smile at them, though in his fear and fatigue he doubted his smile looked like more than an attempt at a pleasant face. Suddenly the men were running, and he had never seen or heard such speed. They flew through the grass and underbrush. The sound of their feet quickly faded, and Chad remained in the moonlit silence. He had just stood his ground against four primitive men who might be cannibals.

The problem was, he and his family were at least twelve hours from being spotted by rescuers. His radio was useless. He didn't know if he should tell Dad and Kate what had happened. Why worry them? But if he did tell them, and he wasn't here when the Brazas came back, would the cannibals come looking for him? What if they found him with Dad and Kate? Would he be endangering his family?

He could only guess whether he had time to run down to the campsite. At least he could tell Dad and Kate about the radio transmission. But first he climbed back into the tree and grabbed hold of the antenna wire. He measured out about ten inches of it and bent it back and forth until that section broke free. He took it back out into the path and wrapped one end around one pole on the battery. Again he felt the buzzing through his fingers.

Chad left the other end of the wire sticking above the other pole. Then he stood and pressed the wire down with his booted foot until it touched the pole. Sparks shot into the air and he let up, releasing the contact. Perfect.

He hurried down to the campsite. As he ran, he tried to think of an excuse to leave Dad and Kate again right away. He would tell them about the radio transmission and that the search party would be looking for them at dawn. But he would not tell them of his discovery of the lighter. If he did, they would wonder why he couldn't build them a fire. No way did he want to provide any kind of sight or smell that might lead the Brazas to his family.

Neither would Chad tell Dad or Kate about the Brazas. It would be the hardest secret he would ever have to keep, but he couldn't think of anything good that could come of their knowing. Dad might not let him go back to meet them, and even if he did, what if Jonga did return with the warriors? Dad would worry, as Chad did, that it was a trick. There was no way to know if Jonga was friendly, if he was still around after all those years. Men in these tribes didn't live long, so by their standards, Jonga would have to be old even if he were only in his forties.

Besides, there was never any indication that Jonga understood the message Dr. Howlett and Mr. Coleman had tried to tell him. It was foolish to think that Jonga might see himself as a friend to Chad's family, even if they could convince him they were friends of Dr. Howlett.

When Chad got back to the camp, Dad was gravely ill. Chad could see in the moonlight that his abdomen was even more swollen, and his forehead was hot. "I think I've got internal bleeding," Dad said, his voice more raspy than ever.

"What can I do, Dad?"

"I don't think there's anything we can do," he said. "I don't even know what kind of medicine is good for this. Besides a bottle of aspirin, we have some antibiotics and penicillin, but I don't think those would do me any good. I don't know how long I have, Chad."

"Can you make it till dawn?" Chad explained to Dad what had happened on the radio. Kate sat up, looking hopeful at last.

"I'll do my best, Spitfire," Dad said. "That'll give me a goal. I don't know how much good it does to just decide to hang on until help arrives, but that's what I'm gonna do. You and Kate pray for me, hear?"

They nodded.

"Chad," Dad said, "no matter what happens, I want you to know how proud I am of you."

"I know." Chad couldn't help wondering what Dad would think if he knew everything.

"I mean it," Dad said. "If I don't make it, you do everything you can to get Kate out of here. And just know that your dad, and of course your mom, loved you kids more than anything on earth."

"Dad!" Kate said. "Don't be talking like that. If you don't make it, I don't want to make it. So if you want me out of here, you have to stay with us."

"I'll try, Kate."

"Just do it!" she said. "Fight!"

Chad knew he had to get back up the mountain, but he wasn't sure he should leave Dad. On the other hand, there was nothing more he could do for him right now.

"Are you cold, Dad?"

"Yeah, but it feels good with this fever."

"You want any medicine?"

"I probably should have antibiotics, but I just don't know if you're supposed to take those when you have internal bleeding."

"How about just some aspirin for your fever and pain?"

"Yeah, maybe that would be good," Dad said.

"No!" Kate said. "You can't have aspirin when you're bleeding. Doesn't aspirin make your blood thinner?"

"You're right, Kate," Dad said. "Good call."

"You're going to make it," she said. "Just try to rest."

"I'm going back up the mountain," Chad said. "I'll be back in a little while."

"You need to rest too," Dad answered. "You've had quite a day."

You don't know the half of it, Chad thought. "I will," he

said. "I just want to make sure everything's set for tomorrow." That was as close to lying to Dad as he ever wanted to get. As he pulled the machete from between two cargo trunks, he asked Kate, "What were those Braza words Dr. Howlett taught us?"

"Who cares?"

"I do. You were just about singing them on the plane, and now I can't remember any of them."

Kate sounded as if she were falling asleep. "Treetzee means friendly," she mumbled. "Shaka means hello. Benboon means gift."

"That's right," Chad said casually, running them over and over in his mind. He filled his pockets with packaged cookies, and then slipped the machete into a loop in Dr. Howlett's denim vest. The long blade brushed against the back of his leg as he started up the mountainside, munching cookies.

About halfway to where he'd left the rigged battery in the path, he looked up into the moonlight and saw at least five silhouettes. One carried a huge torch. Chad could only hope it was the original four spearmen and hopefully a friendly old Braza named Jonga. If it wasn't, then no matter how close he and his family had been to a dawn rescue, they were as good as dead now.

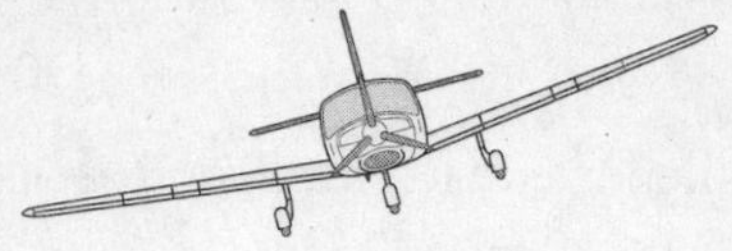

Like Guardian Angels

Chad almost gave up. His body cried out for rest, for sleep, for healing. Every fiber and muscle and bone ached. And even though he was afraid of the cannibals, and worried that they might attack him, or worse, they might find and kill the rest of his family—all he wanted was an end to all this!

His choice, his hope, his prayer was for this to be a friendly meeting and that somehow he could avoid violence. But his confused, tired mind could accept even that, if necessary. He knew he couldn't stay awake much longer. His body couldn't work much longer. He couldn't possibly climb this steep, slippery, overgrown mountainside one more time.

Somehow he had to beat the Brazas to the battery. He had the machete, but he didn't want to pull it out. They could just as easily have replaced their spears. If they all threw at him at the same time, he certainly wouldn't be able to defend himself with a cigarette lighter. He might scare them with sparks from the battery, but he had to get to it before they did. And so he quickened his pace.

Chad wanted to run but he could only limp, lurching up the mountain like an old man. From the other direction the torch and silhouettes grew larger and more distinct in the moonlight. There were indeed five tribesmen, and one appeared older and smaller than the others. The younger four carried spears.

The Braza party stopped about twenty feet above the battery. That was good news, because even moving as quickly as he could, Chad was still double that distance below it. The Brazas were bigger, stronger, healthier, and knew how to walk this terrain. While Chad, besides being younger, smaller, and sore all over, still had an uphill climb.

Just to be safe, he pulled out the lighter and lit it as he approached the battery. Though his little flame was no match for their torch, he knew they were fascinated and afraid of a little flame that could magically appear in a boy's hand.

The Brazas just stood and stared. Chad was tempted to push down on the battery wire with his foot, just to show them a shower of sparks and let them know he still had that strange power. Instead he prayed silently to know what to do. He felt that he should just stand there and wait. He snuffed his light and put the lighter in his pocket.

Without a word, the stooped, older Braza stepped away from the others and walked slowly toward Chad, stopping about ten feet from him. Chad stepped to the left side of the path, which made the old Braza turn and face him from the other side. That also allowed Chad to get a look at his face in the moonlight.

It was a face of fear and confusion, but also of some strength. What looked like a bone or stick had been pushed through his nose horizontally. The Braza held his hands out before him, palms up, and spoke softly in a high, nasal pitch. "Jonga," he said.

Chad was startled. He pointed at the man, which caused the Braza to take one step back. "Jonga?" He wanted to apologize for scaring him by pointing at him, but he knew no words for that.

"Jonga," the man said again.

Chad patted his own chest. "Chad," he said.

"Dahk," the man said.

"Chad."

"Chahk," Jonga said.

"Close enough," Chad said, smiling. Jonga looked confused. "Shaka," Chad said.

The old man flinched. He looked quickly to his companions and then back at Chad.

"Shaka," Chad repeated, and the old man smiled.

"Shaka, Chahk," he said.

"Shaka, Jonga," Chad said. "Treetzee."

"Treetzee?" Jonga said, his whole body seeming to loosen up.

"Shaka, Jonga!" Chad said. "Treetzee!"

Jonga bowed slightly. "Treetzee."

Suddenly Chad remembered the cellophane-wrapped packages of cookies in his pockets. He put both hands in his pockets, and Jonga retreated, obviously frightened.

"No, no!" Chad said. "Um, ah, benboon! Benboon!"

Jonga eyed him warily as Chad pulled out the packages. He held one out to Jonga, who hesitated. "Benboon, Jonga. Benboon."

Jonga accepted the package, turning it over and over as he studied it. Chad, in his enthusiasm, tossed four more packages to the others up the pathway. They jumped away and stared at them as they fell to the ground.

"Benboon!" Chad said, and all eyes turned to him once more. "Look, or I mean ... well ... watch, whatever. Benboon, treetzee!" He opened his own package and ate one of the filled cookies. "Mmm," he said, hoping they would understand.

The younger men crouched and looked at the cookie packages but didn't touch them. Jonga tried to open his. Chad stepped toward him, causing Jonga to stiffen again and the warriors to straighten up and step forward.

"Here," Chad said, "let me show you. Um, treetzee." Chad slipped a fingernail under the cellophane and tore it away from the cookies. Then he stepped back and let Jonga finish opening them. Chad realized that just because he had shown them the cookies were edible didn't mean they would trust him. These were primitive people, but not stupid.

Chad put another cookie in his mouth and gestured to Jonga, but the older man would not eat his. "George-George," Chad said suddenly.

Jonga stumbled and looked as if he wanted to sit. He stared at Chad and spoke quickly. It was all jibberish to Chad except "George-George."

Chad nodded and repeated the name. Jonga was excited, and when Chad said "Man-Man," Jonga dropped to his knees, the cookies falling from his hands. He reached to the sky as if celebrating hearing those names again. He stood quickly then, and pulled the small stick or whatever it was from his nose, holding it out to Chad.

Chad didn't want to touch it, but Jonga was holding it toward the light and pointing at it. Chad looked closely. It wasn't a stick or a bone at all. It was the bottom portion of a plastic ballpoint pen. The clicker and the ink and the point were gone; just the barrel remained. Jonga pointed at the printing on it. Chad leaned close.

Jonga pointed at letters that spelled out Inter-Indonesian Missions, but he said, as if reading, "George-George."

He looked up at Chad with a sparkle in his eye. "George-George benboon," he said, and thrust the pen back through the hole between his nostrils.

Chad now knew for sure that this was the very man Dr. Howlett and Mr. Coleman had talked to so many years before. How he wished he knew more than three words in their language!

Jonga rose and picked up the cookies. "Ah loo," he said. "Ah loo. Jeshuz. Gawd."

Chad squinted at him, and Jonga repeated, "Ah loo, Jeshuz. Gawd."

Chad understood that he was trying to say Jesus and God, but what was ah loo? "Ah loo?" Chad said.

Jonga transferred the cookies to his left hand and thrust out his right, as if he wanted to shake hands. So it was "Hello"! Chad hesitated. If he shook hands with the old man, he would give him an advantage. He could be wrestled to the ground, and be at the mercy of the four warriors. He moved closer to the battery, just in case.

Chad put out his hand, and Jonga reached for it. But rather than shaking Chad's hand, he let his hand slip up to Chad's wrist. As they clasped wrists, Jonga smiled and said, "Ah loo, Jeshuz. Gawd. Gawd blesh choo."

"Hello, Jonga," Chad said. "God bless you too." So Dr.

Howlett and Mr. Coleman had taught the Brazas a few English words while trying to learn their language.

Jonga put the cookies in his mouth and chewed slowly, smiling. The spearmen dropped their weapons and grabbed at the cookies, crumbling them as they tried to open the packages.

Jonga held his arms wide, hands open. "George-George?" he said. "Man-Man?"

Chad didn't know what to say. How could he tell him that Dr. Howlett was dead, but that Mr. Coleman was just over the mountain and would likely be there by morning? He tried to avoid the bad news. "Man-Man," he said, pointing over the mountain. Jonga and the others turned and looked up the path. "No!" Chad shook his head and pointed farther.

Jonga looked puzzled. "George-George?"

Chad motioned for Jonga to follow, then he turned to head down the path. He looked back to see Jonga hesitate and look at his companions. Chad motioned for them again. "Treetzee," he said, and he began the treacherous trip down the mountain. How he hoped this was his last time ever!

Chad turned and saw Jonga and all four spearmen walk way around the battery, keeping an eye on it as they passed. He felt weak and alone as he led them to the valley floor. Except for the machete dangling from the loop in Dr. Howlett's vest and the tiny lighter in his pocket, Chad had nothing with which to defend himself. He had chosen to trust Jonga and his friends. He had read stories of missionaries who were slaughtered by hostile tribes, so all he could do was pray silently.

When they reached the bottom of the path the plane wreckage came into view. "George-George?" Jonga said. Chad nodded sadly.

The warriors held out the torch and looked closely at the plane. Surely they had seen the metal birds flying over through the years, and these men may have even seen the helicopter that was turned away when they were children. But they had never seen wreckage like this.

Jonga peered inside the plane. "George-George?"

Chad knew then that he would have to show him the grave to make him understand. He motioned for Jonga and the others to follow. When they got to the mound of dirt over the shallow grave, Chad pointed and said, "George-George."

Jonga put both hands on his stomach and grimaced, rocking on his heels, looking from Chad to the grave.

Chad pointed straight up and said, "George-George. God. Jesus."

Jonga appeared to understand now, but he looked so grief-stricken that Chad wanted to get him away from the grave. He would introduce Jonga and his friends to Dad and Kate. Once again he motioned for them to follow.

They passed the wreckage again on the way to the pile of cargo trunks and the makeshift lean-to. Jonga and the warriors hesitated as the torch shone on the pile of stuff. Then, as they came around to the other side and saw the two sleeping figures, they were startled.

Dad and Kate appeared sound asleep. Chad went first to Dad, who lay on his back, abdomen protruding. Dad's breathing was so labored that it wouldn't have surprised Chad if he stopped breathing at any moment.

Kate lay on her side, curled up, apparently to keep warm. Chad had to put his ear near her face to hear her breathing. He could only guess that in the absence of medical help, sleep was what was best for them.

Jonga seemed to understand that this was Chad's family, and he had to assume they were all in the plane crash, for what he did next astounded Chad. Jonga seemed to take over. He knelt close to Chad and spoke earnestly, though Chad understood not a word of it.

As Chad watched, Jonga lifted the tiny, cold furnace that Chad had shaped from the nose cone of the plane and tossed it aside. With his hands he swept the area clear and softly gave instructions to his friends. Three of them ran off into the darkness, returning in minutes with twigs and dry leaves and larger pieces of wood. These he piled quickly into a pyramid, then touched the torch to it, and a campfire burst into flames. Even with the light and the heat, neither Dad nor Kate awoke.

Chad had an idea, so he rummaged through Dr. Howlett's belongings and came up with his Bible. "Jonga," he said, holding it out to him, wondering if he had ever seen Dr. Howlett with it. From the puzzled look on his face, it appeared Jonga had not seen the Bible before, but as Chad fanned the pages, the colored pages of the wordless book tucked into the back caught Jonga's eye.

Jonga grabbed it and spoke excitedly, showing his friends. He turned to Chad, pointed to the gold page, then pointed up. "George-George?" he said.

Chad nodded.

Jonga spoke to two of his friends, and they ran off into the night, one with the torch and both with their spears. About half an hour later, one returned with a small wild boar he had killed. With his bare hands he ripped off its skin and propped it over the fire. Despite the cookies, Chad had never been so hungry; and as gross as the skinned boar looked, it smelled so good it had Chad salivating.

About fifteen minutes later the other tribesman returned with Jonga's decades-old, dog-eared copy of the wordless book. Jonga handled the book's pages—now separated into individual sheets with no staples—carefully, as if each one were a prized possession.

A little more than an hour later, Jonga began pulling strips of meat off the boar—again with his bare hands—and everyone who was awake ate. To Chad the meat was as good as the best pork roast.

After they had eaten, Jonga sat near the fire with his legs crossed, the wordless book in his lap. He had apparently instructed his friends to stand guard; they stood at each corner of the little camp, facing out like guardian angels, leaning on their spears.

Jonga pointed to the ground, seeming to urge Chad to sleep. When he lay down near Kate, he watched Jonga for a moment as he sat leafing through the few pages of his old wordless book. Finally, Jonga let them lie in his lap, and he lowered his head and slept.

Chad could barely keep his eyes open, but he wanted to stay awake, still a little wary of the four with their spears. Still, they seemed to obey Jonga, who was clearly a new friend. Chad also wanted to keep an ear open for Dad and Kate, in case their breathing became worse or they had some sort of trouble. What if they awoke to see a Braza sitting by the fire, or four spearmen surrounding them?

But as much as he wanted to stay awake, Chad couldn't. He hoped and prayed they would be spotted at dawn from the air, and now, with a blazing fire going, they would be seen easily. The day's demands caught up with him, and his body shut down. Never had he done so much in so short a time. Soon, Chad's whole world fell silent, and he was out cold.

Chad awoke with a start, squinting against the first sliver of the sun casting a pale yellow on the horizon. Kate had grabbed his collar and pulled. "Chad!" she whispered. "The cannibals!"

Chad was stiff and sore and could hardly move, but he smiled and looked around. The four guardians were seated, spears tilted toward the sky, dozing. Jonga lay on his side next to the dying embers.

"They're friends," Chad whispered, and quickly told her the whole story.

She smiled. "Tell Dad."

Chad slowly rose, trying not to groan and wake anyone. Dad was in the same position as the night before, though his breathing seemed easier. "We should let him sleep. I want to make the fire bigger though. I want the rescue planes to see us right away."

Chad stood and stretched. His ankles and knees were swollen, and his neck hurt no matter which way he turned his head. "Do you need this, Kate?" he said, picking up one of Dr. Howlett's shirts. She shook her head. Chad moved into the underbrush at the base of the mountain and used the shirt as a basket, loading it with more kindling and bigger sticks.

When Chad returned, the Brazas were rising. They looked puzzled that Chad would want a bigger fire, now that the sun was coming up. He didn't know how to explain it.

"Ah loo, Chahk," Jonga said, sitting up.

"Hello, Jonga," Chad said.

The old man smiled and looked at Kate.

"Kate," Chad said.

"Cake," Jonga said, but when Kate put out her hand, he would not shake it. He just nodded to her.

"Maybe they don't touch females or something," Chad said.

Jonga said something in his own dialect about the fire and looked as if he wanted to put it out. Chad hoped he would understand. He pointed to the sky, but not in the same way as when he had tried to indicate that Dr. Howlett was in heaven. This time he waved his finger back and forth and said, "Man-Man, Man-Man."

Could he possibly make Jonga understand that he was waiting for Mr. Coleman to arrive from the sky? From the look on Jonga's face, no. He and his friends stood in a cluster, as if wondering what to do next. Chad looked at his watch. In just a few minutes the search party would leave Bime. They would follow the same course Dad had flown.

The fire would be easily spotted. Chad wondered how the Brazas would react.

Jonga's four companions, if Chad could understand them at all, appeared eager to get back to their own people. It had taken the one warrior forty-five minutes to go and get Jonga's wordless book, and so Chad calculated that their village must be a good twenty-minute hike away.

Jonga spoke quietly to the others, but immediately grew silent as the first search plane could be heard coming over the Great Dividing Range. They all looked up.

Ignoring his pain, Chad immediately began jumping and shouting. Kate struggled to balance on one foot, waving and squealing. Even Dad roused and tried to sit up.

"Can you move away from the fire, Dad?" Chad said. "I want to make it bigger."

Dad winced as he pushed himself away with his left hand. Chad piled everything he had gathered onto the fire, and it began to roar and billow clouds of smoke.

"How'd you start the fire, Chad?" Dad said.

"Our new friends did it with their torch! And don't worry about them. I don't think they're still cannibals, if they ever were!"

"What new friends?"

Chad looked around while still waving at the small plane

heading their way. The Brazas had disappeared. "Jonga!" he called. "Jonga! Man-Man! Treetzee!"

Dad forced himself to a sitting position and waved at the plane. "What in the world are you talking about?" he shouted.

"Long story!" Chad said. "Tell you later!"

The search plane followed the path of their tumble down the mountain; Chad guessed the pilot had seen the metal sheets he'd put on the path. Next, he flew over the wreckage, turned in the direction of the grave, and then circled back around to where the little family waved and shouted. He dipped one wing and then the other to acknowledge he'd seen them. Then he flew back over the ridge.

"No way they can land a fixed-wing plane in here," Dad said. "Hope they can get a 'copter quick."

"How are you feeling?"

"Not good. I feel like my whole system is shot."

"They said something on the radio last night about a mission hospital in Angaruk."

"Good. That's not far."

By now, Kate was sitting again, pain etched in her face. Her foot looked terrible. "I can't wait to get out of here," she said.

Just then two small planes came over the rise. Kate started waving.

"No need to wave any more, honey," Dad said. "It's just the rest of the search party wanting to take a look." Both planes dipped their wings at the family and flew back. "Now, Chad, tell me what friends you were talking about."

As they scanned the horizon, waiting for the helicopter, Chad said, "Dad, you're not going to believe this ..."

Chad told Dad all about the strange encounter with the Brazas, especially Jonga. It seemed all Dad could do was shake his head. Then, within half an hour, the whirring blades of a helicopter cut through the air. It landed between the wreckage and the fire, kicking up grass and dirt. The pilot and two searchers jumped from the chopper and ran to the family. Chad was thrilled to see that one of them was Dave Coleman. Chad told him quickly about Dr. Howlett and the injuries to Dad and Kate.

"Son, let's you and I stay put awhile," Mr. Coleman shouted, "and leave them room to take your dad and sister to the mission hospital right away. That all right with you?"

Was it all right? It was perfect. He nodded and helped them load two stretchers onto the chopper. When it had lifted off, Chad said, "Mr. Coleman, your friend Jonga is not far away."

Mr. Coleman looked stunned. "What do you mean?"

"Jonga!" Chad shouted into the jungle. "Jonga! Treetzee! Man-Man!"

“Man-Man?” Mr. Coleman said. “Where did you hear that?”

“Dr. Howlett told us.” And he told Mr. Coleman the story.

“He won’t recognize me,” Mr. Coleman said. “But I don’t suppose I’d recognize him either.”

“They’re probably afraid of the helicopter,” Chad said. “But they spent the night with us.”

“And they ran off when the first plane few over?”

Chad nodded.

“Then you’re right. They’re probably not far away.” He turned and made a megaphone of his hands. “Jonga! Shaka, Jonga. Treetzee!”

From the underbrush at the base of the mountain came the old man. If the others were there, they hung back out of sight. “Ah loo, Man-Man,” Jonga said softly, and the veteran missionary hurried to him.

They shook hands at the wrist, and they tried to talk with the little bit each knew of the other’s language. Mr. Coleman tried to explain who Chad was, and Jonga said, “Chahk and Cake.”

Chad nodded.

Dave Coleman and Jonga spoke for several minutes and shook hands again. When Jonga retreated into the jungle, Mr. Coleman turned to Chad.

“Jonga accepted our message,” he said. “With just that

little knowledge of the wordless book and what we had told him those many years ago, he believed. He says a few other Brazas also believe, and the whole tribe is more peaceful and no longer cannibalistic. But it sounds like Jonga is basically an outcast. He still has his wordless book, and he wants me to come back."

When the helicopter returned, only the pilot was aboard. "I'm afraid this will be an unpleasant ride," Mr. Coleman said. "We need to take Doc Howlett's body with us. We have a bag for it."

Chad waited on the chopper while the pilot and Mr. Coleman dug up the body and loaded it. It was strange to ride to the mission hospital with the body of a man he had known, but he decided it was no stranger than having had to bury him in the first place.

"You'd make quite a missionary, son," Mr. Coleman said as he climbed aboard. "It takes a man to do what you did. A real man. You saved your dad's and sister's lives, you know."

"I guess."

"No guessing about it. It's clear God was with you, and you can be proud of what you did."

Chad was embarrassed and turned to study the scenery below. He saw the Indonesian mountain jungles with a whole new eye as they flew toward Angaruk. He would never forget this place.

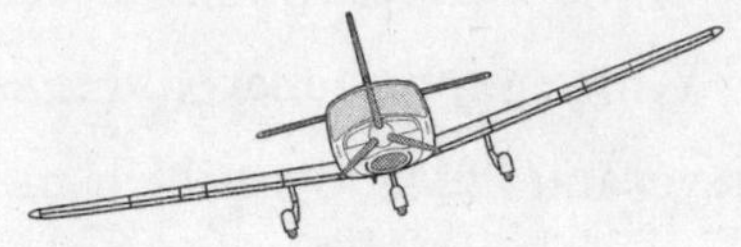

Epilogue

It was bitterly cold the first week of school in Mukluk, but there was not enough snow for the traditional daily snowball fight. Still, when Chad headed out for recess with his now seventh-grade classmates, he suspected the eighth graders were planning something. And Rusty Testor was looking right at Chad as he whispered to his friends.

"Let's play chicken!" Rusty shouted suddenly, suggesting the one game Chad had always hated even more than the snowball fight. In chicken, the two teams lined up facing each other about two feet apart, arms locked. One boy would be chosen from each team, and these two entered the narrow space between the teams from opposite ends. The first one to get to the other end won that round, but the only way to get there was to go through, or over, your opponent. You could tackle him, knock him over, climb over him, whatever you wanted. But you had to scramble past him to the other end before he got up and raced to his end. Teammates were supposed to keep their arms locked, but they could "help out" with their knees and feet.

Chad had been knocked around pretty well in chicken in the past. Usually he had tried to squeeze by his opponent. That proved he was the chicken, and he nearly always got tripped or blasted to the ground.

Today, though, he looked forward to the game. He had enjoyed the instant popularity that came with the newspaper article about his family's adventures in Indonesia, especially when it came out that he was a hero.

"You won't have any cigarette lighter or plane battery to protect you here," Rusty taunted Chad as the teams lined up. The big boy sauntered to one end of the chute of seventh graders. "I'm first, you wimps. Who dares?"

In the past, only two of Chad's friends dared face Rusty, and they always lost. But today, Chad beat them to it. He quickly unlocked arms and jogged to one end without a word. His friends looked at each other in surprise. The eighth graders laughed. Rusty said, "Oh, goody! Jungle Boy!"

Rusty must have forgotten the rules to this game. Because once both players were lined up at either end, they could begin without notice, and before Rusty could even plant himself or start moving, Chad rushed forward. Rusty tensed at the last instant, unable to even take a step before Chad lowered his head and plowed into his stomach. Chad heard a great whoosh of air gush from the bigger boy as he drove him to the ground and scrambled over him. Rusty somersaulted backward, and the first round was over that quick.

Chad expected cries of "No fair!" or "I wasn't ready!" He half expected Rusty to come up swinging. But the redhead lay curled into a ball, moaning and gasping. "I can't breathe!" he mouthed, terror in his eyes. The teams separated and surrounded him.

"Better get some help," someone said.

"Nice goin', Michaels. You hurt him."

"I didn't mean to," Chad said, "and we don't need help. He just got the wind knocked out of him."

"Well, do something!"

Rusty looked panicky as Chad knelt over him. "Lie on your back!" Chad said. "Now!"

Pale and grimacing, Rusty obeyed.

"Lift your knees to your chest!"

When Rusty brought his legs up, Chad straddled him and pushed slowly on his shins. That put slight pressure on his chest until Chad let up, which compressed and released Rusty's lungs. Suddenly the color returned to Rusty's cheeks, and he looked relieved. He rolled to his side and sighed. "Thanks, man," he said. "I thought I was gonna die."

"Sorry," Chad said.

"Are you kiddin'? That was great! You reminded me of me!"

The scare made the other guys lose interest in chicken for the rest of that recess. As they drifted away, Rusty remained sitting on the ground. Chad started to leave, but Rusty spoke.

"You really scared those cannibals with a lighter and shocked one of 'em with a battery?"

Chad nodded. "We're not sure they were really cannibals, you know."

"Yeah, but still—"

They were silent for an awkward moment. "How's your dad doing?"

"Better. He's off the crutches and gets rid of the cane soon. Should be good as new."

"That's good."

Chad could hardly believe his ears. He was having an actual conversation with his enemy. Rusty struggled to his feet and brushed himself off. As they headed back toward the school building, he said, "You know, my cousin was in your mom's Sunday school class last year ..."

Chad continued to walk in silence.

"I'm sorry if you don't want to talk about her," Rusty spoke quietly.

"No, I love talking about her. Your cousin, huh?"

"Yeah, she thinks your mom was really cool."

Chad nodded. "She's right."

"She keeps trying to get me to come to your church."

Chad shrugged. "Any time. You might like it."

"Aw, I don't know. I've got an image, you know."

Chad snorted and chuckled. "Until today."

As Dad was saying good night that evening, Chad talked with him longer than he had for months. He told Dad what had happened that day.

"So no more calling yourself a wimp?" Dad said.

"I guess not."

"Still mad at God?"

Chad shook his head. "I still don't understand though. I don't really see why Mom had to die, and I feel guilty because I'm not sure it's worth it just because some people became Christians at her funeral."

"Chad ..." Dad settled himself on the edge of the bed. "You've been through things that no one your age should have to endure. And I'm not going to sit here and tell you that you'll ever get over your mom's death. It will affect you for the rest of your life." He rubbed a hand over his jaw. "We may never know all the reasons why God allowed it. Or even why we crashed last summer in the jungle." He spread his hands. "But it's our job to trust him, to look for the good that comes from bad. We can let these things tear us up, or we can grow and become what he wants us to be. You proved in the jungle that you could do what you had to do. You've got to face losing Mom the same way you faced those dangers."

"I promise I'll try," said Chad.

Dad swatted Chad's leg. "And I promise not to get you into any more situations where your life is at risk."

"Are you kidding?" Chad said. "That was the best part!"

"You're ready for another assignment then?" Dad pulled a long white envelope from his pocket.

"What do you mean?"

"Kate!" Dad called. "Can you come in here for a second?"

Kate padded in, ready for bed. She looked puzzled.

Dad held up a letter he had received that day from a couple in Washington State. "They're having trouble with the government in a new South American republic, and they want me to fly them in with supplies for a relief organization."

Chad looked at Kate, rolled his eyes, and grinned. "Here we go again."

Discussion Questions for Crash at Cannibal Valley

Chapter 1

1. Have you ever been bullied?
2. Have you ever been the bully?
3. How would you feel if you were talking to an officer like Chad and Kate?

Chapter 2

4. How would your life change if you were in Chad's situation?
5. What would you do if you had the resources Mr. Michaels has?
6. Have you ever been out of the country?

Chapter 3

7. How do you react when you're told to do something you don't want to do?
8. Would you be excited or scared to do this type of work?
9. Do you know any missionaries?

Chapter 4

10. What do you think will become of Waman?
11. Do you know any foreign language words?
12. How would you pray if you were in that plane?

Chapter 5

13. How many do you think survived the crash?
14. How would you try to survive if you were alone in this jungle?

Chapter 6

15. Have you ever had to take care of someone older than you?
16. What do you think is Chad's biggest fear in this situation?
17. What do you think the noise in the underbrush will be?

Chapter 7

18. How will Chad get his wounded family to safety?
19. Have you ever seen a parent in great pain? How did it make you feel?
20. Could you handle Chad's responsibility?

Chapter 8

21. Have you ever been shocked like Chad was when he touched the battery?
22. How would you handle being so exhausted but having so much work to do?
23. Would you have told dad and Kate about the smoke?

Chapter 9

24. Have you ever tried to start a fire without matches or a lighter?
25. Do you think Chad gave the radio operators enough information for rescue?
26. How do you think Chad will survive this attack?

Chapter 10

27. Why do you think the warrior was so scared of Chad?
28. Could you keep such a huge secret like Chad is doing?
29. How will Chad use the few words he knows to communicate?

Chapter 11

30. Have you ever tried to communicate with someone who doesn't speak your language?
31. If the Brazas were hostile, how could Chad have had a chance?
32. Does this story make you interested in missionary work?

TERROR
in Branco Grande

Sam, Maya, Elle, Max, Isaac, Jalen, Micah,
and Chelsea . . . my hearts.

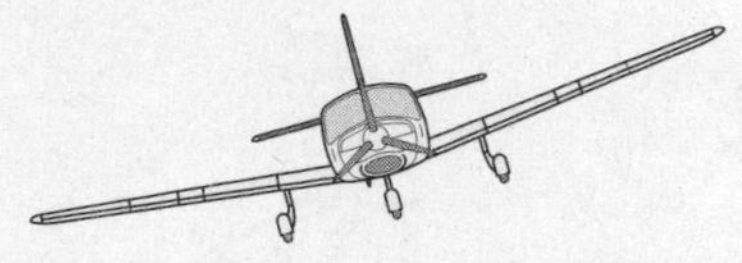

Contents

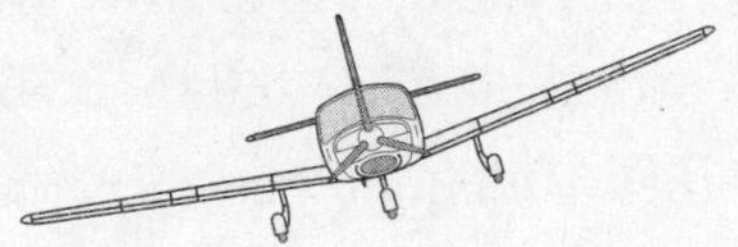

Women's Intuition

"You can't talk to me that way!" Kate Michaels said.

Her brother Chad sneered. "Just stop trying to act like Mom!"

Kate felt her face redden and a sob rise in her throat. She wanted to lash out, but she knew she would burst into tears. "What would be so wrong with acting like Mom?" she said. Just saying "Mom" brought back all the grief and pain of her mother's death six months before.

"Because you're not her! Nobody is or ever will be, so quit trying to be a woman or anything but a kid! And don't forget—you're not Thomas Edison, either!"

That was all Kate could take. She bounded up the steps to her room. As she flew by Dad at his desk, he said, "What are you two arguing about now?"

Kate slammed her door and flopped onto her bed. She allowed herself to cry softly, occasionally pausing to listen for Dad. Nothing. Maybe he was already giving Chad the standard lecture about girls and their emotions. Dad was real big on their sticking together as the AirQuest Adventures team. "We're family. We're all we've got," he always said.

Kate had just started sixth grade at Mukluk Middle School in northern Alaska. She felt older and more mature than ever; sometimes she almost forgot she was almost a year younger than Chad. So if she acted like her mom sometimes, what was wrong with that?

Her mom had been killed by a drunk driver one day when they were scheduled to pick up Dad at the airport. Dad, then an Air Force fighter pilot and owner of his own charter-flight company, was returning from a military assignment.

Since their mother's death, Kate's father had retired from military work and sold the company. Dad, Chad, and Kate had then formed AirQuest Adventures, a team available to Christian organizations anywhere in the world.

Dad was the pilot, of course. Chad, who his dad liked to call Spitfire after the quick and deadly World War II plane, was the computer expert. And Kate, a techie for as long as she could remember, knew a lot about radios and communications. She had won first prize at the school science fair every year since second grade.

Recently, she'd designed a two-way wrist radio that looked like a big watch. She and Chad and Dad all had one. After school Kate had told Chad that it wouldn't take much to add a miniature high frequency band and video camera to the gadget, which would allow for a crude LCD television picture.

Chad didn't believe her, which is what had started their argument a few moments before.

"Yeah, right." Chad had laughed as he followed her into the kitchen after school. "Like we could see each other on our wrist radios."

"Why is that so hard to believe?" she said. "We have cell phones where we can see each other—and even take pictures and make video clips."

"Exactly," Chad said. "So why waste time inventing a two- or three-way radio with a TV screen?"

"Think," Kate said, rolling her eyes. "Where we fly—jungles mostly—have you seen a lot of cell phone towers? Would your fancy phone be able to communicate at all?" She snorted. "You'd never pick up a signal."

Chad frowned. "True … "

Kate smiled. She loved proving him wrong. "Course, when we're talking into the radios, the other person could only see our mouth and nose, but if you held it back a ways, it would give a picture of our face or whole body."

Chad shook his head. "You're dreaming. The smallest two-way radio is ten times the size of your watch, and the smallest video camera is five times bigger than our wrist radios! How are you going to fit the machinery in there to record and send? And think of the antenna you'd need. We'd look like robots with rabbit ears!"

"You're not up on technology," Kate said. "They now make video cameras smaller than the end of your thumb. Batteries today will give you a five-mile range, and I know more than a hundred interference eliminator codes so we can hear each other clearly. Thanks to Dad, I also know the specs for military radios and what's needed to operate in harsh environments. I'm close, Chad, that's all I can say. You used to encourage me. Can't you see how it might work?"

"That's a long time away."

"No, it isn't! A Korean company has already invented a watch with a digital camera and phone. And video cameras in wristwatches already exist. I want to combine the watch and the video, but with a radio transmitter instead of a phone. The picture wouldn't be much, but it would be a start."

Chad shook his head. "It might make something interesting for this year's science fair, but you're years from making all that work."

"Maybe," Kate said. "I'm just saying I've got a feeling I'm on to something."

"You've got a feeling!" Chad spat. "You still think you've got women's intuition like Mom did?"

"Why shouldn't I? I'm a woman."

He laughed. "Not yet! Women's intuition is just a myth, and anyway"—and this is where he'd said it—"stop trying to act so much like Mom!"

Face down on her bed, Kate finally stopped crying. She sat up. The key was the battery! If she could somehow boost the power of those tiny batteries, she could transmit high-frequency radio waves plenty strong enough to produce an LCD readout.

As she started back down the stairs she saw that Dad was still at his desk. "What's up, Kate?" he said idly.

"I don't want to talk about it," she said.

Dad laughed, and she whirled to face him.

"Oh, come on, Katie. Don't give me that look. I just know that when you say you don't want to talk about something, it doesn't necessarily mean you don't want to talk about it."

Kate didn't know whether to smile or cry. Of course he was right. She shrugged. "I'll be in my workshop."

"And I'll be down in a few minutes to talk to you about whatever it is you want to talk to me about but say you don't. Fair enough?"

She rolled her eyes, then nodded and walked away. Men!

As she headed toward her frigid basement workshop, she heard Dad call out. “Spitfire! Got a minute?”

Downstairs, Kate lost herself in studying various combinations of batteries and experimenting with them to see what changes might show up on an oscillograph. She looked up when Chad came down.

“I don’t know how you can stand it down here,” he said, rubbing his arms.

“People think better in the cold,” she said. “It’s been proven.”

“Yeah? So is your wrist TV done?”

“I’m probably a week away,” she said.

“Yeah, well, I’m sorry for what I said about Mom and everything.”

“What you said about *me*, you mean?”

“You know what I mean.”

“Did Dad make you apologize?”

“What if he did?”

“Then don’t bother.”

Chad stared at the floor. “Well, I mean it anyway.”

“Okay then. I accept. You don’t need to hang around. Just go.”

Chad appeared grateful and charged back up the stairs. A few minutes later, Dad showed up in her workshop. “So are you and Chad okay?”

"We're okay." Kate said, sighing. "We just get on each other's nerves."

"You figure you both miss Mom and need someone to take it out on?"

"Maybe."

"You can take it out on me," Dad said. "I can take it. That's what dads are for. You're supposed to give me grief."

"But Chad's easier to fight with and be mad at. He deserves it."

They both laughed. "Let's all try to do what Mom would want us to do, hmm?" Dad said. "That way it's like she's still with us."

Kate nodded and pursed her lips. "You always tell us to do what God wants us to do."

"What God wants us to do and what Mom would want us to do are pretty much the same, aren't they?"

"It always seemed that way," Kate said.

"It's even more true now. Listen," he said, "I need to talk to you about something else. I want to do a short weekend run to South America for that couple who wrote us last summer."

"Oh, Dad!"

"I know you've had a funny feeling about it, Kate, but there's no reason to worry."

"I thought you told them we were all still recuperating from the last trip."

"I did, but they've written again. They couldn't find anyone else to fly them and their relief supplies into that newly formed country down there. Don't worry. It sounds like something right up our alley. We don't even have to bring them back. They're planning to stay down there awhile."

That night after dinner, Dad read out loud the first letter he had received from Howard and June Geist. " 'Our humanitarian organization, New Frontiers, Inc., headquartered in Boise, Idaho, delivers goods to struggling Third World nations. We are looking for someone who can fly us and our goods into Branco Grande, capital city of the newly formed South American country of Amazonia. The country gets its name from the Amazon River.' "

Dad explained that Amazonia was way south, a landlocked country that appeared to have been cut out of the country of Argentina. It lay about midway between Buenos Aires, Argentina, and Santiago, Chile. The country had been formed after a fierce battle for independence from Argentina.

"I thought you already told them we wouldn't do it," Chad said.

"I did," Dad said. "They wrote back. Let me see here, 'We followed your advice and looked into other possibilities for getting into Amazonia with our supplies, but so far we have struck out.' They say the government of the new country is welcoming them with open arms because of the goods and supplies they're bringing." He laid his hands flat on the table. "I'm going to rent a six-seat Learjet and offer to fly them down there for free."

Kate frowned. "Didn't we have a policy about helping only Christian organizations?"

"Remember what Jesus said about feeding the hungry or visiting the prisoners?" Dad spoke quietly.

"You mean—like what we do for others is like doing it for Jesus?" Chad said.

"I know, I know," Kate mumbled. "But it just doesn't feel right ..."

"What?" Dad looked at her closely. "You still got a problem with this?"

"We just don't know these people," she said. "Why can't they find another way down there? How do they get to the other countries they go to?" Kate felt a rising panic. She couldn't bring herself to say it out loud, but she was also worried about getting into another airplane. How could Dad and Chad even think about flying after their crash only a few short months before in Indonesia?

"They sound legitimate to me," Dad went on. "It's a rough time of their year, they say. Donations are down, and people don't know enough about Amazonia to give money for relief work there. They're looking for a one-way ride down there for themselves and less than a thousand pounds of cargo."

"Well," Chad said, "I'm not interested in getting another bunch of shots."

Shots? That's just an excuse, Kate thought. Chad must be scared to fly too.

"I already checked on that," Dad said. "The shots we got for Indonesia cover all and more than we would need for South America."

"You already checked?" Kate said. "So we're going and that's it? Why don't you quit pretending it makes any difference what we think or say?"

Dad seemed to think about that. Chad looked amazed that Kate had spoken up like that to Dad.

"I care what you think, Kate," Dad said. "But if it really is just a feeling, what am I supposed to tell the Geists? 'My son and I are for it and willing even to provide the flight for free, but my daughter has a funny feeling about it, so no, we're sorry'?"

Was she just being a wimp? She knew Chad would never say anything even if he was afraid.

"Should I tell them we'll do it?" Dad said. "Either we all go, or we all stay home. That's been the deal since we formed the company. I won't leave you behind."

Kate was silent. Dad would probably take her silence as agreeing to go, but she could no longer fight for no real reason.

After homework and another hour in her workshop, Kate went to bed, and Dad came in to pray and talk as usual. "Don't feel bad about being cautious, Kate," he said. "Your mom was cautious. Or at least she was thorough. Everything was planned out and thought through. Remember that?"

Kate nodded, hoping Dad couldn't see the fear in her eyes in the low light.

"She always thought I was impulsive," Dad said. "It's okay to be cautious. The Bible calls it being prudent. But in this case I don't think you have any reason to be afraid."

"I'm—I'm—"

"What is it, Kate?" Dad said gently.

"I'm scared, Dad. The plane ... I mean ... your friend was killed, and we almost died."

Dad nodded. "Of course. It makes perfect sense that you'd be afraid."

"Aren't you and Chad? Even a little?"

"I'd be lying if I said no. But flying is all I've ever wanted to do. I can't let fear stop me from being who I am. Besides, we're a team. Does AirQuest Adventures go out of business at the first sign of trouble? When you fall off a horse—"

Kate could feel a lecture coming on. "When do we meet these people?" she said.

Dad smiled. "That's my girl. We meet them in Boise the last Friday of next month, and we take off for South America early the next morning. I'm chartering a small jet that will carry the five of us and their cargo."

Kate hadn't meant to imply she was all for it.

A week later Kate had a breakthrough on her wrist TV idea. When she finally was able to boost the power in the tiny batteries without damaging the other functions, she produced a crude image on a small liquid-crystal display. She yelled for Dad and Chad to come down to her workshop, and they were amazed.

"Will it work on a smaller display so you can fit it on our wrists?" Chad said.

"If I can get the parts I need in time, I'll have three of them made before we leave for South America."

Over the next few weeks she finished fashioning the wrist TVs.

When she finally met the Geists at their home in Boise, Idaho, her fears about them nearly vanished. Howard Geist was a big, burly man with white hair, a red face, and a constant smile. His wife was tall and thin, freckle-faced, and wore no makeup. Her eyes sparkled, especially when she talked to Chad or Kate.

Mrs. Geist showed Kate a scrapbook with snapshots of several deliveries she and her husband had made to various needy countries. Later the Geists showed Dad, Chad, and Kate sample packages of the seeds and medicines they planned to load onto the plane in the morning.

"Listen," June Geist said, "one thing we insist on. We're so grateful for your help that we want to bring meals along for the flight."

"Thanks," Dad said. "We appreciate it."

"The pleasure is all ours," June Geist said.

By the end of the evening, as the AirQuest Adventures team settled into their hotel room to wait for the next morning's flight, Kate's uneasiness was almost gone. Still, she had trouble falling asleep. Maybe she was just nervous about another flight into a mountainous country that would remind her of Indonesia. But like Dad said, "you can't let fear stop you."

Kate's nervousness was still there the next morning, but she tried to be cheerful. Nobody liked a grumpy person, especially at the start of a long flight. The Geists seemed upbeat as they pulled their rented truck into the hangar and began to load their cargo onto the plane.

Dad offered to help, but they insisted he finish filing his flight plan. Kate and Chad tried to help too, but the metal containers that fit so well together were too heavy. The kids piled into the small jet and sat in the back two seats. Kate's heart pounded so hard, she was sure Chad could hear it.

As Mr. Geist hoisted one of the containers in through the cargo door, he called out to Kate and Chad. "Would you mind if my wife and I sit back there? We want to be able to keep an eye on the cargo and the food."

Kate and Chad looked at each other and shrugged. "Sure," they said. Just then one of the cartons slipped out of Mr. Geist's grasp and bounced on the floor. The latches came loose and the top slid off, spilling out three small boxes. Howard Geist turned and hefted one end of another carton, and his wife grabbed the other end. He smiled at Kate and nodded at the boxes on the floor. "Would you mind picking those up for me, sweetie?" Kate bristled at being called *sweetie*, but she picked up the boxes anyway, which she noticed contained seed packets.

Soon everyone was on board. Kate and Chad, now in the middle seats, passed their backpacks to the rear to be stowed with Dad's. The Geists tucked everything in the cargo pile along with their own bags.

Dad checked to make sure the cargo was secure, then started the engines. Kate turned to Chad. "Are you scared? You know, of flying?"

He just stared straight ahead, but his hands were gripping the armrests, and his knuckles were white.

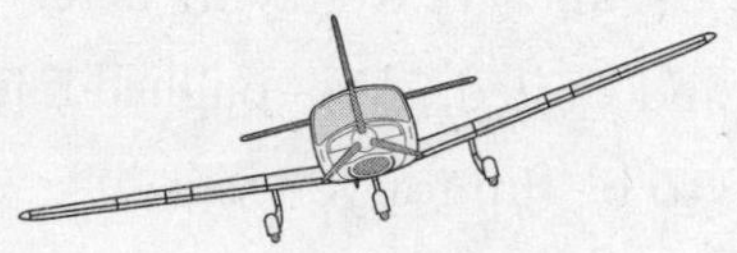

Branco Grande

The Geists sat in the back for the entire flight, while Kate and Chad moved between the middle two seats and the seat next to Dad. Once they were in the air for a while, Kate's tension began to ease. She got to know the Geists better, chatting with them off and on for hours. When the couple wanted to nap, she talked with Chad or just sat next to Dad and pretended to be his first officer.

"Where are we staying, Dad?"

He handed her a brochure from his flight bag. "The Branco Grande Plaza del Rio, a new standard of hospitality in a new country," she read. Inside was a photo of a beautiful hotel under construction in the capital city. One wing was finished, and the brochure showed a pool and a little park beside it. Three other wings were framed up, and an artist had drawn pictures of what they would look like when they were finished.

"Really?" Kate said. "We're staying here?"

Dad nodded and smiled. "We roughed it in Indonesia. I wanted this trip to be fun for you kids."

"Thanks, Dad."

Kate put on her headphones and listened to the radio air traffic as they flew over the larger cities in North America, Central America, and South America. She was grateful that the international language of aviation was English.

Now that she wasn't as nervous, Kate even grew drowsy and fell asleep with the headphones on, occasionally rousing when static or voices came through. When Dad reached over and slid the earphones off her head, she curled up and slept soundly, making up for the restless night before.

Kate didn't know how long she had slept when the landing woke her. Though the jet was air conditioned, heat invaded the cabin. Kate peered out, squinting against the late afternoon sun that made heat waves shimmer off the end of the runway. She peeled off her sweater and found she was already sweating heavily. It seemed strange to see only a few other planes at the Branco Grande airstrip.

"That huge, long runway," her dad said, pointing, "was built for the jumbo jets the new government hopes to begin flying to their new capital city soon."

In the distance Kate saw the airport: a row of low buildings, some finished, some not. The airport personnel wore camouflage uniforms. Kate watched as they unloaded a cargo plane near a crude metal shed. Several open-topped, four-wheel drive jeeps waited nearby. Four men carrying automatic assault weapons were in each jeep. "Dad?" she said, voice quivering.

But Dad had one hand up to his headphones. "Roger, understand," he was saying. "Roger, understand."

Kate grabbed her earphones and listened. Someone was telling Dad in broken English to stay right where he was, to not taxi toward the airport. "We will come and inspect your plane on the runway," the voice told Dad.

"Roger that, understand," Dad said. One of the four-manned vehicles roared out from under a rough shelter of leaves and branches and into the sunshine. The driver swerved recklessly while the other three men desperately held on. Kate heard the jeep's squealing brakes from inside the still-pressurized cabin. The vehicle finally stopped directly in front of the jet.

The jeep's three passengers cautiously stepped out and brandished their weapons while the driver reached for a bullhorn. "Are you carrying any weapons?"

Dad shook his head and raised his hands.

"The others?" the driver demanded.

Kate and Chad and the Geists all followed Dad's example and raised their hands.

"I'm going to talk to ground control and get to the bottom of this." Dad reached for the microphone, but the gunman to their left rattled three loud bursts from his weapon into the air.

Dad quickly raised both hands again, and the driver shouted through his bullhorn. "Don't do that again!" he said. "You want to get yourself and your passengers killed? We could blow you off the runway with one grenade!"

Dad had to know they couldn't hear him, Kate thought, but he shouted back, "There are children on this plane, and we're on a humanitarian mission. We demand appropriate respect and hospitality!"

"Silence!" The driver reached beneath his seat and displayed a grenade. "We know who you are, and we are merely taking normal precautions! We will check your plane and your cargo, and then we will process your passengers in customs."

"Customs," Dad muttered. "I can't wait to see that facility."

"I ask again—do you or any of your passengers have weapons?"

Dad shook his head.

"If we find any, you could be sentenced to death!"

"Chad, did you bring your AK-47?" Dad whispered.

"Not this time, Dad," Chad said. "Seemed like a little too much power."

"Depressurize, and then keep your hands in the air while we do our work!"

The driver stayed in the jeep, and a gunman stood at each wing while the third yanked open the cargo door. "Do not be afraid, everybody," he said, as he dug through the cargo. The muscular young man was dark with long hair and a scraggly black beard. Sweat had soaked through his shirt. "Please face the front, señorita," he said, glancing at Kate. "No problem. No problem." He loosened the latches on the big metal containers and slid off the tops. "Seeds, more seeds, seeds, medicine, more seeds," he said over and over. "*Bueno, bueno, gracias.* Sandwiches! May I?"

"Like we've got a choice!" Dad mumbled.

Mrs. Geist insisted that the man help himself and share the goodies with his friends. He tossed food to his compatriots, then began to search backpacks and suitcases, tossing them on the ground as he finished each one. He ignored the larger cargo containers in the plane.

Dad rapped on the window. "Hey, take it easy with our bags!" he shouted.

The driver tossed the grenade onto the jeep seat and, still holding the bullhorn, he picked up his weapon. He stepped from the jeep and walked directly to the cockpit, where he pressed the barrel against the window. Kate covered her face with her hands and shrank down in the seat.

"Sit up, señorita!" the man shouted, and she did.

"The window is bulletproof," Dad whispered, "and he knows that."

"And you," the man said to Dad. "Unless you keep your hands in the air, I will kill you. Comprendé?"

Dad nodded but stared at the man in disgust. "Why terrorize my passengers? They're civilians and kids!"

"Are you calling me a terrorist?" the man shouted.

"You're terrorizing them."

"No more talking! Paco! You finished?"

The young man in the cargo hold said he was, but then whistled and marched dramatically around to the front of the plane. He held a semi-automatic pistol by the barrel in two fingers. "Look what I find in this bag!" he crowed.

The backpack was Dad's, but the gun was not. "Whose is that?" Dad said, almost under his breath.

Howard Geist's face was redder than ever. "Surely you didn't bring that."

"Of course not. It's a plant."

The man with the bullhorn waved Paco over and peered at the weapon in the sunlight. "American-made Smith & Wesson," he said. "And found in the bag of... " He turned the identification tag over and read slowly, "Bruce Michaels of Mukluk, Alaska. Which one of you is that?"

Dad nodded and gestured to himself. "But that is not my gun. I don't own a Smith & Wesson, and I did not carry a weapon on this plane."

"You may explain it in customs," the soldier said.

"I can't," Dad said. "Someone planted it."

"You would accuse us of such a thing?" yelled the man with the bullhorn. "You bring a powerful firearm into my country, and you accuse me of that? Paco! Drag him out of there!"

Dad dropped his hands and dug in his flight bag until he found his wallet. He pulled out their passports and visas, then slipped the wallet to Kate. "Wrap this in your sweater," he said, "and whatever you do, keep it hidden."

"Hands up!" Bullhorn shouted from the ground. Kate tucked the heavy wallet into the back of her sweater and rolled the sweater up, tying it around her waist. She and Dad raised their hands again as Paco opened the cockpit door on Kate's side. "Move back, little lady," he said.

She unbuckled her seat belt and stepped between the seats to sit next to Chad. As she moved, she felt the wallet pulling on the rolled up sweater around her waist. Would Paco see it? She was afraid it would flop out, and she quickly dropped into the seat.

"You!" Paco shouted at Dad. "Out! Out!"

Paco grabbed Dad's wrist and pulled him over the seat. Dad stumbled out of the plane.

"Hands up! Search!"

Dad raised his hands yet again, and Paco patted him down. "Any more guns in the plane?"

Dad shrugged. "The only one I've seen is the one your people put there."

Paco pressed his weapon against Dad's neck, and Kate froze. "I could kill you where you stand."

"But you have no reason to. You must have planted the gun for some kind of leverage." Dad glanced over his shoulder. "Now that you've got it, what do you want? Or are you just a soldier and not a commander?

"You'll be just as dead no matter which I am. Now move!"

As the men handcuffed Dad and pushed him toward the jeep, Kate heard Bullhorn call on his radio for another vehicle and more help to unload the cargo. Within a minute, more soldiers arrived. The Geists and Chad were herded into one jeep, and Kate was put into the back seat of another—she sat directly behind the driver, the man with the bullhorn. Dad sat in the front next to Bullhorn, and Paco climbed in beside Kate. *Dear God, help us!* She could hardly move; their luggage was stashed all around them. Every chance she got, Kate tightened the sweater around her.

Kate watched the unloading operation, and then the same thing happened that had happened in the hangar in

Boise. One of the containers popped open, and some boxes fell out. The weight shifted, and the two men lugging the container almost dropped it.

"Paco!" Bullhorn said. "Help them."

Paco jumped from the vehicle, and Kate realized no one was watching her. She worked the wallet out of her sweater and stuffed it down between the seat cushion and the back of the seat. Then she pressed her back against it until it was completely buried in the cushion. She hooked her toe into her own backpack and slowly slid it in between her feet. She had packed all three wrist TVs, and she didn't want them found. Kate pushed on the backpack until it was lodged out of sight behind the seat.

"I don't want to be separated from my kids," Dad said. "That's my son in the other jeep."

"We don't care what you want, señor. You have been found trying to smuggle a weapon into our country. Bringing in a weapon is not in itself against our new constitution. Many mercenaries and freedom fighters have come in to help us defend ourselves. But you must declare it."

Dad just shook his head.

"We are not unreasonable people," Bullhorn said. "We will determine why you wanted to smuggle a weapon in, which side you are sympathetic with, and whether you should be sentenced to death or just life in prison."

Kate couldn't believe this! But Dad turned quickly and shook his head at her, as if to say that was ridiculous—the man was bluffing.

"Oh, you think I am not serious, señor? Wait till you see your cellmates. May I assume you sympathize with Argentina?"

"I know nothing about your revolution. From the news and the fact that the United States government is considering recognizing your sovereignty, I can only assume your cause was just."

"That is the correct answer, señor. But gun smuggling does not fit. You had better hope we find no more contraband in your cargo."

Kate could only guess what *sovereignty* and *contraband* meant. The other vehicle had already pulled away with the Geists and Chad aboard. She knew Dad was as anxious as she was to be reunited with Chad.

And what a mess for the poor Geists. Here they were, trying to do something nice for the people of a new country, and they were treated like criminals.

Despite her fear, Kate felt suddenly tired. She only wished she could go back to her nap and discover that this was all a dream. A bad dream.

The Tribunal

Kate's heart raced as she thought about her dad's wallet stuffed into the seat behind her and her backpack hidden deep under the seat. It had scared her to see Chad squatting between Howard and June Geist, who sat in the two back seats of the other four-wheel drive, which was crammed with armed guards and roaring off toward the terminal.

Something felt strange about the way the Geists had seemed to relax in their seats. She was trying to make sense of it when Dad turned to the man with the bullhorn. "I do not want to be separated from my son," he said fiercely.

Bullhorn started the jeep. "Señor, you have no say in — "

Dad jerked sideways. "Okay, fine! I'll walk. I will not be separated!" He swung his legs over the side of the vehicle and staggered onto the runway. But after two quick steps toward the terminal a quarter mile away, he stopped in his tracks at the sound of gunfire behind him.

"Dad!" Kate screamed and covered her ears. It was Bullhorn who had fired into the air. He jumped from the jeep.

"If you are dead," he shouted, "you will be separated from both of your children forever!"

Dad whirled to face him. "I don't know what you people are trying to pull, but we have rights under international law!"

"You may have rights, but I have the weapon." He grabbed Dad by the handcuffs and swung him around, causing him to topple back into the vehicle. "You, your son, your daughter, and your other passengers will be interrogated together, so just calm down."

"Well, get moving then!" Dad said.

Paco had been leaning across Kate all this time, trying to see the action. He smiled broadly now and leaned back against the seat. Kate glared at him, fighting tears. Dad owned handguns—she had seen them. The huge Smith & Wesson was not one of them. She'd prove it was planted if it was the last thing she did.

Kate had seen a new side of her father, and it almost made her bold enough to speak up. But she was not as convinced as Dad seemed to be that these people would not shoot them. Two soldiers had already fired into the air, and she had seen and heard the spent cartridges plink onto the asphalt of the runway.

As the vehicle whipped around and sped toward the terminal, Kate grabbed the back of the seat in front of her to keep her balance. The last thing she wanted was to lean over onto Paco.

Kate's hands were inches from the driver's neck and the weapon strapped over his shoulder. But when she turned to steal a glance at Paco, he chuckled, as if reading her mind. How long could an eleven-year-old live if she attacked an armed soldier? All Kate could do was pray that everything would be straightened out in customs.

When the jeep jerked to a stop in front of the single-story terminal, Chad and the Geists were already being herded inside. Dad turned and gestured with a nod that Kate should stay close to him. *As if I would do anything else.*

Bullhorn and Paco jumped out first and stood on either side of the jeep, weapons in hand. Dad awkwardly stumbled from his seat to the ground, unable to steady himself with his hands cuffed behind his back. Bullhorn gestured to Kate, indicating that she should climb down out of his side of the vehicle, but she ignored him and scrambled into the front and out the same way Dad had gone. She stole a glance back at the jeep and saw a gap between the back and the cushion of her seat. But the wallet wasn't showing. She'd get it when they were driven back to the plane.

Kate realized that none of the vehicles had numbers or license plates and were all the same size and color. If they moved it, she wouldn't know that jeep from any of the others. She trotted to catch up with Dad as he hurried into the terminal, where he turned his head in every direction, obviously looking for Chad.

Bullhorn ordered Paco and a couple of other soldiers to bring in the luggage, and Kate found herself praying again. She could only hope the soldiers wouldn't think to look deep under the seat where they would find her backpack.

When Paco and Bullhorn steered Dad down a long hallway to a large room under a sign that read *Interrogación*, Kate peeked back to study the jeep. The left headlight was broken, and the bumper was creased. She hoped that wasn't true of any of the other jeeps. Soldiers began filing in with their luggage, and she saw no one with her backpack. She turned back around just in time to keep from bumping into Paco, who had stopped before the interrogation room.

Kate heard footsteps and turned to see three men and two women approaching from the other end of the hallway. They wore uniforms, and they all looked neater and less haggard than the soldiers. They filed into the room before anyone else and began setting up a tape recorder and their notebooks at one end of the table.

"Must I sit in there handcuffed in front of my children?" Dad said.

"Silence!" Bullhorn said. "You are now in the custody of General Rafael Valdez, and he will tell you whether you will remain cuffed or not."

General Valdez was a short, powerfully built man who stood quietly to one side as his aides finished arranging everything. He scowled at Dad, then asked Bullhorn a question in Spanish. Kate guessed he had asked why Dad was handcuffed, because Bullhorn was obviously rehashing what had happened on the runway. With a gesture and a nod, the general gave instructions to remove Dad's handcuffs. Paco did so and then stood with his weapon in both hands, as if afraid Dad would try something.

The older of the two women, who looked older than anyone in the room except perhaps the Geists, finally got the tape recorder plugged in. The general sat in the middle of one side of the table, flanked by a man on either side. The women sat at each end. Kate could hardly take her eyes off the younger woman. She strained to read the nameplate above her chest pocket—Eva Flores. Kate couldn't be sure, but she thought she saw a hint of sympathy or encouragement in the young woman's eyes. The rest of the people in uniform were grim-faced and quiet.

"Passports and visas, *por favor*," the older woman sang out.

The Geists produced theirs, and Dad turned over three sets. The woman flipped to the picture in each passport, glanced at the person, and pointed to a chair before the tribunal of officers. June Geist was placed at the far left end of five chairs. Then Howard Geist sat beside her. Dad was in the middle. Then Chad. Then Kate.

That put Kate directly in front of Eva Flores. More than once they caught each other's eyes, and Kate felt strangely warmed. Could she have found a caring person in the middle of this nightmare?

The older woman placed the passports before the general in the order in which the Americans sat. Valdez repeated the routine, peeking at each picture and matching it with the person before him. He glanced at the visas as well, then crossed his arms and sat staring at Dad. Dad did not look away.

Valdez nodded to the older woman, who turned on the tape recorder. In a thick accent, he began, "This is an official investigation by the government of the sovereign South American state of Amazonia into the possible illegal transport of weapons and contraband goods into the airport of the capital city of Branco Grande."

The general read off the number of Dad's rented Learjet and then read into the record the names of the passengers, starting with Kate.

"Kathryn Thompson Michaels, age eleven, a native of Enid, Oklahoma, currently residing in Mukluk, Alaska.

"Chadwick Whiteford Michaels, age twelve, a native of Enid, Oklahoma, currently residing in Mukluk, Alaska.

"Bruce Phillip Michaels, age thirty-five, a native of Kalamazoo, Michigan, currently residing in Mukluk, Alaska."

"Recently retired United States Air Force colonel," Dad added.

"Pardon?" Valdez said. "You, señor?"

"That is correct, sir."

"Then you should know it is a violation of international law to smuggle weapons or—"

"Of course I know that, sir. That's why I wouldn't do such a foolish thing. That weapon was planted—"

"Señor, this trial is only beginning. You will have your chance to—"

"Excuse me?" Dad leaned forward. "So this is a trial now?"

"What did you think it was?"

Kate's breath came in short gasps.

"Surely this must violate your own constitution! I haven't been formally charged, and I don't have a lawyer."

"Our constitution, señor, is still in process. Meanwhile, we are a nation not unlike your own, brought into existence with bloodshed at the hands of our oppressive, tyrannical enemy." He smiled grimly. "You sacrificed a lawyer when you lied about not having a weapon with you. All you had to do was declare it and swear allegiance to our cause. We would not even have required you to surrender it."

"You can have it," Dad said quietly, "because it's not mine."

One of the soldiers who had been rifling through the luggage hurried over and whispered in the general's ear. Valdez shot him a double take and whirled in his chair to talk animatedly with him. When he turned back, his face was flushed and his eyes afire.

"You, señor, will have an opportunity to speak later. Not only have more weapons been found among your luggage, but also cocaine and heroin. My patience with you is at an end."

"Your patience with *me*?" Dad shook his head. "But of course you knew about the drugs before they were found, right?"

"What a bunch of lies!" Chad shouted. "My dad would never do anything like—"

"Señor!" General Valdez shouted. "You will quiet your son, or you will be separated. Any further outbursts will be cause for an immediate judgment against you."

Dad put a hand on Chad's shoulder. "Son, let's just ride this out," he said quietly. "Something's happening here that's out of our control."

Eva Flores squinted, staring at Dad and Chad as if trying to make it all compute. Kate hoped the woman could see through all of this. But even if she had doubts, what could she do? Did she have any authority, or was she just an assistant to the general?

General Valdez picked up the fourth passport and flipped to the picture. "George Kennicott, age fifty-six, a native of Albuquerque, New Mexico, currently residing in Anchorage, Alaska."

George Kennicott? Kate turned to see her father's reaction. Who in the world was George Kennicott? Dad and Chad were staring at Howard Geist, or at least the man they thought was Howard Geist. He ignored them, holding the general's gaze and nodding slightly.

Dad let out a huge sigh and nodded slowly, as if it had all become clear to him. But it wasn't clear to Kate. What had Dad figured out? Were guns and drugs really found in the cargo, and had the Geists—or the Kennicotts—put them there?

The general continued. "Iris Kennicott, age fifty-five, a native of Baton Rouge, Louisiana, currently residing in Anchorage, Alaska."

So the Geists were using fake names, either with AirQuest Adventures or with the passport officials. Here Dad was accusing the Amazonians of framing him, and maybe it was really the Geists—or the Kennicotts—all along. Kate wanted to scream. Dad seemed to just take it all in.

The general turned to take a list from one of the soldiers. He studied it for a minute, then set it in front of him on the table. "Let's start with you, señora," Valdez said, addressing Mrs. Geist. "Mrs. Kennicott, your luggage contains no contraband and your papers are in order. Tell me the nature of your business in Amazonia."

"My husband and I run a humanitarian organization out of Anchorage called New Frontiers. We donate our time, along with medicine and seeds, to emerging countries. We are on file with your foreign ministry, and we were expected."

"How is it that you have traveled with a smuggler of weapons and drugs?"

"We had no idea. We advertised for a flight to Amazonia, and Mr. Michaels here answered the ad. He offered to fly us for free, and we couldn't pass up the bargain."

"That's not true!" Chad blurted, but Dad quieted him. The general continued. "Did you not suspect that someone offering to fly you for free might be using you as a cover for his own smuggling operation?"

"We never even gave that a thought. We had heard that Mr. Michaels was very successful with his business, the Yukon Do It air charter service, and we were grateful that he seemed interested in our humanitarian efforts."

Kate could tell from Chad's body language that he was not going to keep quiet about this. "That's a lie!" he shouted. "They live in Boise and they call themselves the Geists and my dad doesn't even have that business anymore. We call ourselves—"

"Enough!" Valdez shouted. "You will each get your turn."

Dad put a hand on Chad's shoulder and nodded.

"Mr. Kennicott?" the General said.

"Yes, Mr. Michael's manifest will show that he flew a small plane out of Mukluk, where he lives, to Anchorage, where he picked us up and rented the Lear."

"I didn't pick you up until we got to Boise, and you know it," Dad said.

"Anyway," the older man said, "it will also show that we made a stop in Boise, Idaho, which is where we warehouse our goods. As my wife has said, we had no idea that he and his children would be involved in anything but a straight charter flying service. If our papers are in order and our cargo is accounted for, we would ask that we be excused to go about our business."

Kate glared at the older couple. Why were they trusted while her family was treated like criminals? Surely the general would not let these people trick him like this. But he quickly slid their passports and visas down the table to Eva Flores, who began stamping them. The general stood and extended his hand to the couple Kate had known as the Geists.

"Mr. and Mrs. Kennicott, allow me to apologize for having detained you, but you understand."

The "Geists" stood and shook his hand.

"We understand," Mr. Kennicott said.

"And also allow me to welcome you to Branco Grande on behalf of the free and independent people of Amazonia and to thank you for the gifts you have brought us."

The Kennicotts made a big deal of nodding and looking humble as they smiled and picked up their documents, then hurried out.

Kate slumped, puzzled by her dad's sudden silence. If the Geists were the criminals, the real smugglers, and they were free, Kate wondered what that meant for her and her brother and her dad. She knew Dad had brought their original letter, with the name Geist on it, and she thought he had attached a newspaper article with a picture of them posing with some foreign dignitary. That also identified them as the Geists. Would the general change his mind if he saw that? And did she dare suggest that it was in Dad's wallet, stuffed in the seat of one of their own jeeps?

No, Dad had made it clear that she should keep his wallet hidden no matter what. He could always ask her for the wallet if he wanted to produce his proof. What was going to happen to her family? Dad would get his turn to talk, but what could he say? If he tried to blame this on the Geists, or whoever they were, he would get nowhere. The people who now called themselves the Kennicotts were already heroes to the Amazonians.

Kate sat on her hands, rocking on the hard wooden chair, sweating in the oppressive heat. She glanced at Eva Flores, whose forehead seemed knotted as she stared at the three passports still laid out in front of the general.

Kate tried to catch her eye, to find that hint of sympathy or encouragement, but Eva Flores was not looking at her.

The "Hearing"

Kate could hardly believe what had happened since they'd landed. Even if they didn't know who planted the guns and the drugs in their cargo, even if it was done after they landed, they did know the Geists were certainly not who they claimed to be. At the very least they were liars and impostors.

Kate watched Dad as he sat at the table shaking his head, while the general and his aides conferred. But Eva Flores merely listened and observed the others. A soldier approached and turned in yet another list of some kind, then whispered something to Valdez. The general nodded and gestured, and soon several soldiers filed in, pushing dollies containing the metal cargo containers the Geists had loaded onto the plane.

"This will prove we're innocent," Kate whispered to Chad. "Those containers aren't even ours!"

The general looked up quickly and scowled at her, and Eva Flores casually put a finger to her lips, as if to warn Kate to be quiet and careful. Whenever Eva Flores seemed to communicate in some way Kate felt secure; something about this woman made Kate want to trust her.

When the nearly one thousand pounds of metal containers were stacked in a corner, General Valdez turned to the soldiers. “Show me,” he said.

Two soldiers set aside the loose tops and began pulling stuff from the containers. At first all they produced were boxes of seed packets, cartons of penicillin, and two kinds of medicines for what the Geists had said was the treatment of malaria. But then one soldier bent and, leaning his torso deep into one of the other containers, pulled out a wooden rack which held four high-powered assault weapons. The other soldier pulled boxes of ammunition from another container.

Kate peeked at her dad. He just sat there as if nothing would surprise him now.

“If you were bringing these into our country to aid us in the defense of our coup,” General Rafael Valdez said, “you would be a hero to us. But as you have denied bringing them, it is too late to take credit. If it makes you feel any better, they will be put to good use.”

“They are not mine,” Dad said.

"Oh? And how do I know that? These are American-made weapons. A man of your stature in the military would have ready access to these."

"I'm no longer in the military, and anyone in the United States has access to such weapons. The right to bear arms is in—"

"Your constitution, yes, I know. Ours, too. So, if these are not yours, what is your explanation? And never let it be said that I did not give you an opportunity to stage your defense."

"This is my defense? I face so-called evidence I have never seen and must explain why it is not mine?"

"You had better say something, Señor Michaels. Your hours of freedom are fast closing."

Dad sighed and spoke in a flat, even tone. "I don't know who put weapons in those containers. I never saw them before they were loaded onto my plane. My son is correct in that the Kennicotts, as you call them, represented themselves to us as the Geists from Boise. We spent last evening in their home before leaving this morning. If their phony name and location is part of this, then yes, maybe those weapons were in the cargo from the time we left the States."

"You did not supervise the loading of cargo on your own plane?"

"I was doing the preflight checklist while they loaded the cargo—at their request, I might add—and they seemed to have a lot of experience at this sort of thing. I can see why now."

"Don't be pointing the finger at the Kennicotts, Señor Michaels. They are on register with our foreign ministry, and they come with the full authority of the President of the United States."

"What does that mean?"

"Here, look. But do not touch."

The general spun a single sheet of paper and slid it to where Dad could lean forward and read it. "A personal letter of introduction and endorsement from your president himself," the general said proudly.

"All due respect, General," Dad said, "but this is such an obvious phony that even you should be able to see through it."

It was clear the general was offended. He snatched up the sheet and ran his fingers along the embossed letterhead. Then he licked a finger and ran it across the signature. "See, the ink runs! It is an original. What is not to trust about it?"

"For one thing, the president of the United States is so isolated, so hard to get to, that it is highly unlikely any private citizen could get such an endorsement from him. Only an ambassador or an official spokesperson from our government would ever rate something like this. I'm sorry. It's as phony as the Geists, or the Kennicotts, or whatever you choose to call them. If I'm guilty of a crime, it's that I have allowed myself to be royally duped."

"Señor," Valdez said, "you are guilty of much more than that." He wheeled around in his chair to watch as the soldiers began lifting cellophane bags from the containers. "In the Kennicotts' containers, medicines and seeds," Valdez said. "In your containers, cocaine and heroin, as well as weapons and ammunition."

"All those containers belong to the Geists'," Dad said. "My record is crystal clear from childhood. Other than two speeding tickets when I was a teenager, you'll find nothing there for thirty-five years. But I'll bet the Geists' record is not so clear."

"The Kennicotts are not your concern," Valdez said. "Your life had better be your concern. Our country has been in existence for less than a year, and we have executed more than two dozen smugglers of drugs and firearms."

Suddenly everyone grew quiet. Kate glanced at Chad, who looked pale.

Valdez stroked his mustache. "We have a slogan here that we picked up from our neighbors to the north, the Mexicans, and from your own country. It is called zero-tolerance. We do not tolerate threats to our freedom or to our health. Weapons that are not brought in here to help us hold off the tyrannists are here to bring us down. And drugs are brought here for only two reasons—to make the smuggler rich and to weaken the moral fabric of our society."

Suddenly, Dad leaned across the table, arms outstretched. "Listen to me, please," he said. "I agree with this policy a hundred percent. I've seen my own country go from being tough on crime to soft on crime. I know the Mexicans sentence international criminals to life in prison or to death, and they make it stick. But with just a little detective work you can prove or disprove my story."

Dad looked earnestly at the other officials, one at a time, then turned back to the general.

"You just let the real criminals walk free because you were duped like I was. I don't mean to offend or insult you, sir, but if you are sincere about the health of your country, you don't want to pin this crime on an innocent man. The smallest amount of detective work can tell you where those metal containers came from. You could fingerprint the contents. You could check out the, uh, the Kennicotts with the United States government."

"You forget that your government is still dragging its feet in recognizing us as a sovereign state."

"It's just a matter of time."

"We have allocated land for a U.S. embassy, but they have thumbed their noses at us."

"No! I'm certain I've read that it's just red tape, and that they will be appointing an ambassador soon."

"Let me ask you something, Señor Michaels. Do you think you are talking to an imbecile?"

Dad shook his head.

"Do you think you are talking to someone who does not hold your life in his hands?"

"I'm starting to get the picture."

"Are you?"

"Yes, sir."

"Do you understand that I have sentenced men both to life in prison and to death? And that it has been done right here in this room?"

Kate couldn't move, and it felt as if the air had been sucked from the room.

"No trial?" Dad said. "No jury? No lawyer for the accused?"

"Now you really are getting the picture. You do not talk to me with respect even though my men carry weapons. You do not talk to me with respect even though I hold the rank of general in my country's military. You do not talk to me with respect even when you have been caught red-handed, smuggling into my country. Maybe now you will talk to me with respect when you know I hold your life in my hands."

Kate wished with all her might that her dad would try to convince the general that it wasn't a lack of respect but rather the phony charges that were causing such strong reactions. But she knew Dad was not the type to back down from someone who was unfair and unjust.

"Of course I don't want to say or do anything that would cost my children their only remaining parent," Dad said, and Kate heard Eva Flores groan softly. She glanced up at the woman and saw the worried look in her eyes.

"These children have no mother?" General Valdez said.

"No, sir, she was killed in an auto accident earlier this year."

At this, Eva Flores quickly covered her mouth with her hand.

"All the more reason for you to come clean now, Señor Michaels," Valdez said. "If you refuse to take responsibility for your crimes, you will be sentenced to prison either for life or to await your execution, and your children will become wards of the state."

"He didn't do anything wrong!" Kate shouted, but her dad shushed her.

"General Valdez, if you imprison me or put me to death and detain my children, you will have the United States government and the court of world opinion against you. I am a decorated military officer with an impeccable record, a recent widower with two young children. And I am innocent. Even if I were guilty, my government would not allow one of its citizens, especially a retired Air Force colonel, to be tried by a one-man judge and jury."

"You think I care about the court of world opinion? You think I feel threatened by the United States? Had I been in the battle over the Islas Malvinas years ago, they would belong to Argentina now."

Dad looked puzzled. "You mean the Falkland Islands?"

"That may be what *you* call them, but—"

"That was a United Kingdom possession anyway, and—"

"But the U.S. aided them."

"It was long before my time," Dad said.

"As I suspected, you deny everything. Nothing is your fault."

"Well, in the case of this cargo it certainly isn't."

"Señor," General Valdez said slowly, "you have spoken to me with great indignation, as a man who has been wrongly accused."

For the first time, Kate felt hope. The general's voice sounded softer. Was he about to say that Dad could possibly be telling the truth? That was what she read in the eyes of Eva Flores, but were women the only ones with intuition? The Bible said nothing about women's intuition, but Kate knew her mother had had it, and Mom had always said she believed it was a gift from God.

The general continued. "And though I would not willingly forge ahead with charges and sentencing of a man of your stature and face the reaction from your government and possibly the rest of the world, I am a man who has long fought in the face of tremendous odds. I might be tempted to be more sympathetic to what you say if your name were not fastened to every cargo container that carried guns or drugs."

"That's impossible."

The general waved over a soldier who had pulled identification tags from the containers.

The general read out loud, "Bruce Michaels, President, Yukon Do It Air Charter Service, Mukluk, Alaska. How do you explain these?"

"Not mine," Dad said.

The general laughed and pushed the pile of tags toward Dad.

Dad picked one up. "You ask me to speak to you with respect because of your rank, your weapon, your authority. But let me ask you a question you cannot answer."

"Go ahead. This is your day in court."

"Put yourself in my position. Let's say I'm guilty. I'm flying guns and drugs into this country using an air charter service and a humanitarian organization as my cover. Are you with me?"

"Don't insult me. Go on and ask your question."

"Okay, you are me. Would you put your name in with the contraband?"

The general stared, not smiling.

"I told you it was an unanswerable question," Dad said. "Of course you wouldn't. It would be stupid. And you are not stupid, are you, General? You're not stupid enough to go through with this."

Valdez sat seething. "Your children will live better than you will," he said, "at least for the brief time you are still alive."

"You're sentencing me to death? Because it appears I put my name and the name of a company I haven't owned for months on containers of smuggled goods?"

"I want you to think about your children living in one of our fine orphanages. And I want you to explain this." He turned again with a flourish and waved over another soldier who carried three backpacks. One was Dad's. One was Chad's. And the other Kate guessed had belonged to the Geists.

"Look here," Valdez said. "I would bet this is pure heroin." He lifted a huge plastic bag full of white powder from Dad's backpack. Then he looked at the identification tag on the backpack. It read, "Bruce Michaels, President, AirQuest Adventures, Mukluk, Alaska."

"That should be proof enough that this stuff was planted," Dad said. "Why would I use two different identification tags?"

Valdez shrugged and smiled. "The containers are older. You never switched the tags."

He pulled a similar plastic bag out of Chad's backpack. He read the tag. "Chad Michaels."

"That's not— " Chad began, but Dad quickly stopped him with a hand on his knee.

Valdez then pulled a bag from the Geists' backpack and turned the tag over. "Katie Michaels," he read, and Kate nearly jumped from her seat. Only her dad called her Katie, and they would never put that on an ID tag. Anyway, that wasn't her backpack.

"What else is in there?" Dad said, and Valdez turned it over and dumped it out.

Spread out across the table were trinkets and toys and stuff a much younger girl might enjoy. Again Kate wanted to say it wasn't her bag, but how would she ever explain where hers was? And if she did produce it, her radio watches would be proof enough that they were spies.

The Geists were smooth, all right, probably spilling the one container in Boise on purpose to show that they were carrying seeds. And asking to sit in the back so they could keep an eye on the cargo and get the food prepared, all the while switching tags on the luggage. When exactly had they put the ID tags on the cargo containers? Even more curious, had they found old tags or created phony ones?

"Well," Dad said, "you can believe what you want and I know you will do what you want, but I would like to go on record that we have been royally framed by Howard and June Geist of Boise, Idaho. I hope someday they come to justice."

"Señor Michaels," General Valdez said with a tired sigh, "do you think I know no German?"

"German?"

"Yes, do you know any?"

"Not really."

"Surely you know the meaning of the word *geist* in German."

"Can't say that I do," Dad said.

"Ghost, sir. It means ghost. You and I both know that the Geists are a figment of your imagination. They do not exist, and you cannot pin this on them."

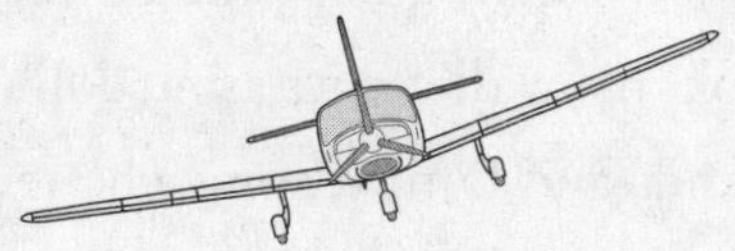

The Escape

Kate had never felt so terrified. She remembered her fear and grief when her mother died. And then there was the plane crash in the jungles of Indonesia. But to hear that her father would be put to death, especially for something he didn't do, and that she and her brother would be sent to live in an orphanage in the middle of nowhere—well, that was too much.

Kate thought her heart would burst. She wanted to grab onto her dad and never let go, and she could see Chad felt the same. What were they going to do? She sneaked a peek at Eva Flores. The woman stared at the floor.

Valdez called on a soldier to search the three yet again and empty their pockets onto the table. Dad stared meaningfully at Kate as she was searched, and he let out a huge sigh when his wallet did not turn up. Clearly he was desperate to know where it was, and Kate wanted badly to tell him.

Chad surrendered his watch, a folded-up computer instruction book, his wallet with nine dollars and pictures of his friends and family, some change, and a key ring with the Yukon Do It logo on it. Valdez raised his eyebrows at Dad when he saw that. But Dad had fallen silent, and Kate wondered if he had just resigned himself to whatever came next.

Dad's pockets were empty, except for some change, a small pocketknife, and a key ring. Kate's pockets held only a couple of pieces of tissue paper and a loose bracelet.

"What were you going to do for money here in Branco Grande?" Valdez said.

Dad said nothing.

"You have hidden some money somewhere? Credit cards? Your identification?"

"You have my passport and visa."

"You see how this appears, Señor Michaels? It appears you were going to use cash from your weapons and drug sales to finance your stay here."

"As a matter of fact, this was an in and out mission. We planned to fly the Geists ... er ... the Kennicotts in, and then turn around and fly back."

"Again you insult me by lying to me? We knew the Kennicotts were coming because we invited them. We knew what they were bringing. They told us how they were getting here and we checked you out. We may be a new country, but we have computers and telephones. It was not hard to find that you had reservations at the Plaza del Rio, of which we are very proud. How were you going to pay for that?"

"We were staying only until Monday," Dad said. "Now I'm through answering your questions."

"All the more reason for me to sentence you here and now."

"I had some money and some credit cards. I'm sure if you search the plane carefully, you'll find them. Or maybe they fell out on the runway."

"I am through being toyed with, señor. I will confer with the other jurors and pronounce sentence."

Kate looked at her dad. Did he want her to tell these people where his wallet was? But what would that help? And if he wanted her to tell, he would say so. But maybe he was afraid she would be punished for having hidden it. What could they do to her? If she were going to lose her father anyway, she didn't much care what happened to her.

Eva Flores was growing more and more agitated. Kate could tell by the look in her eyes and how she rubbed her hands together. Finally, she spoke for the first time, with a tiny, fragile, but melodic voice. "General Valdez, sir, should I not take the children to the toilet before you announce— "

"No! Let them stay! We will determine what to do with them now too."

Dad spoke up. "Sir, let me appeal to your sense of decency. Do you have children?"

"That is none of your business."

"Then you must. Would you want them present when you were sentenced, guilty or not? I beg you not to put them through this ordeal."

Valdez pressed his lips together and appeared frustrated. Eva Flores leaned toward him, pleading with her eyes. Finally he waved her off. "Take them!" he said. "But have them back here in twenty minutes."

"I want to stay," Chad said quickly.

"Me too," Kate said, but Eva looked stricken and shook her head slightly at Kate.

"No, let's go." Eva came around the table to round them up.

"Go, kids," Dad said. "Please. I don't want you to hear this."

"But I may never see you again!" Chad shouted.

"You'll let me say good-bye to them, won't you, sir?" Dad said.

Valdez turned away from his associates. "Yes, of course. Now go!"

Eva hurried from the room, and Chad and Kate followed her down the hall. She herded them into a small waiting room where Kate could see out the window that the sun had begun to set. It was still hot.

"How do they execute people in this country?" Chad said.

Eva looked at him as if she knew she could not evade the question. "Firing squad."

Kate swallowed a whimper. "Do they do it right away?"

"No. Usually thirty days. I don't know why they wait. Nothing ever changes."

"What do you think my dad will get?" Chad said.

Eva looked away and shook her head.

"You think they'll shoot him?"

"I've seen people shot for less."

"My dad is innocent, you know," Kate said.

"Is he?" Eva said, not unkindly. "Tell me."

"Everything he said is true. He's never done a thing wrong in his life! He would never do anything like this." Kate paused, wanting to sound grown up. "Those people told us they were the Geists, and we gave them a free flight down here to deliver the medicine and seeds. I had a feeling something wasn't right about them, and I was right."

"You had a feeling?" Eva said.

"Yeah," Chad grumbled. "She's got women's intuition. Lot of good it'll do us now."

"But everything I just told you is true," Kate said.

"That's right," Chad said. "Dad is completely innocent."

Eva opened the door an inch and looked down the hallway. "I too have intuition," she whispered. "But this time it's more than a feeling. I'm going to tell you why I believe you."

"You believe us?" Kate said. "Why didn't you say so? Why don't you tell the general?"

"I have no say there," she said. "No say."

"Then why are you in there?"

"I'm on his staff, that's all I'll say. But I have seen too much killing. Too much so-called justice. I can't stand by and see a family torn apart like this."

"What can you do?"

"I can show you how to get out of here, but he'll be asking for you in about fifteen minutes. Maybe I can stall another five. I'll say you pushed me down and got away. If he knows I helped you escape, I'll be killed."

Kate glanced at Chad. Could they really leave their dad behind? Did they have any choice? "But why do you believe us?" Kate said.

"The Kennicotts," she said. "I've seen them before. They are friends of the general. What they brought in, they brought in for him."

"Then why didn't they just unload it without us knowing about it and let us go?" Chad said.

"Paco is new. He was not informed. He was not supposed

to find anything in your luggage. We would have checked you out at the Plaza del Rio and made sure you weren't international agents. If it looked like you were going to expose the general, you would have been in trouble. Otherwise, you would have been on your way."

"If you can get us out of here, where would we go?" Chad said.

The woman leaned close and continued in a whisper. "I cannot tell you where to go. I would love to give you sanctuary, but there is no way I can do that without someone telling the general. Don't trust anyone in this city or in this country. If you can get to Santiago or to Buenos Aires, you can probably call back to your own country. Get as far from here as you can."

"We can't leave our father," Kate said. "Where will they keep him?"

"The central prison is downtown, about four blocks from the Plaza del Rio. It's an awful place. Awful. You wouldn't want to see it."

"How can we get our dad out of there?"

"You have to get help for him within thirty days or there will be no hope."

"Then get us out of here," Chad said.

"Here's what we'll do," she said. "I am going to take each of you to the bathroom. When there is no one else in either of the bathrooms, lock both doors from the inside." She pointed at Chad. "Kick out the little door under the sink that leads to the pipes. You can squeeze through there until you're in the women's bathroom. That bathroom has a window that opens to the back of the building. Go straight away from the building and no one will see you. It's about five miles to the city, and by the time you get there, your descriptions will have been sent everywhere. You will stand out with your blond hair and green eyes, so stay out of sight."

"But what—"

"I don't know what else to tell you or how to help you," she said. "And you must hurry."

"Wait," Chad said. "I've got an idea that will give us more time. You come into the bathroom with me and lie on the floor as if we knocked you out. They'll have to break the door down to get in, and they'll find you on the floor, that hole kicked in the wall, and the open window in the other bathroom. But by then we'll be long gone."

"That *will* help me," Eva said. "I will look silly being overtaken by children, but I am a good actress."

Her legs trembling, Kate went into the women's washroom and locked the door. In the mirror she saw a girl so pale, with eyes so huge, that she hardly recognized herself. Through the thin walls, she could hear Chad talking quickly to Eva. "What are common names for kids in this town?"

"Oh, something like Manuel or Manny for you. Conchita for her."

"Can you do us one more favor? Can you get us some hair dye?"

Eva paused. "Maybe."

"Leave it at the counter at the Plaza del Rio. Tell 'em it's for Manny and Conchita."

"You shouldn't go there! They'll look for you, knowing you had reservations."

"I'll figure out something," Chad said. "Just leave it there and we'll find a way to get it."

Kate jumped back when the thin wood wall broke through and Chad climbed into her bathroom. Kate squatted to look for Eva, who peeked through and reached in to take both of Kate's hands. "God go with you," Eva said.

Chad was already climbing through the window. Kate caught up and whispered for him to wait.

"What for? We've got to go! Somehow I've got to call Uncle Bill in Portland."

"Chad! I hid Dad's wallet in that one jeep. My backpack, too, with our wrist TVs and other stuff."

"Great! And we'll need hats until we can get our hair dyed."

"I've got a terry-cloth cap and a sun visor in there."

"How can we get it?"

"We've got to find the jeep with the broken headlight and the crunched front bumper."

"Okay. And then we've got to go, Kate."

She hesitated at the thought of leaving their dad. "I know."

They each climbed through the window and held onto the window sill before dropping to the ground. Then they split up and ran to either end of the building, where they peeked around the side into the gathering darkness. If the jeep was still parked where the men had left it, Kate would be closest. She would make a dash to get the stuff and meet Chad in the back again.

But when Kate got to her end of the building and looked around front, her heart sank. The jeep was gone. She looked back at Chad, who waved at her to come to his end. She could barely see him. That meant no one else could easily see them either. She sprinted to him.

"Look," he said. Six jeeps were parked side by side in front of a metal Quonset hut. "It has to be one of those, doesn't it?"

"Probably, but they all look alike from behind."

"You take one end, and I'll take the other," Chad said. They raced into the darkness. They tried to tiptoe quietly across a patch of gravel, but then they were on asphalt again, and their steps were silent. Kate ran to one end of the line of jeeps, and Chad ran to the other. Chad found the right vehicle, second from the end.

"Here!" he cried softly, and Kate ran to the other end. She pointed under the seat, and Chad pulled her backpack out while she yanked the wallet out from its hiding place. Then they ran off into the darkness.

As they ran Kate finally began to feel the fatigue from the short, restless night the night before, then the long trip, the short nap, the terror, and now the escape. She knew Chad would not slow down until they were a long way from the terminal. She considered herself lucky that she had nothing to carry but the wallet.

And they kept running.

Finding Shelter

"Man, your backpack is heavy!" Chad shouted, panting. "What have you got in there?"

"Lots of stuff," Kate said between gasps. "It probably just feels heavy because you're running and tired."

"Then you carry it for a while."

Chad let the strap slip off his shoulder and caught it in one hand. He slowed enough to allow Kate to catch up, then slung the pack to her. It nearly knocked her over.

"Whoa!" She stumbled and tried to keep running. She handed him Dad's wallet and struggled with the backpack. "This *is* heavy! I've got to rest, Chad!"

"Let's make it to the trees first!"

They slowed to a jog and often looked behind them. There was no activity at the airstrip, at least from what they could tell in the darkness. The lights on either side of the one long runway would have silhouetted anyone running toward them from that direction. They were about a quarter of a mile from a thick cluster of trees.

Kate finally slowed to a walk, shifted the backpack from one shoulder to the other, then slipped both arms under the straps so it lay flat on her back. That made it a little easier to carry, but she could tell there was more inside than she had packed.

Chad was the first to flop to the ground when they reached the trees. "No one can see us here," he said.

Kate joined him. "What do you think they'll do to Dad when they find us missing?"

"We can't worry about that. It's out of our control." Chad leaned against a tree. "Let's rest and then walk to town." He pointed right.

Kate saw faint city lights in the sky. "That's not much light for a capital city. How far do you figure that is?"

"Eva said five miles from the airport, but I'd say it's farther than that."

"Even five miles is too far," Kate said, her heart still banging and her breath coming in short bursts. "I'm thirsty."

"There's no water around here and anything we find in Branco Grande, unless it's bottled or from a well, will probably make us sick."

"Oh, great." Kate fought tears. "Where will we find help?"

“The police could be as crooked as the general.” Chad shook his head. “Somehow we’ve got to get a call through to Uncle Bill. He’ll know what we should do.”

Kate leaned back, pressing the backpack against a tree, and sucked in a huge breath. She looked at the sky. The stars were just coming into view, and the temperature was dropping fast. Her skin was cold, but her body still felt warm from all the running. Half a minute later, however, she started to shiver. She slid out from under the backpack, untied the sweater from around her waist, and pulled it on.

She wrestled the backpack into her lap. “I wish I could see enough to tell what’s in this,” she said.

“Yeah,” Chad said. “Wish we had a flashlight.”

Kate dug into the bag. “Oh, no!” she whispered. “Oh, my goodness! Chad!”

“What?” She handed him a huge pistol. “Whoa!” he said. “Man, I wonder if this thing is loaded!”

“Be careful, just in case. Oh, Chad! Here’s another one!”

“Make sure you keep the barrel pointed away from me,” he said. “What else is in there?”

Kate set the handgun on the ground and pawed through the bag. “Our wrist TVs are here. And the hat and the sun visor.” She found a small but heavy cardboard box stuck down in the corner. She pulled it out. “What do you think this is?” she said, handing it to Chad.

"Bullets," he said. "Too heavy to be anything else."

"And this?" She handed him a floppy plastic bag with something loose and shifting in it.

"Oh, no," he said. "This feels like those bags of drugs the general found in Dad's and my backpacks."

"And in the pack that had my name on it," Kate said. "Shouldn't we get rid of the guns and the drugs?"

"I don't know," Chad said. "They're evidence. Kate, we'd better keep moving."

They repacked the bag, then Chad handed the wallet back to Kate and hoisted the pack onto his back. She peered back at the airstrip a mile away. Nothing. By now someone should have come looking for them and found Eva Flores on the bathroom floor. Kate hoped Eva was as good an actress as she thought she was. The last thing Kate wanted was for Eva to get in trouble over their escape. No matter what happened, they owed a lot to that brave woman.

They started off again, Chad moving quickly, even with the heavy pack on his back. The ground became less even, and Kate felt dust puffing up almost to her knees with every heel-dragging step. She was exhausted and wanted to sleep.

"What are we going to do when we get to the city?" she said.

"No idea," Chad said. "I want to look for a place where we can stop and I can see what else is in the backpack. And we need a place to sleep. In the morning we need to find that hotel, get the hair dye, and see if we can make a call to the States."

They trudged on. Despite the cool breeze in her face, Kate felt her body warming again. She was perspiring, but she didn't want to go to the trouble of taking off her sweater and tying it around her waist. Tired and miserable as she felt, she just wanted to keep going.

An hour later they came to the outskirts of the capital of Amazonia, Branco Grande. From what she had seen in the hotel brochure, she expected a huge, modern city. This was strange. A single neon sign glowed in the night sky, and as she and her brother carefully maneuvered through alleys and back streets, they got close enough to read it. Sure enough, it was the Branco Grande Plaza del Rio. Chad chuckled.

"What's funny?" Kate said.

"Besides the fact that the hotel is the only modern building in this town? I just figured out what it means in English. It's the Big Horse Place of the River."

Kate smiled, but she was too tired to laugh. Anyway, she kept wondering what was happening to Dad. What was the general doing to him? Was he even alive?

The hotel sign was the brightest thing around. Only about a third of the street lights were lit. So far, they had seen no one. Then they heard voices from a few streets away.

They stayed in the shadows and circled around the back of the unpaved road that separated the city from the desert. Several hundred yards away sat a small gathering of adobe-type buildings with vehicles parked outside. A light burned in one of the windows, and a single bare bulb hung in what looked like a combination garage and stable attached to the lighted building.

"We might be able to hide in there and even sleep," Chad said. "Come on."

Kate felt like a robot, but somehow she forced her legs onward. When they got within the ring of light from the bulb at the end of the larger building, Chad let the backpack slip off his shoulders and set it on the ground.

"Is that a well?" Kate said, pointing to a small structure nearby. Her throat was parched.

"Yeah, wait here," Chad said.

"Be careful. There's got to be people in there."

She watched as Chad crept around the other side of the building in the darkness, then came around again and peeked in the window of the tiny house attached to the stable. She held her breath and prayed no one would see or hear him. He ducked quickly away from the window and scampered back around the buildings toward the well. Then he slowly and quietly lowered and raised the bucket. He untied it and carried it to Kate and they both drank. Kate had never tasted water so sweet and refreshing.

"There are a bunch of guys in there," he told her, "most of them with their shirts off like they're ready for bed. They're eating and drinking and playing cards, and there are bunk beds crammed in there. The name on the building is the same as the one on the sides of those trucks and jeeps. So they must work for this company and live here."

"What's in the garage?"

"One old truck or tractor or something, a cow, and a couple of goats. The goats are in a pen, and the cow is tied to the wall. There's room enough in there for us to sleep."

"But what if they find us?"

"I don't want to think about it."

"Shouldn't we at least wait until they're all asleep?"

"Probably," Chad said. "I'm going to take the bucket back over there, then let's just sit here awhile."

They watched for an hour, Kate dozing and rousing every time she heard a car or truck in the distance. "It's nothing," Chad would say as they sat in the shadows. "No one can see us here."

Finally he nudged her awake. "The light just went off where they were playing cards," he said.

She stood, dizzy and disoriented. "Chad, I'm so tired. I have to lie down."

"Me too," he said. "Let's sneak into the stable, but be quiet. They won't be sound asleep for quite a while."

As they crept out of the shadows and down the street, a noisy window fan came on in the bunkhouse. "That's good," Chad whispered. "They won't hear anything, but we still have to be careful."

Just then the door swung open. A young man in a flannel shirt came out and headed for the well. Kate and Chad stopped. Kate held her breath and couldn't hear Chad breathing either. They were out in the open but still in the dark.

The young man grabbed the bucket, but it quickly came loose of the rope, and he nearly dropped it down the well. He muttered something angrily in his own language, then looked around. He retied the rope to the bucket, drew some water, and headed for the stable.

Kate let her breath out. "I hope he's not sleeping in there," she whispered.

They heard noises from the stable, as if the man was watering the animals. Soon he returned the bucket, padded back to the bunkhouse, and slammed the door. Kate and Chad waited a few more minutes, then tiptoed to the stable.

The big wood door was open only about three inches. Since Chad was carrying the heavy backpack, Kate put Dad's wallet in her waistband and pushed on the door with both hands. It creaked loudly, so she stopped and tried again. It made noise each time, but she stayed with it until it was open enough for them to squeeze through.

Kate could hardly stomach the stench, but she knew they didn't have any choice. It would be cold enough inside; she didn't want to think about sleeping outside. They stepped into the stable, but then the cow began to moo.

"Oh, no," Chad whispered. "Shh, moo cow," he said. "Shh!"

"She probably doesn't understand English," Kate whispered.

"Shh isn't English!" Chad said. "Be quiet-o, el cow-o!"

Kate laughed so hard she had to cover her mouth. But what if the workers heard the cow and came to investigate? Chad and Kate looked at each other in the sliver of light coming from the bulb outside. They stood still and silent, and suddenly the cow turned away and fell quiet.

Kate touched Chad's arm and pointed. A makeshift ladder of planks nailed to the wall led to a tiny hayloft about eight feet overhead. She couldn't see much hay up there, but at least they would be out of sight in case someone came in.

"Let me get started up there, and then hand me the backpack," Chad whispered.

He climbed a few steps, then held on with one hand and reached with the other for the pack. Kate lifted it over her head in both hands and felt the pain in her shoulders and upper arms. When Chad grabbed it, it nearly swung him off his perch.

"Whoa!" he whispered.

Chad tried to swing the backpack into the loft ahead of him, but it was too heavy and kept pulling him away from the wall. The cow turned to stare at them, and the goats in the pen stirred and stood.

"You're going to have to push," Chad said.

Kate made sure Dad's wallet was secure at her waist and then started up the ladder. The planks were nailed flat against the wall and didn't angle out away from the wall like a normal ladder, so it was harder to climb. She didn't think she could climb with only one arm.

Kate moved slowly up the ladder to just below where Chad stood. She planted her feet and held on with her left hand, then pushed on the backpack with her right, and Chad was able to go up one more rung. Then she had to grab with both hands again to keep her balance. They did this for every rung until Chad finally curled his left arm around a vertical plank on the floor of the loft. Kate gave one last push and the backpack tumbled into the hayloft, the guns inside thudding against the wood.

Chad helped Kate the rest of the way up.

"What now?" she said, almost passing out from the fatigue.

"I was just wondering what the cow and goats would think if one of those guns went off!"

Kate collapsed into a heap. “It wouldn’t make much difference what the animals thought. The guys inside would sure come running.”

“We’d hold them off with the guns,” Chad said.

Kate was too tired to respond. She knew he was kidding, and it was supposed to be funny, but she didn’t have the energy to laugh. They should never have come on this trip in the first place. Why hadn’t her dad or Chad listened to her?

Moonlight shown through a two-foot-square opening in the wall. “Let me see Dad’s wallet,” Chad said. While he held it up to the light, Kate began pulling stuff out of her backpack. She left the guns inside. Chad had been right; the heavy little box contained, according to the label, twenty bullets for a nine-millimeter Luger. She pulled out the heavy plastic bag filled with powder.

“This looks darker than the stuff in the other bags, doesn’t it?”

Chad looked at it. “Yeah. It looks brown, but maybe it’s just too dark in here to tell.”

“Looks brown to me,” she said. “Like wheat flour. Maybe it’s not drugs at all.”

“Kate,” Chad said slowly and dramatically. “Do you know what Dad has in his wallet?”

“Money and travelers checks and credit cards, I suppose.”

"Right. Of course, the travelers checks and the credit cards won't do us any good, because we can't match his signature and no one would accept them from kids anyway. But Kate, Dad's got fifty twenty-dollar bills in here."

Kate calculated silently. "A thousand dollars? What for?"

"I don't know. Emergencies, I guess."

"Well, they don't use American dollars here anyway, do they?"

"Actually, American dollars are valuable everywhere. In fact, in a lot of places they're illegal because they're worth so much. If you get caught using American currency in some European countries, you can be in big trouble. They probably use some sort of Argentinean or Chilean money here. I wouldn't think they'd have their own currency yet. But American dollars have to be like gold."

"We'll find out," Kate said. "We're not going to get far without paying somebody something, are we?"

"That's for sure. Let me see those hats."

Kate pulled out the floppy terry-cloth cap and the sun visor.

"If you put your hair up and stuffed it into this one, would it hide it?" Chad said.

Kate used both hands to push her hair up, then held it in place as Chad plopped the floppy hat on her head. Blond curls peeked out from underneath. "Not too good," he said, as he put the sun visor on. "What do you think?"

"There's no hiding it," Kate said. "You look like a blond American boy wearing a visor."

"Let's hope Eva leaves some dye for us," Chad said.

But Kate did more than hope. As she curled up in the hay, shoulders hunched against the cold, she prayed as she always did before sleeping. But this time it was without Dad there. She prayed for him and she prayed for Chad. She prayed for herself. And while the prickly hay and the hard floor made the most uncomfortable bed she could remember since the jungles of Indonesia, she finally fell asleep.

She awoke when Chad turned in his sleep and kicked her. She had no idea what time it was, but the loft was stifling from the early morning sun. As she sat up and squinted against the harsh light streaming through the cracks in the walls, she heard footsteps below. She lay back down and silently rolled onto her side so she could peek through the crack in the floor. The cow was gone, and she watched a young man close the goat pen. The goats scooted out, and then something seemed to catch the man's attention. He looked up, as if staring straight into Kate's eyes.

He looked puzzled and moved toward the ladder. The backpack! One of the straps hung over the side, and he was coming to investigate. He climbed two steps and reached to grab the strap. Kate rolled quickly and wrapped the backpack in her arms, burying her face in it. She kicked

Chad hard and he sat up. She put one finger to her lips and pointed downward.

She felt a yank as the young man continued to pull on the backpack. He was strong, and she had to hook her feet around a sturdy post to hang on. He would discover them, there was no doubt of that. But she would not let him have their stuff without a fight.

The young man yanked on the strap again, and Kate grimaced and hung on with all her might. As the bag pulled her closer to the edge, she stiffened and tightened her feet in a desperate attempt to hang on to the post.

By now Chad had stuffed Dad's wallet into his pocket, bent over Kate, and grabbed the backpack. Kate hung on even tighter. Now it was their four young arms against the muscular laborer in a tug of war that could cost them their lives.

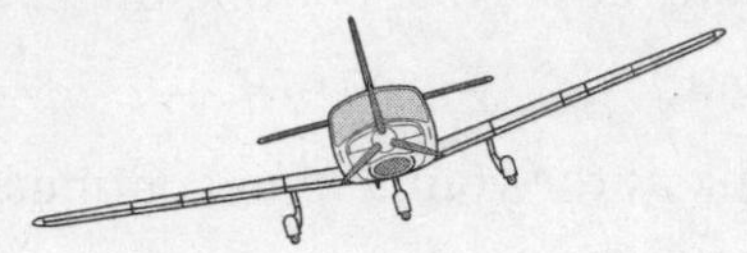

Close Calls

Kate grunted as the young man in the flannel shirt pulled on the other end of the backpack strap. She peeked around the bag and peered down at the Amazonian. He hung from the backpack with his toes barely touching one of the ladder planks. Kate and Chad were tugging against his entire weight.

Suddenly his feet slipped off the plank. "Left!" she shouted, and Chad pulled and jerked the bag a few inches. The young man held on and was yanked away from the ladder.

Success! His feet slipped free and he dangled a couple of feet off the ground. But now Kate heard threads popping on the backpack as the young man's weight strained the straps. She and Chad were wedged together, arms enveloping the bag. They would have the advantage if they could hold out only a few seconds more.

Kate rocked, which caused the man to swing, and finally he lost his grip. He shrieked as he toppled onto the hard dirt floor, his seat smacking, the back of his head banging, and his feet flying over his head. Kate and Chad watched him somersault into the door of the goat pen, which slammed shut so hard that it flew back and hit him again, knocking him flat onto his stomach.

He lay there shaking his head as if to make the world stop spinning, but Kate knew they couldn't take any time to see if he was hurt. She jumped to her feet and started down the ladder.

"No!" Chad shouted. "You'll never get past him. C'mon! We have to jump!"

Chad slung the backpack out the opening in the wall, turned around and slid out. He hung by his hands, and when he was fully stretched out, he dropped the rest of the way to the ground.

Kate stepped into the opening. Eight feet looked like a long way down! Chad gathered up the backpack while she tried to decide how best to get down. She heard a bang on the floor behind her and whirled to see both hands of the young man grabbing the boards. He wasn't even going to try the ladder this time. He swung up with the toes of one booted foot and struggled to pull himself into the loft. But before he could get his other leg up, Kate ran over and kicked his foot off the ledge.

"Ayeee!" the young man shouted as he swung back down. He landed again on his seat and somersaulted back into the goat-pen door. Kate was afraid she might have killed him, but when she peeked down, he just lay there as if he had given up. She stepped through the opening and hung there, and Chad reached up to put a hand under each foot. They had never practiced anything like that, and soon she had fallen onto him. Immediately they scrambled to their feet.

"Let's go!" Chad said.

They ran, the backpack hanging between them, each holding one of the straps. Kate looked back to see the young man watching them from the hole in the hayloft.

They ran as fast as they could. Kate looked back as the young man hung by his hands and then dropped the rest of the way to the ground.

"He's coming!" she shouted.

Kate guessed he twisted his ankle, because he staggered and smacked into the well, finally tumbling to the ground. Kate and Chad raced away in the morning sunlight.

Branco Grande seemed bigger in the daylight, but it was still a dusty, crowded place that looked half-finished. Kate knew people would by now be on the lookout for the two blond kids who had escaped from the guards at the airport. For all she knew, there might even be a reward for finding them.

What a way to start a day! She was warm again but realized she wasn't wearing her sweater. "Oh, no! Chad, I left my sweater in that barn!"

"Big deal! You can get another one."

"Yeah, but it's evidence. It proves we were there and that we're probably here in town. I feel like everybody is looking at me and knows who I am."

"Nobody's looking at you," Chad said.

"They will be. We'd better stay out of sight or do something about our looks, and right now."

Kate and Chad stayed in the alleys and side streets, crossing any time they saw anyone who might pass them. Finally they came upon the worst part of town, where drunks slept in the street and little bands of people hung around. Some drank. Some smoked. Most just talked and laughed among themselves. These people, Kate guessed, were probably the type who wouldn't ask any questions because they didn't want any asked of them.

Still, she and Chad stayed in the shadows. While these people might not turn them in, they might want to steal anything they had of value. And to save Dad they needed everything in that backpack—including those guns.

"I need a bath," Kate said, squatting in the cool shade of a tree.

"You and me both," Chad said. "But first, we need clothes."

"A woman over there is selling clothes out of a cart. Should we see what she's got?"

Chad nodded, but Kate suddenly grabbed Chad's arm and pulled him behind a tree. "Look! A jeep from the airport!"

He peered around the trunk. "How do you know that's where it's from?"

"Paco's driving! Maybe the general sent him to look for us."

"Maybe." Chad shaded his eyes. "He's got a couple of other soldiers with him. I wonder if they're going to do a house-to-house search."

"Yeah," Kate said, "and I wonder if they've already been to that place where we slept. If they have, they know we're here."

Kate and Chad waited until the jeep turned toward the center of town before moving again. They crossed the street to where the old peasant woman had her used-clothing stand.

"We'd better not be seen together until we get some disguises," Chad said, and Kate nodded. "Wait over there," he added as he dug the floppy, white terry-cloth hat from the backpack. He jammed it down over his head.

Kate watched from a nearby alley as Chad approached the old woman's stand. The woman looked at him warily as he picked through her racks of hung clothes and her table of folded stuff. Then he spoke to her, and she quickly looked in every direction before leaning close to him, nodding and whispering. She reached behind the cart and slapped two pairs of sandals onto the table. Then she slid two pairs of long pants from the middle of a pile and laid them out beside the sandals. Then two button-type shirts, the least colorful of the ones she had. Chad asked her something else, and she dug around in a box, finally pulling out several caps and hats.

Once Chad seemed to have everything he needed, he turned his back to her and carefully pulled out one of the American twenty-dollar bills. When he turned back and offered it to her, she grabbed her heart. Again she looked this way and that and tried to explain something to him. He waved her off, and she clutched the bill to her heart.

Suddenly Kate heard the roar of an engine. She froze when it stopped behind her. Had they been discovered? Was it Paco and his compatriots?

A man directly behind her spoke out, "Pardon, señorita!"

She jumped and turned slowly, only to discover that she was merely in the man's way. He was picking up trash. Kate decided that a heart attack could not feel much worse than the way her chest felt right then. She looked into the street. Chad was jogging toward her in that stupid-looking hat, his bundle of clothes and sandals under one arm. Behind him the woman was packing up her stuff and preparing to move her stand. The twenty American dollars must have been more than she usually made in a week.

Kate and Chad ran off to the shady area of a rundown park where Chad relayed what had gone on with the woman.

"She hardly understood English," he said. "I asked if she took American dollars, and she just about went ballistic on me. She looked around to see if anybody was watching, and then she said something about no change. I figured she meant she couldn't break a large bill. I said that was okay, and then I started asking for shoes and hats, besides the shirts and pants I found."

"Everybody around here seems to dress colorfully," Kate said. "These look pretty drab. Will we blend in?"

"The people in this area dress plainer," Chad said, "because they're obviously poorer. I think we need to look like peasant kids, don't you?"

"I guess."

"Put this stuff on over your clothes, and later, when we find a place to wash up, we can wear just the new stuff."

"The new *old* stuff, you mean? These are rags."

"Yeah, but at least they're clean."

Kate and Chad put their shoes into the backpack, which was now heavier than ever, and put the big, baggy peasant clothes on. They laughed when they looked at each other in the huge, wide-brimmed sombrero-type hats and thick-soled sandals.

"Now we don't have to split up," Kate said. "No one can see our hair or our pink skin."

"Yeah, unless they look at our hands and feet. Listen, Kate, we're going to have to take a risk if we want to get anywhere. One of us will have to go into the Plaza del Rio Hotel and ask if anyone left anything there for us, or we'll have to pay somebody to do it."

Kate nodded. "Chad, what did you say the name of that hotel means in English?"

"I was just guessing, but Branco sounds like bronco, which is a horse. Grande means big. Plaza is place, I think, and Rio means river."

"You think the hotel is really on a river?"

"Maybe. At least the brochure showed a fountain in the plaza."

"I wouldn't mind taking a bath in that fountain," Kate said, "but I don't suppose I'd ever get away with that."

"No way," Chad said, "but we should be able to follow the river out of town until we find a place where we can get cleaned up."

"I'm sure getting hungry."

"Me too. Let's see what we can find on the way."

They moved toward the center of town and saw the big hotel and the plaza in the distance.

"The river runs along behind it," Kate said, "just past that boulevard. See?"

"Yeah. Let's not get too close to the hotel yet. Let's just circle back and follow the river."

A man was selling roasted corn on the cob at a little stand on a street corner near the edge of town. It was Kate's turn to do the bargaining. She left Chad with the backpack and the wallet and shoved a twenty-dollar bill into her pocket.

"You've got to try to get change," Chad said. "If we keep spending American twenty-dollar bills all over town, we won't stay under cover for long."

Kate approached the man. "Speak English?" she said.

He held up his thumb and finger a half-inch apart.

"A little?"

He nodded, but so far she hadn't heard any of it.

"Take American dollars?" she said.

He nodded vigorously, but looked up and down the street, the same way the clothes lady had.

"Four corn." Kate held up four fingers and pointed to the cobs.

The man quickly took four sharp sticks and stabbed the cobs.

"How much?" She looked hungrily at the corn.

"One American dollar," he said slowly.

"One?"

He nodded.

"Change?" she said. "Change for twenty?"

"Twenty?" He shrugged. "Twenty okay!"

"No!" she said. "Need change!"

He squatted next to a cigar box and opened it. It was full of local currency—bills and coins. He pointed to the box and then to Kate. "Change, twenty," he said.

She had no idea how much the change was worth, but she took all he had, and the corn, and gave him the twenty. The man immediately began closing up his cart. *He's probably going off to buy a house*, Kate thought.

"Sir?" she said. "Can you tell me where the prison is?"

"Prison?" His eyes narrowed.

She nodded, hoping he wouldn't report her.

He pointed down the street. Just as Eva had said, about four blocks this side of the Plaza del Rio stood a block-long complex. Her heart ached; Dad was probably in that prison. Had he already been tortured and beaten—or worse?

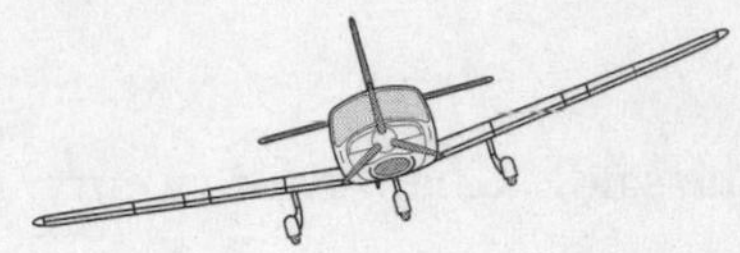

The Plaza del Rio

When Kate pointed out the prison to Chad, he stopped and stared. She understood his look. It didn't look like a prison at all. The structure was as long and wide as a whole city block and made of adobe and wood beams. As they got closer they saw bars on openings in the walls; the place was obviously built for some other purpose and then converted into a prison.

People could walk right by the prison, and though heavily armed guards hung around and could have shot anyone trying to escape, the whole thing looked pretty casual.

"We'll look obvious with this backpack, even in these clothes," Chad said. He suggested they hurry past the prison on the other side of the street and head out of town to the river, where they could wash up. Then he tucked the backpack under his huge shirt, and they made their way down the street.

Kate was nearly overcome by the smell as they walked past the prison. It was worse than the smell in the barn the night before. "What *is* that?" she wondered aloud.

"Smells like they don't have any plumbing," Chad said. "Yuck!"

"You think Dad's in there?"

"I hope not."

"If he is, we've got to get him out of there."

They were nearly a block past the prison when Kate whirled around. "Chad, look!"

It was Paco again, slowly driving a jeep past the prison. The young man who had almost caught Kate and Chad that morning sat beside Paco in the front seat. Tied around his neck was Kate's sweater.

"Let's get out of here!" Kate said.

Kate and Chad darted down an alley, circled around the prison, and kept running until they were about a mile outside of town. "Did you see what I saw?" Chad asked when they slowed. "At the back side of the prison?"

"What?"

"All those little kids crowded around the windows."

"No, I didn't."

"If we can dye our hair and somehow keep from looking so light-skinned," Chad said, "we can blend in with those kids. The guards were right there, but it looked like the kids were talking to the prisoners, maybe even selling them something."

"Let's check that out," Kate said.

No one was around, and the river looked clean and inviting in the heat. They were both surprised at how cold it was. They washed quickly and put on their new South American clothes. Then it was off to the Plaza del Rio to see if Eva Flores had left them any hair dye.

"How are we going to get in there?" Kate said. "You know they'll be watching for us."

Chad nodded. "We've got to keep the backpack out of sight. In fact, maybe we should get some kind of a new bag."

"I like this bag!"

"But it could get us caught."

On their way back into town, this time circling wide of the prison, Kate and Chad came upon a small storefront where leather goods were sold.

"I'll hang onto the backpack," Chad said. "See if you can get a leather bag with the change you got from the corn guy."

Kate entered and looked around. Despite her clothes and the hat hiding her hair, there was no pretending she was South American. A woman approached and said, "Español?"

Kate shook her head. "English."

"Okay," the woman said, but she did not seem comfortable with that.

"Leather bag?" Kate said.

The woman looked puzzled and shook her head. Kate pointed to a big leather bag on a high shelf. "Oh, bueno," the woman said, and used a long pole to pull it down. Kate put the strap over her shoulder and smiled.

"How much?"

"Much?"

Kate made a gesture with her thumb and fingers. The woman responded in Spanish. Kate didn't understand. She produced the change she had in local currency, which she hoped totaled more than fifteen dollars in American money.

The woman took it and carefully counted it out. "No," she said. "No. More."

Kate held up one finger to tell her to wait, left the bag, and hurried out to Chad. "Let me have another twenty," she said.

Back in the store the woman looked at the twenty, quickly folded it, and put it in her pocket. "Okay," she said, nodding. "Okay."

But Kate had learned. "Change." And she thrust out her hand. The woman shook her head, so Kate moved as if to give the bag back. The woman reached in another pocket, looked around, and then quickly gave Kate, of all things, five dollars change in American currency.

"We can use that," Chad said a few minutes later as they emptied the backpack into the leather bag. "I hate giving twenties to people who would be thrilled with five." Chad fingered the bag of brown powder that had been planted in Kate's backpack. "I still wonder what this is."

When they finally came into view of the hotel, Kate said, "We're still too obvious. We need to split up."

"Let's get someone to go to the desk in there and see if anything has been left for us," Chad said.

"How will we find someone who speaks English?"

"Lots of these people understand English," he said. "It must be their second language."

"Let's find a kid who wants a little money," Kate said.

"A bunch of kids are playing over near the fountain, but one of us should stay out of sight."

"I'll go," Kate said. "I'll find someone."

"When you do, offer them a little of that local change to get something in there that was left for Manny or Conchita."

Chad stayed on a bench near a small cluster of trees, while Kate slowly approached some children frolicking near a fountain in the plaza. "English?" she said. "Anybody speak English?"

The kids looked shyly at her. Some smiled, some scowled. None, it seemed, understood. She kept moving, speaking quietly. "English?"

Finally, a little girl smiled at her and pointed at an older boy. "José," she called out. "English. English."

"Sí," he said. "Yes. What?"

"You speak English?"

"A little. What you want, Yankee?"

"You want to earn some money, José?"

"Money?" He straightened his back and looked doubtfully at her.

Kate dug into her pocket and pulled out three bills of the local currency. She had no idea what they were worth. The boy's eyes lit up, but then he grew wary again.

"How I make money?"

"Just go into the hotel and ask at the desk for a delivery for Manny or Conchita."

"Manny or Conchita?"

"Yes."

"Why?"

"To earn the money, José."

"You give money first."

"No way, José."

Kate almost laughed, but José had apparently never heard that before.

"Who's Manny and Conchita?"

"Too many questions," Kate said, and she turned to leave.

"No. I do! I do! Ask for delivery."

"Right."

"Okay, Yankee."

José ran toward the front of the Plaza del Rio, but before Kate could see whether he had moved all the way inside, she heard, "Conchita! Conchita!"

She spun and saw Chad waving frantically at her from the shadow of the trees. "Run, Conchita! Run!"

Kate wanted to wait for José and get the hair dye, but Chad wasn't the type to get excited over nothing. She jogged toward him, but he waved all the harder, so she began sprinting. Before she reached him, he began running too. She knew she could never catch him unless he let her, so she just followed him. They ran down one street after another, through alleys, and eventually came to the poorer section of town again.

Finally Chad slowed and stopped behind a brick building. Kate reached him and dropped to the ground, panting. "What's up?" she said. "I found a kid and he's in there getting the package. What's wrong?"

"The Geists," Chad said, sucking for air. "They weren't a hundred feet from you. They parked a small car in front of the hotel and stood there looking all around before they hurried in. I thought for sure they'd seen you. They were staring right at you. I waited until they went inside before I called you. If they're friends of General Valdez, they'll tell him where we are."

"But now what do we do about the dye? If José has it, he'll think I was a liar and won't have any idea what I was up to. What if he throws it away?"

"He wouldn't do that. He might sell it, though." Chad hoisted the leather bag to his shoulder. "We've still got to try to get it."

"I'm going to go back and find him." Kate scooped some dust and dirt into her hands, clapped, and then rubbed her feet and ankles. She did the same to her face. "Is it working?"

"Is what working? You look dirty, if that's what you wanted."

"I just don't want to look so white."

"It's working. You look like a dirty American. Kate, be careful. If you see the Geists, don't let them see you, whatever you do."

Kate wasn't so sure about being this far from Chad. What if one of them got caught? The other would be left to fend for herself or himself. Since Chad was staying with the big leather bag, the guns, and what they thought might be drugs, she would get out their wrist TVs and see if they worked from that far away.

From three blocks away, Kate could still hear Chad and even see a faint image of him on the tiny TV screen.

"This is too cool," he said. "But I probably shouldn't talk to you when people are around and can hear the static."

"Right," she said. "And don't let anyone see it. Keep it tucked up under your sleeve."

Kate felt a lot better now that she knew she could call Chad for help, and it also gave her an idea. If Dad was in the nearby prison, maybe they could somehow get a wrist TV in to him. If there were enough light, she could see him and he could see them. If he had any privacy at all, maybe he could tell them what to do.

When Kate got back to the plaza in front of the hotel, she kept an eye out for the Geists. But she soon realized that José was nowhere to be found. What must he have thought—a "Yankee" promises him money to do an errand and then runs away as fast as she can go?

"José?" she asked the children in the area. "José?"

They shrugged. Some frowned as if they knew she had promised him money and then run out on him.

Kate kept searching for José, then found a spot that was out of sight but still dangerously close to the hotel. She clicked the switch at the side of her wrist TV and whispered, "Chad, are you there?"

"I'm here," he said. "You okay?"

"I'm okay, but no José. Can you see me? I have no picture of you."

"Yeah, I can see you a little," he said. "Not too well."

"What kind of a car were the Geists driving, and where did they park?"

"It's a Japanese four-door, and they parked right in front of the hotel at the top of the circle drive."

"They're still there," Kate said.

"How do you know? Are you that close?"

"See for yourself," Kate said, and she held her wrist toward the front of the hotel.

"That's the car!" Chad said. "If it's red, that is."

"It is," Kate said.

"Then get away from there."

"They can't see me. I'm all right."

"You've got to find José."

"I know, but I don't know where to look. I'm thinking about going into the hotel myself and seeing whether he picked up the package."

"No! Don't risk it!"

Suddenly a voice from the shadows startled Kate. "Psst! Are you Conchita?"

Kate flinched and stared at José. She quickly dropped her arm so that her sleeve covered the wrist TV. "José!" she said, "I'm sorry I had to run off."

"Where you go?" he said.

"No questions," she said. "Did you get the package?"

"I got it." He patted his pocket. "How much?"

"I already told you." She reached into her pocket and pulled out the three local bills.

"Not enough," he said. "Could sell this for more."

"But it's not yours to sell," she told him.

"It is now."

"That would be stealing."

"How do I know you not steal it anyway? You no Conchita. You no even from here."

"How much do you want?"

"Want American dollars."

"I can give you five."

"Five American dollars?" he said. "Let me see!"

She found the five. He reached for it, but she pulled it back. "Give me the package first."

Suddenly José's eyes grew cold. He scowled at her. "I could break you into pieces," he said. "I could take all your money and keep your package."

Kate casually reached up under her sleeve and turned on her wrist TV. "I'm not alone," she said.

"What?" José said, looking around.

"My brother is here with me, and my father is in town too."

"I see nobody."

"If you listen closely, they will tell you you had better

give me the package and take the five dollars and get away from me."

"Ha! I'm listening!"

From under her sleeve came Chad's low, gravelly voice as he tried to imitate an adult. "José! Give Conchita the package now, take the five dollars, and get away from her!"

José grabbed the paper bag from his pocket and tossed it to Kate, then dashed away.

"Your money!" she called after him, holding the five-dollar bill at her side so as not to make a scene.

José stopped and turned around. He eyed her carefully, then ran back and grabbed the five on his way past.

"I got it," Kate said into her wrist TV.

"Then get back here fast," Chad said. "What was that all about?"

"I'll tell you when I get there," she said, "but I want to check something out first."

Branco Grande Prison

Something about the Plaza del Rio had caught Kate's eye. Their best hiding place might be right under the Geists' noses. The hotel's unfinished wings jutted several hundred feet out the back of the building in a straight line. The section closest to the main lobby was almost finished, and workers were busy there. The next three-story section was walled and roofed, but no windows had been installed. The last section looked like a wooden skeleton and still lacked walls and a roof. Kate felt the second section was promising.

She sidled around the back, careful not to draw attention to herself. When she'd moved out of the workers' vision, she went up to where the windows would eventually be installed and peeked in. The floors were bare plywood, the bathrooms had no fixtures yet, pipes and wiring were visible, and electrical outlets had no cover plates. Open stairs led to the second floor. If she and Chad could sneak in and make their way upstairs, they'd be protected from the weather. More important, they couldn't be seen.

She started back to Chad, but then skidded to a stop outside the first section. Near the fountain, Mrs. Geist was talking to the same group of kids Kate had talked to earlier! Kate crouched behind a pile of dirt and bricks and watched. Kate guessed Mrs. Geist spoke Spanish, because they talked a long time and no one seemed to have trouble understanding.

When she was finished, Mrs. Geist looked around and then slipped the children a dollar each. They ran off laughing and squealing, while she hurried back into the hotel. It wouldn't be long, Kate knew, before Mrs. Geist found José, or he found her.

When Kate returned to the poorer part of town, Chad congratulated her on a good job and agreed they would need to check out the unfinished hotel section. Then Chad and Kate ran back to the river to see if the hair dye would work. Kate had only peeked in the sack to be sure it contained dye. She hadn't noticed anything else, and so she was as surprised as Chad when he pulled a tightly folded sheet of paper from the box.

"What's this?" he said.

"Probably the instructions," she said.

"No. It's from Eva, but it's written in Spanish."

Kate read over his shoulder: "Gnirif dauqs yadseut. Teg pleh kciuq. Eraweb. Stsieg kniht uoy evah kcapkcab htiw erup, tucnu nioreh htrow erom naht eno noillim nacirema srallod. Stsieg gnikool rof ti ta lla stsoc."

"What in the world is this?" Chad said.

"Let me see." Kate studied it for several minutes while Chad pulled out the hair dye.

"This isn't Spanish!" Kate said. "It's English!"

"That's English?" Chad said.

"Yes. C'mere and read each word backward."

They sat and read Eva Flores' message together. " 'Firing squad Tuesday. Get help quick.

Beware. Geists think you have backpack with pure, uncut heroin worth more than one million American dollars. Geists looking for it at all costs.' "

"We've got to bust Dad out of there!" Chad said. "I mean, I still want to try to call Uncle Bill, but we won't have time to wait for him. What are we supposed to do with this dye?"

"What do the directions say?"

"They're definitely in Spanish. And look, it's black dye."

"Oh, brother."

"Guess we can't be picky. I was hoping to use a little of it on my skin. But not even black people are *that* black."

Kate and Chad quickly mixed the dye and worked it

through each other's hair. "Don't rinse," Kate said, "or it might all disappear."

But she needn't have worried about that. When they finished, their hair was so ridiculously jet black that they would have laughed their heads off at each other, had they not been in so much trouble.

"Your eyebrows are still blond," Chad said.

"So are yours."

So they each dipped a finger into the remaining dye and smeared it on the other's brows. Now they looked so ridiculous to each other that they couldn't help but giggle. Streaks of black ran down their foreheads, and their hands were stained black.

"Oh, now we'll really blend in," Chad said.

Kate wanted to laugh, but she wanted to cry too. Dad had till Tuesday, and the brown powder they hadn't recognized made their own lives worthless too. If it was worth as much as Eva said, the Geists wouldn't hesitate killing them to get it back.

"We've got to hide that heroin in case the Geists catch us," Kate said.

"We could bury it."

"As long as we can find it later," Kate said.

"I'd like to just dump it in the river. That way it will never hurt anyone."

"Me too, but wouldn't it harm the fish?"

"No, this river is so huge it would probably dilute the drug into a harmless level."

"Let's do it then," said Kate. "Otherwise, it's just a million dollars' worth of misery—if it were to be used by anyone."

"You're right! But let's just save out a little for evidence," suggested Chad. "And maybe a little more to tease the Geists."

"How would we do that?"

"I don't know yet, but the prison is so close to the hotel. We've got to get them away from there so we can get help for Dad. Let's keep trying to think of a plan." Chad took the big cellophane bag of brown powder and looked at Kate.

She shook her head. "I wonder if anyone has ever dumped a million dollars in a river before," she said.

"You want to do it?" he said.

"Go ahead," she said. "Just remember to save some for evidence."

Chad held the bag by one end and carefully shook it back and forth. The powder poured out and the slight breeze carried it out over the river and into the water. He saved a small amount of the powder in the cellophane bag.

"Let's hide that inside a sock," Kate said, pulling a pair from the leather bag.

Next they smeared their faces, hands, and feet with dust.

Kate felt ridiculous as they walked toward town. She kept a careful eye out for Paco and the Geists as they neared the Branco Grande Prison.

"I'm gonna see what those kids are doing around the back," Chad said. "Whatever it is, the guards seem to leave them alone. Wait here."

Kate looked around at all the people sitting on the ground. Some were almost in the street, and others sat with their backs against the buildings across the street from the prison. Kate backed up against a wall and slid down, exhausted. With the sun directly overhead, she was sweating. She was also starving again. She watched from several feet away, hiding under her huge hat and baggy clothes. Her dirty, sandaled feet stuck out in front of her. She prayed for Chad and her dad. And she prayed they could get hold of Uncle Bill and that he would know what to do. She also came up with an idea of how to distract the Geists.

A few minutes later Chad returned and motioned for her to follow him back into an alley. "They're selling stuff to the inmates!" he said. "And they share the profits with the guards so they'll look the other way."

"What are they selling?"

"Well, you won't believe it, but it looks like hot potatoes. They go up to the window and call out, "Papas calientes! Papas calientes."

Kate's stomach growled. Chad grinned. "Yeah, food sounds good to me too."

"Well, *we* can buy food, but Dad won't be able to buy anything. Don't those prisoners get fed?"

"Not enough, I guess. They really went for those potatoes."

"How do the prisoners pay for them?" Kate said. "Dad didn't have any money."

"Well, somebody's getting money in there, because the prisoners were handing money out through the bars."

"Where are those kids getting the potatoes?"

"From a vendor down the street."

"I'm gonna try it," Kate said. "We've got to know for sure if Dad's in there. If he is, I'm going to slip him some money and food." She took some local currency and the third wrist TV.

"Be careful!" Chad said.

Kate used two single bills of local currency and bought five roasted potatoes from the vender. She ate one of them, ignoring the slightly burned taste, saving one for Chad and planning to give the others to her dad. She moved around to the back of the prison and peeked in the first empty window she came to. The stench nearly knocked her over. No wonder! There were no bathrooms in there. It almost made her vomit. Not even any separate cells. And no beds. The floor was made of dirt. Hundreds of men milled around or lay around in clusters. They wore no uniforms. They were probably all wearing whatever they had on when they were sentenced and tossed in there.

Kate heard yelling and what she assumed was cursing in Spanish. A fight broke out at the far end, and most of the other prisoners drifted away from it, but then another broke out at the near end. Kate saw no sign of her dad. As kids crowded around the windows to watch, prisoners jostled for position to snatch a free potato or at least get the chance to buy one. Once they got one, they quickly stuffed it into their mouths.

Kate knifed her way closer and closer to a barred window opening. Finally she was close enough to see the huge, dark, open area. She looked and looked but no one even resembled her dad.

Finally she called, "Papas calientes," but she guessed she wasn't loud enough. The men in front of her ignored her and reached past her, buying potatoes and passing coins to the other kids.

"Spitfire!" Kate hollered, and a couple of men looked at her quizzically, then ignored her. She alternated between saying "papas calientes" and "Spitfire." Suddenly, from the edge of the crowd of prisoners pushed a lone figure. He shouldered his way past some and through others, causing them to grumble and threaten.

"Spitfire," Kate repeated as her father's haggard, unshaven face came into view. His eyes were desperate, as he reached through the bars and grabbed her wrist. She didn't want him to say her name. "I'm Conchita!" she whispered. "My brother Manny and I are selling potatoes. You want one?"

He nodded. He wore the same clothes he'd flown in, but he was barefoot, as were all the others. His shirttail hung out and his pants were torn.

"Have you eaten anything?"

Dad shook his head, and she handed him a potato with a wrist TV wrapped around it. No one else seemed to be listening, and if they were, they did not understand. Others were busy making their own transactions, buying food and cigarettes and who knew what else from the kids at the window.

"And here's your change, señor." Kate slipped Dad a handful of local currency. He stuffed the TV and the change into his pocket and quickly gorged on the potato.

"Stay out of sight, Conchita. Don't come here again. Call Uncle Bill. Go!"

"In a minute. I've got two more—"

But other kids elbowed her out of the way, and her dad disappeared. As much as Kate wanted to stay with her dad, she did what he said and took off running. A guard stopped her with a straight arm to the chest. "Señorita!" he said, sticking out his hand. Had he recognized her? What should she do? She didn't want to say anything. He rubbed his fingertips together as if he wanted money. She pulled out a single bill and handed it to him. He turned away, and Kate ran off to Chad.

"He's there!" she said, gasping. "Chad, he looks awful! I gave him a potato and a wrist TV and some money. It's terrible in there. No chairs, no bed, no plumbing, no light. They all just hang around on that dirt floor and try to get stuff from the kids on the street. He hadn't eaten."

"Then he needs more than one potato!"

"I know. I got shoved out of the way before I could give him the rest."

"Give me those!" Chad grabbed the potatoes and stood.

"Don't say your name," Kate said. "Go by Manny! Here, take him some more money. Take a bill for the guard too."

Kate hung back out of sight and watched Chad work his way to one of the windows. But then she was stunned to see a jeep skid to the curb. Paco was at the wheel. Most of the kids scattered, and the guards became quickly diligent. Chad was one of the last to notice that he needed to get away from the barred opening.

"Manny!" Kate screamed when she saw the Geists' car pull in behind Paco.

Chad took off running, but away from Kate. He followed the other kids down the street and into an alley. Where would she ever catch up with him? She didn't want to follow right away because she would have to pass Paco and the Geists. Despite her dyed hair, disguise, and new bag, she didn't want to risk that.

Paco had leaped out of his jeep and was screaming at the guards. He handed a sheet of paper to one of them. Someone unlocked an entrance to the prison while one of the guards read from the sheet: "Arguello! Michaels! Sanchez!" He then rattled off a bunch of instructions Kate didn't understand.

She staggered from the prison, lugging the leather bag, when she heard Chad on her wrist TV. "Meet me at the hotel!" he said. "The kids were all saying, 'Busque, busque.' I think it means search."

"Oh, no," Kate said. "I hope Dad had time to get rid of the wrist TV." And she hoped those kids were right and that this was *only* a search.

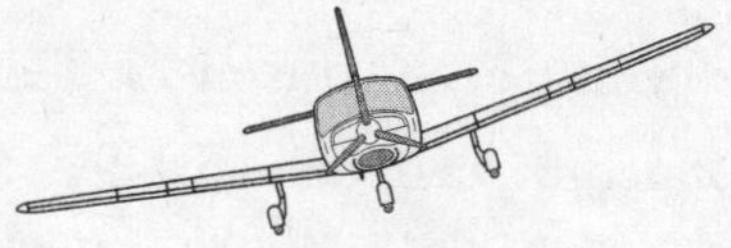

The Plan

As Kate hurried through back streets toward the hotel, staticky noises came from her wrist TV. She ducked into an alley and set the bag down, then leaned against a building and tried to tune in whoever was on the other end.

A faint, jumpy image came from the liquid-crystal display, and she held it out into a stream of sunlight. Someone was messing with Dad's wrist TV, and it wasn't Dad! From what she could make out, it appeared someone was studying the wrist TV near a window in the prison. Occasionally she saw a face peer at the TV, as if he was trying to make it work. When he turned the TV over, Kate could see light, then a dark wall, the floor, bare feet, then his clothes. He wore no uniform! It wasn't a guard.

Had Dad lost the radio or given it to someone to hold for him? She saw the man reach toward the screen as he stared at it, pushing buttons. Suddenly the tinny sound returned, and she heard noises from within the prison. It sounded like the guards were yelling at the prisoners. She heard whacks and screams as if people were being beaten. She prayed it wasn't Dad.

It was clear the man on the other end of the wrist TV could see her now. He looked shocked and kept staring. Kate didn't feel like smiling, and she didn't know enough Spanish to tell him anything. "Hello," she said, praying the man wasn't standing near a guard who might hear her.

He raised his eyebrows and tried to repeat the greeting. "Alloo."

"Is my dad okay?" she said.

He frowned and shook the watch.

"Speak English, and stop shaking the watch!" Kate cried. "Is there an American there?"

"Alloo," the man said, grinning.

Kate wanted to burst into tears. "Adios," she said finally.

"Adios, poquita," he said.

She turned off the TV, telling herself to remember the word *poquita*.

Kate met Chad a block from the Plaza del Rio, and they agreed that he would go check out the nearly completed second wing to see if they'd be as well hidden as Kate thought. He ran off then to see if he could get in and out without being noticed.

"We can get in there without being seen," Chad said when he returned twenty minutes later.

"Good work. Let's go settle in." Kate followed her brother, and they covered the blocks in silence.

Before they got to the hotel, Kate used a little more of the local currency she had left to buy two small bouquets of flowers from a woman on the street. "I'll explain later," she told Chad.

Kate followed Chad around to the back of the hotel. He glanced over his shoulder before entering the half-finished wing. They found a room near the back from which they could watch the plaza and the fountain after dark. Kate let the heavy bag drop and sat on the floor. "This is going to be hard sleeping," she said, then added, "Chad, I have an idea. It's why I bought the flowers. I say we go to the desk with flower deliveries, one for the Geists and one for the Kennicotts. Only one of those names is registered here, right? I mean, they had to use one name or the other. We leave the flowers for them with notes and a little bit of the uncut heroin. We tell them where we'll meet them and when." She shrugged. "Maybe that will get them out of our hair for a while, and we can work on getting help for Dad."

"Great." Chad sat in silence. "Hey," he said finally, "when they tell us one of those names isn't registered in the hotel, we can take the leftover bouquet and have it delivered to

Eva Flores at the airport. Tell her where we are. See if she can call Uncle Bill."

"How would you get it to her?"

"I know. I'll ask the guy who drives the hotel shuttle back and forth to the airport. Bet he'd do it for American dollars."

Kate lay on her side and rested her head against the bag. His idea bothered her for some reason, but she couldn't put her finger on it. "I need to rest," she said, and she rolled onto her back and breathed heavily in the late afternoon heat.

Chad gently tugged the bag out from under her head, making her less comfortable. "Gotta find something to write with," he said. "These flowers won't last long in this heat."

Kate rolled suddenly to her side. "Chad, you know what we should have done with the heroin? We should have used it to buy Dad back."

"What do you mean? Give it to the guards?"

"No, that wouldn't be right. But we had a million dollar's worth of the Geists' stuff. And they're in this thing with General Valdez. We had the advantage."

Chad stared at her. "As far as they know, we still do. They don't know we threw it away."

Kate and Chad heard noises from their wrist TVs at the

same time. They crawled over to the window opening, and Kate tried to tune in the transmission.

"Manny, Conchita," a voice spoke through the TV. It was Dad. "Do you read?"

The tiny screen was black.

"We're here," Kate said. "Go ahead."

Dad must have been hunched in a dark corner somewhere, whispering into the radio. "What's happening?" he said. "Where are you?"

Kate told him, then, "Did you get searched?"

"Yeah, but not before I got a guy to hold the wrist TV for a while. I don't think he had any idea what it was."

"Did they beat you too?"

"I'm all right."

"But did they?"

"Don't worry about it. Just get help and get me out of here."

"We're trying!"

"Over and out," Dad said.

Kate wanted to keep him talking, but she didn't want to get him in trouble. Maybe someone had noticed him or was approaching. She would not try to make contact. They would just wait to hear from him. "Now what?"

"We do whatever we have to to get him out. What do you think of this?" Chad showed her the note he'd written to the Geists. It read, "We have what you want, and you have what we want. Ready to deal?" It was signed, *Your young "friends."*

"Good," she said.

"This should send them on a wild goose chase so we don't have to worry about them all the time," Chad said.

"But eventually we have to meet with them," Kate said. "If they think we have their million dollars' worth of drugs, we can use that to get them to talk Valdez into letting Dad go."

"I don't know, Kate. Sounds too risky."

"I know they have guns, but we've got guns too. They don't know we wouldn't use them."

He finally nodded. "Where should we tell them to meet us?"

"Somewhere out in the open so we can see if they bring soldiers with them. And where they can see only one of us, so they think the other one has their drugs. We have to convince them that if one of us doesn't get back to the other one safely, they'll never get their drugs."

"Wow, Kate, how do you think of all this stuff?"

"I don't know," she said. "Women's intuition, I guess."

Chad shook his head. "I can't see Valdez just giving Dad the plane back, giving him fuel, and letting him leave the country. Somehow we've got to get Uncle Bill to let the U.S. government know what's going on."

Kate and Chad settled on two locations for their meetings, one with the Geists, one with Eva Flores. They would tell the Geists to meet them at the bend in the river, near where they had dumped the drugs. The Geists would be instructed to come together but to bring no one else. They'd have to park at least a quarter mile away and walk to the spot, so Kate and Chad could see if they brought anyone with them.

Kate and Chad would also give Eva Flores the names of two cross streets in town, along with directions to a back alley. The note to Eva asked that she meet them at sundown. He put Eva's note with her flowers. They would meet the Geists an hour after talking to Eva. And they would stick together. While Chad negotiated with the Geists, Kate would be up a tree behind him.

Chad added the meeting location to the Geists' note. Then he sprinkled a small amount of the leftover heroin into the envelope and placed it in with their flowers. Chad headed down to the front desk, and Kate listened by wrist TV.

"English?" he said to the girl.

"Sí. I mean, yes!"

"Flower deliveries for two guests. Geist and Kennicott."

There was a long pause, then, "I'm sorry, *poquito*, but

there is no one here under the name Geist. Are they at another hotel?"

"Maybe," Chad said. "I'll check."

"Kennicott is in room 514. You want to deliver them yourself?"

"Are they here?" Chad said. Kate knew that was unlikely. They had just seen the Geists at the prison.

"Let me ring their room and see," she said. "Oh! Their car just pulled up! Wait here and you'll get a tip."

"No, I've got to get going," Chad said. "More deliveries."

Kate heard him run away. She knew he wouldn't risk coming back to where she was for a while—it was too close to the Geists. She crawled to the window opening and peeked out. There was Chad, running as fast as he could with a bouquet of flowers in his hand. Soon Mr. Geist appeared, but he wasn't running. He scanned the area and then turned back into the hotel.

"You're not being followed, Manny," Kate transmitted. "But you'd better stay out of sight for a while."

"That was close. Can you see their car?"

Kate craned her neck. "Yes. It's in the side lot near the front."

"Let me know if they leave so I can get Eva's flowers and note to the shuttle guy. And I'll try to find us some food."

"Good, I'm starving." Forty minutes later, Kate let Chad

know the Geists were on the move. Not long after that he sneaked back up to their perch.

"Worked perfectly," he said. "The guy was thrilled."

"But will he do it?"

"Why not? He even said he knew who Eva Flores was and would deliver the bouquet himself." Chad unrolled the edge of his baggy shirt to reveal the food he'd bought.

"What's that?" Kate said, smelling cooked meat and onions.

"*Flautas*, I think they call them. Meat wrapped in tortillas."

Kate wolfed down two. Spicy or not, they tasted great. "Should we tell Dad what we're up to?" she said.

"No! If we call him at the wrong time, someone might hear the wrist TV and he'd be in trouble. We have to wait to hear from him."

Kate and Chad sat on the floor, resting, sweating, and discussing what Chad would say to the Geists if they showed up an hour after sundown.

"By then," Kate said, "Eva should have had time to make a phone call. Do you know Uncle Bill's number?"

"No, but Dad's address and phone book is in the bag with his wallet." He dug it out and found the number.

"Let me see that wallet again," Kate said. She picked through it for a minute, then proudly held up a plastic card. "Bingo!"

"Dad's phone card!" Chad said. "Perfect! Eva should be able to use this to call the States from just about any phone. And it won't show up on a phone record no matter where she calls from."

"Yeah," Kate said, "but remember where we are."

"It has to work," Chad said. "I just know if she can get through to Uncle Bill, he'll know who to contact and we'll get some action."

Their wrist TVs crackled then. "Spitfire?" Dad whispered.

"Spitfire here, go ahead."

"Guys in here tell me executions take place a minute after midnight. Next one is scheduled for twelve-oh-one Tuesday. That's a minute after midnight tomorrow night. And I think I'm the target."

"They'll have to kill *us* first," Kate said. "If we can't get help by then, we'll come down there with these guns."

"No! Don't do anything stupid. Now— "

"We'll do whatever we have to do," Kate said. "And I mean it!"

But Dad's TV had fallen silent.

Dark couldn't come soon enough for Kate. The day was hotter than the one before, and besides, she had never been one for sitting around and doing nothing. She had no idea where the Geists were or what they were up to. General

Valdez was apparently determined to have Dad put to death with no trial and little time to reconsider. Paco seemed to be all over town trying to find the "escapees" and make up for his mistake of finding the stuff he wasn't supposed to find.

Occasionally Kate or Chad would peek out the window to see whether the Geists' car was there or not. They could do little else until it began to grow dark. If the Geists' car was at the hotel when Kate and Chad left, they would walk in a different direction so they wouldn't be noticed so easily. But if the car was not there, it could be anywhere, and they would have to be on the lookout for the Geists all the time.

When the sun finally began to dip below the horizon, Kate and Chad grabbed the bag, checked the window, and headed out. The Geists' car was back in place, and Kate and Chad left the hotel through the back way. They circled around the side streets to get to the location where they hoped to meet Eva Flores.

Kate kept peeking behind her as they hurried through the city. As far as she could tell, no one was following them. But when they were within a couple of blocks of the prearranged spot, Chad suddenly stopped. Kate wasn't looking and bumped into him. He immediately shushed her.

"What?" she said.

He pointed. There, parked on the side of the street, was a military jeep identical to the ones at the airport. Kate and

Chad quickly ducked into an alley and circled around to where they could see the jeep from the front. The headlight was broken and the bumper creased. Kate and Chad stared at each other. They were still two blocks from where they were supposed to meet Eva.

They went the long way around, keeping on the alert for soldiers all the way. But they saw none. Kate couldn't imagine why anyone from the airport would be in that area unless they had followed Eva or knew where she was going. Chad walked Kate to the opposite end of the alley where they were supposed to meet Eva.

There, ramrod straight as a statue, stood a soldier in a camouflage uniform.

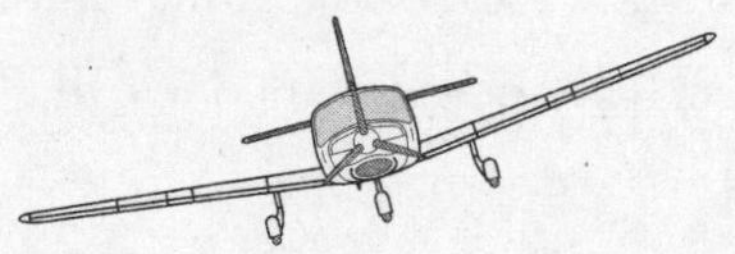

The Meetings

"Wait!" Chad whispered. "Back up. I don't think he's seen us."

"We're dead," Kate said. "I'll bet they have us surrounded."

"He doesn't know it's us yet," Chad said. "We'd better make a run for it before that guy spots us and tells his friends we're here."

"Back to the hotel?"

"Anywhere. We can't just walk into a trap. Should we split up?"

"Maybe. You want to take one of the guns?"

"What are you, crazy? What're we gonna do, go blast Dad out of prison?"

"We might as well try, Chad. I'm telling you, I've got a feeling we're surrounded."

"All right, let's go. If we get away, I'll meet you at the river in an hour."

And with that they took off running. But before she had gone twenty feet, Kate heard someone call, "Conchita! Manny! It's me!"

Kate skidded to a stop and whirled. In full camouflage, her hair tucked up under a helmet, Eva Flores waited for them near the alley to their right. They ran to her.

"Hello, kids," she said. "I brought these extra clothes and changed after I was away from the airport. I often drive to town on errands." She looked up and down the alley in both directions. "I'm sorry we have to meet here, but you can't be seen with me. People are all over the place looking for you. The Kennicotts are at the Plaza del Rio."

"We know," Kate and Chad said in unison.

"You were spotted at a barn on the edge of town."

"We know."

"Paco says someone even thought he saw you at the prison. Your father was searched and beaten. I'm sorry to tell you—he is to die just after midnight tomorrow night."

"No!" Kate cried. "Eva, we have to get him out of there. Can you call the United States for us?"

"Maybe. It is very dangerous."

"You can make the call with my dad's phone credit card," Chad said.

"Still, it puts me in grave danger," Eva said. "Maybe you can do something for me in exchange."

"What can we do?"

"Can you get me asylum?"

"Asylum? What's that?"

"Refuge. Sanctuary."

Kate and Chad looked at each other, confused. Kate had heard those words but wasn't sure what they meant.

"How do we do that?"

"It's simple," Eva said. "If we can somehow get your father out of this mess, you help me get back to my home country."

"Which is?"

"Ecuador. I met Valdez in military training there and worked for him all the way up to when he became a rebel and began opposing established military regimes. But now it has gone too far and I see him for who he is. I want to return to my family, but I need a way out."

"We have to trust you," Kate said. "We hardly know you, but we know you risked your life to help us escape. And if you can do anything to help us get our dad out of prison, we promise you he will get you to Ecuador."

Eva knelt in the alley. "Then I will risk everything," she whispered. "Tell me what to do and I will do it."

Kate and Chad gave her their dad's phone card and the number for their Uncle Bill in Portland. "Tell him everything that's going on. He'll know what to do."

"What will he do?" Eva said.

"He'll get the United States government and even the military involved, if he has to."

"I'll do it," Eva said. "Even if I have to risk doing it from a phone at the airport, I will do this. But I must not be revealed as one who has helped you until it is clear I can go with you and not be in danger. As corrupt and criminal as Valdez is, he will accuse me of an act of treason punishable by death. I should have turned him in to President Guillen months ago. Our president is an honorable man, but he does not know everything about Valdez."

Kate and Chad nodded. "I just know this is going to work," Kate said. "Dad will be free. We will be free. And you will be free."

"I'd better go," Eva said.

"Meet us back here in two hours," Chad said. "And Eva, if we're not here, do whatever you have to do to get our dad free, and tell him we promised he would take you to Ecuador."

Kate and Chad then headed toward the river. "Maybe we should just forget about the Geists," Kate said as they ran. "Let them show up and wonder where we are."

"No," Chad said. "We should go through with the plan. Make them ask Valdez to release Dad so they can get their million dollars' worth of dope back."

"But what if he says we have to turn over the drugs or he'll execute Dad?"

Chad just shook his head. "All I know," he said, "is that we need to buy some time in case it takes a while for Uncle Bill to get hold of somebody who can do something. Don't forget this is Sunday."

Kate shuddered. "And let's not forget we've got only a little more than twenty-four hours to work with."

They arrived at the river half an hour before they were supposed to meet the Geists. Chad helped Kate lug the leather bag up a tree about forty feet behind the spot he'd told them to meet him. "Just watch and listen," he said, moving away.

Kate and Chad whispered to each other over their wrist TVs while they waited for the Geists. "Let's not do anything stupid," Chad said.

"What if they grab you and force you to tell them where their drugs are?"

"They won't. They know that if they want their drugs back, they have to deal with me."

"I wish I knew how to use these guns," Kate said.

"Well, you don't, so don't even think about it. They're not loaded, and I wouldn't know how to do it."

"These are just clips," Kate said. "All you do is snap them in."

"Well, don't."

"Don't worry."

It was pitch black when Kate and Chad noticed headlights turning off the main road, onto the dirt road, and then down a narrow path toward the river. A couple of hundred feet from Chad, where the ground became rough and uneven, the car stopped. Kate could hardly hear from that distance, but it sounded as if the Geists had left it running. The lights were still on, and the car was parked facing the river, maybe ten feet from the bank, which was steep at that point.

Though the headlights pointed more toward the river than toward Chad, Kate could make out two figures headed toward them. They slowly came closer, and when they were within about a hundred feet, Chad shouted, "Are you alone?"

"We're alone, you little dirt ball," Mr. Geist called. "Are you?"

"Yeah, I'd be stupid enough to meet you two alone out here in the dark in the middle of nowhere."

"Well, you're pretty stupid to think you can walk off with something of ours."

"Oh, that was yours? It was in my sister's backpack."

When the Geists were about twenty feet from Chad, he told them to stop.

"How about you just give us back our stuff and we promise you won't die when your dad does?"

"Sounds like you don't really want your stuff back," Chad said.

"Just tell us where it is."

Chad's voice sounded more confident than he was, Kate knew. "Oh, sure, that would be smart. Here's the deal. We'll give you back your guns and ammunition and the rest of the drugs when my dad's plane is fueled up, cleared for takeoff, and we're all allowed back on it. Dad will even pay for the fuel."

"Why don't we just take you and make your sister buy you back with what belongs to us?"

"You could never catch me," Chad said.

"How do you know we don't have you surrounded?"

"How do you know we didn't already flush your dope down the river?"

"You wouldn't be that stupid," Mr. Geist said. "You know it's your only hope of getting your dad out of prison."

Kate had heard enough. She dug into the bag and pulled out a Luger. She knew it was empty, but it felt heavy and ugly and cold in her hand. "How do you know I don't have your own gun pointed right at your head?" she hollered.

The Geists looked up quickly, but Kate knew they couldn't see her in the tree.

"Listen," Mrs. Geist spoke for the first time, "we know you have no reason to believe or trust us. But we're here unarmed. You don't need to shoot us."

Kate alternated pointing the gun at Mr. Geist and then Mrs. Geist. What would it be like to pull the trigger? She put her index finger on it, but of course, the empty gun would make only a metallic snapping sound, and then they would know she was sitting up there with an unloaded weapon. Suddenly an idea hit her. She put the weapon back in the bag and quietly climbed out of the tree. It was totally dark other than the light from the car's headlamps. She circled far outside the Geists' and her brother's fields of vision, heading for their car.

She wanted to know whether it was running and if anyone else was around. She listened on her wrist TV as Mrs. Geist talked on. "We have no influence over what happened to your father. It was not what we intended. We thought you would stay a few days and fly home none the wiser. Something went wrong. It wasn't *our* fault. We didn't want to see your father go to prison. We know he is innocent. We just used him."

"You think I don't know that you're in this deal with General Valdez?" Chad said. "You tell him to let our dad go. That's the only way you'll see your stuff again."

Everything was silent for a moment. "How do we know you'll keep up your end of the bargain?" Mr. Geist finally asked.

"Why wouldn't we? All we want is our dad back."

Kate reached the Geists' car, which was still running. No one else was around. She tiptoed up and peered in the window of the back door. There on the seat lay two high-powered weapons.

Kate was suddenly overcome with bitterness toward this couple. She didn't know what their real names were. She didn't know their history, what they were up to, or why they had lied to get her father to fly them to Amazonia. All she knew was that they had treated her so nice in Boise that she had put away all her doubts and misgivings about them.

She was mad at herself, angry at them, and scared they would try to do something to Chad or to her just to get their precious drugs back. What were these weapons all about? Did the Geists plan to come back and shoot them? Kate didn't know, but she knew she had to do something.

She could holler at Chad that the Geists had weapons in the car. She could throw the weapons in the river. Why had they left the engine running? Were they planning a quick getaway?

Kate impulsively opened the driver's-side door and grabbed the gearshift. She tried to shift the car into drive, but it wouldn't budge. Then she remembered that on her dad's car, he had to push on the brake pedal to shift into drive. One foot still on the ground, she stepped into the car and placed her right foot on the brake pedal. But standing awkwardly like that didn't give her enough leverage.

She slipped into the car and sat behind the wheel. She looked back at Chad and the Geists. She could hear them talking on her wrist TV, but she couldn't see them. "Why don't you let us drive you out to the airport and we'll talk this over with the general?" Mrs. Geist was saying.

"You must think kids are stupid," Chad said. "No deal. You get my dad out of that prison and out to the airport and then we'll come there."

"I'll tell you what I'm going to do, you little slime," Mr. Geist said. "I'm gonna break your neck and see if your little sister has the guts to shoot me. What do you think of that?"

Kate sat in the car with her left foot still on the ground. She pushed on the brake pedal and shifted into drive. She felt the gears engage. All she had to do was let her foot off the brake and the car would head toward the river, just a few feet away.

On her wrist she heard Chad's less than confident voice. "If you hurt me, my sister might shoot you. But even if she doesn't, you'll never get your stuff back."

"I'm through messing with you," Mr. Geist said.

"Don't do it," Mrs. Geist said.

Kate let up on the brake and jumped out of the car. It began rolling slowly, crunching the dry ground. When the front wheels of the all-wheel-drive car dropped over the edge of the river bank, the wheels continued to turn, but they gripped only air. The car's headlights now pointed into the water, and the under-carriage of the car had become hung up. The car teetered on the edge of the bank.

It rocked there, and every time the back tires touched the ground they moved the car forward another few inches before it rocked some more, pulling the back tires off the ground. Kate ran straight back about a hundred feet. She could hear the Geists swearing and knew they were running toward the car.

She stood still in the darkness as they approached. "What the devil!" Mr. Geist shouted. "Did you leave it in drive?"

"I wasn't driving, you idiot," his wife said. "You were."

"Well, I didn't leave it in gear!"

"Get the rifles," Mrs. Geist said.

"I've got to get the stuff from the trunk first! Do you realize what we have in there? We can replace the weapons, but we're talking over ten million bucks in the trunk!"

"Be careful," she said.

"Shut up! Where are the keys?"

"In the ignition, stupid."

"Can't I pop the trunk from a switch in the glove box?" he said.

"I don't know! This is a rental car. Just do what you have to do!"

"You're a big help."

"You're the one who didn't want to risk leaving the stuff in the hotel!" she snapped. " 'Nobody will find it in the trunk,' you said."

"Just get out of my way," he said.

Mr. Geist hurried to the other side of the car and carefully opened the front passenger door. He pushed the button on the glove compartment, which made the car teeter a little farther forward.

"Careful!" Mrs. Geist hollered.

"Shut up!" he shouted.

He pushed another button and the trunk flew open, shifting the weight of the car and making it rock enough so that the rear wheels grabbed the ground solidly one more time. Mrs. Geist rushed toward the open trunk as Mr. Geist jumped away from the moving car.

With great squeaking and scraping and crunching, the car plunged straight down into the river. The gigantic splash drenched both the Geists.

"No! No! No!" Mr. Geist yelled as he tore at his hair and jumped up and down.

The car must have flipped over, Kate decided, because the bobbing headlights now faced the bank. With a gurgle and bubbles, the car began to sink.

Kate raced back to the tree to get the leather bag, hoping Chad was still there and was all right.

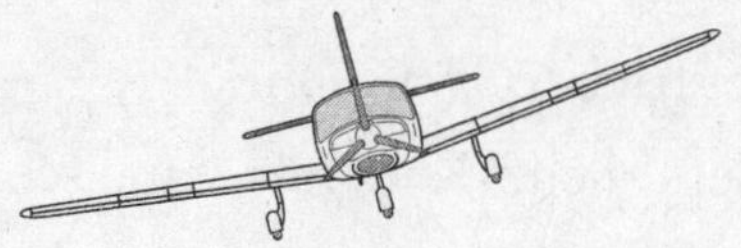

The Rescue

Kate found Chad calling for her from the tree she'd hidden in. "I'm right here," she said.

He scrambled down. "Where have you been? Mr. Geist was trying to kill me."

"Who do you think put their car on the edge of the river bank?"

"You? Why?"

"It got their attention away from you, didn't it?"

"For a while. We've got to get out of here."

Kate and Chad stared into the distance where the car lights were quickly disappearing under the water. They heard a splash, then Mrs. Geist telling her husband to be careful, and him telling her to shut up again. He must have jumped into the water to salvage whatever he could.

"There were high-powered weapons in there," Kate said, as they ran off into the darkness, farther and farther from town. "You think they'll come after us?"

"Not without light. We'd better be careful not to get lost. We've got to get back to Eva soon."

"Let's wait here then," Kate said, "and see if we hear anything. Then we can circle around and get back to town."

Kate and Chad sat panting near a grove of trees, and Kate pulled out the gun she had pointed at the Geists. "Can you see this?" she said.

"No, what?"

"The Luger."

"You made them think you were actually pointing it at them."

"I was! It's not loaded, Chad. You told me that yourself."

"You know Dad says there's no such thing as an unloaded gun."

"Yeah, but I wasn't going to pull the trigger. You think I wanted them to know it wasn't loaded?" She pointed the gun into the air. "It would have made a sound like this." And she pulled the trigger.

The boom was so deafening that both kids hit the ground. Kate's right ear rang, but she could hear enough out of her left.

"I can't believe you did that!" Chad said. "You were pointing that gun at the Geists for real?"

"Yes," she said, feeling sobs invade her throat. "And I had my finger on the trigger, too!"

"Kate!"

"Chad! The clip isn't even in it! Feel!"

She handed him the Luger. "You're right!" he said. "Maybe it's a trick gun or something. Whatever it is, don't touch it again."

"You think the Geists heard that?"

"They had to."

"Then let's get out of here."

Kate was shaky. What if she had shot someone? It didn't matter if it was the Geists, Chad, or herself, she would never have gotten over it. She felt so stupid! "I'm sorry, Chad. That was really dumb."

"It sure proves Dad's point about guns, doesn't it?" He laughed.

"What's funny?"

"I was just thinking ... if you had shot the gun into the air when you were in the tree, the Geists would have fainted."

"So would I," Kate said.

Half an hour later they arrived at the edge of town. They stopped when they heard a crackly noise from their wrist TVs. "Spitfire?"

"Dad! Can you hear us?"

"I heard all of that! I didn't want to call until I was sure you were alone. What in the world were you doing, meeting with the Geists? Don't you realize how dangerous they must be? I mean I appreciate it, but you've got to get to Uncle Bill."

"We're trying," Chad said. "But they left drugs in Kate's backpack and we found out it was worth a million dollars."

"Just get rid of it and get help," Dad said. "These people will stop at nothing. How did Kate get her backpack anyway?"

"I'll tell you later," Kate said. "You probably know it was the young woman at the tribunal who helped us escape."

"I wondered. I heard you overpowered her, but she didn't seem hurt. It didn't add up to me, and it probably won't add up to anyone else either. You're all in danger."

"She's helping us," Chad said, "and we need her, Dad."

"Quiet!" Dad said. "Someone's—"

His TV transmission cut out, and they didn't dare risk transmitting to him until they heard from him. Kate worried the Geists had already gotten to Valdez and he had sent someone to the prison to beat him again—or worse—for what she and Chad did.

They ran to where they had agreed to meet Eva. She was there, sitting in the darkness.

"Eva!" Kate hurried to her side. "Did you reach our uncle?"

"I did," she said, "and I did not have to risk using an airport phone. I remembered a distant relative on the outskirts of town who has a phone. It took half an hour to get a line out of the country, but I did talk to your Uncle Bill. He did not trust me and insisted on talking to one of you."

"We'll talk to him, but when and where?"

"Get into the jeep and stay down out of sight. I will take you to the phone. I also reached President Guillen and told him everything. I think he believes me. He wants to keep the United States out of this at all costs. For one thing, he is afraid Valdez might attack, pretending it is self-defense, if Americans land at the airport. The president wants to solve this himself. He wants me to call him back to finalize a plan."

"Do you trust him?" Chad said.

"I have to. I have no choice anymore."

Kate and Chad lay down on the floor of the back seat of the jeep, and Eva roared to the outskirts of town. "Do you believe her?" Chad whispered. "Or do you think she has already been caught and is taking us somewhere for Valdez?"

"No way," Kate said. "Eva is with us. She would not betray us."

"How can you be so sure?"

"Women's intuition," Kate said.

Soon the jeep braked behind a small house in a remote area. Someone peeked out the window, and Kate and Chad jumped down and followed Eva inside. Her relatives, a shy couple with a bunch of children, herded all the kids into another room and left Eva, Kate, and Chad alone with the phone.

Eva got connected with the international operator in Spanish. She read off the card numbers, while Kate and Chad waited impatiently beside her. "Let me talk to him," Kate whispered to Chad.

"That's fine," he said. "Just be quick and tell him everything."

Eva hung up. "The operator will call me back when she's made the connection." She went into the other room to talk with her relatives, then brought them all out to meet Kate and Chad. None spoke English, so Eva translated.

The phone rang and Eva answered. "Yes, sir, your niece is right here."

"Uncle Bill?"

"Kate, honey, are you all right?"

"Yes, Uncle Bill. Let me tell you—"

"Before you say anything, let me ask you some questions. Is anyone else on the line?"

"No."

"Are you sure?"

"Pretty sure."

"Is the woman who called me really Mrs. Geist?"

"No!"

"You're sure?"

"Totally."

"Is she really a friend who helped you escape?"

"Yes, Uncle Bill. Everything she told you is true."

"And you're not just saying this because you're being threatened?"

"No!"

"Praise the Lord!" he said. "Listen, Kate. The U.S. government knows all about the Geists. Someone called here looking to get hold of your dad not too long after you guys took off from Boise. They wanted to warn him about the Geists, that they were phonies and drug runners. They were taking some of their uncut stuff down there to show the Amazonians how they processed heroin and cocaine. U.S. agents had been tracking them for months, but our government didn't learn of their trip until the last minute."

"So what did you do?" Kate said.

"Just in case the woman who called me was telling the truth, I told the military and our government everything. They've had planes in Chile and Argentina since yesterday anyway, knowing the Geists are down there, and they're ready to make an air strike if necessary. The state department is prepared to insist that it will not recognize Amazonia as an independent country until your dad has been released."

"You'd better talk to Eva about that," Kate said. "She thinks the president of Amazonia will help us."

"Would he turn over the Geists to the U.S. government?"

"Talk to her, Uncle Bill."

"Honey?"

"Yes."

"Is Chad there?"

"Sure. You want to talk to him?"

"Better not take the time right now. Just tell him we love you guys, and we're praying for you, and we will get you all out of there safely."

Kate handed the phone to Eva and began to feel optimistic for the first time since the family had landed in South America.

Eva listened a moment, then said, "Sir, let me talk to our president about that. I do not believe there will be any reason to bring warplanes in. Let me give President Guillen your ideas and get him in touch with your government and military. Thank you, sir."

"Let me talk to him," Chad said.

Eva looked troubled, like she did not want to take any more time. But she handed Chad the phone.

"One more thing, Uncle Bill," he said. "We promised Eva she could get back to Ecuador if she helped us."

Eva spent the next hour on the phone connected to the president's vacation home a hundred miles away. They seemed to be concocting an elaborate scheme. When she hung up, she smiled at Kate and Chad. "I might not have to go back to Ecuador after all. I might want to stay here and continue working for the president. He is a good man. He is going to do the right thing. He says if you have evidence, he will make Valdez pay."

Eva told them the plan on the way back to the meeting place, where they would split up. "Lay low tonight," she said, "and I will arrange for you to be captured here tomorrow morning, probably by Paco."

Kate jerked. "What! Why?"

"You will not be in danger. The president will tell Valdez that he is coming to the airport to meet and honor the American couple who helped expose an arms and drug smuggler. He will also say that he wants the prisoner there to be publicly humiliated by the ceremony." She turned a corner. "I will tell Valdez that you called the airport and have said you would surrender if it might help your father's cause in any way. That way he can have your father and his children there as a surprise for the president." Eva turned down the alley. "The Geists will be there, of course, for their honor. At the proper time, the tables will be turned."

Before leaving, they turned the guns, ammunition, and remaining dope in Kate's sock over to Eva. "Do you know anything about weapons?" Kate asked their new friend.

"Sure."

"Why would a Luger like this fire when there is no clip in it?"

"Because one shell remains in the chamber when a clip is removed. You always have to be careful and check that."

"No kidding," Kate said.

The kids sneaked into their uncomfortable, unfinished hotel room that night but found sleep impossible. In the morning they heard a commotion and peeked outside to see the well-dressed Geists proudly climbing into an airport military jeep. The excitement of what the day would bring was almost unbearable to Kate.

Once the Geists were gone, she and Chad packed their leather bag and ran to the meeting place. Two jeeps waited, loaded with soldiers. Kate was terrified that these military men might take justice into their own hands and kill them, just for the honor of it. She shook when Paco leveled his weapon at them and ordered them into a jeep.

"Good to surrender," he said, as his driver roared off. "Right thing to do. Can't help father, but now live in state orphanage."

Neither Kate nor Chad responded.

When they arrived at the airport it seemed every soldier wore a clean, pressed uniform. Many worked around the grounds, sprucing up the place for the president's visit. They saw a review platform being hastily built near the runway. When Kate and Chad were ushered inside, General Valdez and his tribunal, including Eva Flores, were waiting for them in the interrogation room. The Geists were not in sight, but soon after Kate and Chad were seated, Valdez asked the guards to bring in their father.

It broke Kate's heart to see how terrible he looked. His face was bruised and scraped, and one eye was swollen. He limped, still barefoot. He had not shaved, and his clothes were filthy. But he communicated to Kate and Chad with his eyes. It was clear he had no idea what this was all about, and Kate wanted with everything in her to tell him it was almost over, and he would soon be free.

General Valdez, in his dress uniform, looked delighted. "Here we all are again," he announced. "And *el presidente* is on his way."

Dad looked surprised, but he said nothing.

"The prisoner is not so talkative today, eh?" Valdez said.

"No, sir," Dad said. "I beg your mercy on my children."

Kate didn't want to see him beg, but she knew he believed it was his last hope for them.

"Send them back to the United States to be with people who love them," Dad added.

"Silence!" Valdez said. He turned to the others. "Allow me to be alone with the prisoners."

The older woman, the other two officers, and Eva Flores gathered up their papers and notebooks. Eva stacked her tape recorder and her papers on a table near the wall, then followed the rest of the officers and several soldiers into the hall.

Soon the AirQuest Aventures team was alone in the room with General Valdez. "Your children are going nowhere, señor," he said. "As I told you before, they will be guests of one of our fine orphanages."

"Don't do this," Dad said.

Now Valdez was angry. He stood. "This will be a great day. The *presidente* will honor me and the Kennicotts in front of your face. You proclaim your ignorance, and yet you stole what the Kennicotts brought me."

"I didn't steal—"

"Your children, señor! Your children! What would they be doing with a million dollars' worth of contraband? Even if you did nothing, you should die for their theft."

"We didn't steal anything," Kate said. "Your friends put it into my backpack. I didn't even know I had it."

"But now you know, and you know it is mine. And I want to know where the rest of it is."

"I dumped it in the river," Chad said.

Valdez appeared ready to explode. "I do not believe that," he said. "You will tell me when you see your father tortured to within an inch of his life."

Valdez called for guards to take the family to a waiting area. They were not allowed to speak. Kate was bursting, wanting to wink at her dad, to smile, to tell him everything. But she could not. Soon they heard a plane landing, and the family was led out into the sun for the ceremony.

President Guillen was a small man with a thin mustache and vivid, dark eyes. He was not dressed in a uniform but wore a suit. The Amazonian airport military stood proudly in a line as Valdez introduced the president and his entourage of personal bodyguards. They saluted smartly, and he walked down the row inspecting them.

The president placed his hands on each officer's shoulders and leaned close for a personal greeting. Kate noticed that Eva spoke briefly with him and then slipped him a small package.

The Kennicotts waited proudly on chairs on the platform, where they were joined by Valdez, Guillen, and the tribunal, including Eva Flores. The Michaels family waited off to the side, guarded by two soldiers.

General Valdez took the microphone. "We are proud to welcome our leader, the honorable President Manuel Guillen. He has come to honor our efforts in apprehending an American smuggler and to also honor those Americans who aided in the arrest. President Guillen."

Guillen thanked the general and began. "First, I would ask that the soldiers guarding the prisoners be replaced by two of my own men, so that they may join the rest of the airport military."

The soldiers looked at Valdez, who nodded.

Guillen spoke directly to the guards. "You may leave your weapons there."

Again the guards looked to Valdez, and again he nodded.

"And General Valdez, I would like to have your troops leave their weapons where they stand and move directly in front of me."

"I don't understand," Valdez said, standing.

"It will become clear to you, General, if you please."

Valdez gestured to his troops, and they left their weapons on the ground and paraded in front of the podium to stand in front of President Guillen.

"And now I would ask that my men arrest the airport troops, including General Valdez and his officers, and the American couple on the platform."

Valdez stood, flush-faced and sputtering. "But, sir, I— "

"General, I know what has gone on here, and it will not be tolerated. The sovereign state of Amazonia will be run by men and women who cherish the law and freedom."

"But, sir, I— "

"Or perhaps you would prefer that I play a tape of the conversation you just had with your prisoners, in which you admit that the smuggled goods belonged to you." Valdez fell silent and was handcuffed. "We will determine later how many of your troops should be tried along with you, Señor Valdez."

Dad stood there with his eyes wide and his mouth open,

and Kate began to jabber at him. In a little more than a minute she gushed the whole story, right up to nearly shooting the Geists, setting up their car to drop into the river, and talking to Uncle Bill on the phone.

"A United States military plane will land here in a few minutes," President Guillen said. "It will extradite the Geists for trial in their own country and make sure the Michaels family is healthy before they return home as well."

"I want to go home now," Dad whispered.

"But you can't," Kate said. "You need someone to look at your wounds, and you need at least two days of rest."

Dad looked at her and shook his head. "I'd rather rest at home."

"You can rest there too, but you need at least two days before you fly a plane again."

"What do you think, Chad?" Dad said.

Chad shrugged. "Don't look at me."

Kate grinned. "Dad," she said, "I don't think Chad will ever argue against women's intuition again."

Discussion Questions for Terror in Branco Grande

Chapter 1

1. When was the last time you had to apologize to a sibling?
2. Have you ever had a really bad feeling about something?
3. How should Chad have responded to Kate's plans?

Chapter 2

4. What would you have done if you were on the plane?
5. Do you pray when you're scared like Kate did?
6. What were your impressions about how Dad reacted to the situation?

Chapter 3

7. Have you ever been wrongfully accused?
8. What do you do when your situation is unfair?
9. What do you think of Eva Flores?

Chapter 4

10. Do you believe General Valdez would execute Mr. Michaels or is he bluffing?
11. What would you say to try to escape the situation?
12. What would the kids' lives be like if their father was taken away?

Chapter 5

13. Would you leave your dad and try to escape?
14. How should we help wrongfully accused people in prison?
15. How would you avoid being spotted in a foreign country?

Chapter 6

16. What would you have done with the guns and drugs?
17. What could Kate and Chad do if they are discovered?
18. Kate prayed for Chad and her dad. Whom do you pray for?

Chapter 7

19. What's the most scared you've ever been?
20. How would you try to get to the prison?

Chapter 8

21. Have you ever had to wash in a river?
22. Have you ever tried to communicate with someone who doesn't speak your language?
23. How will they use Kate's watches to help their dad?

Chapter 9

24. How would you conceal your identity?
25. Was it a good idea to dump the drugs into the river?
26. Have you ever been to a prison (Turkish or otherwise)?

Chapter 10

27. Do you think Kate's plan will work?
28. If unable to call for help, what would you do with the resources Kate and Chad have?

Chapter 11

29. Do you think Eva Flores will succeed?
30. Could you be as brave as Chad was during his meeting with the Geists?
31. How do you think the Geists will react to what happened to their car?

Chapter 12

32. What should be done to General Valdez and the Geists?

DISASTER
in the Yukon

To David Van Orman, who wanted to go to Alaska and wound up in Abania.

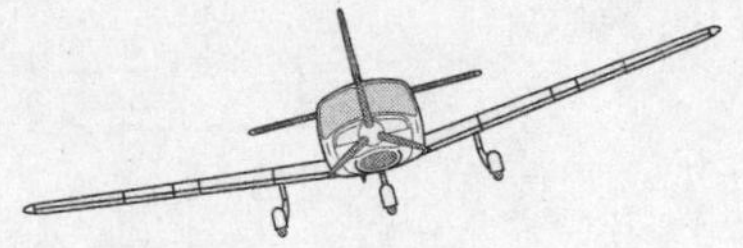

Contents

Kate's Friend

It wasn't the news Chad Michaels wanted to hear.

"Suzie Q and her family are moving to the Yukon!" his sister Kate exulted one night at the dinner table.

Of course Kate would be thrilled. She and Susan Quenton had been playmates the first six years of their lives, back in Oklahoma. But that was five years ago, and all Chad remembered was Suzie Q as a spoiled brat.

"No kidding?" Dad said. "I told her dad Old Sparrow Christian Boarding School was looking for a president, but I had no idea he'd actually go for it, the school being so far into Yukon Territory."

"How far?" Kate said, her mouth full. "Will I get to see her a lot?"

Dad squinted. "Old Sparrow is near the Canadian border, at least two hundred miles east." He smiled. "I can't imagine Suzie Q in that environment, can you? I mean, those mountains, the river frozen most of the year, and snow, snow, and more snow."

"We all love that, Dad," Kate said. "Why shouldn't they?"

"Oh, *they* will," Chad said. "It's that spoiled only child who's in for a surprise."

"Chad!" Kate said, slamming her fork on the table. "You don't know Suzie anymore. She's not still six, you know."

"Come on, Kate. I'll bet she's still a dumb little kid."

"Now Chad," Dad said, "Kate's kept up with Suzie by email all these years, and—"

"And she's sweet," Kate said. "And wonderful."

"I'll believe it when I see it," Chad said, looking away from Kate's withering stare.

"How's she doing with her—what is it—diabetes?"

"Yeah," Kate said. "She gives herself shots every day. She says her mom is shipping a six-month supply of insulin up here before the heavy snow season."

"The heavy snow season is already here," Dad said. "Hope she knows that. When do they arrive?"

"They'll be at the school by the end of the week," Kate said.

Dad raised his eyebrows. "Something different for Hugh; he's been an Air Force chaplain for so long. But he'll do fine. I do wonder how Margie will do in this climate."

"Let alone Suzie Q," Chad said, shaking his head.

"Leave her alone," Kate said. "You've never given her a chance."

Chad smirked. "Maybe she'll grow up one of these days."

"She's already grown up, Chad," Kate said. "You're just too critical. How would you like to have to give yourself shots every day?"

"I'm not saying I don't feel sorry for her. But why does she have to be such a—"

"You have no idea what kind of a person she is now," Kate said. "Just be glad you're not judged by how you acted five years ago."

Well, that was true, but Chad wasn't about to admit it.

Dad stood and signaled the kids to help clear the table. "Kate," he said, "have Suzie Q tell her parents that I'll email them. We have to get you two together soon."

"When, Dad?"

"Soon. If we wait even until November, it'll be too hard to drive that close to Canada. Wouldn't surprise me if the Porcupine River is already frozen and snowed over."

That night before going to bed, Chad spent some time online keeping up with his sports statistics from the lower forty-eight states. Then he checked the saved email files to see what Kate and Dad had written to the Quentons. Kate had written, "Chad doesn't say so, but I think he's as excited about seeing you again as I am."

Could she really think that? No way. It wasn't like Kate to lie. Maybe she just wanted Susie Q to feel welcome in the Yukon or something. Or maybe Kate thought he was hiding some secret interest in Suzie Q. If she believed that, she couldn't be more wrong.

Kate also told Suzie Q about the wrist radios she had converted into wrist TVs. "They work for only about a mile, and the picture's fuzzy. We can't watch each other on our wrists from two hundred miles away, but at least we can play with them when we're together."

Dad's email message congratulated Hugh and Margie Quenton on the new assignment and said he looked forward to seeing them and Suzie Q again. He thanked them again for their condolences after Chad and Kate's mom's death eight months earlier, then added, "While it won't be the same without her when we get together, we'll have lots of fond memories to share. Don't hesitate to talk about her, as so many people around here do. I suppose they think it's too painful for me, but the truth is, there's nothing I'd rather do than think and talk about Kathryn."

Chad scrolled down to read the rest of Dad's message.

"We'll give you time to settle in and get your bearings, and then we'll try to drive over there the weekend after next. We'll leave Friday after school and probably see you late that night. The kids are out of school on Monday and

Tuesday, so we'll leave Kate there and come back and get her Tuesday afternoon, if that's all right with you."

Chad checked the file where Suzie Q had attached her picture. He was stunned. Sure, she had braces, but what a smile! What eyes! What hair! Then he woke himself up. It was still Suzie Q, the little brat. And he didn't like girls anyway. Chad shook his head and shut down the machine.

Two Fridays later it had begun snowing just before Mukluk Middle School let out. Huge flakes darted about as Chad and Kate helped Dad pack the four-wheel-drive all-terrain vehicle.

Chad had grown tired of Kate's excitement over seeing Susie Q again. It was all she talked about lately. She'd counted the days and then the hours. "Good grief," Chad would say. "It's only Suzie Q."

"Well, we've been here five years, and I've never made a friend like her."

The drive would take only about four hours, and Chad and Dad were planning to stay only one night, but packing survival equipment was their most important task.

People in northern Alaska didn't make a big deal about it, because surviving the cold and snow was a way of life. They got a kick out of people from the lower forty-eight complaining about zero-degree temperatures or even ten- or twenty-degrees-below-zero wind chills. That was everyday stuff for them from the fall to the spring, and when things got really nasty, they imagined outsiders just curling up and dying in the elements.

The family packed foodstuffs, extra clothing, extra boots, snowshoes, backpacks, petroleum jelly to protect exposed skin, first-aid stuff, and every other item necessary for survival in the arctic climate. They packed enough stuff that the entire cargo area of the ATV was full. Dad would have to use the outside mirrors on either side to see behind them on the highway.

The Michaelses pulled out into what was now a driving snowstorm. Dad drove the speed limit for the first hour and a half, but then the snow began to accumulate and he had to back down a few miles per hour. The big four-wheel-drive tires bit into the snow, and Chad felt as secure as ever. He and Kate turned on their individual lights and read as the ATV hummed along in the darkness. About an hour from the Canadian border the snow let up, Dad sped up, and they cruised into Old Sparrow County near midnight.

Old Sparrow Christian School was easy to find. Its buildings were the only ones on the north side of the road for miles, just beyond the sign that pointed east and said, "Old Sparrow 48 kilometers." The school and the dormitories were dark, but a light burned in the living room of the main house. Hugh and Margie Quenton greeted them warmly.

"Where's Suzie Q?" Kate said, looking around.

"I'm afraid Sue finally fell asleep waiting," Margie said. "But she insisted we wake her up the minute you arrived."

Kate looked disappointed, but Chad was surprised when she said, "No, let her sleep. We'll have the next few days together."

Chad was relieved to put off seeing Suzie Q till morning. When the Quentons finished going on and on over how much Kate and Chad had grown and how pretty and handsome they were, they were finally shown the spare room.

Chad laid out his sleeping bag, but as soon as he was snuggled inside it, his head near the door, he heard Margie Quenton burst into tears.

"I feel so bad about Kathryn!" she wailed. "It has to be so hard for you and the kids. How are they taking it?"

"Pretty hard. What could be worse than losing your mother? But we know she's with God. Heaven has never seemed more real to us."

That's for sure, Chad thought. To him, heaven used to be just an idea, part of a story. But now he imagined Mom there. He found himself often wondering what she was doing, what she could see and hear, if she knew what he was up to.

Mrs. Quenton tried to tell a funny story she remembered about Mom, but she wound up in tears again.

"I'm sorry!" she said. "This isn't going to work! I cry either way!"

"That's all right, Margie," Dad said. "One of these days, we'll talk about Kathryn without crying. Meanwhile, tell me what's happened with you three since we saw you last."

That was enough to make Chad drowsy. The last thing he wanted to listen to was boring adult conversation. He drifted off to the muffled sound of laughter.

Chad awoke when sunlight peeked through the heavy curtains. He didn't realize what had awakened him until he felt the door lightly brush his head. He sat up. In the semi-darkness he saw the form of a girl.

"Suzie Q?" he whispered.

She laughed. "No one calls me that anymore, Chad. Call me Sue."

"Okay, Suzie Q."

"Chad! So how are you anyway?"

"I'm all right. I was sleeping though."

"Sorry. I was just so eager to see you guys."

"To see Kate, you mean."

"Well, both of you, silly. Why not?"

Chad wished he could see her better. "You want me to wake Kate?"

Suzie Q seemed to think about it. "Nah," she said. "If she wakes up, she wakes up. I'll talk to you, if it's all right."

Chad shrugged, then realized that Suzie Q couldn't see him.

"I've been praying for you," she said.

"Really?"

"Course. Losing your mom and everything."

"Yeah." Chad squirmed.

"You don't want to talk about it?"

"I don't mind, but I like the good memories, not the sad ones."

"Tell me some of them."

Suzie Q sounded genuinely interested and seemed to really listen. Chad couldn't remember the last time he had talked so easily and casually with a girl, other than Kate. Could this really be the girl who gave him so much grief when they were little?

He told her the story about the time his mother had taken him out for lunch, just the two of them, on his birthday. For some reason, as simple as the story was, it made Suzie Q cry. He felt a little emotional himself as he talked about Mom.

"Well, Chad," she said finally, "to tell you the truth, I was always jealous of you and Kate because you had each other. Being an only child has its good parts, but it's lonely too. When I heard about your mother, I felt so guilty for any bad feelings I'd ever had about you. It was as if I grew up in one night. I was so thankful for my parents and so glad that you and Kate had each other. Can you imagine going through something like that without Kate?"

Chad just shrugged and grunted. As for Kate, he'd had lots of frustrating times with her lately. Every day certain things irritated them about each other. But to go through losing Mom without her? Suzie Q was right.

The girl in front of him had changed, all right. He could tell she wasn't just being friendly. Still, he felt awkward and wished Kate would wake up soon.

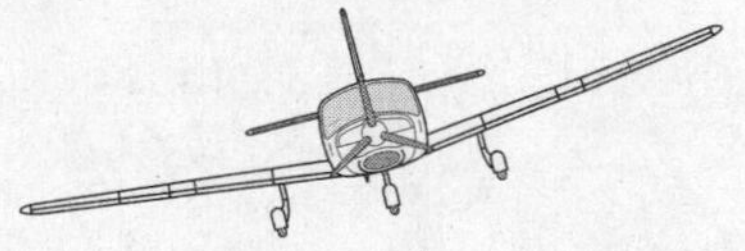

Storm Warnings

Their talking finally woke Kate, and she jumped up to hug Suzie Q. Chad decided this was a good time to slip away. He found Dad alone at the kitchen table, reading his Bible.

"Hey, Spitfire," Dad said. "The girls up?"

Chad nodded. "How soon can we get out of here?"

Dad snorted. "Suzie Q on your nerves already?"

"Nah. It's just that this place will be boring."

After a big breakfast, the Quentons had to sweep snow away from their walkways and driveway. In the harsh, sunlit white of the day, Chad noticed how Mr. and Mrs. Quenton had aged since he saw them last. They were a few years older than his dad anyway, but now he saw lines in their faces and around their eyes. Both were tall and light-haired with glasses and perfect teeth.

Both families toured the little compound where a couple of hundred kids from kindergarten to eighth grade lived during the school year. Many of their parents were missionaries to the Indians and Eskimos of northern Canada and Alaska.

Chad kept finding himself stealing glances at Suzie Q. She was as pretty as her last picture on the computer, but Chad tried not to get caught staring at her. He knew those braces would make her teeth as perfect as her mother's, and her freckles and long, strawberry-blonde hair almost made Chad forget that he hated girls.

"Do you have a CB radio in your ATV?" Mr. Quenton asked Dad, as the six of them trudged through the snow to the main buildings.

"Oh, yeah. You have to in these parts. Too much open space between towns. No decent cell coverage either. Can't risk getting stuck in the middle of nowhere with no communication."

"Did you hear anything last night about the weather that's supposed to be coming this way?"

Dad shook his head. "Truckers and people around here don't talk about it much unless it's out of the ordinary. Blizzards don't bother us much—"

"We heard it was supposed to be quite a storm coming in tonight," Mr. Quenton said. "A snow thunderstorm, something I've never heard of."

Dad smiled. "Pretty common. I'll keep an ear open when

Chad and I head back later this morning, but I wouldn't worry about it. In fact, you'd better get used to it. The next six months are going to be mighty cold and snowy."

Hugh Quenton wanted to hear all about AirQuest Adventures. After Dad told him how the little family organization was born, Hugh asked Chad about their adventures. "I hear you were the hero in the Indonesian jungles and that you and Kate helped rescue your dad in South America."

"Yeah, I guess." Chad was proud of his part in both those adventures, but what was he supposed to say? "What sports do you have in the Yukon?"

"Lots of basketball and volleyball in the winter and softball when the weather clears."

Kate and Suzie Q ran off to explore and to meet Suzie Q's new friends. Mrs. Quenton left to check on the infirmary. Chad, Dad, and Mr. Quenton went to the gym, housed in a huge Quonset hut building. Boys' and girls' basketball and volleyball games were being played all over the building at the same time.

"I'd get you into one of the games, Chad," Mr. Quenton said, "but this is an intramural league setup, different dorms against each other."

As Chad sat in the bleachers behind his dad and Mr. Quenton, he wished he could play basketball, but mostly he just wanted to get on the road toward home. It would be nice to have Dad all to himself for a few days. He hadn't been alone with Dad for more than a few hours for a long time.

"I'm sure glad you spotted this job opening," Hugh Quenton said, and Chad leaned forward to listen. "I think we're really going to like it here. Would you ever send your kids to a place like this?"

"Not on your life," Dad said. "As happy as I am for you getting this job, I frankly don't agree with places like this. I mean, if the missionary kids have to go somewhere, I'm glad it's a nice place with good leadership, but what a thing to do to a kid."

"You know, Bruce, I agree with you. In fact, I told the mission board that when they were interviewing me. I told them they should take the salary they were offering me and add some to it so teachers could be sent to the remote mission posts to teach the kids there." He glanced back at Chad. "That way they wouldn't have to be sent hundreds or even thousands of miles away from their parents for months at a time."

"What did they say?" Chad said.

"They showed me what that would cost, but they also told me that someone with my view was the kind of guy they would like running the place." He ran a hand through his thin hair. "Margie and I have already tried making this place as much like home as possible. We brought a bunch of used computers with us after we heard they had broadband high-speed access here."

"They do?" Chad said. "Clear up here in the boonies?"

"Yup." He waved toward the students. "These kids need low-cost daily contact with their parents, and we plan to make sure it happens."

"Good for you, Hugh," Dad said. "Is Margie running the infirmary?"

"Yeah, her nursing and my seminary training gave the mission board just what they wanted. The place used to count on circuit-riding nurses and the occasional doctor from a clinic in Old Sparrow. This is good for Margie. She had to work off base in Enid because she wasn't military. We like working together."

"I noticed Suzie Q, sorry, Sue, doesn't stay in the dorm. Or was she just trying to wait up for Kate last night?"

"No, because of her diabetes we like to have her with us at night. We try not to baby her, but we can't take chances yet either. They tell us that this child-onset type of diabetes will stabilize as she gets older and she'll be able to regulate her own medicine better."

"She's sure growing up into a beautiful girl."

"Kate, too."

"Thanks."

Chad was bored again. All this stuff about girls growing up and becoming beautiful was making him sick. It was true about Suzie Q, of course. He could see that. And people in Mukluk all thought Kate was cute, but he couldn't see it. His sister?

A sweaty little roly-poly boy with jet black hair and a red face ran up to Mr. Quenton and thrust a note into his hand. "Message for you, sir!" he said.

"Thanks, Oliver," Mr. Quenton said, and he excused himself.

"Can we get going, Dad?" Chad said.

"It won't be long, Spitfire. Pick a game and enjoy it."

"I can't tell what the score is anyway, and I can't play."

"You want to shoot some hoops at the church when we get home?"

"Yeah!"

"We'll leave within the hour."

Mr. Quenton returned. "Margie says the infirmary is full this morning. Some kind of a bug. I'll have to go into Old Sparrow to get some antibiotics."

"You're out?"

"No, but we didn't plan on all twelve beds being full today. If we get any more cases, we're going to have problems."

"Why don't we leave early and pick up the stuff in Old Sparrow?" Chad said.

"I couldn't ask you to do that," Mr. Quenton said.

"Shouldn't you stick around here?" Dad said.

"Probably, but I could just as easily send a staffer."

"No, let us do it," Dad said, and Chad silently cheered.

"If you wouldn't mind, Bruce, see if Sue's medicine has come in too. It's a pretty expensive supply, but I'll give you a note and they'll bill us."

On their way out of the school grounds, Chad noticed a huge machine. "What's that contraption?" he said.

"Looks like a combination snowplow and snowblower." Dad chuckled. "Looks as old as the hills, doesn't it?"

"I'd like to check it out," Chad said.

"You stay away from that thing. It looks like it hasn't been used in years."

In Old Sparrow, Dad filled the gas tank and asked the attendant what the Christian school used for snow removal. "They got an ancient plow out there," the man said. "Makes more of a mess than anything, but somehow they get it to fire up when they need it."

At the drugstore Dad showed the pharmacist the note from Hugh Quenton. "How's that new president workin' out over there?" the man said. "Seems like a good guy. Former military, you know."

"I know," Dad said. "I used to serve with him."

"You a chaplain too?"

"No, sir. Former fighter pilot."

Chad couldn't have been more proud and watched for the man's reaction.

"You don't say."

"Anyway, Hugh seems to be working out fine."

"Well," the pharmacist said, "we're low on antibiotics, but I'll give you what I have. His daughter's stuff hasn't come in yet. Last we heard it was airborne, but you know we get our stock from Edmonton. They fly a route that takes 'em through northwest B.C. and then up into the Yukon. They have stops in eight or ten places before they get to us."

Chad whistled. "So when will it get here?"

"Supposed to be tomorrow. We'll get more antibiotics then too, but we got word last night the pilot's hung up in Whitehorse in weather and can't promise when he'll get out."

"That so?" Dad said. "Well, at least that weather system is heading away from us."

"Yeah," the man said, "but haven't you heard? Something huge is brewing in the Brooks Range."

"The Brooks Range?" Chad said. "Isn't that a long way from here?"

The pharmacist leaned on the counter. "Yeah, but they get to us eventually. Nobody's traveling in the mountains up there, so they say."

"They seldom do," Dad said. "I wouldn't worry about snow in the Brooks."

"You're probably right, but when you hear about weather that far away, it sounds like something out of the ordinary."

"Even for here," Dad said as the man bagged the medicine.

"Yes, sir," the man said. "Even for here."

Forty minutes later Chad and Dad pulled into the Old Sparrow Christian School again. The sun rode high in a cloudless sky, and the modest, rambling complex of buildings actually looked pretty and serene. Suzie Q and Kate were waiting to say their good-byes. Hugh Quenton thanked Dad for the package and the news and said, "Margie sends her best and apologizes that she can't leave the infirmary just now. She'll look forward to a little more time with you when you come back Tuesday."

"Tell her I understand."

Dad and Chad hugged Kate, and Suzie Q actually hugged Chad. He couldn't remember the last time he had hugged a girl other than his sister, and he froze. He just stood there as she giggled at his discomfort. "See ya," he said.

As he backed away, Suzie Q looked right into his eyes, smiling. He turned and bumped into Dad.

"Whoa there, big guy," Dad said, and Chad felt himself blushing. Boy, was he glad his friends weren't here to see this.

Chad had not slept well the night before, and he became aware of it as soon as he settled in for the long ride home. He lowered the front passenger seat and tried to stretch out, thinking this was at least more comfortable than the sleeping bag on the floor last night. But the sun was so bright he had to hide his eyes. And Dad kept the CB on the whole way to monitor the weather. So Chad didn't really sleep. He just rested.

"Hard to believe they're talking about weather when you see a sky like this," Dad said.

"Um-hm," Chad mumbled. He hadn't seen a cloud. It was cold though, despite the harsh sun. The windows were edged with ice, and the ground was snow covered, but it sure didn't look like anything close to a blizzard was coming.

Over the CB came a warning from the weather bureau, predicting that the massive storm over Meat Mountain in the Brooks Range would still pack a wallop when it swept all the way to the Yukon Flats, Alaska, by nightfall.

"That's hard to believe," Dad mumbled as he grabbed the microphone. "This is Fighter Pilot westbound out of Old Sparrow, en route to Mukluk. Anybody seeing any of this weather yet?"

"Negative, Fighter Pilot. This is Fat Fox comin' at you from the west in an eighteen-wheeler. Lookin' fine from here, pardner, but there's also somethin' brewin' from the west."

"Repeat?"

"Hughes, that little town on the Koyukuk south of the forks, is buried."

"Ten-four," Dad said, then clicked off. "Chad, that makes no sense. One system coming down at us from the Brooks, and another sweeping east out of Koyukuk. They can't be the same storm front, but they appear to be on a collision course."

It was obvious Chad was going to get no sleep. He sat up and raised the seat back. "What happens then?"

"Don't think I've ever seen it," Dad said. "Don't think I want to either. We'll just speed it up here and plan on getting into Mukluk before either one of those fronts hits."

Though the heater in the ATV worked perfectly, icy drafts seeped in around Chad's window, making him hunker down in his down-filled parka.

"Cover the temperature without looking, Dad," he said. "Let's guess."

"Well, didn't we just hear it on the radio?"

"I didn't. But if you think you did, go ahead and guess."

"Low teens," Dad said, fingers covering the readout on the dash.

"Lower than that," Chad said. "Single digits."

Dad pulled his hand away. Five degrees. "What do you win?"

"I get to drive."

"Not a chance," Dad said smiling. "But let's guess how long it will take for the temperature to drop. I say we'll be down to zero within two hours."

"It's the middle of the day. I say it stays the same until late this afternoon."

"But we're heading toward two storms, Spitfire."

Chad shrugged. "So, if I'm wrong, you get to keep driving."

"Very funny."

Chad sat, shoulders hunched, drowsy in the blasts from the heater. It made him think of one of his and Kate's favorite phrases—"cotie, cotie"—their childhood way of saying "cozy." It had begun when their mother made a fire once when Dad was away. In their footie pajamas and blankets, they had settled in front of the fireplace with popcorn, singing, telling stories, and cuddling with Mom until Dad got home and joined them. Mom had said, "Isn't this cozy?"

And Kate had repeated, "Cotie."

Chad added, "Cotie, cotie."

And now "cotie, cotie" was how the whole family

described such settings. When they were together and huddled against the cold, comfortable and warm and protected, the situation was “cotie, cotie.”

But a glance at the horizon told Chad it wouldn’t be that way in the ATV for long.

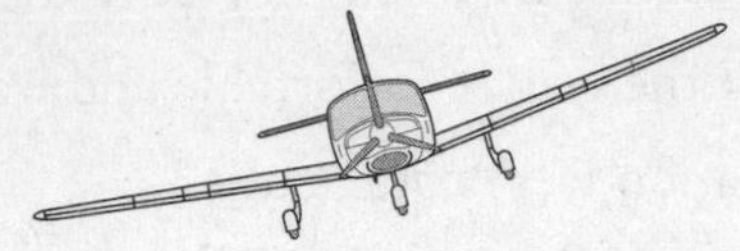

White on White

Chad stared. He'd never seen anything like it.

Dad got back on the radio. "This is Fighter Pilot in an ATV heading west, midway between Spike Mountain and Chandalar. Anybody coming east with a black cloud behind you?"

"Roger, ATV," came an immediate answer. "It's supposed to be just a snowstorm, but it looks like the thundershowers we used to get in Nebraska."

"Midwest boy, eh?" Dad said.

"Roger. You?"

"Michigan," Dad said.

"Close enough. This thing hasn't caught me yet, but I can see it. I'm trying to outrun it, hoping it turns one way or the other. You're going to run right into it. Where you headed?"

"Mukluk, over."

"A couple more hours if it stays dry."

"Dry as a bone right here," Dad said. "You may escape it altogether unless it runs you down."

"I'm keeping an eye on it in my rearview mirror, and I gotta tell you, it's coming fast. Black in the distance and cloudy above me already."

"You see clouds other than on the horizon?" Dad said. "I must be in a funny spot. Here it's just sun and blue skies, but dark on the horizon."

"You're in for a good show, Fighter."

"Wave at us when you pass," Dad said. "Red ATV."

"Roger, Fighter. I've got a big orange wrapper, heading for the railroads."

"How far out of Mukluk are you?" Dad said.

"About half an hour east," came the answer.

"Everything clear there?"

"It was. I gotta guess Mukluk is getting hit already."

"Should I dig in and hole up somewhere?"

"Where? There's precious little between where you are and Mukluk. I'd keep chugging. Still looks like just thunder clouds to me."

"Question is, is it the one out of Koyukuk or the one out of the Brooks Range?"

"Gotta be Koyukuk. Can't see anything out of the Brooks coming this low, can you?"

"Hope not."

"Good luck."

About forty-five minutes later Chad spotted the orange eighteen-wheeler in the distance. "There he is, Dad."

"Greetings from the Fighter, Orange Man," Dad said. "You copy?"

"Ten-four. I'm outrunning our dark chaser for now, but I understand it's hit Mukluk pretty heavy."

"Will I be able to get in there?" Dad said.

"Probably. I'm not seeing much traffic coming from your way. Other people scared to be out?"

"There's never much traffic up here, man," Dad said. "You ought to know that."

"I guess. But it's never this light except at night. Anybody ahead of me?"

"Come to think of it," Dad said, "we've passed only a couple of trucks and maybe three cars. You've got the road all to yourself."

"Don't know how good that is if the storm catches me."

"Take a big storm to stop you, Orange."

"Ten-four."

With that the big rig swept past them heading east. The driver waved and blew his huge air horns. Dad and Chad smiled and waved, and both drivers clicked their transmitters.

"This is fun," Chad said.

"For now," Dad said. "We don't want to get caught in a storm."

"If that rig can make it, we can."

"Oh, no. We're a whole lot lighter. We may be more maneuverable, but it takes a lot to stop a semi. We can pick our way through water and snow and ice, but if we get a whiteout, we're in trouble."

"Why? What happens?"

"It's impossible to see anything. Your headlights are useless. They just point directly into the swirling snow and shine right back into your eyes. And it doesn't make any difference whether it's day or night. The blizzard blinds you." He turned the heater down a notch. "During the day, the sun only makes everything whiter. At night, your headlights make it impossible. The only advantage at night is that you can sometimes see other headlights coming at you. But you never know if the other driver has seen you. All you can do is pull off the road as far as you can and keep your flashers on."

"Not your headlights?"

"They might be able to see your headlights better, but you risk blinding them too. If they don't see you till the last minute and you blind them with your lights, you're just as likely to get hit." Dad pressed his lips together, checked both side mirrors and the rearview mirror. "I'd turn back, but we're well over halfway home. And it might not be that bad. I've never seen a storm yet that I couldn't get through."

"I still say this is fun. It's kind of scary, but exciting. I wouldn't mind being caught in a blizzard again."

"You've never been in a real blizzard."

"Sure I have, Dad. I walked home through a huge snowstorm once."

"Did someone actually call it a blizzard?"

"Yeah."

"Well, a *real* blizzard is when there's so much snow that you can't see in front of your face. When you lose your orientation, have no idea which direction you're heading. We never would have let you walk home from school in a real blizzard."

"Don't you think it would be great though, Dad? To have to fight your way through the weather?"

"I thought so when I was a kid," Dad said. "Back then I thought everything turned out the way it was supposed to. TV shows and movies and books all seemed to have happy endings. But life's not like that, is it?"

Chad shook his head. He wasn't going to argue, but he still thought it would be fun to be stranded. Maybe not too far from home, but stranded anyway. How would they get out? What would they do?

His eyes felt heavy, so he closed them and thought about trekking through the frozen tundra. He woke sometime later with a start. It was cloudy and getting dark. "That came up awfully quick," he said.

"Not really," Dad said, driving more slowly. A freezing rain was hitting the windshield. "It's been building, and the road's slick. I just hope it dissipates as it heads east. It'd be nice if both those storms, whether they meet or not, would peter out before they hit Old Sparrow."

"How far are we from home?"

"About fifty miles."

The clock on the dash said three o'clock, and Chad went back to sleep. When he awoke in what seemed just a few minutes, Dad was hunched forward in the seat, his face even with the steering wheel.

"Whoa!" Chad said, peering into pitch blackness. "Welcome to Alaska. How long did I sleep anyway?"

"About an hour and a half."

"No kidding. How fast are you going? Or should I say how slow?"

"You tell me. I don't dare take my eyes off the road—or what I can see of it."

Chad studied the speedometer. "It's hardly registering. How much farther to Mukluk?"

"Less than twenty miles," Dad said. "But don't get your hopes up. At this rate it might take us all night, if we get there at all."

"We'll get there," Chad said. The temperature gauge read below zero. "How can it snow when it's this cold?"

"I guess it's just used to it." Dad grinned but kept his eyes on the road. "Nobody ever told Alaska it was too cold for snow."

A bright light suddenly flashed in the distance. "What was that?" Chad said.

"Lightning," Dad said.

"Is that what Mr. Quenton was talking about?"

"Must be. Snow thunderstorms are supposed to be pretty common in the mountains. I've heard of them, but I've never been in one. They remind me of the tornadoes in the Midwest, so I don't like them much."

"I love them! I love storms! Especially when we're safe and warm and together. Cotie, cotie."

"Yeah, I hope," Dad said. "I'd rather be cozy in our own house, wouldn't you?"

"Yeah, but it wouldn't be as exciting."

"Driving like this is not exciting. The only two vehicles

I've seen were heading the other way. A snowplow and a squad car, lights flashing."

"A snowplow going the other way?"

"Surprised me too, Spitfire. Go figure."

"We could sure use one going *this* way."

"I'd settle right in behind him," Dad said. He kept his eyes forward but rolled his head around, appearing to try to loosen his neck muscles. "Get on the CB and see who you can rouse."

"Are we too far from Old Sparrow to get the Quentons?"

"Oh, sure. Just ask for anybody traveling within fifty miles of Mukluk."

"Breaker, channel nineteen," Chad said, "this is Spitfire with Fighter Pilot, heading west into Mukluk. We going to make it?"

"Where are you, Spitfire?" came the reply.

"Twenty miles east," Chad said. "What's your handle?"

"ASPERN."

"ASPERN?" Chad repeated.

"Alaska State Police Emergency Radio Network. How many in your party?"

"Two," Chad said, "and it's no party."

"What're you driving?"

"Four-wheel ATV."

"Ten-four. Deep snow where you are?"

"Roger."

"You're going to have tough going, Spitfire. Consider pulling off and waiting this out. Emergency vehicles are busy in Mukluk. No electricity, power lines down, lots of accidents. If you're not hurt, try not to ask for help."

"Give me that," Dad said, taking the mike without looking.

"This is Fighter Pilot, ASPERN," he said. "Any advice on where we should go to wait this out?"

"If you're east, there's nothing till you get here. You live in Mukluk?"

"Roger."

"Better try to make it then. Got a generator at home?"

"Roger."

"You might want to get that going to keep your pipes from freezing."

"We're looking forward to relaxing by a warm fire, ASPERN."

"Roger. I know the feeling. I've been called to Venetie, and they don't even think it's the same storm."

"You're kidding! Is it the one that was supposed to have come out of the Brooks Range?"

"Roger. Don't know how it could have gotten past this front so fast and gone so far south. It's the bigger of the two, though. High winds, whiteouts, twisters, you name it."

"*Twisters*?"

"Well, not tornadoes, but close to it, they say. Better keep this frequency open, Fighter. Seventy-twos to you and Spitfire."

"Same back at ya," Dad said. "You'll be passing us here in a while if you're headed east. We're in a red ATV."

"Ten-four."

Half an hour later, as the ATV crawled along the covered roadway and Dad picked his way through the snow, trying to stay on course, Chad saw flashing police-car lights coming toward them. "That you, Fighter?" came the radio message.

"Ten-four."

"Deep drifts ahead of you. If you get hung up, are you prepared?"

"Ten-four."

"Need anything? I've got a few flares and some survival blankets."

"Got all we need, ASPERN."

"All the best."

Dad clicked his microphone twice, and they rolled slowly on into the storm.

Within minutes Dad had to downshift and weave across the road to stay in the shallowest drifts. Some were as deep as three feet already, and Chad tried to talk him into driving right through them, but Dad would have no part of it.

"Plowing through them might be fun at home, out of the storm, and on our own property," he said. "And we both know this rig can handle it. But we've got to get home. I hope this thing blows through and dies so we can get back to Old Sparrow by Tuesday."

"Storms around here never last long, do they?"

"Not usually, and it's a little early for one this severe. But sometimes they follow one right after another. That could strand us for days."

"Kate wouldn't mind. No school!"

"She'd have to go to school there, Chad. Those poor kids probably never get snowed out of school."

"Yuck."

"Let me show you what I mean about the headlights," Dad said and flashed the brights. They seemed to shine straight up. Chad squinted at the brilliant white light gleaming off the driving snowfall.

He nodded. "Wow."

Suddenly, no matter where Dad drove, the snow was two or three feet deep. Chad always loved to see his dad in action, doing whatever he had to do. He played with the controls, feathered the gas pedal, downshifted, steered this way and that, and kept driving. He was slipping and sliding, but the ATV was still upright and moving, though awfully slowly. Even with the oversized tires and the high ride, they could hear the snow scraping the bottom of the ATV.

"Hang on," he told Chad. "If we don't pick up some speed, we're going to get stuck in one of these drifts. Let me know if you see anything coming. I'm deciding right now to head right if we see anything coming at us."

Dad downshifted one more time and gunned the engine. The tires spun, then bit, and the car lurched. They probably weren't going more than twenty miles an hour, but after crawling along, to Chad it seemed they were flying. And for the first time he wondered what would happen if something appeared before them? Going this fast, would Dad be able to stop or swerve?

"If I can just get through this stretch and onto some clearer road," Dad said, "I think we can make it."

Dad ran smack into a five-foot drift, and the ATV nearly toppled, but he steered into the lean and they bounced and hit another drift. "Cool!" Chad shouted, but it wasn't as cool as all that. They couldn't go much farther unless they found shallower snow.

“Does it feel to you like we’re still on the road?” Dad said.

“No clue!”

“I don’t think we are,” Dad said. “All I see is white. Just pray there are no ditches close by.”

But there were. And Dad found a deep one.

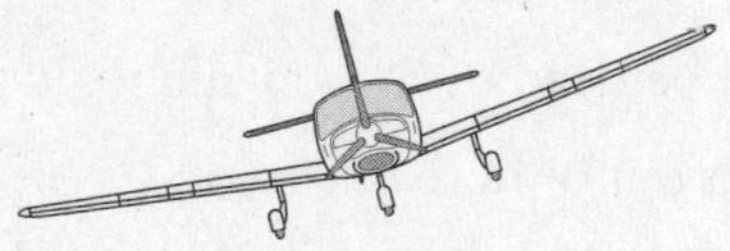

On Foot

The ATV slipped off the steep shoulder, bouncing from one huge drift to another and then sliding backward into the ditch at the side of the road. Chad's head snapped back and his neck pressed hard against the headrest. He sat stunned as the headlights illuminated a tiny avalanche. Great chunks of snow slid over the hood of the car, covering the lights. In the eerie dimness, the light dancing in crazy directions as the lamps were covered, the last big wave of packed snow spread across the windshield.

Darkness engulfed them until Dad flipped on the inside lights. "You okay?" he said.

"Just whacked my head on the dash," Chad said, feeling a bump rising on his forehead.

Dad shifted into reverse and gunned the engine, then into drive and did the same. They were hung up, going nowhere. He shut off the engine.

"We'll freeze!" Chad shouted. "Turn that back on!"

"If I do, we'll be dead of carbon-monoxide poisoning. We've got to get out of here."

Dad unstrapped his seat belt and tried to open the door. It wouldn't budge. Chad pushed on his door. It opened about two inches. "I'm going to turn on the key just long enough so we can lower the windows," Dad said. "We'll have to dig out."

Dad pushed all four window buttons at once, and they whined down. Snow tumbled in around them. Something gave way above them with a thump, and Chad knew more snow was pressing on top of the car.

"There's not a lot of air left," Dad said. "Don't panic. Breathe normally and steadily, but start digging out. We don't know which way is softer or more shallow, so you go out your window and I'll go out mine."

"Where do we put the snow?" Chad said.

"Right behind us inside the car."

Dad crouched in the driver's seat and pulled on his huge mittens. He turned toward the open window and the snow pushing in around him and began pawing at it like a dog, sending it flying behind him onto the seat.

"Dad! Don't we need our stuff out of the back?"

"We'll come back for it! We need to tunnel out of here first."

Chad put on his gloves and hat and zipped his parka all the way to his neck. He copied his dad's position and started scooping snow behind him. Dad seemed to be getting nowhere but it wasn't long before Chad was able to crawl out and begin tunneling toward the surface, wherever that was.

He turned and hollered, "Dad, this way's easier! Follow me!"

Dad scrambled out through Chad's window and pressed up behind him. But the snow around the car was deep and soft. "Stand on my shoulders," Dad said, "and dig through to the top."

Chad grew panicky. Was he short of air? He was breathing heavily, but maybe it was just the work. Surely this was not like a real avalanche where the snow packs so tight and heavy that you might as well be encased in cement.

Chad struggled to step onto his dad's knees as Dad leaned back. A faint pinging noise in the car told him he hadn't shut his door after opening it a crack. The dim interior light was all he could see. He was fast growing claustrophobic and dug frantically, making the snow shift and fall all around Dad.

Strangely, it was cold, but not bitter; the avalanche protected them from the howling winds. When Chad reached the surface, he would be in the snowstorm, huge flakes blowing every which way and the wind stinging and freezing his exposed flesh. He wondered how far they were from home.

Chad set one foot on Dad's hip and reached higher, digging through the loosely packed snow and making it fall on his head, into his face, and down his body onto his father. "Sorry, Dad."

"Just keep going!" Dad shouted, as he grabbed Chad's boots and pushed. Chad was amazed at his dad's strength; it was as if he stood on a strong ladder, his dad pushing him higher as he scooped and scooped, trying to break through.

Finally Chad realized he was standing straight up, his dad with a hand under each boot, arms fully extended. He felt Dad's arms shaking; he surely couldn't hold Chad for long. Chad felt his own arms weakening as the blood rushed away from them. He pawed and scratched and dug with all his might.

Then, with one hand he broke through the snow. "I'm through!" he cried.

"Can you crawl out?" Dad said.

Chad stood on his tiptoes and reached with both hands, trying to gain purchase on the soft, shifting surface of the snow. He grabbed and pulled himself away from his dad, but as soon as he put all his weight on the snow, it crumbled beneath him. He seemed to be swimming, trying to stay above the drifts without pushing too much more down onto Dad.

"Dad! Are you all right?"

"I'm coming!" Dad shouted.

Chad barely heard the muffled sound. He decided to try to find some footing atop the snow and crab-walk away from the hole. Unfortunately, he had pushed chunks of snow behind him and into Dad's way.

"Just keep going!" Dad yelled. "I'll find you!"

Chad stretched out on the surface, trying to distribute his weight as evenly as possible so he wouldn't plunge back through. He wriggled and half crawled to where he thought the ATV was buried. He hoped it would provide a more solid base. The wind and snow bit into his face and his eyes stung. He brushed the snow away with his glove, but just smeared his vision more. Still, he thought he could make out the faint glow of the headlights under the snow.

Chad thought he heard Dad scratching his way to the surface behind him, but the wind was so strong and the snow so thick that he was afraid it was his imagination. He didn't know whether to move back to help Dad or stay where he was and let Dad find him.

"Dad!" he shouted.

"Stay where you are!" he heard faintly.

But Chad felt himself sliding, drifting with the shifting snow. He struggled to stay over the buried car, and when he felt his feet dropping, he windmilled with his hands, trying to stay upright. His boots finally stopped at something solid, and he realized he was standing tiptoe atop the ATV. The snow was up to just under his shoulders. Though encased in the snow bank, the lower part of his body felt warmer than the upper, which was exposed to the wind and watery snow. He oriented himself by the power-line poles, faced the road, and waited for his dad.

Soon a mittened hand thrust up out of the snow about six feet to his right, and Chad tried to reach it. He couldn't move. "Dad!" he shouted. "Over here!"

Dad thrashed and fought his way to the surface, then crab-walked until he slipped down into the snow and stood atop the ATV. Being a head taller than Chad, Dad stuck farther out of the snow.

"Now what?" Chad shouted above the violence of the storm.

"Now we breathe awhile," Dad said.

"How are we going to get home, Dad?"

"We'll need backpacks with some food. Flashlights. Snowshoes. Compasses."

"That's all in the car."

"I know. We'll have to dig down and get it, or we'll be stuck here. I'll make the first attempt."

"And what happens if the snow caves in on you?"

"Then you'll have to come and get me."

A few minutes later, Dad said, "Stay here."

"Like I've got a choice," Chad said, waving to show that only his arms would move.

Dad tunneled toward the passenger-side window and was soon out of sight. "Can you hear me?" he shouted.

"Yes!"

"I'm trying to keep an open area above me so I can breathe and come back the same way. I'll start tossing stuff to you. Be watching for it."

Chad thought he heard an engine in the distance, maybe a truck or car heading their way. He tried to clear his eyes and scan the horizon, but he saw nothing. He just felt the vibration and heard something.

"Dad! Can you hear that?"

No reply. Suddenly Chad heard the ATV start up. "Dad! What are you doing?"

Soon Dad returned to the surface, pushing two pairs of snowshoes and ski poles ahead of him. "Grab these!" he said.

"Why'd you start the car?" Chad said.

"It might melt some snow and be easier to pull out later.

I have to keep an eye on it though, because if there's snow packed in the exhaust pipe, it'll cause a backup, overheat, and maybe catch fire."

Dad went back down. The wind shifted and calmed, and Chad thought he detected two headlights far in the distance to the west. Before he could say anything, Dad tossed him two backpacks and shouted, "We're overheating! I've got to turn it off!"

"But Dad!" Chad said too late. Dad had disappeared.

The truck sound grew louder, and a snowplow came into view. It was moving more slowly than Chad had ever seen one go. The drifts before it were so huge that it couldn't just blast through as usual. This plow would get up some speed, then seem to waver and even wobble, then slow and start again.

Finally, about a quarter mile from where Chad stood anchored in the snow, the snowplow began to pick up speed. Soon it was noisily humming along, pushing four- and five-foot drifts ahead of it and off to the side. There was only one problem—it was on the wrong side of the road!

The driver couldn't possibly see Chad—the snow was so deep. But the plow was in the westbound lane, heading east and pushing snow off to its left. Chad stood right in the path of the hurtling snow.

Chad waved and shouted and then screamed as the

snowplow bore down on him. He knew the plow blade wouldn't hit him, because if the truck got that close to the edge of the road, it would tumble down into the ditch with the ATV.

The driver wasn't slowing. Chad wished he had a flashlight. "Dad!" he shouted, and then the plow came roaring by going at least forty miles an hour. He hid his face with his arms, and rocks and dirt and snow blasted him. The plow dumped hundreds of pounds of snow in the ditch, covering him. He had no idea how deep the snow was above him now.

"What was that?" Dad shouted, sounding far away.

"Snowplow!" Chad hollered.

"You all right?"

"Buried!" Chad said.

"Dig yourself out again, Spitfire. You're not under big drifts now. I've got everything, and I'm coming up!"

Chad huffed and puffed as he dug and scrambled up. Scraping through the freshly plowed snow and dirt and rocks was the hardest part of the ordeal so far. But, finally, he reached the howling wind and gulped the frigid, but precious, air. He crawled nearer the road, up out of the ditch to where he could stand on the plowed road. He turned to wait and watch for Dad.

When Dad's head finally popped up out of the snow, Chad waved.

"Where are the rest of our supplies?" Dad yelled.

"Under the snow somewhere!"

"We've got to have them, Spitfire! Help me dig."

Chad was so exhausted by the time they had spread-eagled their bodies and picked through the snow for their supplies that he could hardly get up. "We don't need the snowshoes, do we," he said, "now that the road is plowed?"

"We don't know how far it's plowed or how long it'll be clear," Dad said. "We'd better take them anyway. We have to keep moving. Just be glad you don't live near the South Pole."

"Why?" Chad said. They were on solid ground now, strapping on their backpacks, checking their flashlights, and tying their snowshoes around their shoulders.

"The South Pole hovers around one hundred degrees below zero during the winter, especially during the months when the sun doesn't shine. Then in the summer, the temperature shoots as high as sixty or even thirty degrees *below*. They think it's balmy."

Somehow, talking about a place even more frigid and miserable than where he was didn't make Chad feel any warmer. "How far do you figure we'll have to walk?" he said.

"We're less than ten miles from home," Dad said, "but I sure hope we'll see someone on the road before we have to walk that far. Let's each eat a granola bar or some trail mix. We're going to need the energy."

They trudged off into the darkness, eating and leaning into the wind. At one point Dad stopped and dug out some petroleum jelly, which he smeared on both their faces. Snow was drifting across the road again, and they soon had to stop and put on their snowshoes. Chad had always compared walking in snowshoes to walking with tennis rackets tied to your boots. They took some getting used to, but it was a lot easier going than sliding a foot or two into the snow with every step.

Two hours later Chad didn't feel as if they had gone far at all. They were wet, cold, exhausted, and hungry again. Dad found two more granola bars in Chad's backpack, and they ate them quickly.

"Can we make it all the way?" Chad said.

"We have to, Spitfire. There's no shelter anywhere but back at the car, and if we cleared the snow around it, it could get buried again. We just have to put one foot in front of the other until we get home. Just through those trees over there you can see the lights of Mukluk."

It sure looked far away. But just then all the lights in Mukluk went out.

"They'll come back on," Dad said. "Remember the trooper told us the power was off hours ago. It came back on then. It'll come back on again."

"I'm glad you're so sure," Chad muttered. "Because I'm not."

"Keep trudging, big guy," Dad said. "Sometimes tough times get easier when you're down to fewer options. Right now we have only one. Keep going."

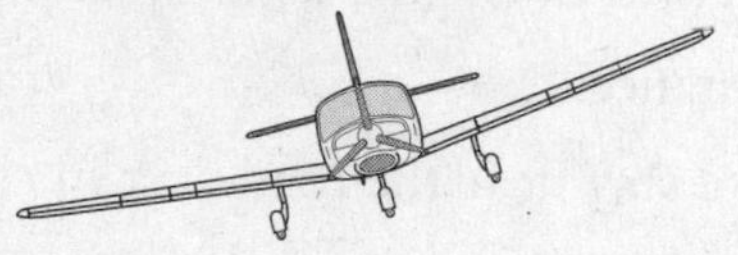

Home

Dad tried to motivate Chad as they marched through the blowing snow. "*Left*, right, *left*, right, *left*." He made up silly ditties to keep them moving. "*Left*, right *left*, right. I *left* my wife and thirty-one children at *home* in the kitchen without any gingerbread *left*. *Left*, right, *left*."

The petroleum jelly smeared on his otherwise exposed cheeks helped a little, but still Chad was cold to the bone. His feet felt like huge blocks of ice attached to the wide snowshoes, but he forced himself to keep lifting his knees and trudging along. Dad stopped occasionally to shine his flashlight on the compass.

"If I have it figured right, we're on a direct course to our house."

Chad saw no cars, no trucks, no snowplows, no lights, no moon, no stars, no anything. Suddenly Dad turned off the highway and started through a wide-open plain toward a forest in the distance.

"Shouldn't we stay near the road, just in case?" Chad said.

"We might as well walk in a straight line toward home, rather than on the road. You want to sing?"

"Dad, the last thing I want to do is sing."

"You want me to sing?"

"Check that. The second to the last thing I want to do is sing. The very last thing I want to do is hear you sing."

Dad laughed. "I wonder how far the storm extends."

"This one or the one out of the Brooks Range?" Chad said.

"Either. I just wonder if the snow has hit Old Sparrow yet."

For several hours — Chad guessed three or four — they trudged on. Dad flashed his light between trees to areas they could walk, calling out frequently to encourage Chad or stopping for water. The woods seemed to protect the ground from the bigger drifts, and while they were still probably two feet above the soil, at least they weren't slogging through the really deep snow.

Finally, as they came into a clearing, they looked up and the storm had blown over. No more snow. No more cloud cover. The wind was even slowing. Chad was struck by the beauty of the early-morning sky. It was a velvety blue-black. The stars were still ablaze.

"We should be home within the hour," Dad said. "It'll still be dark, but we'll get there."

Chad picked up his pace with that news. He and Dad ate the rest of the trail mix and granola bars, and he felt a brief surge of energy. Sometimes he shut his eyes and pretended he was sleepwalking. He no longer had to fight the wind and the watery flakes, so he could breathe easier, but he still didn't know how he could keep going for another hour. He was numb. Every muscle ached. Like a toddler in a snow-suit, he walked stiff-legged, carefully lifting his feet enough to make the snowshoes work the way they were designed.

Dad wrapped an arm around Chad's shoulders. "When we get home, we'll make a big fire in the fireplace and I'll get the gas generator going. We'll see if the phones are working, and I'll try to call Old Sparrow. We'll change our clothes and sleep in front of the fire under the biggest quilts we have."

"I wish I could sleep now!" Chad muttered.

"Me too, Spitfire," Dad said. "Me too."

Nearly an hour later, Dad said, "Chad, would you like to see the prettiest sight I've seen in a long time? Look straight ahead."

Dad shined his powerful flashlight beam into the distance, and Chad could barely see the outline of the small hangar at the edge of their property where Dad kept two of his remaining double-engine planes. "Thank God," Chad said. It still looked a long way off.

"Come on," Dad said. "Just stay steady, and we'll get there."

When they finally got to the fence outside the hangar, Dad held the barbed wire down so Chad could flop over. One of his snowshoes got hung up, and he fell face first into the snow. He quickly brushed himself off, thinking how predictable that had been. As if they hadn't already been through enough.

Dad paused. "I don't even want to think about how frozen those engines are in the unheated hangar."

Chad walked on alone, his eyes on the garage and then the back door of the house.

"The hangar doors are frozen shut and drifted over," Dad said, catching up.

Chad couldn't even grunt. All he wanted was to get inside.

The garage was also entombed in snow, and when they reached the back door of the house, they had to dig several feet of snow away before it would open. Chad staggered up the steps. Everything was dark, and the house was cold, but it was warmer than being outside.

"Get out of those clothes and get dried off," Dad said, starting to peel off his own stuff. "Massage your fingers and toes to get the blood circulating. I'm going to get the generator going."

A few moments later, wood was piled high in the fireplace, and the radio was tuned to the emergency weather station. Chad laid quilts out in front of the fireplace while his dad lit the fire. When the lights came on, Dad started heating cider in the electric coffee pot.

"Phone lines are dead," Dad said. "Bring your laptop down."

"What if my battery's low?"

"I have another socket on the generator."

Chad shuddered. "Let me get warm first."

"Fair enough. I don't suppose there's anything we can do for anybody right now anyway, no matter what they need."

Chad curled up in a sleeping bag under a quilt. He watched as Dad unplugged the answering machine from the wall. He plugged it into the generator, which was vented to the outside so the exhaust wouldn't create carbon monoxide in the house.

The generator was so loud that Chad couldn't hear the clicking of the machine as it reset itself and Dad played back the messages. "Chad!" he said. "Come and listen."

Chad was finally warm and comfortable and almost asleep, but he crawled out from under the covers and leaned in toward the answering machine. The message was from the Old Sparrow Christian School.

"Bruce, this is Hugh Quenton. It's pitch black here, and it's the middle of the afternoon. The forecasts are scary. Thunder snowstorms are coming from two directions and are expected to converge. They're predicting twister-type winds, several inches of snow, closed roads, and probably power and phone outages. Your daughter is at the computer now, trying to bang out a message to you so you'll get it before we lose power."

Chad would have to check his email right away.

"We've got a problem here, buddy, some kind of an epidemic. A lot of our kids and staff have come down with it, and we don't know what it is. Kate and Sue both show symptoms. I'm not feeling so hot myself, and though Marge won't admit it, I think she's coming down with it too."

Dad frowned. "Oh, Katie," he whispered.

"Seems like anybody who had any contact with the infirmary or with people who were in the infirmary are getting it and getting it quick," Mr. Quenton said. "We've got a call in to the druggist in Old Sparrow, but he says the last he heard his air shipment made it as far as McDougall Pass. That's about a hundred miles to the east of him. By the time he gets the stuff, if he does, it's unlikely we'll be able to get to him or him to us."

"Dad! We can get it!"

"*Shhh!*"

"We need antibiotics, and we need them in a bad way. And Sue needs more of her insulin sometime within the next two days." Mr. Quenton paused, and Chad heard a dim rumbling. "Did you hear that? That's thunder! Never heard thunder in the winter before." Heavy static crackled on the line. "It's starting to rain here, Bruce, of all things. Looks like a heavy sleet on the windows, and like I say, it's dark as night here."

Chad didn't like the sound of Mr. Quenton's voice.

"I'd better get off the phone, but if you could call someone, let authorities know, get us some help or something, I'd sure appreciate it. Hope you and Chad get home all right and that your place is spared whatever's coming at us. Call us if you can and— "

Mr. Quenton was cut off by a huge boom, more static, and then nothing. The next message was from the Mukluk Sheriff, asking Dad if he could help with emergency relief in town. "We don't expect to have power much longer, Bruce, but call us if you can."

"I can't call anybody," Dad said, checking the phone again. "I can't believe Katie's sick already. I wish she were with us." He paused. "Come on, let's pray."

After praying for everyone sick at the school, Dad ran an extension cord from the generator to the radio and set the radio near the fireplace, far enough from the generator that they could hear it.

"I'd like to get word to the state police about our car," Dad said. "And I'd like to offer to help with the relief effort in town."

"Get some sleep," Chad managed. "You can't help anybody now."

"You're probably right." Dad collapsed into his bedroll and was asleep before Chad. Chad fell asleep listening to local weather reports and emergency bulletins that merely told him what he had walked through.

Chad slept so soundly that when he awoke several hours later he was in the exact position as when he'd gone to sleep. He dragged himself out of his sleeping bag and stoked the fire, adding logs until it burst back to life. Dad stirred, rolled over, and kept sleeping. Chad sat near the fire, still tired and achy, but feeling a lot better. It was snowing, not heavily, but enough to cover the drifts with a fresh blanket.

Chad checked the phone. Still dead. He went to his cold room, grabbed his laptop, set it next to the generator and booted up. He found several email messages, mostly junk except for Kate's. He'd never seen her so urgent.

"We all have fevers," she wrote, "and huge storms are coming. If I wasn't sick and if I couldn't tell from the others how much sicker I'm going to be, I'd love being stranded here with Suzie Q. She only has a little medicine left, and her parents feel guilty about that. But they did all they could. They arranged for more to be flown in, in plenty of time, but who knew the storms would come? We're supposed to lose power too. I feel so achy and sick. I hope they get some medicine in here soon. When you come back, call me on your wrist TV when you're within a mile or so. Write back as soon as you get this."

Chad quickly answered, wondering if Kate would be well enough to read it. He went back to the fireplace and listened to the radio, keeping the volume low to let his dad sleep. What he heard gave him chills all over again.

"This is the last report from the United States Weather Bureau headquartered in Beaver in the Yukon Flats. Even by northern Alaskan standards, the twin thunder snowstorms that have ravaged the northeastern part of the state have been record breaking. A huge front rolling out of the Brooks Range north of the Kobuk Valley has caught, overtaken, and mixed with the same sort of storm front that seems to have originated in the Bering Strait, swept through Kotzebue Sound, gained momentum in Koyukuk, and blasted through Mukluk yesterday.

"These twin storm fronts, either of which alone has the potential for mass destruction, now form one giant weather pattern that has hugged the frozen Porcupine River bed. The new hybrid storm picked up steam, rolling over Spike Mountain near the Canadian border, dumping several inches of hail, ice, rain, and snow on the area in a direct line with McDougall Pass.

"Old Sparrow and everything to the west is under heavy drifts, and the snow continues with high winds, downed power and phone lines, impassable roads, and communications virtually at a standstill. Except for infrequent shortwave radio traffic, no news is going into or coming out of the region."

Chad leaned closer to the radio.

"Ironically," the newscaster continued, "yet another huge blizzard has settled in McDougall Pass and threatens to join the others to form a three-headed monster, the likes of which even this area has never seen. One can only imagine the destruction. Emergency medical technicians and power and phone company employees are working to bring relief to tiny Mukluk. Power is being returned slowly, though phone lines may be down for days."

Chad wished Dad had heard this. But on the other hand, he was glad Dad was still asleep. Dad had this thing about wanting to be in the center of the action, going where he was needed, doing whatever needed to be done. That was all well and good, but he needed his sleep—and it was still dangerous out there. Chad didn't know where and when they would be needed, but if his dad got his rest, he would be ready when the time came.

There would be plenty of work to go around, and Chad knew Dad would be eager to somehow get back to Old Sparrow. Those people, including Kate, were in deep trouble. If this bug and Suzie Q's diabetes could not be treated, they faced dangers worse than the snowstorms.

Venturing Out

In the morning Dad did wonders with the electric skillet. Although they had only bacon and eggs, Chad couldn't remember such a tasty and filling breakfast. After checking the dead phones again, Dad assigned Chad the task of packing everything they would need for a flight into the storm area.

"A *flight*?" Chad said.

Dad nodded. "We'll use the ski plane. There'll be no driving in there, maybe for days. We can't leave those people stranded. I may be the only one who can get into town if those medicines do arrive. And if they don't, I may have to meet the delivery pilot in McDougall Pass."

Chad slowly shook his head.

"You don't have to come along if you don't want to," Dad said. "But I could use you on the radio while I'm keeping an eye on the weather and the ground."

"Of course I want to come. I can just hardly believe you're doing this."

"Chad, my only daughter is in there with a family I've cared about for years, not to mention all those kids I don't even know. If I were a parent of one of them, I would want to believe somebody was making an effort to get in there with help."

"But aren't the authorities doing that? They have to know that the school is stranded."

"I'm sure they do, Chad, but what can they do? You know every law enforcement and emergency team is overloaded just trying to restore power and make the roads passable."

Chad packed food, first-aid stuff, extra clothes, gloves, boots, and hats. He also gathered their snowshoes and snowmobile suits. And, as Kate suggested, he included their wrist TVs.

Meanwhile Dad rigged up his gasoline feeder to allow a supply of fuel to run continually to the generator. It had an automatic shutoff when electrical power to the house kicked back on.

"How long can it run?" Chad said.

"Nonstop for forty-eight hours. We'll run some electric heaters to keep the water pipes from freezing."

As Chad tied the bundles he would load onto the ski plane (the one with landing skis as well as retractable wheels), he saw Dad shoveling snow from in front of the hangar. He jogged out to help. The snow had diminished to just flurries, but it was bitterly cold.

"Finish this patch here so we can roll the plane out," Dad said, "and I'll see if I can get this door open."

Chad knew the hangar door to be stubborn even in the best of weather. It was a huge, corrugated steel thing that ran on wheels and slid across the opening. It was old, heavy, creaky, and ornery, and now it was frozen in place.

Dad yanked on it, kicked it, then rammed it with his shoulder. Chad ran over and added his own shoulder. When it seemed to break free a bit, Dad shook it and tried to drag it open, but it wouldn't budge. He went through a side door and began banging on the big door from the inside. Soon he came back outside carrying one of the pressurized tanks filled with deicer that was usually used on the wings. He sprayed it all over the door.

When it finally opened, Dad slipped inside the frigid Quonset hut and slid the door shut again.

"What are you doing?" Chad said.

"We've got a lot of work to do on the plane before we can back it out of here," Dad said. "We don't need that cold wind."

"Why didn't we work on the plane before we opened the door?"

"For the same reason we're not going to load the plane until we make sure the engines work. What if we couldn't open the door after getting the plane ready? We would have wasted our effort."

Dad sprayed deicer directly onto the engine and began tinkering with all the various parts—spark plugs, coils, propellers, everything. "It's going to work," he said finally. "You can start loading up."

"And can I open the big door?"

"You may."

After Chad's third trip from the house with the supplies, he was shivering and his face stung. It reminded him of their all-night walk, and he really wanted to forget about that. Dad had jumped inside the tiny cockpit and tried to fire up the engines, but only the right one came to life. He shut it off, then stuck his head out and motioned to Chad.

"Hand crank the left prop and then get back!"

Chad turned the left propeller with both hands the way he had watched his dad do it many times. When he felt it tighten and ready to spring, he jumped out of the way and Dad flipped the switch. Soon both engines roared and began that high-pitched hum. The wind gusts caused by the powerful blades blasted against the sides of the hangar and threatened to push Chad outside.

Dad signaled that Chad should step aside and shut the door after the plane was outside. As the noisy thing passed him, Chad pressed his back up against the wall. Once outside on the packed snow, Dad retracted the wheels. He settled the plane down on its landing skis and waited until Chad had rolled the big door shut, locked it, and climbed aboard.

Dad taxied into a clearing near the house and sat, letting the engines whir as he radioed into town. He reached the Alaska State Police Emergency Radio Network and found the chaos he'd expected. Everyone had been working twenty-four hours, he was told. Dad informed them of the approximate location of the ATV, adding, "I don't expect to see it soon, but I want you to know it's buried out there so we don't lose it forever."

"No promises," he was told. "But thanks. We'll watch for it and let you know."

Then Dad filed his flight plan with the local airport control tower. "You're going where, over?" he was asked.

"Trying to get as close to Old Sparrow as possible."

"You know about the weather there?"

"Fully informed," Dad said. "They have medical emergencies, and no one else is getting in or out."

"And you're going to do it with a ski plane?"

"No choice."

"We can't forbid you, but the odds are against you."

"I'll be careful. I should be able to put down anywhere."

"But you realize what could happen if—"

"Totally cognizant," Dad said, and Chad could tell he was getting frustrated. "The longer I talk to you, the worse the weather gets over there."

Chad wasn't confident about getting off the unevenly snow-packed ground. With wheels on dry ground, it was easy. But sliding along on skis over packed and drifted snow—he wasn't so sure.

As was his custom, Dad prayed before they took off. He asked for guidance and safety and for God to make a way where none seemed to exist.

Dad cranked the throttle up full, and the little craft seemed to sit on its haunches, just waiting to break free. Rattling and vibrating at full tilt, the little plane seemed to paw at the ground and flit around in the wind. Dad maneuvered the controls quickly so they began their takeoff at top speed. Chad sat there, tightly buckled in, gripping the sides of his chair, his eyes fixed on the snow-covered ground.

The craft cut through the tops of high, powdery drifts, then dipped to bounce off deep, more tightly packed snow. Chad knew there was no turning back. There were no brakes with the skis down, so even if Dad had aborted right then, they would have slid wildly to a stop. With snow like this, who knew what would happen if he dropped the wheels so that they could dig into the snow and come to a halt? Dad was playing the controls like a big musical instrument, and Chad knew the flaps were dancing, trying to direct the air stream and push their overgrown hummingbird into the air.

Chad felt the plane rise only a bit, then a little more. Finally, they swept into the air, the fuselage shuddering and the little plane breaking free of gravity. Chad had been holding his breath, and now he let out a huge sigh. "Thank You, Lord," he said aloud.

Dad smiled. "Never a doubt," he said.

"Maybe not in your mind," Chad said.

Dad laughed.

Chad studied the ground. "It took us all night to walk nearly ten miles in the snow after driving several hours. How long a flight is this?"

"We'll be able to go as the crow flies, in other words, in a straight line. We don't have to follow the highway, which was built to follow the curves of the river. So if we fly all the way to the city of Old Sparrow, I'm guessing it's about 250 miles. Not a long flight."

"Are you going to fly all the way to Old Sparrow?"

"We'll see after we talk to the Quentons, provided I can rouse them on the radio. I have to know the medical situation and if they know whether the medicine has arrived in the city. If the medicine has no way of getting to the school and the school has no way of getting to it, then yes, we'll try to put down near the city so we can pick it up."

The first hour and a half of the flight was uneventful. Chad peered down on the river, the highway, and the tiny villages, and nothing seemed to be moving. It was as if northeast Alaska had been turned into a ghost town, but rather than dust and dirt covering everything as it did in Old West ghost towns, mounds of snow lay over the frozen cars, trucks, buildings, and ground. Here and there a plume of smoke from a vent atop a house puffed out the news that someone was trying to keep warm. The occasional snowplow worked slowly with front-end loaders, clearing small sections of highway at a time.

"I don't like what I'm seeing on the horizon." Dad glanced at his watch. "Almost three, and look at that sky."

Although daylight was nearly gone, the horizon looked particularly dark and ominous. "How far from the school are we?" Chad said.

"Should be reachable by radio. See if you can raise them."

Dad had assigned to the ski plane the call letters of the plane destroyed in Indonesia the previous summer. Chad announced, “November, November double Hotel forty forty-eight to ground at Old Sparrow Christian School. Do you read? Over.”

Chad and Dad heard nothing but static. Chad repeated the call. Still nothing.

“Change frequencies,” Dad suggested. “Just stay off the emergency band, because the local authorities will be all over that.”

Chad tried a couple of other channels. Finally he heard the voice of a young man “Hello? Hello? Are you calling us?” the man said, his voice cracking.

“Calling Old Sparrow Christian School,” Chad said.

“That’s us!” he said. “I’m supposed to be manning the radio, but I don’t really know what I’m doing. This is the first call I’ve got. Who is this, and what do you want?”

“My name is Chad. My dad and I are on an airplane coming at you from the west. We’re friends of the Quentons. What’s your name?”

“Mike.”

“Listen, Mike, we need to talk to Mr. or Mrs. Quenton.”

“They’re real sick, just like most everybody here. I don’t feel so good myself, but there are about twenty or so of us who aren’t sick. We’re waiting for medicine from Old Sparrow.”

Dad took the microphone. “Mike, this is Chad’s dad. I’m the pilot. Where’s everybody staying?”

“In their rooms and in classrooms. There’s only room for about twelve in the infirmary. They started putting people in classrooms, but they ran out of cots. They were trying to keep the infected people from exposing the others, but they finally had to let people just go to their own beds. I guess we’ve all been exposed to this by now.”

“What is it? Do you know?”

“Mrs. Quenton said it’s called strep-something. Anyway, it’s highly contagious and strong.”

“Does she think it’s deadly?” All he could think of was Kate. “Do you know anything about my daughter, Kate? She’s staying with the Quentons.”

“Sorry, no, I don’t. Mrs. Quenton doesn’t think the virus is deadly, but she’s worried about what might happen to people who carry high fevers too long. We need antibiotics from Old Sparrow.”

“Any word on whether they have a supply?”

“Yes! We heard from the drugstore there that they met the flight somewhere near McDougall Pass and got back as far as Old Sparrow, but they can’t come any farther. The roads are closed and snowed and drifted over, and there’s no power in Old Sparrow now either.”

“How did you get power?”

"Mr. Quenton hooked the radio and some heaters up to a generator, but we're low on gas. He's only running it every other half hour."

"How's he doing?"

"Not good. He just tells us what to do from his bed. He's got the fever and chills like everybody else."

"How's the food supply?"

"We put the frozen stuff outside, and there seems to be enough for a while. The sick people aren't hungry, and the well people are scared. It's still snowing and blowing here. That storm last night and this morning was unbelievable."

"You know you got two of them at the same time."

"Three, actually. We got the McDougall Pass front too."

"Wow."

"It was awful. We thought the roof was going to blow off the main building. The Quentons' house lost most of its windows and part of its roof. Nobody can be in there now."

Chad grabbed the mike. "How's Suzie Q?"

"Who?"

"Sue Quenton!"

"Not good. She's real low on her medicine. She's got some other kind of a disease, you know, and they've cut her doses in half, but I guess it's not working. The drugstore in Old Sparrow has what she needs too, but we've got to have it fast."

"We're over you right now," Dad told Mike. "We're going to try to put down in Old Sparrow, get Sue's insulin, and bring it back to you. What else do you need?"

"Gas!" he shouted. "We're low. We've been running the generator on gas from the cars. They can't go anywhere anyway."

"Tell the Quentons we're on our way!"

But when Chad and Dad came within visual range of Old Sparrow, Chad could hardly believe his eyes. The town appeared to have been destroyed by a tornado. He'd heard that twister-type winds were part of at least two of the three storms that had converged on the little town, but he hadn't expected to see houses in pieces and roofs torn off several structures.

Worse, from what Chad could see, there was nowhere to land their plane and be certain that it wouldn't hit debris under the snow.

Plan B

"You've heard of Plan A and Plan B?" Dad said.

"Yeah," Chad said. "But I guess I never knew what it meant."

"Well, Plan A is your original plan—the easiest, most logical solution to a problem. Our plan was to fly to Old Sparrow, get the medicine, fly to the school and deliver it, and see what we could do about helping those people."

"And bring Kate home."

"Of course. As soon as she's able to fly. But look what happened to Plan A."

Chad looked down at Old Sparrow again as Dad circled. "Snow happened to Plan A," Chad said.

"Worse than snow," Dad said. "That was some kind of major storm, maybe three at once."

Chad nodded. "So what's Plan B?"

"We've got to find a place to put down and then walk into Old Sparrow to get that medicine. Suzie Q's life is in danger, and who knows how sick Katie is? And all those adults and other kids who need antibiotics—who knows what might happen to them? This thing may not be fatal, but how can we know what damage it's doing to their systems?"

"But Dad, look," Chad said, pointing. The ground was covered with huge drifts for miles in every direction surrounding Old Sparrow. "If we find a place to land, it will take us hours to get into and out of Old Sparrow. And how do we know if anyone is still alive down there or if the drugstore is open or even if we can get through the drifts on foot? We should have brought snowmobiles."

"Shoulda, woulda, coulda never gets you anywhere," Dad said. "We couldn't fit a snowmobile in this plane, and it would have been too heavy anyway. We'll just have to scout out a place to put down as close as possible and take our chances. That's Plan B. There are no alternatives. Meanwhile, see if you can raise anybody on the radio in Old Sparrow."

Chad tried every channel, getting no response.

"They may be on batteries only," Dad said, "and on the air only a few minutes every hour. Keep trying. And try the emergency channel if all else fails."

Dad was now flying back toward the Old Sparrow Christian School, thirty miles west of the town of Old Sparrow. The plane circled in wider and wider arcs as Dad looked for open areas. Chad finally raised a medical technician on the emergency channel.

"Roger, I read you November, November double Hotel," he said. "Unless your call is urgent, we need to keep this channel clear."

Chad told him the situation.

"Nothing's getting in or out of that area for at least twenty-four hours," the emergency medical technician said. "And we're warning small aircraft to stay out of there too. More weather is coming from the pass soon."

"McDougall?"

"Roger. Something's building in there again."

"That's all we need."

"Roger," the EMT said. "Wish we could help, but the snowplows are moving mighty slow. We've had limited radio contact with Old Sparrow, but their power is down. They're on batteries the first ten minutes of every hour. Several deaths there, lots of injuries. They're our top priority, but we appreciate knowing about the school too. Nothing we can do there for at least twenty-four hours." He signed off.

"Chad, look," Dad said as he circled a wide open field. "That looks pretty smooth. I don't detect anything beneath the surface."

Chad studied it. "Sure seems a long way from Old Sparrow. I can't even see the town from here."

"If you look back this way you can," Dad said. "About twenty miles."

"We're going to walk *twenty* miles into town, and *twenty* back to the plane?"

"We're going to do what we have to do, son."

"Won't it be dark by then?"

"We've got flashlights."

"Wait. We're closer to the Christian school than to the town, right?"

"Oh, yeah."

"Then why don't we put down closer to the school and see if we can get that old snow remover of theirs working?"

Dad frowned. "It's a long shot."

"It's worth a try. It would take us the whole day to walk twenty miles each way through this stuff, especially after last night. And with another storm coming? And who can say we would even be able to get past all the drifts?"

Dad rubbed his forehead. "You're right, " he said. "Try to get Mike back on the radio. We need to find out if they've siphoned the fuel out of the snow remover."

Chad got no response. Then suddenly the radio crackled to life. "November, November, double Hotel forty forty-eight airborne, do you read? This is Old Sparrow, over."

"Go ahead, Old Sparrow."

"We're on just a few minutes an hour here—down to batteries—but we got word from an EMT that you were trying to reach us."

"Yeah." Chad quickly ran down the situation at the Christian school and what they planned.

"I'll get in touch with the pharmacist and see what he's got, November Hotel. No one's heard from him since he got back from McDougall with the stuff, just before the twisters hit."

"You think he's all right?"

"Couldn't tell you. The store seems all right, but of course it's not open. Nothing's happening here. Relief is on its way from state and federal agencies, they tell us, but we've got a mess."

"Ten-four. We'll probably see you later today to try to get some of that medicine."

"I don't know how you'll ever get in here, but good luck."

They were soon within sight of the Christian school. It looked as lifeless as Old Sparrow but without as much destruction. A long smooth stretch of snow lay on both sides of the main buildings. Dad buzzed the complex, and

Chad heard a staticky transmission on his wrist TV. He pulled his sleeve back and tuned it in. "Kate?" he said. "Are you there?"

"I'm here, Chad," came his sister's hoarse voice. The LCD picture was fuzzy. "What are you guys doing up there? Do you have the medicine?"

"Kate!" Dad yelled over the engine noise. "Are you all right? You sound awfully weak."

"I'm okay, Dad, really," she said. "Or I will be."

Chad brought her up to date and told her their plan to try to get into Old Sparrow in the dilapidated snowplow.

"They say that thing has been used only a couple of times in the last few months," she said. "I don't even know if it would get that far. Mr. Quenton only uses it to plow the driveways and get the drifts away from the front of the buildings."

"Well, it's Plan B, but it's all we've got," Chad said. "Dad wants to know if there's gas in the snowplow."

"We'll let you know," Kate said.

"When will Mike be back on the radio?"

"The first half hour of every hour," she said. "But I can tell you over the wrist TVs."

"That's only if we're close enough," Chad said. "It's hard to hear. We'll be landing pretty soon, but we don't want to be exposed to anybody who's sick. Just have him tell us whether the thing is gassed up or where the gas supply is if it's not."

"We're low on gas, I know that," Kate said. "Because of the generator. We've got food—"

"Outside, yeah, I know," Chad said. "Mike told us. Have him call us on the radio at the top of the hour. That's just a few minutes from now."

"That's the snowplow right there, isn't it?" Dad pointed at a snow-covered contraption near one of the buildings.

The huge old truck had a plow on the front, double tires on each back axle, and a gigantic snowblower built onto one side. It was a dump truck, but the bed appeared empty except for snow.

"Looks like it," Chad said. "You think it'll get us anywhere in this snow?"

"It's our only hope," Dad said. "I just hope you're up to helping me shovel salt or gravel or dirt or something up into the back of that thing. If that truck bed is empty, we'll slide all over the roads and likely bounce right out of the cab. If we can fill it, it should drive through anything."

"How long will it take to fill it?"

"I don't want to think about it. I sure hope there are chains on the tires."

"There have to be, right?"

"Not necessarily. Those are big tires with deep treads,

and if they only use it here on the complex, they might not have put chains on it. Those are probably old tires though, so if chains are available, I'll want them."

Dad made one more pass over the school complex.

"How are we doing on fuel?" Chad said.

"We're fine," Dad said. "We have plenty to get us back home if we don't go anywhere else."

"Sure wish we were flying to Old Sparrow."

"Me too. But wishing doesn't get us anywhere. The Lord has been with us so far, even last night. Just keep praying."

"I still can't believe we made it all the way home."

"I know, Chad. We could have easily been buried in the ATV or frozen to death on the road." Dad scanned the ground. "That looks good, right there."

The plane's descent felt too fast to Chad. "Should you slow down a little?" he said.

"Can't risk stalling. The engines would never refire in this weather. If you think it's cold out there, imagine the windchill we're generating at over a hundred miles an hour. I've got lots of room to slide once we touch down. I just hope it's all smooth and that there are no surprises under the snow."

The plane turned and dipped, then leveled off before starting to rapidly descend. It felt like they were diving straight down, and Chad's heart pounded just like when they'd crashed in Indonesia earlier in the year. He hung on and prayed.

Dad leveled off again, and all Chad could see was white. The ground was snow covered, of course, but even the sky, cloud covered in the middle of the afternoon, looked white to him. How could Dad keep his bearings, his perspective?

At the first touch of the skis to the snow, the plane bounced and swerved left. Dad straightened it in the air, and then they touched down again and began a long, fast slide. The plane glided smoothly along the snow, hardly seeming to slow.

"Perfect," Chad said.

"Not yet," Dad said. "What's that up there?"

Chad stared straight ahead. Something loomed in front of them now that hadn't been visible from the sky. The snow-covered mound had somehow blended in with the ground when looked at from above.

"I don't know!" Chad said. "Can you miss it?"

"Have to try," Dad said, playing with the flaps. With no brakes on landing skis, all he could do was try to turn, but at that speed, turning could easily flip the plane.

Dad went into a slow turn in a large arc, and as they slid past the mound in the snow, the wing missed it by inches. They looked at each other. Their obstacle was a snowman.

When the plane stopped, they were facing the compound,

a little over a quarter mile away. An adult and two kids stood by the snowplow.

"We don't want to be exposed to them, even if they're not sick yet," Dad said. He got on the radio, but the school's unit was not on. Chad jumped out and waved at the people to move away from the truck. They went inside.

Chad climbed back in the plane. Dad kept the engines running and skimmed along the ground toward the snowplow.

"Wish we could just keep going like this all the way to Old Sparrow," Chad said.

"That would be nice," Dad said, "but we'd have to go airborne over every drift or mound. We'd never make it."

They looked at their watches. It was four o'clock, and the radio crackled to life. "This is Mike to December or whatever."

Chad smiled. "That's us."

"Mr. Quenton thinks the truck is about half full of gas. The gas pump is behind the kitchen at the end of the dining hall. He thinks you should try to put something heavy in the truck bed."

"We already thought of that," Chad said. "Is there a dirt pile or gravel somewhere?"

"There's some junk, old bed frames, and a sandpile near the barn. Shovels are in the barn."

"We'll try to make that work. Dad wants to know if the truck has chains on it."

"They're not on the tires, but they're in the truck, behind the seat. Mr. Quenton has one more request, but he wants to wait until you're ready to go."

"What is it?" Dad said, taking the radio.

"He doesn't want to tell you until the truck is gassed up, the truck bed loaded down, the chains on, and you're ready to pull out."

"What's the mystery?"

"I don't even know, sir," Mike said. "He said he'll try to make it out here to the radio to talk to you himself as soon as you're ready."

"Well, we should be ready to go in an hour or so. We'll come back to the radio in the plane at five."

"Okay. I mean, ten-four."

"Wait!" Chad said, leaning over the radio. "Just have Mr. Quenton speak to us from Kate's wrist TV."

"He and Kate aren't in the same room."

"Yeah, but it has to be easier to get the wrist TV to him than to get him up and to the radio."

"Good point. Five o'clock then?"

"Well," Dad said, "get him the radio now, and we'll call him when we're ready. If we can get away from here before five, we want to."

Dad signed off, and they climbed out.

Dad used deicer to startle the truck engine into waking up. The thing barely turned over but then rumbled noisily and finally caught. Dad backed it up, slipping and sliding, to the gas pump, where he filled it and told Chad he had left very little fuel for the generator. "We'll have to be quick and successful," he said.

Chad began shoveling sand and throwing junk into the open bed of the truck. It was hard, cold, miserable work, but he knew it was important. Dad left the truck running, and they jumped inside to get warm every few minutes.

A half hour later, Dad had the tire chains draped over the tires and was ready to hook them together. He told Chad how to drive the truck forward just a few inches, so he could link the chains. It took several tries, because the truck was a stick shift and Chad had to put in the clutch and shift every time he wanted to move the truck. But by quarter to five, they were ready to roll.

Dad and Chad sat up in the cramped cab of the truck, trying to keep the heater working correctly. Chad got on his wrist TV. "Mr. Quenton," he radioed. "Are you there?"

"I'm here," Mr. Quenton managed, his voice weak. "How do you work this thing?"

"Just press the upper right button to speak and let go to listen."

"Bruce?" Hugh Quenton called.

"Go ahead, Hugh," Dad said.

"I need a big favor." Chad heard the tremble in his voice.

"I'm listening."

"I need you to take Sue with you."

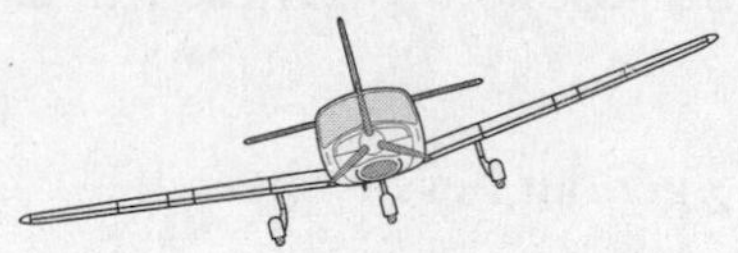

Over the River

"Repeat please?" Dad said into his wrist TV while glancing at Chad.

"I know it's a lot to ask," Mr. Quenton began, "and I know I'm putting you at tremendous risk. But this bug has wreaked havoc with Sue's blood-sugar levels, and she took her last dose of insulin this morning. We don't know when you might get to Old Sparrow or when you'll get back, but she'll need the insulin as soon as you can get to it."

"No options?" Dad said. "This cab is cramped and drafty."

"I don't see any options, Bruce. You know I wouldn't ask if I wasn't desperate."

"I know. Do you have surgical masks we could wear?"

"I think we could find a couple for you, and we'll put one on her too. Problem is, you'll have to be careful even opening them, because someone here will have to touch the boxes."

"Can Suzie Q get out here by herself?"

"We'll get her to the door. She's pretty weak, but she has eaten a little and she's medicated the best we know how. We'll bundle her up. Hopefully she'll sleep. Will you take her?"

"Of course. But I hate to think what might happen if we get stranded. One of us will have to stay with her."

"Bruce, if there were any other way ..."

"I understand."

"One thing we know for sure," Mr. Quenton said, his voice breaking. "If we have to wait any longer than necessary, she runs the risk of a diabetic coma ... and then almost certain death."

Chad glanced at his dad, who pressed his lips together and seemed to be fighting his own tears. "We'll do everything we can, Hugh."

"I know you will. But she must have the insulin as soon as you can get it. And of course, the rest of us need the antibiotics as soon as you can get back."

"Gotcha," Dad said. "You'd better get her out here as soon as you can."

Chad and Dad sat in the idling truck for a few minutes, trying to stay warm and watching the door at the back of the dining hall. “When she gets here,” Dad said, “let’s put her between us so she can stay warm.”

“There’s room for her to lie down behind the seat,” Chad said.

Dad looked back. “It’s bare metal on the floor, Chad, and we’ll be bouncing. I wouldn’t even want you there, and you’re healthy.”

The door opened and Suzie Q emerged slowly, a student on either side guiding her out, then letting go of her arms. She took slow, seemingly painful steps and stared at the truck, not turning her head. She wore a surgical mask and carried two more in small boxes.

Dad jumped out of his side of the truck and motioned for Chad to do the same. Dad took the two boxes from Suzie Q. He gave one of the boxes to Chad and told him to get out the mask and put it on. Dad put his own on, and the three of them climbed into the truck.

At one time, Chad could never have endured sitting that close to Suzie Q, but she seemed so fragile and he felt so sorry for her that he really didn’t mind. He just wanted her to feel better, to get well, and to get the medicine she needed. He didn’t know what a diabetic coma was, and he didn’t want to find out.

Besides, Suzie Q had been nice to him the other morning, and he thought Kate might be right about Suzie Q growing up. She was friendly and pretty, and she really seemed to care about other people. All that silliness he remembered seemed to be gone.

The three of them sat in the truck, shoulder to shoulder, lap belts fastened, and Suzie Q had said nothing yet. "Do you mind if we call you Suzie Q?" Dad said. "We notice your parents don't call you that anymore, and I assume you don't go by that nickname here at the school. But it's a hard habit for us to break."

"Actually, I kind of like it, Mr. Michaels," Susie Q spoke softly. "Only the people who knew us in Enid call me that, so it takes me home in my mind."

"Then Suzie Q it is, at least for this trip. Are you going to be all right?"

"I'm feeling a little queasy, actually," she said. "I'll let you know if I have to throw up. You think maybe I should sit by the window with Chad in the middle?"

"It's pretty cold by that window, hon." Dad said, smiling. "We'll move fast if you get sick."

"I'm freezing already," she said. "I think I can let you know in time for Chad to get out of my way."

Chad laughed, and he could see from Suzie Q's crinkled eyes above her mask that she was smiling.

"I'm so tired," she said.

"You need anything right now?" Dad said.

"No, let's just go."

Dad depressed the clutch and shifted into low gear. The truck groaned and lurched as he let out the clutch and the gears engaged. The old beast rumbled slowly around the building and up the drive, heading toward the main road. The truck rattled and shook and bounced even where the road was fairly smooth, so Chad could only imagine what would happen when they tried to blast their way through heavy snowdrifts.

Suzie Q, her arms folded in front of her, tried to stay steady, but she tipped and swayed and would catch herself by grabbing the dashboard or leaning on either Chad or Dad. And she kept apologizing.

"Suzie Q," Dad said, "if you apologize every time you bump either of us, you'll never shut up. Let's just all apologize at once here and let it stand for the whole trip, okay?"

She laughed. "Sorry."

"There you go again. Now hang on."

They were near the end of the drive and about to pull out onto the highway, which was covered with about two feet of snow for as far as Chad could see. "I need a little speed here," Dad said, "and we're about to make a sharp left. Hang on."

Suzie Q braced herself on the dashboard, but as Dad picked up speed, downshifted, and hurtled the plow onto the road, all three passengers were thrown to the right. Suzie Q was pressed against Chad, pushing him toward the door. His head was plastered up against the iced-over window, and he expected his door to fly open.

Susie Q looked at him and started to say something.

"Don't apologize!" he hollered. "I understand!"

The truck straightened, they all sat up, and off they went down the road at between twenty-five and thirty miles an hour, bouncing like a crazy carnival ride. Twice Chad's head hit the ceiling, and he saw Dad press his left hand up there to make sure he didn't do the same. Suzie Q bounced up and down and up and down but didn't reach the ceiling because she was shorter than Chad. Once, though, when one bounce coincided perfectly with the next, all three of them were in the air, their seats off the bench, when the next bump came. They came down as the truck came up, and the bounce threw all three of them straight up into the ceiling of the cab. As they tumbled back down, Dad's foot slipped off the gas and the engine died.

"Oh, no!" Suzie Q cried.

"It's all right," Dad said. "I just lost contact." He turned the key, and after a few grinds on the engine, it fired up again. "Everybody all right?" Dad said.

Chad and Suzie Q looked at each other and nodded.

"Dad," Chad said, "I'm afraid I'm going to take this mask off and take my chances."

"Why?"

"It stinks. The smell is making me sick. I may be the first one who throws up."

"They do smell awful, don't they?" And Dad tore his off. Chad immediately followed, and Suzie Q asked if she could get rid of hers too.

"I think it's safe to say they weren't helping much anyway," Dad said. "Let's just hope God protects us, or you're already past the contagious stage."

For the next hour they chugged along. Sometimes the drifts were so large that Dad had to lower the plow and make his own path. Other times he engaged the snowblower and sent showers of dirt and ice and snow high into the air. Twice Suzie Q thought she might have to throw up. She whipped off her seat belt and climbed over Chad, hanging her head out the hastily lowered window, but both times were false alarms.

"It's all this bouncing," she said.

"I wish I could make it smoother," Dad said.

"I understand," she said. "There's no easy way to do this."

Finally they came to a mound of snow in the road that the plow couldn't budge. Dad tried attacking the seven-foot drift from two different directions with both the plow and the snowblower. "It would take at least two trucks and maybe more," he said. "I can't see them opening this for days."

"What are we going to do?" Suzie Q said.

"I'm going to have to go off the road for a while," Dad said. "That's why we weighted down the truck bed and put the chains on. I just hope this old buggy can make it through."

Dad downshifted to low again and turned off the roadway. The heavy truck plunged down a ravine and up the other side, as he kept clutching and shifting and punching the accelerator. For several minutes Dad drove as if on an obstacle course, looking for the points of least resistance. They weren't moving that fast, but it seemed they would never stop jostling up and down. Dad tore through fields, avoiding the deepest drifts, and when a shallow spot looked smooth, he drove right through it, even though it was clear they were hitting rocks, tree stumps, and even half-buried fence posts along the way.

For a ten-minute period, the way seemed almost smooth. The snow was only about a foot deep for a few miles, and Dad took the opportunity to increase his speed and make up some time. It wouldn't be long before nightfall, and he told Chad and Suzie Q that he didn't want to be driving in unfamiliar terrain after dark.

"How will we get back then?" Suzie Q said.

"That'll be easier. Well, not easier. Certainly not much smoother. But we will have been there before. We'll go back the exact way we came. All this work now is building us a path for the way back."

"As long as it doesn't get snowed under or drifted over," Suzie Q said.

"Hey!" Dad said. "None of that kind of thinking!"

And she smiled.

But soon, Suzie Q was asleep. She seemed to conk out in an instant, just as Chad was trying to think of something to talk to her about. One minute she was hanging onto the dashboard and occasionally slamming into him, and the next her arms lay limp in her lap, she was flopping back and forth, and her head was hanging.

"Is she all right, Dad?"

Dad looked at her. "Exhausted, I would guess. Her color looks all right. You could put your arm around her though, Spitfire. Otherwise she's going to bang into something."

"Dad!"

"Chad, it doesn't mean anything. I promise not to tell anyone. I'd put my arm around her, but I need one hand to shift with."

Chad looked at Suzie Q. He'd never sat with his arm around anyone except his parents. "Do it!" Dad said. "She won't even be aware of it, and she's going to get hurt if you don't!"

Chad reluctantly put his arm up behind Suzie Q on the back of the seat, but he didn't touch her. "Thatta boy!" Dad said, obviously not realizing that Chad still didn't have ahold of her. They hit a bump, and Suzie Q bounced toward Chad. He grabbed her shoulder and held tight, keeping her from banging into the dashboard or lurching back toward Dad. He still felt uncomfortable, but it wasn't anything romantic, after all.

The longer they sat like that and the more progress Dad made pushing the plow through the snow, the more brave and protective Chad felt. Suddenly Suzie Q's body went limp and she leaned over, settling in against Chad, her head on his chest. Whoops! This was more than he'd bargained for. He didn't know what to do, so he just sat there, his arm still around her shoulder.

"Dad?" he said.

"Just hang onto her," Dad said. "She's not going to bite you, and it's not going to kill you."

Chad whispered, "If she wakes up, she'll be embarrassed."

"Hm?" Dad said.

Chad didn't want to say it again, and certainly not loudly enough to wake her.

"Nothing," he said.

Suddenly Dad slammed on the brakes, and Chad hung onto Suzie Q tighter to keep her from flying forward. "What?" Chad said.

Dad shook his head. "Look at this. And we were making such good progress. I'm guessing we're halfway there."

Chad stared out at a wall of snow. It stood higher than the truck as far as they could see to the left. To the right it extended all the way to the frozen-over and snow-filled Porcupine River. There was no way they could remove it or go through it.

"Do we have to go back, Dad?"

"I hope not."

He backed up and turned so he could flash his headlights far to the left. Nothing but a wall of snow. He turned to the right. The wall ended only at the river bank. "We've got to try it," Dad said.

"Try what?"

"Crossing the river. This is a mighty heavy truck, but that river isn't deep and has to be solid ice. It should hold us."

"Dad!"

Dad pointed across the river. "There's a woods on the other side where the snow has to be shallower. If we can pick our way through there, we'll be on our way to Old Sparrow."

He drove to the river's edge and eased the truck over the bank. It rolled and hurtled toward the ice, which seemed to hold it without any trouble. Dad drove straight across, which took only a few minutes. "We'll have to cross back again at some point," Dad reminded Chad, "because Old Sparrow is on the other side at the fork where the Porcupine splits. But we'll make it."

As they drew close to the other side and saw the woods looming, it became obvious that the bank was steeper on that side. Dad shifted and accelerated, and when the front tires hit the other side, the truck flew through the air, dumping half the weight from its bed and sending the debris sliding down the frozen river.

They settled back down and headed for the woods, but the jarring didn't even wake Sue. "Dad," Chad said, as he studied her, "Something's really wrong."

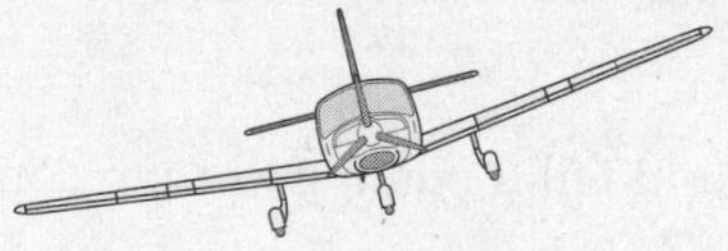

And through the Woods

Dad put the snowplow in neutral and set the brake. He turned on the inside light and leaned close to look at Suzie Q. She was pale, her eyelids fluttering, her lips bluish.

"Is she just cold?" Chad said.

"I don't think so," Dad said. "And I'm afraid this is more than whatever flu bug is going around."

"Does she need that diabetes medicine her dad talked about?"

"Insulin? Probably. I know a little about this because my grandmother was dependent on insulin. I haven't got time to explain it all to you now, but because her body is not producing insulin, her blood-sugar level is too high."

"Mr. Michaels," Suzie whispered weakly, obviously trying to focus on his face, "I've never needed insulin this badly in my life. If I don't get some soon, then . . ."

"Then what?" Chad said.

"You don't want to know," she said.

"Yes, I do."

"My heart could fail. I could go into a coma and have a stroke. It wouldn't be good." She struggled to sit up. "Mr. Michaels, don't worry about making me sicker or bouncing me around. If there's insulin in Old Sparrow, we have to get there soon."

That was all Dad needed to hear. He lowered the snowplow, turned on the noisy snowblower, shifted into low, punched the accelerator, and popped the clutch. The big old truck tires and chains dug into the snow and earth, and they began bouncing through the woods.

It was dark in among the trees, and Chad wondered how his dad could see far enough ahead to make his turns. The snowblower rattled and squealed as it ground up twigs and branches and pushed huge mounds of snow off to the side. Dad would get the truck up to twenty-five or thirty miles an hour, pushing big drifts ahead of him, then he would raise the plow and the truck would run up the pile in the way, bounce down the other side, and keep going.

Chad put both hands on the lap belt across his lap and held on. Suzie Q was bouncing all over. She grabbed the dashboard, but her hands flew loose. She pressed her palms flat on the ceiling to try to keep from hitting her head.

"You sure you're all right?" Dad shouted as he shifted and clutched and turned and plowed.

"Yes," she shouted. "Keep going!"

Chad thought he saw a clearing at the other edge of the woods, but just before the opening was a rim of short, thin trees. The thickest might have been five inches around, and they were no more than fifteen feet tall.

Dad jerked the truck this way and that, avoiding big trees, dipping into holes, and sideswiping medium-sized trees. With the clearing in sight, he lifted the plow, turned off the blower, and shifted into high gear. The truck was flying. Dad, Suzie Q, and Chad were bouncing around and banging into each other. They must have been going nearly forty miles an hour through underbrush and between trees in the snow.

Ten feet from the last of the big trees, Dad came full throttle to the rim of thin saplings encircling the forest and suddenly had nowhere to turn. The truck couldn't fit between the small trees, and Dad was going too fast to stop. He bore down, ran over two small trees, and then hit a slightly bigger one head on.

The tree nearly stopped the truck. The force of the old machine as it rolled over the tree almost bent it all the way to the ground, but while the plow tore the bark from the trunk to the branches, the truck was barely moving. The tree rumbled and scraped beneath it, as if struggling to straighten itself again. As the truck rolled forward, the tree lifted the back tires into the air, and nearly flipped the truck over frontward.

Chad saw the snowy ground out the windshield directly below him and was certain they were about to flip end over end. He hung on, Suzie screamed, Dad grunted, and the tree slid to one side of the underbelly of the truck and made them tip to Chad's side. Now they were about to roll that way, and Chad wondered if he would wake up in heaven. Who would take care of Kate? Would he see his mother? What would the Quentons think? Who would ever find them in these woods? What if more snow covered their tracks and even the truck? They might lie frozen in this thing for days!

As Chad thought about all this, somehow the truck righted itself and bounced down on both axles, the four tires in the back and the two in the front now solidly in the snow again. Dad had never taken his foot off the accelerator, so the back wheels had spun at top speed while suspended by the little tree beneath them. When they again hit the ground, they dug a huge hole and shot the truck forward even faster.

Suzie Q hollered, "Go! Go!"

Chad's heart banged inside his chest, and he tried to stop thinking about how they might die. As Dad took a hard left to head back to the Porcupine River, which he would have to cross again to get to Old Sparrow, Suzie Q was thrown almost into Chad's lap. Only her lap belt kept her from landing on him.

As she was flung into him again, he felt a strange lack of tension in her body; she was either spent or had given up trying to protect herself from the bouncing. Her infection and her diabetes must have sapped all her strength. Chad put his arm around her again, and she settled against him, her mittened hands clasped in her lap.

If he didn't hold onto her, she would be thrown all over the cab and could really hurt herself. Suzie Q was awake, and sometimes Chad sensed her eyes on him from close range, as her head bounced up and down on his chest. He was embarrassed and a little uncomfortable, but he kept one arm around her shoulder and the other firmly on the dashboard.

"Everybody all right?" Dad said, not taking his eyes off the path he was creating.

"Yeah," Chad said.

"Suzie Q?"

"Yup, I'm still here," she said.

"I figure we're about four miles from Old Sparrow. If I keep getting lucky and finding places to push this rig, we should be there inside half an hour."

"This isn't luck, Mr. Michaels," Suzie Q said. "I'm praying my heart out."

"Me too," Dad said. "You're right."

Dad was now pushing the snowplow through a field covered with a shallow layer of snow, and though it was not a paved road, it seemed more bouncy than it should have been. "Dad," Chad said, "are we bouncing even more than before, especially in the back?"

"Could be," Dad said, searching for the best spot to cross the frozen Porcupine again. "I don't know how much weight we lost out of the truck bed."

"I'll check," Chad said, lowering his window. Suzie Q dropped her head and put her hands up to cover her face against the blast of cold air and snow. Chad pulled his arm away from her shoulder, and she sat up, allowing him room to turn and crouch on the seat. He thrust his head and torso out the window and stood on the seat, squinting and peering over the back of the trailer.

Chad slithered back into the cab and shut the window. "Empty," he said.

"Completely?" Dad said. "That explains the bouncing."

The truck chugged along, rattling and bouncing, and Chad automatically put his arm around Susie Q again so she wouldn't go flying. She settled in, leaning against him, her hands in her lap. He wouldn't have wanted anyone else but Dad to see him in this predicament. Certainly not Kate or any of his friends.

"Once we get across the Porcupine again, we can head for the road and see if it's any better," Dad said. "I'd sure like to get into Old Sparrow on the main drag."

Dad pulled the truck near the bank of the river, but it was hard to tell where the field ended and the drop-off to the ice began, because of the drifting snow. He must have seen a good entry point then, because he angled the truck to the left and rumbled down toward the river. Chad kept expecting to hear cracking ice and then the gurgling sound of a sinking truck.

But the truck rode the smoothest since they had left the Christian school. In some spots on the river the snow was only six inches deep, so if Dad maintained the right speed, they sailed along, the tires cutting through the snow and the chains biting into the surface of the ice.

"Do you trust the river?" Chad said.

"Sure! Why not?" Dad said. "Ice has to be a couple of feet thick. It's been frozen over for a month, and the temperatures up here have averaged below zero for weeks."

"I don't know," Chad said. "Just gives me the creeps being over water in this heavy thing."

Suzie Q seemed to be sleeping. Her eyes were closed, her body relaxed, and her breathing even and deep. He looked close to make sure her eyelids were not fluttering or her lips blue. She looked fine. Maybe this was best for her. She was sick, out of diabetes medicine, and exhausted. Now, if he could keep her from getting bruised up on this crazy ride …

"There's the highway." Dad pointed ahead and to his left. "It actually looks passable, though it hasn't been plowed in a while. I'm going to try to get over there."

The bank on the left side looked steeper than where they had slid down onto the river. They needed to find a gentle slope and gather enough speed to make it up. Chad pointed out a spot about two hundred yards ahead. "Does that look good?" he said.

"From here it does," Dad said, and he increased his speed, angling toward the place.

Chad noticed underbrush above the snow line, something he rarely saw in northern Alaska or Canada. The exit area was looking better all the time.

Dad maneuvered the truck into position to shoot up the shallow slope and onto the bank. He accelerated, then suddenly he slammed on the brakes, sending the truck into a skid. What had appeared to be a short snow bank was really a boulder! If Dad hit it at top speed, they'd be killed!

The truck slid in a straight line. Dad quickly let off the brake so the front tires would roll, then he jerked the wheel to the right. The tires were turned, but still the truck slid forward. When they were just a few feet from hitting the boulder head on, the truck finally slowed enough and, following the direction of the tires, lurched to the right.

The truck went into a huge slide, missing the boulder but cutting a huge circle through the snow and on the ice. Chad felt as if he might pass out as they spun around and around. He held tight to Suzie Q, who did not budge or awaken.

This would have been fun if Dad had done it on purpose. Of course, had they not been on ice, anything they'd hit during this kind of spin would have tipped them over and spilled them out.

The truck finally came to a stop, and there they sat in the middle of the frozen-over Porcupine River, not far from the U.S. Canadian border, a few miles from Old Sparrow. Again Chad imagined the ice cracking and that monstrous old snowplow sinking slowly into the frigid waters with him and his dad and his friend inside.

Friend. Yes, that was what Suzie Q was now.

Dad shifted into low gear but had difficulty getting the tire chains to move slowly enough to gain traction on the ice. Finally they were moving again, and Chad could see that just upriver was an opening. If Dad could generate enough speed and there were no more hidden rocks, they just might be able to make it out of here alive.

Facing the Wall

As they bounced up the bank and then turned toward the highway, Chad wondered what this crazy ride was doing to his spine, not to mention his dad's or Suzie Q's. At any other time, he might have thought this was fun, but after a couple hours of it, he had had enough. It was noisy, it was painful, it was cold, and he was still embarrassed sitting there with his arm around Suzie Q as if they were a couple.

Dad steered the truck off the plains and through some drifts onto thc highway. The snow was deep, and there was no evidence that any cars or trucks had driven along the road for hours. Occasionally they passed a car or truck in the ditch or at a crazy angle at the side of the road, buried under the snow. But finally, for the first time, they seemed to be making good time. For about five minutes, Dad averaged thirty miles an hour.

Chad caught Dad straining and looking puzzled as he stared into the distance. “What?” Chad said.

“Is that what it looks like?” Dad said. “Or is it my imagination?”

Chad leaned forward and scraped the film of frost off the inside of the windshield. He couldn’t believe his eyes.

“Have you ever seen anything like that?” Dad said.

Chad couldn’t speak. He just shook his head and stared. He had walked all night through snowdrifts to get home. He had ridden in an ancient snowplow across drifted plains, through the woods, and across a frozen river twice. But Chad had never before seen what lay ahead of them—a wall of snow twice as high as the truck stretched across the entire highway, plus as far as he could see on either side of it.

It was as if someone had recreated the Great Wall of China out of snow. “So that’s what happens when three storm fronts converge.” Dad took his foot off the gas and allowed the truck to roll slowly, closer and closer to the wall of snow. He stopped about a hundred feet from the blockage and looked to the left and to the right. “There’s flat nowhere to go,” he said. “I can’t believe we’ve come this far and can go no farther.”

Chad looked both ways as well. There was no going around this thing.

His dad laid his arms on the steering wheel. "It looks like the twister-type winds from one storm hit the same winds from another storm, while the third storm provided the snow."

Chad was almost afraid to ask. "How far are we from Old Sparrow?"

"Not more than a mile," Dad said with a sigh. "So close."

Suzie Q awoke. "What's happening?"

"Look," Chad said.

"Oh, man!" she said. "What are we going to do?"

"There's nothing we can do in this truck," Dad said. "I'm going to have to try to walk around or over this thing." Dad reached behind the seat for his snowshoes. He slathered a huge dollop of petroleum jelly all over his face, tightened his hood, zipped and buttoned and snapped everything that could be fastened on his snowmobile suit, tossed the snowshoes out on the ground, and stepped out. As he struggled into the snowshoes, he said, "Chad, keep your wrist TV on, and I'll let you know how it goes."

Chad noticed Suzie Q's hands shaking. "Cold?" he said.

"Nervous," she said. "Terrified actually. I don't have much time. Mr. Michaels, I can wait here if you need Chad to go with you."

"I couldn't do that, hon," Dad said. "I'll be worried enough about the two of you without worrying about you alone. I don't know what Chad's going to do if you have another crisis, but we sure can't leave you alone out here. There's plenty of gas to keep the heater going, and I'll go as fast as I can."

Dad leaned in and turned the heat all the way up. When he shut the door the cab began to get warm, and Suzie slid over behind the wheel. "Thanks for keeping me warm," she said.

Chad felt his face flush. "You're welcome."

"While the truck's not moving, it's not so drafty, so I'm okay now."

"Good!" he said. "I mean, I didn't mind, I mean, it was all right, but— "

"I understand," she said, laughing. "You never expected to have to keep your old enemy warm."

"You're not my enemy," Chad said.

"I used to be."

"Not really."

"Now tell the truth, Chad. You always thought I was a little brat."

Chad turned toward the window to watch his dad. "Yeah, I guess I did."

Dad looked left and right, and then headed straight up the wall of snow. Climbing in snowshoes was no easy task, but there was obviously no other way to get up there.

He fell twice and rolled once and had to come back down another time to retrieve a snowshoe. But finally he reached the summit.

“Chad, come in, please,” came Dad’s staticky voice on Chad’s wrist.

“I read you,” Chad said.

“Look at this.” Dad turned his wrist to give Chad a blurry, LCD readout view of what he saw from the top of the wall of snow. Chad showed Suzie Q.

They both said, “Wow.”

“It’s hard to see, Dad,” Chad said, “but it looks like that would be a great place for a sled.”

“Wish I had a toboggan,” Dad said. “It just angles down for a quarter of a mile or so, and it looks like you can almost see pavement at the end. The road looks passable, but I don’t see anyone coming this way. They’ve probably got all their snow-removal equipment in town, trying to dig out. This will take a week.”

“Should be easy walking though, right, Dad?”

“Hope so. This seems firm enough, so by the time I get to the road I should be able to make good time. You guys all right?”

“Yeah.” Chad watched his dad start down the other side of the wall of snow. He didn’t want to worry Suzie Q, but if that snow wasn't as firm as his dad hoped, he could drop through and be buried alive.

"Suzie Q?" Dad said. "You okay?"

"Yes, sir," she said, leaning over to talk into the little contraption on Chad's wrist. "I'm fine for now. I'll sure feel better when I know you're on your way back with the insulin."

"Me too," he said. The picture on the TV screen disappeared. It was toasty now in the cab of the truck, yet Chad still shivered. When was the last time he had sat in an enclosed place with a girl other than his sister and had to carry on some kind of intelligent conversation?

"I was a brat," Suzie Q said. "I was jealous of Kate because she had a brother, so I pretended I didn't like you and tried to make life miserable for you."

"You were pretending?"

"I had just decided I didn't like boys, that boys weren't as good as girls, and so I did everything I could to annoy you."

"You succeeded. To tell you the truth, I couldn't stand you."

"I don't blame you. I don't know what was wrong with me then. Maybe I was feeling sorry for myself because of my diabetes. When I was eight, I had to start giving myself my own insulin shots."

"Yuck."

"Yuck is right. I'm used to it now and I know how important it is, but it's never been fun, never anything you'd wish on anyone."

"Has the diabetes kept you from doing things you want to do?"

"Not really. I have to be careful what I eat and when I eat, and I have to keep track of my blood-sugar levels. I stick my finger, and then a little machine measures the glucose in my blood. Honestly, I hate doing that all the time, even more than I hate giving myself the shots."

"I'd hate to have to do either one."

"Don't feel sorry for me though. I don't want pity."

Chad nodded. "I can understand that. Kate and I got a lot of pity when Mom died."

"I felt sorry for you too," Suzie Q said.

"That's fine, but we're trying to do what Dad does. He remembers the good times and talks about her all the time. We know she's in heaven, and we can't wait to see her someday."

"See, that's sort of how I feel about my diabetes now. My parents are always trying to find positive things about it. With my mom being a nurse, well, what could be better than that? When I was younger, she did everything for me. She sang and talked to me about fun stuff to get my mind off the shots."

"You have to do that every day?" Chad said.

Suzie Q gave a tired smile. "I get four shots per day on a normal day, usually when I eat my meals."

"Four! You get the shots in the leg, huh?"

"Yeah. Usually above the knee, or on the arm or even the stomach. It has to be a place where there's more fatty tissue."

"It doesn't hurt?"

"Not bad. I'm so used to it. The needles are tinier than they've ever been and are getting sharper all the time. Sometimes they slip in so easily I really don't feel them." She sighed. "I think I hate watching my diet more than anything. Hardly any junk food or sugar allowed."

Chad turned to face her. "Have you ever gone this long without insulin before?"

"I don't think so. I mean, actually I have, but I didn't need it as much. The older I get, the more I need. And if I get tense or upset or sick, then I need more. That's the problem right now. I had enough insulin to last a few normal days, but with being sick, and then the blizzard and everybody else getting sick, I had a couple of close calls."

Chad scowled. "What if you have another one of those?"

She shrugged. "You never know. Once when playing softball, I was waiting to hit, and I felt this tingling in my tongue and in my fingers. That was a sign I was having circulation problems because of my blood-sugar level. But I ignored it—stupid thing to do—and hit the ball hard. I hit a home run!"

"Couldn't you have called time out?"

"I could have, but it would have been so embarrassing. I just moved into the batter's box, hoping the pitcher would give me anything close. The first pitch I could reach I blasted over the left fielder's head. I ran so fast around those bases I think she had just gotten to the ball when I was rounding third. Everybody thought I was running so fast because I wanted a homer.

"My teammates were all waiting to slap my hand at the plate, but I just ran right through them. I was so excited and pumped, but I was shaking bad. Mom just reached over the fence and gave me my shot, right through my uniform pant leg."

"You can do that?"

"You're not supposed to. It's not the most sanitary. But time is what's most important." She paused. "Chad? Will you forgive me?"

"Forgive you?"

"For being such a brat when we were little and then for never apologizing before now? I had lots of chances, with all those emails I've sent to Kate. I'm sorry."

"It's all right."

"Then you accept my apology?"

"Sure."

"You think we can be friends?"

Chad smiled. "As long you don't tell anybody."

"Well, it's not like we'd be boyfriend and girlfriend or anything like that," she said.

"I know, but I don't have any other friends who are girls."

"That makes me special," Suzie Q said.

"That's not all that makes you special." Chad could hardly believe he'd said that.

"What?" she said.

"Nothing."

"Don't say 'nothing.' I heard what you said. What did you mean?"

"Nothing, now really. Please."

"Chad, come in, please," Dad said over his wrist TV, and Chad sighed with relief.

Crisis in Old Sparrow

"Go ahead, Dad."

"Chad? I've run into trouble here. I'm in Old Sparrow, and it looks as much like a ghost town down here as it did from the air. They've got snow-removal equipment trying to clear the main drag, but it has huge drifts. Power is still out, everything's closed up. I just went over to the drugstore, and it's sealed up tight. I'm going to have to hunt down the pharmacist and find out where his shipment of medicine is."

"Ten-four," Chad said. "I can't see you, by the way."

"Well, it's dark here already. Anyway, the high frequency radio waves will not go through that snow mountain you've got in front of you, Chad," Dad said. "The low frequency transmitter Kate built into these things works fine from this distance."

"Ten-four."

"How's Suzie Q doing?"

"She's a little shaky. I should let her speak for herself."

"I'm trying to hold up," Suzie said into Chad's wrist transmitter, "but I don't know how much longer I can make it."

"I'm coming as fast as I can, Suzie."

"Thanks."

Just talking about Suzie's condition made Chad nervous. But he'd rather talk about that than what he had stupidly brought up a minute before about her being special. Why had he even said that in the first place?

A few minutes later Chad realized that Dad had left his transmitter on. They heard his steps and even his heavy breathing as he fought his way through the elements looking for someone in Old Sparrow to talk to. But just as Chad was about to signal Dad and tell him to turn off his sending mechanism, he heard conversation.

"Evening, gentlemen," Chad's dad said. "Might have guessed the only place open in town would be the bar." He was met with whistles and shrieks and laughter. "How you keeping warm?"

"Hooch!" somebody hollered. "Booze! Have yourself one!"

"No, thanks," Dad said. "Those heaters safe?"

"Who knows? We'd be dead without 'em."

"Listen, I'm looking for the pharmacist. Anybody know where he is? His place is closed."

That was met with more laughter and shouting. Then Dad said, "Who? You?"

Apparently the pharmacist had been pointed out to his dad. Chad heard footsteps again, then, "Hey, there, partner, you awake? Sit up here a minute. I hate to wake you or bother you, but do you remember me?"

"Remember you? No! Leave me alone."

"I wish I could, but I can't. I was in your store the other day, looking to pick up a shipment of medical supplies, antibiotics, and insulin. Remember? C'mon, pal, stay with me a minute here. The Old Sparrow Christian School got word the shipment had arrived here, and that's why I came. People are sick back there. We need it bad, and we need it now."

"I got cleaned out," the man said. "Looted, you understand? My burglar alarm wasn't working, and somebody came in and cleaned me out."

"What are you talking about?" Dad said. "I was just by your place and it was locked up tight."

"So that wasn't my place that got busted into?"

Chad glanced at Suzie Q. Every minute counted, and they were losing critical time.

After another chorus of laughs, somebody said, "You from that Christian school?"

"Yes, sir, I am."

"Well, they reached somebody on the shortwave a little while ago over at the station. They were looking for you, saying you were going to be in town this afternoon and to give you a message."

"What's the message?"

"Something about they still need the medicine and all, but some of them are starting to get better, and they don't see it as life-threatening or anything."

"That's great news. Anything else?"

"No, but they wanted to hear from you as soon as you got here."

"I can talk to them from the gas station?"

"They're closed—everybody's working on the roads and power and such."

"Not *everybody*," Dad said, obviously referring to the drinkers in front of him. "None of you guys willing to pitch in and help?"

"This was an act of nature," somebody yelled. "We didn't have nothin' to do with it."

"So you're just going to roll over and let everyone else do the cleanup work? Now as for you," and Chad knew he must be talking to the pharmacist again, "you're coming with me and opening your store."

"And what if I don't?" the man slurred.

"Then I'll break into your place and find the stuff. I've got an emergency situation, and I've got to have that medicine."

"I just heard him tell you it wasn't a big deal anymore."

"I'm talking about the insulin," Dad said in a tight voice. "I need it right now. Either you come and give it to me, or I'll find a way to get in there."

"Oh, all right!" the man muttered, and Chad and Suzie Q heard him grumbling to himself as the men's boots crunched the frozen snow until they reached the drugstore. They heard the jangle of keys and a lot of fumbling around.

"Just show me which one it is and let me do it," Dad said in a disgusted tone.

Soon they heard the door open and the two clomp inside. "It's no warmer in here than it is out there," the pharmacist said.

"At least we're out of the wind," Dad said. "Now where's that shipment?"

"I don't know. It's here somewhere. I drove all the way to McDougall myself, you know, when that storm had just started. I was lucky to get back alive."

"I'd be more impressed if you were trying to dig your town out of this mess."

"Well, Sonny," the man said, "we all react to trouble in our own way, don't we?"

"I guess we do. Now if you're not going to look, tell me where to look. Where'd you put the stuff when you got back here?"

"You know, I don't remember bringing it in from the car."

"What are you saying? You left fresh medicine in the car to freeze?"

"Oh, don't get your mind in a bind. It comes in insulated boxes. It's all right."

"Well, let's go! Where's your car?"

"I didn't take the car. I took the truck."

"Then where's the truck? Come on, man! This is an emergency!"

"It's out back."

Chad looked at Suzie Q, who appeared weaker and more fidgety. She held up a hand, anticipating Chad's question. "I'm okay," she said.

Over the wrist TV they heard Dad's footsteps, firm and alone, out the door and into the snow again. "Hey there!" Dad said.

"Hello," came the voice of a young man.

"Name's Bruce Michaels."

"I'm Sam. My dad's the pharmacist here."

"Your dad's a heavy drinker."

"Don't I know it. What can I do for you?"

"He said a shipment of medicine is in this truck. A lot of it is for the Old Sparrow Christian School, and I'm getting it for them."

"You'll never get over there until they clear the highway, probably some time next week," Sam said. Dad quickly filled him in on how he had gotten there and about the urgent need for the insulin. "Well, then, let's find you that stuff and get you on your way."

Chad and Suzie Q heard them rooting around in the truck. "Nothing here," Sam said.

"Sam," Dad said. "This is an emergency. Maybe you can communicate to your father better than I can. I have got to have that stuff, and right away."

"I'll try."

"I'll wait here," Dad said.

They heard Sam move away and Dad said into his wrist TV, "Chad?"

"Yeah, Dad, we hear you. In fact we've heard everything since you were in the bar."

"It was the only business in town where I saw any smoke rising from the chimney. How's Suzie?"

"I'm fine," she called out, a little too loudly.

"To tell you the truth, I'm worried about her," Chad said.

"Why?" she screeched. "I'm fine! I said I was fine! I'm fine!"

"Suzie," Dad said. "You sound a little hyper."

"I'm not! I'm fine."

"Hurry, Dad," Chad said.

"Ten-four. Here comes Sam, and he doesn't look too pleased."

"Leave your watch on, Dad," Chad said quickly, but it was too late. The signal suddenly ended and the sound disappeared.

"Now what?" Suzie Q said. "Is he in trouble? I hope he's not in trouble, because if he's in trouble, I'm in trouble."

Chad sat back and stared at her.

"What?"

"Can you hear yourself?" he said. "Something's wrong with you. You talked normally after Dad left, but now you're totally wired."

Suzie began to cry.

"I'm sorry, Suzie, I didn't mean to upset you. It's just that—"

"No! It's that—I don't want to be this way. This is how I get when I'm not producing insulin and my blood is full of sugar!" She was still crying. "You're such a good friend, Chad."

"Yeah, okay."

"No! You are! Let me tell you what a good friend you are!"

"Okay, Suzie. Take it easy now. Dad will be back soon."

"You don't know that! We don't even know what happened to him!"

"Suzie, please, you have to calm down. My dad was a fighter pilot. He's been in every kind of situation you can imagine, and he can handle himself."

But Suzie wasn't listening. She covered her face with her mittens and rubbed her forehead, rocking back in the seat.

"Are you all right?" Chad said.

"I'm fine" came the muffled shout from behind the mittens. "I told you and your dad I'm fine, so I'm fine, okay?"

"Okay, okay. Sorry."

Suddenly Suzie Q pulled her hands away from her face and spoke calmly and seriously. "Listen to me, Chad, I'm all screwed up with glucose and insulin. You can't take personally anything I might say or do, okay?"

"Okay."

"Promise? You understand?"

Chad nodded. "Suzie, listen to me," he said. "I completely understand, all right? Don't worry about anything. Just try to stay calm and stay warm, and let's pray my dad gets back here with your insulin."

The wrist TV crackled. "Chad, I'm on the street with Sam. His dad finally admitted he sold the stuff to some guy at the gas station."

"Sold it?" Chad shouted.

"Oh, no!" Suzie Q wailed.

"He wanted some money, and the guy said he would sell it to the rescue workers for a profit and split it with him."

"What are you going to do, Dad?"

"Sam's taking me to find the guy. I'll try to get on the radio back to the school."

"Why'd he sell the stuff when he knew it was the school's?"

"He said he knew we'd never make it to Old Sparrow."

"He didn't know us, did he, Dad?"

"Suzie hanging in there?" Dad said.

"Not really. She needs the stuff as soon as we can get it."

"Ten-four."

"And Dad, leave your TV on."

Suzie had buried her face in her mittens again and was rocking in the seat. What if she collapsed or lost consciousness? How would he know if it was a coma or whether she was dying? What if she had heart failure? It was more than he wanted to think about. All he knew was that he could not, *would not*, let her die.

He wanted her conscious when his dad returned with the medicine, because neither he nor his dad knew how to give her the injection. Sure, he had seen doctors and nurses use hypodermic needles before, but he certainly never thought he'd have to do it himself.

"How big a dose do you need?" Chad said, just in case.

"I need a lot," Suzie Q said, "but my first dose after a long time can't be more than thirty units, or it'll be too much for my system."

"Thirty units," he repeated.

They fell silent, and Chad listened desperately for his dad on his wrist TV.

Racing the Clock

Suzie Q leaned back on the headrest and seemed to fall asleep, though her fingers were still moving and her hands shaking. On his wrist TV Chad suddenly heard Dad's new acquaintance, Sam, talking with someone at the gas station. Then he heard Dad on his shortwave radio to the Christian school.

"I have good news," Dad said. "We should be heading back soon." He told them where Chad and Suzie Q were. "Once I get the medicine, we'll be on our way. Ten-four. Over and out."

"Not so fast," someone was saying. "I didn't say I'd sell you the stuff."

"I don't have to buy it from you," Dad said. "It was ordered by the Christian school, and it's going on their bill."

"Then you don't even have the cash for it?"

"Like I said, it goes on the school's account."

"Then give me one reason I shouldn't just sell it to the rescue workers and make my profit in cash, like I planned."

"Because it's not yours to sell."

"I bought it from Sam's dad."

"You paid him already?" Sam said.

"I didn't say that. I'll pay him from the profits."

Sam's voice was like steel. "You heard this man say that the Christian school has a crisis and a little girl just outside town is gonna die if she doesn't get her medicine, and you're not going to do the right thing?"

"Sam, the right thing is none of your business. It's my stuff, and I'll make that decision."

Chad heard Sam whisper to Dad, "Are you prepared to run?"

"I'll do whatever I have to do, Sam, and I appreciate your help."

"Let me do this," Sam said, and Chad could tell by his loud voice that he was talking to the man with the medicine. "Let me check the supply and see what it's worth, and then we can talk about a proper price. Fair enough?"

"I guess," the other man said.

Chad was fascinated. He could only imagine what was going on. It was quiet for a minute, then Sam shouted,

"Go!" He heard fast footsteps, shouting, a door slamming, running, and finally, Dad.

"Chad! Chad! Come in please!"

"I'm here, Dad!" Chad said. "What's happening?"

Dad was clearly running; he was already panting. "I'm trying to get far enough from these yokels to get my snowshoes on."

"What's going on?"

"Sam got the stuff from the guy, handed it to me, and motioned that I should get going! We owe him a big thanks."

"Can you outrun those guys?"

"Sure!"

Chad heard a loud pop. "What was that? It sounded like a gun!"

"That's what it was," Dad said. "They can't catch me, so one of 'em's shooting!"

Chad shouted, "Leave your transmitter on!"

"I wish this case wasn't so heavy!" Dad said, his breath coming in short bursts.

Chad heard another shot. "Dad!"

"I'm all right! They're just trying to scare me. I have to keep moving! They can't even see me now!"

"Save your breath and just get here!"

"I'm coming!"

Chad couldn't believe what this trip had turned into. He

could just see Dad lurching through town, trying to get back to the road where he would put on his snowshoes and climb the huge incline and then scamper down the other side to the snowplow. Dad had to still be a mile away, and while the lazy locals may have given up chasing him, he had to keep running. He must be exhausted. Chad thought about climbing to the top of the drift in the road to watch for him, but he couldn't leave Suzie Q.

He turned to her. "So what do you think about that?"

She didn't stir. She seemed to be sound asleep. How could she have slept through his yelling over the TV transmitter? Had she slipped into a coma? He felt for a pulse in her wrist. It was faint.

"Suzie Q? Are you all right?"

"Hm?" she said, still sounding asleep.

"Are you all right?"

He thought she nodded, but he wasn't sure. Maybe sleep was good. Maybe he should leave her alone. He didn't know how long it would take Dad to trudge back through the deep snow with the medicine.

"Chad!" Dad called.

"Go ahead."

"I'm on the outskirts of town, a little less than a mile from you. I'm going to rest here a second and get my snowshoes on."

"Dad, what was the good news from the school?"

"A lot of them are getting better. This thing was highly contagious, but it's only a forty-eight-hour bug. They still need the antibiotics, but they're encouraged."

"Good."

"I'm on the move again. How's Suzie Q?"

"She doesn't look good. She's sleeping. She doesn't seem to hear me."

"Does she look calmer than before?"

"I guess."

"Let her be, she just needs the insulin," Dad said. "Hang on till I get there."

What else could he do?

Chad heard the crunching of Dad's snowshoes, the steady, quick gait of a man in a hurry.

Suddenly Suzie Q turned, opened her eyes, and looked Chad full in the face. She seemed to want to say something, but nothing came out.

"You okay, Suzie?" Chad said.

She just continued to stare, as if she were sleeping with her eyes open.

"Suzie!" he said, louder this time.

"Chad," she said quietly.

"Yeah?"

"Chad?" she repeated.

"What, Suzie?"

"Do you know what CPR is?"

"Yeah."

"I mean, do you know how to do it?"

"Perform CPR, you mean?"

"Yes."

"Yeah, we learned in health last year. Why?"

"Because I think I need it."

"Are you kidding?"

But Suzie didn't answer. She just stared at Chad, not blinking. She coughed twice, causing her little body to bounce, but still she stared.

"Suzie Q! Are you serious? You need CPR?"

She didn't move and her eyes seemed to freeze. Her pupils were huge, and Chad wondered if that's what doctors on TV meant when they described someone's pupils as "fixed and dilated."

Now he was scared. What was he supposed to do? He felt for her pulse again, but this time he felt none. He put his ear to her mouth and heard nothing. Had she died right in front of him? He felt the pressure points beneath her lower jaw at the neck. Nothing!

"Suzie!"

Her head rolled to one side, and she began to topple. He grabbed her shoulders and she leaned heavily on him.

Chad pulled his knees onto the seat and knelt there, trying to guide Suzie onto her back. But she was too close to the driver's side door. Chad scooted over to the other side and put his hands under her arms, pulling her across the seat on her back. He reached to open the passenger-side door, then stood on the step, leaning over her. She lay still, staring blankly at the ceiling.

"Suzie!" he yelled, then decided not to yell at her again. She couldn't hear him. The wind was icy, and the sky was dark, but suddenly Chad's life seemed to be moving in slow motion.

"God, help me!" Chad prayed. He flipped on his transmitter. "Dad! Hurry! I think Suzie's dying!"

"What's happening?" came the reply.

"No pulse, no breathing."

"Start CPR!"

"I will!"

"You know what to do. I'll get there as fast as I can!"

Suzie's knees were up, her boots pressing against the driver's side door. Chad needed to shut his own door or they would both freeze. He crawled inside and knelt with his back to the dashboard, facing the seat. He tugged on Suzie until she was stretched out before him, her head resting on the passenger seat. Then he shut the door.

Chad whipped off his gloves and tore at the buckle at her waist that kept her snowsuit tight around her. Once that was loose he untied the string under her chin and pulled down her hood. He bunched it up under her neck and moved her head back a little to keep the windpipe open.

Suzie went rigid now, her arms and legs straight. Her eyes were still open but lifeless. Her mouth was slightly open, her teeth clenched. Chad forced a finger between her teeth to open her air passage.

He unzipped her snowsuit to her waist, then tipped her head back and covered her mouth with his. He blew air into her until her cheeks puffed and her chest rose a little. Then he clasped his hands together and placed them just below her sternum. He pushed firmly but not too hard.

He alternated between forcing air into her lungs and pressing on her sternum, stopping every third time to listen for breathing or for a pulse.

"Anything?" Dad said over the transmitter. "Don't answer until you have a pulse. Don't take time out to talk to me unless you know you can."

"No!" Chad shouted.

"Keep working, Chad. I'm praying for you, and I know you can do this."

"What if she dies?" Chad squealed.

Dad sounded surprisingly calm. "You know what to do, so just keep doing it."

Chad could hear his dad gasping as he ran through the frozen wilderness. "I'm on the highway!" Dad said.

Chad couldn't respond. His own heart was pounding enough for both him and Suzie Q. He had to do something to get her breathing and to get her heart beating again. When he had taken CPR training he had hoped he would never have to use it. He'd wondered if he could, and he'd always hoped that someone else would be around who could do it instead.

Now he had no choice. Suzie Q's life depended on him. He breathed into her mouth, and he pushed against her breastbone. He looked for any signs of life. Her face was pale, her lips blue.

"C'mon, Suzie Q," he whispered. "C'mon!"

How long could she hang on with no heartbeat, with no air? He would never give up, but he wanted something to happen. "God, please!" he cried out.

He was massaging her heart when he sensed her body relax a little. Her arm moved! When he tried to breathe for her again, she turned her head and sputtered.

"Suzie!"

He felt for a pulse. It was faint. And then it was gone, and he began again. Several times he felt he had brought her back, only to lose her again. He was panicky, but he would not lose control. He couldn't. He had to hang on.

"Dad!" he called. "I don't know if I'm doing any good!"

"As long as you're doing anything," Dad said between gasps, "you're doing good. Keep it up!"

"Where are you?"

"Halfway up the incline!"

"Hurry!" Chad said and blew into Suzie's mouth again.

It seemed like an hour since Chad had begun, but it had to be only minutes. Suzie blinked and looked at him, this time as if she could see him. She tried to speak. He felt for a pulse. It was a little stronger, but not yet steady. She jerked and thrashed, and he thought that was a good sign. But he knew she could still die on him any second.

Chad heard two thumps on the truck and whirled to see Dad's snowshoes clatter over the hood and into the snow. He leaned out and saw Dad in the fading light at the top of the drift, a black case in both hands. Dad dove from the top and tumbled down the drift, rolling and flipping until he flopped onto the ground with a loud grunt.

Chad pushed the door open, barely missing Dad, who was reaching for the handle. "Do you have a pulse?" Dad said.

"Yes, finally."

"Suzie!" Dad called out.

She didn't respond.

"Give me the insulin," Chad said, and Dad cracked open the case, tossing aside everything that didn't say "insulin" on the label. Finally he found a vial. Chad reached past him and grabbed a hypodermic. He tore at the paper and whipped the plastic end off the needle.

Dad had just opened the vial when Chad grabbed it and held it up to the interior light. He drove the needle through the rubber opening, turned the vial upside down and, checking the gauge on the side, drew into the needle 30 units of insulin.

He pulled the needle away from the vial and let the vial fall to the floor. Pressing the plunger, he cleared the needle of air, shooting a fraction of the insulin into the air. Then he jammed the needle right through Suzie Q's snowsuit and trousers and into her inner thigh. He quickly pressed the plunger. He was surprised at how hard it was to push the liquid into her.

Chad began CPR again, but within seconds Suzie roused and began to lift her head. "Stay right there, girl," Dad said. "Stay right there."

She was groggy, but she was awake. She was breathing. Her heart was beating. Chad dropped onto the floor and sobbed.

"What happened?" Suzie said, her voice thick and her words slurred.

"Just take it easy," Dad said.

But Suzie fought to sit up. "I'm all right," she said. "Did you bring my medicine?"

"You've already gotten it," Dad said. "Chad saved your life."

"He gave me the insulin?"

"He also gave you CPR."

"He did?"

Dad nodded. Chad fought to gain control. He was spent. The CPR was one thing. But he had injected insulin into Suzie Q. And she seemed to be doing fine. He could hardly move.

Dad helped Suzie Q sit up, then pulled Chad from the floor and propped him up too. He shut the door and ran around to get behind the wheel. Suzie was breathing deeply. "I'm not going anywhere," Dad said, "especially back the same way we came, until I'm sure you're up to it."

"I feel pretty weak," she said. "But I'm up to giving Chad a hug."

"Do you have to?" Chad said.

"Yes, I do," she said. And she did.

Secretly, Chad didn't mind a bit.

Epilogue

Dad didn't attempt the drive back to the school until he was sure Suzie Q could make it. It wasn't quite as bouncy a ride this time. He followed his own tracks and drove along the path he had cleared on the way. They arrived back at the school in about half the time it had taken to travel east.

The antibiotics sped the recovery of those who were ill from what Mrs. Quenton said was an outbreak of Streptococcus pneumonia at the school. Chad was treated like a hero. This time, however, he didn't enjoy the attention. He wanted to shake the memories and the terror of Suzie Q coming so close to death right in his arms, but he knew the experience would be with him always.

Suzie Q and even Kate seemed to understand that Chad would rather not talk about the ordeal. He was grateful for that, and he changed his opinion about girls—at least those two girls.

Chad felt as if he had grown up almost overnight. He was thankful God had been with him when he needed him the most.

The Michaelses flew home a few days later, but when the roads were passable in a couple weeks, they traveled back to Old Sparrow, where Dad personally thanked his new friend, Sam, for his help. "You had as much to do with saving Sue Quenton's life as any of us did," Dad told him.

And Chad knew it was true.

He had made it through the experience of having another person's life in his hands, and Chad knew that was something he would never take lightly. This had been an incredible adventure for AirQuest Adventures—what more could the future possibly bring?

Discussion Questions for Disaster in the Yukon

Chapter 1

1. Have you ever had to move away from a good friend?
2. How did you stay in touch?
3. Why do we sometimes feel awkward when talking to the opposite sex?

Chapter 2

4. How much one-on-one time do you get with either of your parents?
5. What's the biggest storm you've ever seen?
6. What's the longest you've been away from your parents?

Chapter 3

7. Would you be scared of this weather or excited like Chad?
8. Whom would you like to have in the ATV (along with Dad) if you were Chad?
9. What is the one piece of equipment you would want to have in the ATV?

Chapter 4

10. What's the coldest you've ever been?
11. What skills come in handy in this situation?
12. What's the farthest you've ever walked?

Chapter 5

13. When have you fallen asleep near a fire?
14. What do you do in your house when the power goes out?
15. How can Chad and Dad help the stranded students?

Chapter 6

16. How do you think Chad felt riding in a plane after having been in a crash not long ago?
17. Why is Chad so concerned about Susie Q?
18. How will they land the plane with no safe clearings?

Chapter 7

19. How do you feel when plans change?

20. When have you had to work as hard as Chad did to help with the truck?

21. Why do you think Mr. Quenton needs them to take Sue?

Chapter 8

22. What's the roughest ride you've ever taken?

23. Would you choose the river route or try to blast through the huge drift?

Chapter 9

24. Why is Chad so uncomfortable with Susie Q?

25. If they get stranded, who should stay with Susie Q and why?

26. How do you pray when you're scared?

Chapter 10

27. What can you do to help someone with Susie Q's problems?

28. When have you apologized?

29. When is the last time you forgave someone?

Chapter 11

30. How do you respond to trouble?

31. Would you help out or sit back?

32. Whom in your life do you feel the need to protect?

Chapter 12

33. How would you perform CPR? Do you know how?

34. How would you respond if someone's life were in danger?

35. Why do you think Chad started sobbing when it was all over?

We want to hear from you. Please send your comments about this book to us in care of zreview@zondervan.com. Thank you.

ZONDERVAN.com/
AUTHORTRACKER
follow your favorite authors